ISLAND BLISS

ISLAND BLISS

Rochelle Alers
Marcia King-Gamble
Carmen Green
Felicia Mason

St. Martin's Paperbacks

ISLAND BLISS

"From the Heart" copyright © 2002 by Rochelle Alers.
"An Officer and a Hero" copyright © 2002 by Marcia King-Gamble.
"Our Secret Affair" copyright © 2002 by Carmen Green.
"Heart's Desire" copyright © 2002 by Felicia L. Mason.

ISBN: 0-312-97893-6

Printed in the United States of America

St. Martin's Paperbacks edition / February 2002

St. Martin's Paperbacks are published by St. Martin's Press, 175 Fifth Avenue, New York, NY 10010.

10 9 8 7 6 5 4 3 2 1

CONTENTS

From the Heart

by Rochelle Alers

Beloved, let us love one another, because love springs from God and whoever loves has been born of God and knows God.

—1 John 4:7

ONE

Aimee Frasier downshifted her late-model Audi, following a road sign indicating the number of miles to St. Simons Island. Rolling her head in a circular motion, she tried easing the tightness in her neck and along her shoulders. It had taken her four hours to drive from Atlanta to Savannah, where she'd stopped to rest, fueled up her car, and enjoyed a leisurely lunch. The hour delay had refreshed her—but only temporarily.

She then left Savannah and continued along I-95, but a four-car pile-up had stalled traffic for miles before it began to inch along at a rate of about fifteen miles an hour. The total trip, which should have taken about six hours, had taken her more than eight.

She'd been up before sunrise, making certain she had everything she'd need to catalogue the contents of an early—eighteenth century house on historic St. Simons Island. The trunk of her car was packed with her laptop computer, printer, scanner, notebooks, clothes, and personal items. She'd packed enough to last her a month. Her luggage contained a few outfits better suited for dinner at an upscale restaurant. What she did not intend to do was spend all of her time on St. Simons, because she'd contacted several old friends for a brief reunion.

A smile tilted her full lips upward. She missed Savannah and had called the sensual city home when she attended SCAD—or, as the locals and students called it, the Savannah College of Art and Design. After graduating, she'd returned to Atlanta—her birthplace and permanent home—with bachelor and master of fine arts degrees in art and architectural history. She had assisted her mother with her antique enterprise until she joined the staff of the Georgia National Trust for Historic Preservation.

The Trust's curator had summoned her a week ago, informing her that a direct descendant of George Monroe had taken up residence at his grandparents' home on St. Simons. Leland Monroe had contacted the Trust because he'd discovered documents and artifacts dating back two hundred years. The present-day Monroe wanted the pieces authenticated before he loaned them to designated museums throughout the country.

Aimee hadn't hesitated accepting the assignment because it had been more than three years since she'd catalogued the contents of an entire house. Leaving Atlanta for a month also offered her the break she needed to put some distance between her and Jeremy Robinson. A year before, the Atlanta police captain had proposed marriage and she'd agreed to become his wife, but hours before leaving Atlanta she'd returned his ring. They'd traded acerbic words when he complained about not seeing her for a month. And when she tried explaining that this commission was certain to become the highlight of her career thus far, Jeremy drawled that she should consider a career change.

Her blood had run cold when she stared at him in shock. He knew how hard she'd worked to advance her career, but in a moment of utter selfishness he'd let her know exactly how he felt about her work. It was his turn for an expression of shock to freeze his features when she twisted the diamond ring off her left hand, leaving it on the table in his kitchen. And without a backward glance, she walked out of Jeremy Robinson's house and his life.

What troubled her about her relationship with Jeremy was that she'd dated him steadily for two years despite the fact that she wasn't in love with him. She'd questioned herself why she'd continued to see him and could only conclude that now, at thirty-six, her biological clock had begun to toll. She wanted children, but not without being married. Biting down on her lower lip, she squinted through the lenses of her sunglasses. It had taken a full twenty-four hours, but now she realized she'd made the right decision not to marry Jeremy Robinson.

* * *

Leland Monroe saved what he'd typed on a disk, and then turned off his computer. Leaning back on his chair, he exhaled audibly. After several false starts, the scene had gone better than he'd first anticipated. Glancing up at the large calendar on the wall above his computer, he noted the number penciled in under the date. He was ahead of schedule. He would be able to make his deadline easily, because he'd completed more than half the book that had an October 15 due date. It was now the second week in August, and that meant he had a little more than two months to turn in a projected 800-page manuscript.

Rising to his feet, he stretched his arms above his head, while at the same time flexing his fingers. He was tempted to print out what he'd typed, but decided against it. Not superstitious by nature, he'd established a habit of writing for six hours each day, saving what he'd written, and then printing it out the following morning. There were occasions when he edited what he had written until it was spare and tight, and there were days when he did not have to change one word.

The soft sound of meowing disturbed the silence in the room Leland had set up as his studio, followed by the appearance of a tiny orange-colored kitten. Her bright yellow-gold color reminded Leland of marmalade—for which the feline was aptly named. She crept toward her master, her green eyes fixed on the tall man who had folded his arms over his chest. Marmalade sat in front of Leland and stared up at him.

"I suppose you're ready to eat," Leland said, glaring back at the feline. She meowed in response, her tail flicking from side to side. He wasn't overly fond of cats, but somehow Marmalade had become the exception. The orphaned kitten had captured his heart.

Leland had found Marmalade—barely days old—wet and shivering, outside his front door early one morning several days after he'd come to St. Simons to move into the house that had belonged to his grandparents. He'd wrapped the kitten in a towel, fed her warm milk with an eyedropper, then called a local veterinarian for an appointment. The vet checked the kitten thoroughly, declaring her healthy, and then handed him a bill for several hundred dollars and a schedule for the animal to receive a series of shots. Leland wrote a check, gave it to the nurse, scheduled an appointment, and returned home with Marmalade Monroe asleep on a soft blanket in the cargo area of his SUV. The cat had succeeded where so many women had failed—she shared a roof with Leland Monroe.

Bending down, he picked up his pet and walked out of the studio. Waning sunlight filtering through a copse of towering trees at the rear of the house threw long and short shadows along the back porch as he prepared the cat's dinner. Marmalade ate quickly, lapped up a meager portion of milk, stretched, and then ambled over to the cushioned softness of a wicker bed to sleep. Leland had placed the bed in a corner that took advantage of maximum sunlight coming into the space.

He knew the hour without glancing at a clock or his watch. It was after three. A slight frown furrowed his smooth forehead. The woman who was to catalogue the contents of the house had called him yesterday, introducing herself and confirming her arrival for one o'clock the following day.

She's late!

That was her first strike. And because he ran his life by a clock, Leland usually expected the same from everyone else. Aimee Frasier had only two strikes left before he sent her packing. What he didn't want or need was a distraction—not at this time in his life, not when he was attempting to complete what his editor believed was his finest literary project to date.

The soft chiming of the doorbell brought Leland out of his reverie. Marmalade's head came up and she jumped out of her bed and followed her master as he made his way to the front door.

Aimee stood on an expansive porch, admiring the aged quality of a quartet of mahogany rockers, two positioned at each end. Judging from the workmanship on the arms and back, she estimated they were probably made in the West Indies during the early eighteenth century and then shipped to the American colonies.

She raised her hand to ring the bell again when she saw the outline of a tall man's approach as she peered through the mesh on the door. She hadn't realized she was holding her breath until the door opened and she stared up at a face she had seen on the dust jackets of several best-selling novels.

Straightening her spine, she pulled herself up to her even six-foot height, raised her chin, and met the gaze of Hayden Lawrence as he opened the door.

He was more attractive than his photographs. Tall, several inches above her own towering height, his large brown eyes were mesmerizing. They were the perfect complement for his sable-brown complexion. They narrowed slightly and she noticed pinpoints of gold in their mysterious depths. It was apparent that his eyes changed color with his mood, and she wondered just what he was feeling at that moment. His features were overtly masculine and perfectly symmetrical. His nose was straight, his mouth full, cheekbones high and prominent above a lean jaw and strong chin. His hair was close-cropped, the black strands covering a well-shaped pate. She forced her gaze not to linger below his strong neck. A stark-white T-shirt and khaki walking shorts failed to conceal a large, muscled, well-toned body.

"Good afternoon. I'm Aimee Frasier. Could you please let Mr. Leland Monroe know that I'm here?"

Leland knew he was gawking, but he couldn't help it. She couldn't be the woman who was to spend at least a month under his roof researching and cataloguing the items he'd discovered in the attic of his grandparents' house. How was he expected to complete his manuscript when a woman who looked as if she'd just come from a shoot for the cover of *Vogue*, or strutted down a Paris or Milan catwalk, moved into a bedroom several feet from his own? A white cotton sleeveless blouse with a matching slim skirt that ended at her knees was simple and elegant. Her bare legs and groomed feet in a pair of off-white leather sandals drew his lustful gaze.

She'd said her name was *Amy*, but she'd pronounced with an accent. And she'd said her last name as if it had an S instead of a Z. That didn't matter, because she was the most exotically beautiful woman he'd ever met. She was tall, her height almost matching his, slender, but not skinny. Her face was a flawless sable-brown with red undertones. And it was her face that captured his rapt attention. It was a perfect oval, and was set off by her short, natural haircut. Her large black eyes slanted upward, her nose was short and tiny, while her mouth was full, lush. His gaze lingered on her rounded chin with a slight indentation. It wasn't quite a dimple, but couldn't be called a cleft either.

"I'm Leland Monroe," he said after a noticeable silence.

Aimee's professionally waxed eyebrows lifted slightly. "I assume Hayden Lawrence is a pseudonym?"

He inclined his head. "You assume correct, Miss Frazier."

"It's Frasier," she corrected, stressing the *S*.

"And it's not *Amy*?"

She smiled, revealing a set of perfectly straight teeth—teeth that had been straightened with the aid of orthodontic apparatuses throughout her adolescence.

"It's Aimee. There's an accent on the first E, even though I don't use it anymore. It's too confusing for most people when they try to pronounce it."

Leland extended his right hand. "Welcome to St. Simons."

She placed her slender hand in his larger one, feeling its strength and protection. "Thank you, Mr. Monroe."

He smiled, and attractive lines fanned out at the corners of his deep-set eyes as he turned her hand over to examine her long, slender, professionally manicured fingers before releasing it.

"Leland will do."

Her smile matched his. "Leland it is. I'd like to settle in as soon as I can. If it's all right with you, I'd like to begin work early tomorrow morning. I usually begin at eight, take a break for lunch, then continue until four. And I don't work weekends."

Leland resisted the attempt to salute her. She sounded like a drill sergeant giving orders. His mind whirled in confusion. When he'd set up arrangements with the curator, he'd agreed to provide lodging for the architectural historian. But that was before Aimee Frasier showed up on his doorstep. The woman was too beautiful, and definitely much too much of a distraction to have around for eight hours a day.

Suddenly a thought hit him. Aimee would stay on Monroe

property, just not in the house she was researching. "Would you mind staying in the guest house? It has a bedroom, bath, a small kitchen with a dining area, and a front porch."

Aimee wavered, trying to comprehend what she was hearing. She had been told that she would live *in* the house, not in an outbuilding. Well, it didn't matter that much, because after meeting Leland Monroe, she realized she didn't need to see more of him than was necessary. She'd come to St. Simons Island to complete a research project, not ogle the man who'd commissioned her professional services.

"I wouldn't mind at all."

"Good. If you drive your car around to the back of the house, I'll help you with your bags."

Aimee returned to her car, turned on the ignition, then maneuvered around the back of the well-preserved three-story structure. Her jaw dropped slightly when she spied a small cottage set several hundred feet away from the main house. It was perfect. It would provide her with enough privacy when her day ended. It would also provide her with enough distance from the elusive Leland Monroe.

She turned off the engine, pushed open the door, and stepped out onto a thick carpet of grass. Her gaze narrowed as she spied Leland's approach. For a tall, large man, he claimed a sensual walk. He had the fluid grace of a dancer. A secret smile touched her lips, and she wondered how many people were aware that the mysterious, reclusive Hayden Lawrence was in reality Leland Monroe of the St. Simons Island Monroes. And she wondered how he felt being a direct descendant of one of the Georgia Sea Isle's most infamous slave owners.

TWO

Leland slipped a key into the lock of the door to the cottage. It turned smoothly. The clean smell of pine and lemon-scented wax wafted through the open door. He'd hired a college student to clean the main house and cottage once each week. She was quick, efficient, and he paid her well for her services.

Retracing his steps, he walked down the four steps leading off the porch. Aimee had opened the trunk of her car. Several pieces of lightweight luggage sat on the ground beside her sandaled feet. He handed her the key.

"Why don't you go in and look around? I'll bring your bags in."

She smiled up at him, and surprisingly he returned it with one of his own. Seeing him smile sent a warming shiver through her. The expression was so devastatingly sexy that it sucked the breath from her lungs. His firm lips parting and flattening against the upper ridge of his teeth held her rapt attention.

"Please be careful with my electronic equipment." Aimee pointed to a large case that held her laptop, printer, digital camera, and scanner.

Leland arched a thick, curving black eyebrow. "I can assure you that I won't drop it." Bending over, he picked up one bag, and then cradled another under his armpit while reaching for the case with the electronic equipment. His gaze mirrored amusement when a slight gasp escaped Aimee's parted lips.

Her slanting eyes narrowed. "You'd better not drop—"

"I won't," he said, cutting off her warning.

They stared at each other for a full thirty seconds before Aimee turned on her heel and made her way up the steps to the porch. She felt the heat from Leland's gaze on her back. She halted at the open door, turned, and found him standing motionless, staring at her. Her fingers curled into tight fists, the key biting into her tender flesh. A shiver of awareness rushed through her like the heat of the summer sun. There was something about Leland Monroe that indicated danger—a danger to her and her agitated emotions. His presence reminded her that even though she'd once pledged her future to Jeremy, her ex-fiancé hadn't been able to make her feel what she didn't want to feel with only a glance at this striking man.

Living in the cottage for the month was what she needed to keep some distance between her and her temporary employer.

The guest house was larger than it appeared on the outside, and when Aimee walked in and out of the rooms, she felt as if she'd stepped back in time. A cursory glance indicated that most of the furnishings were post-antebellum.

The parlor was small, but intimate. Off to the right of the parlor was a kitchen with an eat-in area. The windows in the kitchen faced the rear and offered a picturesque view of the water and a stretch of beach. The bedroom was the largest room, boasting a mahogany four-poster bed, matching armoire, rocker, cheval glass, and an overstuffed club chair and ottoman covered in a floral chintz fabric. The bathroom was a little larger than a water closet. It contained a commode, a tiny basin, and a claw-foot tub. However, there were several shelves on the whitewashed walls for her to store her grooming aids.

She returned to the parlor, finding all of her luggage near the door. Taking several steps, she walked out onto the porch. The trunk to her car was closed and Leland was nowhere in sight. From where she stood she could see the rear of the main house. A smile curved her mouth. The guest house was perfect, what she'd seen of St. Simons Island was perfect, and visually Mr. Leland Monroe was near perfect.

It took less than two hours for Aimee to settle into her temporary lodgings. She was pleased to find the refrigerator clean and fresh smelling from boxes of baking soda on each shelf. She filled the bathtub with water, added a handful of perfumed sea salts, then stepped into the tepid water. The sensual fragrance of scented candles and the music coming from the small-wave radio made her bathing ritual complete.

Twenty minutes later she stepped out of the tub, wrapping her body in a luxurious bedsheet she'd found in a narrow linen closet outside the bathroom. The shelves in the closet were filled with antique linens, blankets, and quilts stored in stacking plastic containers. After drying her body, she moisturized her arms and legs with her favorite scented body cream. She had to find a supermarket and purchase enough staples to sustain her for breakfast and lunch. And because she hadn't planned to spend most of her time cooking, she would dine out for dinner.

Clad in a loose-fitting tank dress in a flattering tangerine-orange and a pair of sand-colored espadrilles, she gathered her neutral crocheted shoulder bag. Turning on a table lamp in the parlor, she locked up the guest house and headed for her car. She looked up seconds before she opened the door and saw Leland sitting on the steps at the rear of the house, holding a piece of string just out of the reach of a tiny orange kitten who jumped at the piece of twine.

Brilliant orange rays of the setting sun turned him into a statue of molten gold. Aimee nodded, eliciting a smile from him.

Rising to his feet, Leland closed the distance between them, Marmalade scampering behind his heels. "Did you settle in all right?"

"Yes, I did. Thank you." Her gaze shifted to the kitten. "It's adorable."

Bending overly gracefully, Leland picked up the fluffy ball of yellow-orange fur. "This is Miss Marmalade Monroe. Marmalade, Miss Aimee Frasier." The kitten meowed softly as if she understood what Leland was saying.

Aimee extended her arms. "May I hold her?"

Leland placed the kitten in her embrace, and Marmalade curled against Aimee's breasts, purring. "It appears that she likes you."

Tilting her chin, she smiled up at Leland. "That's because I like most animals."

Pushing his hands into the pockets of his shorts, Leland stared down at the damp curls clinging to Aimee's scalp. "Do you have any pets?"

She shook her head. "No. I'm not home enough to give them the care they need."

He arched an eyebrow at this disclosure. "You do a lot of traveling?"

"At times."

"How often do you have to authenticate the contents of a house?"

"It varies. The last time was more than three years ago. But what I usually do is travel to different cities several times each month to meet with antique dealers or curators from museums." She glanced at her watch. "I'm sorry, but I have to be going. I want to make it to the supermarket before it closes."

"Which one are you going to?"

She shrugged a bare velvety shoulder. "I don't know. I'll find one somewhere on the island."

"Come with me. I'll take you."

"But . . . that won't be—"

"No buts," he said, interrupting her. "It'll be closed by the time you find it. St. Simons is not Atlanta, where some of the supermarkets stay open all night."

He hadn't given her much of a choice, and she followed him around to the other side of the house, her gaze fixed on the firm muscles in his strong calves. For a man who earned his living sitting at a desk, his body was as toned as an athlete's, making her wonder whether he worked out on a regular basis.

He stopped beside his truck and opened the passenger-side door. "Marmalade stays."

Aimee handed him the kitten, while he cupped a free hand under her elbow to help her into the truck. She waited, staring through the windshield at Leland when he opened a door and disappeared into the house. Two minutes later, he sat beside her, the heat and scent of his large body nearly overwhelming her with their potency. His aftershave was as masculine as he. It pulled her in and refused to let her go.

I made a serious mistake, she thought. She shouldn't have

permitted him to accompany her to the store. Well, it was too late now, but she promised herself that it wouldn't happen again.

She glanced at his right hand as he shifted gears. His arms and hands were so deeply tanned by the summer sun that they appeared nearly black. His long, well-shaped fingers didn't grip the gearshift, but caressed it. Shifting to her right, she turned her head and stared out the side window rather than look at the man sitting less than two feet from her. Unconsciously she found herself comparing Leland to Jeremy and the latter coming up on the losing side of the ledger.

Jeremy Robinson was attractive. Leland Monroe was gorgeous.

"We live on the southern tip of the island," Leland said in a quiet voice, breaking the comfortable silence. "You can walk to most of the restaurants, bars, and shops in about half an hour."

"What's on the other end?" Aimee had asked the question without looking at him.

"The eastern edges of the island claim the best beaches—flat expanses of hard-packed gray sand touched by a soft, almost placid surf. You can swim down where we are, but the waters are rough and sometimes quite dangerous."

She turned and stared at his distinctive profile. And it was then it suddenly hit her. Other than his coloring, remnants of Leland's white ancestry were quite obvious in his features. The only exception was his mouth. His lips were slightly fuller than those who claimed European ancestry.

"How are you related to George Monroe?"

"I'm told that I'm a grandson four or five generations removed."

"You're not certain?"

He gave her a quick glance. "I really don't care."

Aimee heard the venom in his tone and decided not to press the issue. She was certain she would be able to glean enough information about the deceased Monroes from the artifacts in the house.

"I can't believe I've never visited St. Simons," she said, deftly changing the topic. "I lived in Savannah for six years while attending college, yet never bothered to come here."

"Do you like what you see?"

She stared at houses nestled under towering trees draped in Spanish moss. Older structures were a vivid contrast to the newer subdivisions constructed several hundred feet back from the narrow paved roads.

"Very much."

"You spent all of your time in Savannah?"

Aimee shook her head. "No. I always spent my holidays and recess at home in Atlanta, but whenever my friends and I looked for a little excitement, we drove down to Jacksonville."

"So, the hot 'Lanta party girl likes the bright lights."

She registered the censure in his words immediately. "What's wrong with big-city life?"

He shrugged a broad shoulder under his T-shirt. "Nothing, if that's what you want."

"And you prefer to hide out, Mr. Leland Monroe, a.k.a. Hayden Lawrence."

Leland's eyebrows met in a frown over the bridge of his nose. "I wouldn't call it hiding. It's more like coveting one's privacy."

"Do you get it here?"

"Absolutely," he said firmly.

"Good for you," Aimee mumbled under her breath.

A smile softened the harsh lines in his face. "Thank you, Miss Frasier."

"You don't have to be facetious, Leland."

"I didn't know I was."

"Well, you are."

He sobered immediately. "If I was, then please accept my apology."

"Apology accepted," she mumbled reluctantly.

All conversation ended when Leland maneuvered into a parking lot to a supermarket. It wasn't as large as the superstores in Atlanta, but it would do.

She waited for Leland to turn off the engine, then come around the Pathfinder to help her down. Instead of extending his hand, he curved his fingers around her waist and swung her down in one smooth motion. But instead of releasing her, he held on to her waist, their breaths mingling when she raised her head to look up at him.

His eyes widened, permitting her to see the gold in their mysterious depths. "How tall are you, Aimee?"

"An even six foot." Inhaling deeply, she forced a smile. "How tall are you?"

"Only six-three."

"Only?"

"Dad is six-six, while Mom is five-three. There's not much height in her family."

"Do you have any siblings?"

"I have a sister. Ivy is five-six." His arms fell away from her body before he closed the truck's door. He reached for her again, this time cradling her hand in his, leading her to the supermarket's entrance. "Who did you inherit your height from?"

"Both parents."

Leland gave her a sidelong glance. "How tall is your father?"

"My mother told me he was six-four. She's five-ten."

He stopped. "She told you?"

Aimee nodded. "I never knew my father. He was killed in Vietnam a month after the U.S. officially entered the war." Her free hand went to her neck and she withdrew a small rectangular piece of gold hanging from a matching chain between her breasts. "This is a replica of the dog tag he wore around his neck when they shipped him back to the States in a body bag. My mother has the original one, photographs of him in jungle fatigues, his lieutenant's bars, Silver Star, Purple Heart, the American flag that covered his casket, and her memories."

"She never remarried?"

"No," Aimee whispered. She didn't know why she'd whispered except that Leland had.

"Why? She must have been a very young woman when she was widowed."

"Momma was only twenty-six. She said she never wanted

to marry again because she was a woman who could only love one man. And my father was that man."

Leland wanted to ask Aimee if she was like her mother, but decided not to. It was too personal. And he didn't know what had possessed him to delve into her personal life, because of his own penchant for privacy.

He forced a smile. "I think he would've been proud of you. The curator at the Trust said you're one of the best in the country."

Aimee felt tears prick the back of her lids. She didn't think she would ever get used to not having or knowing her father. She even envied her friends whose parents were divorced or separated. At least they knew their fathers existed, somewhere out there, while hers lay in a grave, his mangled bones bleached white from the passage of time. Lieutenant Emery Frasier had taken a direct hit from a rocket fired into the foxhole where he was hiding with a dozen men under his command.

She and Leland walked into the store, holding hands. Leland released her hand and reached for a shopping cart. "I'll push it for you."

Her eyes crinkled in a smile. "Now, what would your readers say if they knew that the creator of some of the most popular men's adventure novels written today was seen pushing a cart up and down the aisles of a supermarket?"

Leland's velvet gaze caressed her face slowly before moving lower to her throat and breasts. "I'm not certain the more macho readers would appreciate it, but I believe the women would like it. What do you think?"

Aimee wrinkled her delicate nose. "I'm willing to bet they would."

THREE

Aimee woke up before her alarm went off, rolled over on her back, and stared up at the ceiling. She was surprised she had slept so soundly in a strange bed. Usually it took her several nights before she was able to sleep in a bed other than her own. That was why she never spent the night at Jeremy's house. The first time she shared his bed, she wound up tossing all night while he lay on his back snoring loudly.

She smiled in the dimness of the room when she recalled shopping with Leland. He'd filled the cart, matching her item for item until it nearly overflowed. And when they reached the checkout, he pulled out a credit card and paid for everything. He ignored her protests once they were in the truck, saying he thought it only fair that he offer room, board, and also meals. She'd opened her mouth to come back at him, but he gave her a warning expression that said, *Don't argue with me.*

She didn't know what it was about Leland Monroe, but she felt so comfortable around him—as if she'd known him for years instead of hours. Pushing back the sheet covering her body, she sat up and swung her legs over the side of the bed. Ten minutes later, after brushing her teeth, splashing water on her face, and slipping into a pair of shorts, racing bra, tank top, and a pair of running shoes, she opened the door and headed for the beach. It was only a little past five and pinpoints of light had begun to pierce the sky as the soft sounds of birds calling to one another heralded the start of a new day.

The sound of dirt, sand, and gravel grating under her shoes sounded unnaturally loud in the hushed silence. Golden light spilled from the windows of a house along the path, indicating someone else had gotten up early too. She'd taken a cursory glance at Leland's house, but all of the windows were dark. She hoped he would at least be up by eight.

Her pulse accelerated when she anticipated seeing the inside of his house for the first time. What would she find? What secrets would she uncover that would change the history of St. Simons Island?

She made it down to the beach. There was now enough daylight to see that she was the only one on the beach for at least a quarter of a mile. Resting her right foot on a large boulder, she began a series of stretching exercises before changing legs. Then she began jogging in a smooth, loose-limbed pace, her arms pumping rhythmically at her sides.

The sound of her soles hitting the sand became a wordless, nameless song as she felt the heat of the rising sun on her back. Seagulls floated above the wind currents before skimming the water in search of breakfast. She jogged past an open space set up for outdoor picnicking and barbequing. She jogged past the business district, where restaurants, bars and souvenir shops beckoned locals and tourists. She met another jogger coming in the opposite direction, and they exchanged smiles.

The sand changed color and the surf rushing up to meet the beach was calmer, and Aimee knew she was nearing the eastern edge of the island. The water along this stretch of the island was very different from where the Monroe house was constructed. It was placid, calm, while the waves crashing up against the large boulders on the southern end were angry, almost hostile. She'd noticed the signs warning swimmers about the dangerous currents and undertow.

Slowing her pace, she came to a complete stop, and then sank down to the sand. Aimee sat, catching her breath and staring out into the Atlantic Ocean, and breathing in a lungful of sea-scented air.

She sat on the soft sand for half an hour, then stood up and brushed particles of sand off her shorts. Taking a deep breath, she turned and retraced her steps.

* * *

Leland lay in bed, eyes closed. It was six o'clock and time for him to get up, but he'd delayed rising because his thoughts were filled with the image of Aimee Frasier. After they'd returned from the supermarket, he had berated himself for going shopping with her.

Was he losing his mind? He'd put her up in the guest house so he wouldn't see her, but then turned around and offered to take her food shopping. A muscle throbbed spasmodically in his jaw as he clenched his teeth tightly. Perhaps—just perhaps—because he was spending so much time alone, he unknowingly craved female company. Since relocating from Augusta to St. Simons, he hadn't interacted with more than three people in six months. He saw the young woman who came to clean the house, the elderly man who'd been responsible for cutting the grass for the past twenty-five years, and the widow who was his closest neighbor. Other than his parents, who'd retired and lived in Hawaii, and sister, who lived in an L.A. suburb with her orthodontist-to-the-rich-and-famous husband and three preteen children, the only others he corresponded with were his New York–based agent and editor, and they always communicated with one another by telephone, e-mail, or fax.

And he almost couldn't remember the last time he'd been involved with a woman. There was a time when he thought himself in love: however, that relationship had ended unexpectedly when Lorraine left him because he would not commit to marrying her. That had been eleven years ago. He'd just begun his first novel, and he hadn't been willing to sacrifice his new career or share his life with anyone at that time.

Opening his eyes, he stared up at the ceiling. Times had changed, and his career had changed. He'd left his teaching position at a junior college and had written three best-selling novels, all of which had made the *New York Times* list. His literary success was nothing short of being phenomenal, while the only thing in Leland Monroe's life that changed was that he was older and more reclusive. He was forty, unmarried, claimed no children, and hadn't slept with a woman in more than six months.

Aimee Frasier's presence had evoked a repressed desire—

a desire not to be the last St. Simons Island Monroe. He'd achieved the success he sought, but at what cost?

He closed his eyes again, and whispered an oath. After he completed this novel, he needed to reestablish his priorities. It was time he found a woman to love and marry; it was also time he fathered a child.

A soft mewling let him know that Marmalade had squeezed through the slight opening in the bedroom door. He opened his eyes and sat up. Seconds later he swung his legs over the side of the bed and knelt on a hand-woven cotton rug several feet away. "One, two, three." He began counting as he executed push-ups. He followed the fifty push-ups with sit-ups, and after reaching twenty-five, he made his way to the bathroom to shower and shave.

His step was light as a smile creased his handsome face. For a reason he could not fathom, he looked forward to seeing Aimee again. He wanted to feast on the perfection of her incredibly beautiful face and body. But what he refused to acknowledge was that she appealed to his maleness, had elicited a modicum of sexual awareness that he hadn't felt in a long time.

Yes—he'd done the right thing to put her in the guest house. Sharing a roof with Aimee Frasier was too temptingly challenging. He would only interact with her when necessary.

When Aimee stood on the porch to Leland Monroe's home a few minutes before eight o'clock, she was able to discern in the full sunlight what she'd missed in yesterday's afternoon shadows. The structure's design was a classical version of the Southern vernacular farmhouse. Three evenly positioned columns rising upward to the second-story veranda flanked the front door on either side. Twin ancient oak trees, draped in Spanish moss, stood like silent sentinels guarding the house, and her pulse quickened when she anticipated documenting and authenticating items from a long-ago period in the American South—a period where her ancestors were at the center of issues of race, culture, politics, and economics.

Leland appeared at the door as she raised her hand to ring the doorbell. He was dressed in what she would come to recognize as his "work attire"—shorts, T-shirt, and running shoes.

His eyes crinkled attractively as he offered her a friendly smile. "Good morning." He pushed open the screen door, holding it until she stepped into the entryway.

"Good morning." Aimee returned his warm smile.

Her gaze lingered on the exquisite beauty of a Queen Anne mahogany drop-leaf table, which she estimated was circa 1765, facing a mahogany lolling chair covered in a pale green watered-silk fabric. There was no doubt that the fabric wasn't the original covering for the chair, but just a glance at the bold serpentine crests shaped on its rectangular arms, reeded legs, and lined inlay accents inset panels of maple indicated that the chair was not a reproduction.

While Aimee's gaze swept slowly over the furnishings, Leland stared boldly at her exquisite face, and it was not for the first time that he'd found everything about her perfect. This morning she wore a white man-tailored shirt with a pair of slim black capri pants and matching ballet-type shoes. She'd rolled the shirt cuffs back to just below her elbows, and the flesh covering her slender forearms shimmered from a scented cream that was subtle and hypnotic.

Her expression changed, her smile fading, as she arched her right eyebrow when she turned and caught Leland staring at a spot just below her neck. She resisted the urge to glance down to check whether she hadn't buttoned enough buttons on her shirt.

"It's eight o'clock, Mr. Monroe, and the clock is running." Her tone was cold, the words exacting.

Leland's head jerked up at the same time his mouth tightened into a thin, hard line. "I'm more than aware of the hour, Miss Frasier," he drawled sarcastically. "Follow me and I'll show you where you'll be working."

Turning on his heel, he walked out of the entryway, through a narrow hallway, and to a room off a formal living room, Aimee following. He'd thought of setting her up in a room near the back porch, but it was too close to where he'd established his studio. He would move her only if she complained about not being comfortable enough.

Aimee came to a complete stop when she examined the many mullioned windows facing east and south that allowed unlimited sunlight during the daylight hours. Floor lamps, a small, round mahogany table with four priceless Chippendale carved mahogany side chairs were positioned in the center of the room, and a Queen Anne mahogany block-and-shell tall-case clock in the corner were the space's only furnishings.

A satisfied smile tilted the corners of her mouth. "It's perfect."

You're perfect, Leland mused, staring at the softly curling hair on the nape of her incredibly long neck. He forced a smile he didn't feel.

"I've packed up everything in boxes. I'll bring down the first one."

Aimee nodded, tracing the smooth surface of the priceless table with her fingertips. She didn't know how, but she felt as if she could connect with the many black hands that had polished the piece of furniture. She wondered if they'd sang when they'd gone about their daily tasks. Or if the ones who had come to the Americas in the belly of a ship cried for their loss of freedom, family members, and all that had been familiar to them? Or had they resigned themselves to another place, culture, and a lifetime of servitude?

Standing motionless, she closed her eyes and whispered a silent prayer for the souls of her deceased ancestors who were born, lived, and died without sampling a taste of a freedom intended for everyone from God. She was standing in the same position when Leland returned, cradling a large plastic crate against his chest.

He placed the crate on the floor beside the table, his gaze fixed on the distressed expression marring Aimee's delicate features. "Are you all right?"

She blinked once. "Yes."

He didn't believe her, but he shrugged a broad shoulder. "I've packed up everything that I found in the crawl space that doubles as an attic. All of the books are in one crate; photographs, jewelry, letters, and documents in others. There're at least half a dozen paintings I found wrapped in burlap."

"How many crates are you talking about?"

"A total of four."

She nodded. "One for each week."

"Do you think you can research everything in four weeks?"

"I'm hoping I can. I won't know for certain until I see what I have to work with."

"What about the furniture?"

She touched the table's surface again. "That's easy. If the pieces are originals, then they should be stamped with a manufacturer's name, or the name of the artisan. I'll catalogue the furniture last."

"I'll bring everything down and put it in a corner. That way you can determine what you want to catalogue first."

She nodded again. "Can you get me a tablecloth?"

Both of his eyebrows raised. "A tablecloth?"

"I want to protect the table. If this table and chairs are indeed authentic Chippendale from the School of Job Townsend, Senior, of Newport, circa 1750, then you could expect to fetch a minimum of a hundred to a hundred-fifty thousand for each chair at a Christie's auction."

Leland's jaw dropped and he stared at her as if she'd lost her mind. "You're telling me that if I sold these four chairs at an auction, I could get more than half a million dollars?"

"At least a hundred thousand for the table, six-hundred thousand for the chairs, and between three- and five-hundred thousand for the clock."

Angry lines formed between his eyes. "That's disgusting! Some people work all their lives and don't earn half that much, while some idiot would pay half a million dollars for an old clock."

She lifted her shoulders in a delicate shrug. "What can I say, Leland? Different strokes for different folks."

He took a step, bringing them within a foot of each other. The gold lights in his eyes sparkled like pyrite. "How about you, Aimee? Would you pay half a million dollars for a clock?"

She thought of the exquisite workmanship that went into the construction of the magnificent clock—a clock that was probably more than two hundred fifty years old—a clock whose beauty could not be repeated, not even by the most talented modern clock maker. She also thought about how many people could be fed with half a million dollars.

"No," she said after a swollen silence. "No piece of furniture is worth that."

Her answer seemed to please Leland, because he gave her a sensual smile that made her heart beat just a little faster. Heat flooded her face before it moved downward, warming her throat, and still lower to her breasts.

Their gazes caught and held until he turned and walked out of the room, leaving her staring at the space where he'd been. When he returned to the room, carrying another carton and a tablecloth, she had taken a ledger wrapped in oilcloth out of the crate and was examining the fading signature and date on the first page. What had astounded her was not Jacob Monroe's signature, or the 1822 date, but the fact that she was holding a document that recorded the purchase and sale of human cargo.

Closing her eyes, she bit down hard on her lower lip to compose herself. Aimee did not know why she felt so connected to the Monroe artifacts; never before had she experienced the emotions coursing through her now. Was it because perhaps one or some of the slaves owned by the descendants of George Monroe were also her relatives? Her mother and father could trace their families back more than one hundred years—and all of those years were spent on Georgia soil.

She opened her eyes, blinking back the moisture; she then spread a large oval antique linen cloth over the surface of the table before sitting down to begin a meticulous perusal of the contents of the first of many cartons she would come to know intimately over the next month.

FOUR

Leland's concentration was slipping. He'd spent hours gazing out the window rather than typing, and without looking at a clock, he knew by the lengthening shadows in his studio that it was close to the time when he would quit for the day. His gaze shifted to the page number along the lower ruler of the computer program. He'd managed to complete four pages—four pages in six hours. And it didn't take the I.Q. of a rocket scientist to conclude that his less than productive day had been because he was distracted—distracted by the presence of a woman working in another room several hundred feet away. He saved what he'd typed, then stood and penciled in the page number on the wall calendar.

It'll be better tomorrow, he mused. It would take some getting used to, having another human being share his home. And since he'd moved into the house, he hadn't had any visitors. He didn't count the young woman who came to clean the main house and the guest house cottage.

He walked out of the studio and made his way to the kitchen. Marmalade met him as he walked over to the pantry and took a can of cat food off a shelf. He opened the can and emptied it into a clean saucer before filling another saucer with fresh water. The feline pounced on the food as if she hadn't eaten in days. Leland watched her for several minutes, then turned and walked out of the kitchen to the staircase leading to the second floor. He hadn't planned on dining out, but he knew he had to get away from the house—even if it was only for an hour.

Half an hour later, showered and dressed in a pair of khakis with a matching short-sleeved shirt and sand-colored deck shoes, he started up his truck and headed for Frederica Road.

Aimee, registering the sound of an automobile's engine, glanced up from what she was reading, and then looked at her watch. It was after six. She'd worked two hours past her quitting time. She'd been so engrossed in the entries of three volumes of the five journals that she'd lost track of time. The entries were meticulous—the authors indicating the day and time of each, along with detailed descriptions of every business transaction dating from 1822 to 1898. The volumes had held her spellbound. She'd gotten up once to return to the cottage to eat a hastily prepared salad of red-leaf lettuce, cherry tomatoes, cucumbers, and croutons tossed with a vinaigrette dressing. She'd rushed back to her project and pored over the journals while entering notes in a thick spiral notebook. The notes would be entered into her laptop computer with a printout for Leland and the Trust.

She returned the journals to their carton, turned off the floor lamp, and left the house, closing the door behind her. Her step was slow, her head filled with facts as she tried sorting out what she'd uncovered in only three historical documents. What she could not understand was why she'd become so emotionally involved. It was as if she could hear the sound of the auctioneer's voice as he extolled the physical and artistic attributes of human beings as they were paraded along Savannah's Factor's Walk, and see hundreds of bales of cotton piled high along the waterfront area for shipment to Europe and northern mill towns.

She'd also imagined she could hear the moans and cries of men, women, children—families torn apart and sold in the same manner as a farmer purchased livestock. There was an entry about a recalcitrant father who refused to work because his wife and children were sold to a Virginia tobacco farmer, and was subsequently beaten unconscious when he attacked an overseer. The man had lingered in a coma for a week before he died.

Aimee opened the door to the cottage, made her way to her bedroom, and fell across the bed, sobbing uncontrollably. She lay facedown, motionless, crying without making a sound. It was forty-five minutes later that she made her way to the bathroom, where she filled the tub with water and bubble bath. Stripping off her clothes, she stepped into the tub, sank down, closed her eyes, and willed her mind blank. Once the water cooled and the bubbles disappeared, she picked up a bath sponge and scrubbed her body until her flesh tingled, and when she left the tub, she felt as if she'd washed away the pain and the lingering memories of a part of history that would remain in the hearts and minds of African Americans—forever.

She moisturized her body before pulling on a pair of shorts and a tank top. She'd changed her mind about dining out, and instead prepared a fruit salad of sliced peaches, cantaloupe, and watermelon for dinner. Somehow she'd lost her appetite.

Now that she was back in control, she knew her tears weren't solely for the departed souls who'd lived out their lives in bondage. The tears were also for Aimee Frasier. She'd given a man two years of her life and never really took the time to know him, while refusing to acknowledge his sometimes overbearing manner. She saw only what she wanted to see: a man she wanted to marry because she wanted children before she became too old.

Aimee sat on the porch, watching as dusk settled over St. Simons Island. The scene was reminiscent of someone pulling down a diaphanous lace fabric over a window to provide for a modicum of privacy. A shadowy darkness shaded her as she sat motionless on a cushioned rocker, listening to the incessant chirping of insects and the distinctive croaking of frogs. A smile softened her mouth when she saw the first firefly. She remembered that she and the girl who grew up next door to her and her mother always made a wish when they spotted their first firefly of the evening. They'd made a pact never to reveal their wishes, and Aimee's was always the same—she wished for a father.

Once she entered adolescence, her wish changed—she wanted to fall in love with a tall, handsome boy, marry him, have his babies, and then live happily ever after. And as she matured, so did her aspirations. Completing her education and establishing a professional career had become a priority. Her choice in a career had become an easy one. For twelve years she'd come to her mother's antique shop every day after classes ended, and spent time identifying different periods of furniture, silver, and wallpaper patterns at a glance. At twenty-two she lived in France for a year, studying architecture while perfecting her rudimentary French until she was fully bilingual.

Inhaling, she breathed in a lungful of ocean air, and then let out her breath slowly. Nightfall was complete as a spray of twinkling stars littered a navy-blue sky. Unfolding her legs, she rose gracefully from the rocker as the sound of a car's engine, grating sand, and the sweep of a pair of headlights lit up the night. The outline of Leland's truck came into view as he slowed and parked it alongside the main house. He turned off the headlights and engine, and opened the passenger-side door at the same time that Aimee closed the door to the cottage. If she had waited on the porch, she would've seen Leland standing beside the truck staring at the space where she'd been.

Her bare feet were silent on the faded woven cotton rug on the parlor floor as she walked over to the table beside the sofa to check her cellular phone. It had one voice mail message. Pressing a button, she listened to the message from her mother, asking that she return the call.

She dialed Constance Frasier's number, smiling when she heard her mother's beautifully modulated voice.

"Hello."

"Hello, Momma."

"How are you?"

"Good." And she was, now that she'd recovered from her earlier crying jag.

"How's St. Simons?"

"From what I've seen of it, it's beautiful. I'm planning to tour the island this coming weekend."

"Don't forget to take pictures of some of the historic sites."

"I won't."

Constance told her that she'd sold a pair of five-shell-base circa 1760 Georgian sterling silver candlesticks and a pair of 1825 Warwick vase wine coolers to a young California couple that had recently become collectors of antique silver pieces.

Aimee could understand her mother's excitement, because anyone who came into the shop and inquired about the candlesticks usually wanted to negotiate for a lower price for the exquisite silver pieces. But Constance could quickly assess the value of an article from any era as well as the experts from Christie's or Sotheby's. Aimee had been introduced to the antique trade from one of the best in the business—Constance Brown-Frasier.

"Jeremy called me last night," Constance said, changing the topic of conversation. "He wants you to call him."

Aimee's delicate jaw hardened. "I have nothing to say to him. And if he wants to talk to me, he can call me directly. What is he asking you to be—the mediator?"

"He sounded so sad, honey. I think he's sorry for what he said."

"That's too bad, Momma. He should've thought of that before he berated my profession, telling me to grow up and stop playing with dollhouses."

"He just doesn't understand our business."

Aimee wanted to scream at her mother for being so soft and forgiving. "Exactly. That's why I'm not going to marry him. There are a lot of women in Atlanta who would give up a kidney just to marry Jeremy Robinson. Let him go find one."

A slight gasp came through the earpiece. "When did you get so uncompromising, Aimee?"

"How does my being independent become synonymous with being uncompromising?"

There was a noticeable pause before Constance spoke again. "You're right, honey."

"I'll call you tomorrow," Aimee promised her mother.

"I'm going up to Charleston tomorrow to pick up a few items from another dealer who's going out of business. I plan to be there for a couple of days."

"Then I'll call you at home Sunday evening."

"Good."

"Good night, Momma. I love you."

"I love you too, honey."

Pressing a button, Aimee ended the call, her lips thinning into a tight line. How dare Jeremy! How dare he call her mother with his sad tale of woe. She was tempted to call him and give him a piece of her mind, but decided against it. That's what he wanted her to do—call him.

No!

Never!

FIVE

After her second day on St. Simons Island, Aimee established a pattern of rising early and jogging along the beach before she returned to the cottage to prepare for work. She ate a light breakfast of fresh fruit with a bowl of wheat flakes and a cup of tea. Leland made it a habit to leave the front door unlocked for her, and a day had passed without her even getting a glimpse of him. It was as if she was alone in the large house. But she knew he was in attendance, because the wafting scent of his haunting aftershave lingered in the entryway, and one or two times she heard his distinctive whistle that sent Marmalade scurrying from under the table in the room where she pored over the well-preserved documents from another century.

However, that all changed at the end of the week when she walked into the Georgia Sea Grill on Mallory Street and found Leland waiting to be seated at the seafood restaurant. Seeing him surprised her, because it was the first time she'd seen him dressed in a pair of slacks. He stared at her as if he'd never seen her before. She offered him a smile, seemingly breaking his entrancement.

Closing the distance between them, Leland detected the subtle fragrance of the perfume that had lingered in the room long after Aimee left to return to the compact cottage behind his home.

He'd thought she'd followed him to the restaurant, but dismissed the notion as soon as it entered his mind. He'd left the house an hour earlier to mail a letter to his parents, then stopped at a stationer to purchase several reams of paper before driving to the restaurant. He didn't know why, but he'd wanted her to follow him. His male vanity wanted her to be as intrigued with him as he'd become with her.

His eyes widened as he took in the very sight he'd sought to avoid since meeting her for the first time. She was classically attired in a sleeveless white linen dress with tiny covered buttons running from the scooped neckline to just below her knees. The slimming garment ended mid-calf and permitted him an unobscured view of her long, bare, shapely legs and groomed feet in a pair of high-heeled, sling-back black sandals. Tonight she'd added a touch of makeup to her flawless face—a vibrant orange-brown lipstick and a coat of mascara to her long, full lashes.

She's stunning in white, he told himself while staring openly at her oval-shaped face with the slight indentation on her delicate chin. The color was the perfect foil for her sable-brown face with a hint of copper undertones.

A slight smile touched his strong mouth. "Are you dining alone tonight?"

Aimee tilted her chin, returning his smile. "Yes."

She hadn't realized that she was holding her breath, while marveling that a man could look so stunningly virile in just a shirt and a pair of slacks. A finely woven black short-sleeved shirt was the same fabric as his black linen pants. Her smile widened. He'd changed his casual shoes for a pair of black Cole-Hann slip-ons.

"So am I," he said in a quiet tone. "Would you mind sharing a table?"

Her smile slipped. "Do you really think that's a good idea, Leland?"

He arched a curving eyebrow, shaking his head. "What's wrong with it?"

"I'm working for you."

A flash of humor crossed his handsome face. "You're employed by the Georgia National Trust for Historic Preservation, not Leland Monroe. Besides, your workday is eight to four, and . . ." He glanced at his watch. "And it's six-thirty, which means it's after hours."

Aimee did not want to share a table, or, for that fact, any meal with Leland Monroe. All she wanted to do was complete her research and leave him and St. Simons Island behind. What she could not and refused to admit to herself was that she'd found him a little too attractive. She'd just ended a two-year liaison, and year-long engagement to one man, while within days she'd found herself attracted to a brilliant, reclusive man who stirred emotions her ex-fiancé couldn't.

"What if we discuss business, Aimee?"

"Perhaps another time," she said, hoping to dissuade him.

Vertical lines marred his smooth forehead. "Are you always this uptight, Aimee?"

Her mother thought her uncompromising, Jeremy said she was bullheaded, and Leland had just called her uptight. Were they right? Did they see something in her personality she refused to acknowledge? She remembered dating one man who said that if things didn't go her way, then it could be no way.

"I don't think of myself as uptight."

"What do you call not being able to relax?"

"Being professional," she countered.

A young man approached them, smiling. "Your table is ready, Mr. Monroe."

Leland nodded, reaching for Aimee's hand and pulling it into the curve of his elbow, tightening his firm grip when she attempted to pull away.

"The young lady is dining with me."

The waiter stared at Aimee, then nodded. "Follow me, please."

Leaning down from his impressive height, Leland pressed his mouth against her ear, his warm breathing sweeping over her flesh. "Tonight we'll be very professional. Over dinner you can tell me about what you've uncovered among my family heirlooms."

Aimee missed the admiring glances from men and women as she and Leland were shown to a table in a secluded portion of the restaurant. Her dark eyes flashed fire. Didn't he know he was a walking, breathing mass of temptation? She had come to St. Simons Island to research a project, not lust after a man.

Leland seated Aimee, lingering behind her longer than necessary. His gaze swept over the delicate gold chain around her long neck and the softly curling black hair covering her head before he rounded the table and sat opposite her.

Their gazes met over the small space separating them, neither willing to look away. The burning candle flickered over their features, distorting, then flattering them, as the flame danced and dipped with each breath they took.

The liquid gold in Leland's eyes competed with the hot flame as his gaze moved as slowly as a drop of heated wax from her face, to the curve of bones in her clavicle, and down to her chest before reversing itself. His delicate nostrils flared slightly as he found himself drowning in the beauty of the woman sharing his space and temporarily his property.

"What made you decide to eat here?" he asked, breaking the sensual spell.

Her large glossy eyes crinkled in a warm smile. "I discovered it when I jogged down here this morning."

His eyebrows shifted. "You jogged this far?"

"This isn't far. I usually jog an average of thirty miles a week."

He studied her with an intense curiosity before his gaze shifted to her hands. He noticed the narrow band of lighter color on the third finger of her left hand. It was apparent she'd worn a ring on that finger.

Aimee saw the direction of his gaze, curbing the urge to place her hands in her lap. She picked up the menu on the table in front of her, pretending interest in the selections.

"You appear quite fit for someone who spends so many hours sitting," she said without glancing at him.

Leland picked up his own menu. "I do push-ups, sit-ups, and go bike-riding on the weekends."

She peered up at him. "A stationary bike?"

"A *bicycle* bike." He managed to sound slightly insulted.

"Where do you bike?"

"Around the island. There's a bike path starting at the Ft. Frederica National Monument that winds around Frederica and Demere roads. At Demere you can go west to Kings Way to the St. Simons Causeway, or you can make a circle around Mallory Street and go east along Ocean Boulevard to the Old

Coast Guard Station. Perhaps you'd like to join me early one morning before it gets too hot."

"What will I ride?" Aimee asked, staring directly at him. "I don't do handlebars."

Leland laughed, the deep sound rumbling up from his broad chest. "You'll have your own bike."

"I'll think about it," she said, refusing to commit.

"Is that a promise?" His voice lowered with his gaze.

Smiling sensually, Aimee said, "Yes."

"You should do that more often."

Her smile faded. "What?"

"Smile."

"I smile," she said defensively.

"Not enough."

"That's because you haven't seen me enough to know that I do."

Resting a muscular arm on the tablecloth, his eyes widened until she could see the dark brown centers of his large gold-brown eyes. "When *can* I see you?"

Aimee knew she had fallen headlong into a trap of her own making. He'd thrown down the gauntlet and she'd picked up his challenge. She didn't know whether it was the charming ambiance and natural beauty associated with St. Simons Island, or the powerful magnetism of the overtly virile man sitting several feet from her, but something unknown and mysterious made her want to see more than glimpses of Leland Monroe. She knew more about his ancestors than she knew about him.

"Sunday. We can have dinner together," she said quickly before she could change her mind.

His expression was impassive. "Are you cooking?"

Her delicate jaw dropped slightly before she recovered from his query. "I hadn't planned on cooking."

"What *do* you have planned?"

"I'd planned to make reservations at one of the restaurants on the island."

Leland shrugged a broad shoulder under his shirt. "If that's the case, then I'll cook. It's tourist season and the restaurants are always crowded on Sundays."

Aimee's expression softened as she smiled, her slanting eyes tilting beguilingly. "I'm impressed. You write and cook. What other creative gifts do you claim?"

"That's it," he said in a modest tone.

All conversation ended when a waiter came over to take their orders.

SIX

Aimee swallowed a portion of broiled scallops from an assorted seafood platter, smiling, while Leland wound several strands of pasta around on his fork and extended it to her.

"Taste this." Reaching across the table, he cradled her chin in one hand as he guided the fork to her parted lips, watching her sexy mouth as she chewed and swallowed the linguine. "What do you think?"

Closing her eyes, Aimee shook her head. "It's incredible." She opened her eyes and offered Leland the smile he'd come to look for. He'd ordered linguine with lobster in Alfredo sauce.

"This is why I come here."

"What about the other restaurants?"

He took a sip of chilled white wine, meeting her gaze over the rim. "CJ's is good if you want Italian food. The Crab Trap is the place if you want generous portions of very fresh seafood. George's Mediterranean Café offers wonderful dishes from the Greek Isles. Then there's Frederica House, and dozens of others."

"How many restaurants are on the island?"

"At least thirty-five—give or take a few."

Aimee picked up her wineglass and took a sip of her fragrant white zinfandel. Her lids lowered slightly and she looked at Leland through a fringe of lashes. "How much time did you spend here as a child?" Her question seemed to startle him as he sat up straighter.

"I used to spend my summers here. My mother used to drive my sister and me down the day school ended, stay for two weeks, then drive back to Augusta to spend a month with my dad. Then they would come down together the last two weeks of our summer vacation. Dad and Grandpa would spend most of their time together fishing, while Momma and Grandma cooked and canned for the winter months.

"A couple of days before we returned to Augusta, we'd have a party to celebrate the end of the summer. Those were the times when we'd eat so much that wherever we lay, we slept. There were quite a few times when Dad and Grandpa never made it up the stairs to their bedrooms. Grandma said it was because they were drinking the hooch one of their neighbors used to make in his toolshed. I didn't know what they were talking about until I turned fourteen and drank a small portion that someone had left in a cup. It made me so sick that my folks had to delay our return trip because I couldn't stand up or stop throwing up. Once Grandma found out what I'd drunk, she forbade moonshine in her house ever again."

Aimee laughed, the throaty sound sweeping over Leland and pulling him in where he was ensnared in her innocent web of seduction.

"I didn't know people still made that stuff."

"Some people prefer hooch, or white lightning, to the finest scotch, champagne, or brandy."

She sobered when she realized she and Leland were talking about everything except her research. But suddenly that wasn't paramount, because she wanted to know everything about Leland Monroe—the man and the writer, not the direct descendant of George Monroe.

"What made you decide to become a writer?"

Leland's long fingers toyed with the stem of his glass as he stared over Aimee's shoulder. "I can't remember when I wanted to be anything else. As a kid I made up stories in my head even before I learned to write. Once I entered school, I used to lock myself in my room and spend hours writing. By the time I turned ten, I'd filled up more than twenty-five note-books with an ongoing saga about an action-hero reminiscent of the ones featured in DC Comics." A wry smile curved his mouth. "And before you ask—it was terrible."

"What made you think I was going to ask if it was good?"

"Your eyes. They give you away. They crinkle even though you try to keep a straight face."

Aimee wanted to ask if he could see that her eyes liked what she saw. "Speaking of faces," she began, segueing smoothly, "I found half a dozen daguerreotypes and more than twenty photographs of various Monroes in a tin box this morning. Most of them are identified as to who the subjects are, but there are a few with missing names and dates. Do you happen to have a family Bible?"

Leland nodded. "I have two in my studio. One is so old that I had to put it in a plastic box to keep the sea air from totally destroying it. The later one dates from 1932. What else have you uncovered?"

"George Monroe was born in Scotland, but came to Georgia when he was six with his parents and two sisters. His father, a shipbuilder, settled in Savannah, and eventually became quite prosperous designing and building ships for merchants who plied their trade between the American colonies and Europe. George changed the family's source of income when he used his inheritance to purchase large tracts of land to plant cotton. And as a landowner, he needed someone to plant and harvest his crop. That's when he became a slaveholder. He diversified his crops when he added rice and indigo.

"Even though most farmers in Georgia owned no more than an average of twenty slaves, the Monroe ledgers indicate that they were the exception. At one time they owned more than two hundred fifty African men, women, and children. And judging from the names listed for the various censuses, more than half the children born on the plantation were fathered by the owners."

Suddenly Leland's face was a glowering mask of anger. A muscle twitched noticeably in his jaw as he clenched his teeth. "I suppose it was cheaper and a lot more pleasurable to get a black woman pregnant than it was to purchase slaves at an auction."

Closing her eyes, Aimee leaned back in her chair. "Going through the ledgers has been very difficult for me." When she opened her eyes, they were glistening with unshed tears. "The entries were so descriptive that I felt as if I'd been transported back in time. I've been an architectural historian for ten years, and . . ." Her words trailed off. She couldn't continue, or she would dissolve into tears again.

Leland stood up and circled the table. He'd heard the grief in her voice, saw it on her beautiful face, and in that instant he wanted to take her in his arms and ease her distress. Extending his hand, he pulled her gently to her feet and curved an arm around her waist.

"Let's go, Aimee," he whispered close to her ear, releasing her long enough to drop several large bills on the table before leading her out of the restaurant.

Aimee walked out of the Georgia Sea Grill, leaning heavily against Leland as he steered her onto Mallory Street. The sidewalk was crowded with casually strolling tourists, some who stood around in small groups trying to decide where to dine.

The unyielding strength in his arm around her body was both comforting and frightening. She was grateful for his attempt to console her, while at the same time she registered an awareness of his overt sexuality that hadn't been there before. Aside from shaking his hand when she'd introduced herself, and their holding hands when they'd made their way to the supermarket her first night on the island, he hadn't touched her again.

And for the first time since coming to St. Simons, she admitted to herself that she wanted him to touch her—everywhere. Something foreign and unknown had communicated that she wanted to know Leland Monroe—know him in every way possible; know everything about him: if he was involved with a woman, if he'd been married, whether he had fathered children.

His publicist had revealed very little about Hayden Lawrence, the best-selling novelist. Readers only knew that Hayden Lawrence was a pseudonym for a Georgia native who'd taught literature at a state college before he became a fiction writer.

Placing a hand on his solid chest, Aimee eased back, forcing a smile. "I'm sorry, Leland, about getting emotional back there."

Curving both arms around her waist, he pulled her closer

and pressed his mouth to her hair. "There's no need to apologize." His words were soft, his voice soothing.

Leland was aware that they were standing on a sidewalk along one of the busiest streets on St. Simons, but he ignored the curious stares and glances as he cradled Aimee Frasier to his heart.

"I don't know what it is about your family's records," she said, her voice muffled against his chest, "but this is only the second time since I've entered this field of study that I've become emotionally involved in my research. Perhaps it is because some of the people owned by your ancestors may have also been my relatives. It could be possible that some of the descendants of those little black children who were fathered by the slave-holding Monroes are my distant cousins."

A soft smile curved Leland's mouth. "I hope not, Aimee. I don't want to think of you as a relative."

Pulling back slightly, she stared up at his smiling face. "Why not?"

His smile faded as a serious expression crossed his handsome features. *What I'm feeling now—what I'd like to do with you would amount to incest if you were actually a relative.*

"You could never be a Monroe," he said glibly.

Vertical lines appeared between her large eyes. "Why not?"

"You're too uptight. Monroes are generally laid-back."

She smiled at his attempt at levity. "Perhaps a little moonshine will help me unwind."

Throwing back his head, Leland laughed, the sound rumbling in his chest. "I can't guarantee whether I'll be able to find someone who still makes white lightning, but I know another method that is practically foolproof."

"What is it?"

He sobered, staring down at her. His eyes changed color, darkening with a rising lust he was unable to conceal. "I'll have to show you."

Her gaze widened at the same time her breathing faltered, then stopped completely as she stared at him in astonishment. "Leland." His name came out like a breathless whisper after she'd inhaled to force air into her constricted lungs.

He arched a curving eyebrow. "You didn't know?"

Her lush lips parted. "Know what?" she asked, answering his question with one of her own.

"Why I've stayed away from you?" She shook her head. "You're quite a distraction, Miss Aimee Frasier. A very sexy, very beautiful distraction."

"I'm sorry." The apology sounded trite, even to her ears.

Leland's upper lip flattened against the ridge of his upper teeth when he smiled. "I'm not, Aimee Frasier."

They stood on Mallory Street, embracing and staring at each other as a vague light of awareness tightened, binding them together. Admiring gazes lingered on the tall, attractive couple who seemed oblivious to everyone and everything around them.

"Will you share dinner with me tomorrow night?" Leland asked, his gaze fusing with hers.

Aimee's lashes fluttered wildly. He was asking her for a date—a date she would not be able to accept. "I can't. I've made plans to meet a friend in Savannah."

Leland wanted to ask whether the friend was a man, but decided against it. He had no right to question Aimee about anything or anyone. "Are we still on for Sunday dinner?"

She flashed a brilliant smile. "Yes."

His hands fell from her slim, fragrant body. "Where are you parked?"

Aimee felt his loss immediately. "I'm around the corner."

"I'll walk you to your car."

They walked side by side, not touching as they made their way down the street. Leland waited for Aimee to get into her Audi, start up the engine, maneuver smoothly out of her parking space, and pull away before he turned to go back to where he'd parked his truck.

He'd told Aimee the truth—she was a distraction, one that reminded him of how empty his existence was. He had his writing, but he needed more. And it was only now that he realized the more was Aimee Frasier.

SEVEN

Aimee shared a cushioned love seat with Pamela Hill, cradling her friend's four-month-old daughter to her breasts. The pleasant smell exclusive to babies wafted in her nostrils. Closing her eyes, she smiled.

"She's so precious, Pam."

Pamela affected a slight frown. "You wouldn't think she's precious at three in the morning when she wakes up crying to be fed. I'd promised myself that I wouldn't breast-feed again, but I felt so guilty depriving her of what I'd given her brothers."

Aimee opened her eyes and stared at her ex-college roommate and best friend. Pamela hadn't changed since the two met as incoming freshmen at SCAD, except to add a couple of inches to her narrow hips and tiny breasts. But after giving birth to three children in eight years, it was expected that the waif-thin commercial artist would gain a few pounds.

"And before you ask," Pamela said quickly, "Alicia definitely is the last one. I made certain of that before I left the hospital this time." She and her husband had decided to have two children, but after two sons, they relented and decided to try for a daughter.

"Three is a nice number," Aimee said with a smile.

"One is also a nice number." Her gaze shifted from Aimee's impassive expression to her left hand, where the lighter band of brown flesh was still visible. "I can't believe you're not getting married. You know that Clyde and I planned to have this baby six months before you were scheduled to be married because I didn't want to look like a beached whale waddling down the aisle as your matron of honor."

"It took me less than twenty-four hours to conclude that I'd made the right decision not to marry Jeremy. I had no idea that he was harboring so much resentment about my career."

Staring at Aimee, Pamela folded her arms under her milk-filled breasts. She and Aimee were complete opposites in appearance. Aimee was tall, she petite, barely five-one. She'd inherited her fair skin coloring and soft charcoal-gray eyes from her paternal grandmother, while Aimee claimed a rich, dark sable-brown complexion with large, slanting obsidian eyes. They'd bonded quickly from the first day they shared a two-bedroom apartment a week before they began classes at the Savannah College of Art and Design. Both were popular with the opposite sex and never lamented that they couldn't find dates for most of the college's more important social events.

Aimee remained at SCAD, earning a graduate degree, while Pamela returned to Charlotte, North Carolina, after obtaining her own undergraduate degree. However, four years later she returned to Savannah when she accepted a position as a commercial artist for a Black-owned advertising agency. A May–December romance with the head of the company resulted in a New Year's Eve wedding, and now at thirty-six, she was a happily married mother of three young children.

She remembered Aimee's telephone call, informing her that she was engaged to be married, but Pamela also remembered not hearing the breathless joy she knew Aimee was capable of exhibiting. She'd never met Jeremy Robinson, but something told her that her friend had *not* chosen wisely. She'd almost breathed an audible sigh of relief when Aimee revealed that she had ended her engagement.

"Tell me about your latest commission."

Aimee stared through the mesh of the screened-in second-story veranda in the Hills' stately home in the city's historic district. An overhead fan barely stirred the humid air as the setting sun failed to claim the lingering heat with its descent.

"I'm cataloguing the contents of the summer residence of one of Savannah's most infamous slaveholders. I've read hundreds of pages of journal entries where the Monroes claim they treated their slaves well because they gave their 'property' a limitless supply of shoes, clothes, and foodstuffs—including flour—while slaves on most other plantations died or nearly froze to death during the winter because they weren't clothed properly or fed enough."

A scowl distorted Pamela's pretty face. "Oh, how generous," she spat out.

Aimee was sorry she'd mentioned anything about slaves and slaveholders. She hadn't understood Pamela's proclivity for dating men who were nearly jet-black in coloring until Pamela made her aware of how much she resented the complexion and eye color she'd inherited from her grandmother. However, all of Pamela and Clyde's children were a beautiful copper brown with dark eyes.

"I've only seen one room in the house, but the furnishings are priceless." She told Aimee about the clock and the table and chairs that would probably appraise close to a million dollars. She also told her about the cottage where she was staying. What she didn't reveal was that best-selling fiction author Hayden Lawrence was a pseudonym for Leland Monroe.

"A grandson who is a direct descendant of the former slaveowners now lives in the house?"

Aimee nodded. "He made it his permanent residence about six months ago."

"Does he plan to sell any of the furnishings?"

This time Aimee shook her head. "I doubt it. He told my boss that he'd like to loan them to museums that feature exhibits relating to the African experience in the Americas."

"I hope he loans a few pieces to the Ralph Mark Gilbert Civil Rights Museum and the King-Tisdell Cottage here in Savannah. Our children need to be reminded of our state's rich African-American heritage. I think most of them forget that the wealth of this country was based on an economy that stripped the African of everything he had except his will to survive. I preach to my kids every day that they are descendants of survivors and they'd better not disgrace our ancestors, or I'll make them sorry they ever drew breath."

Aimee laughed as she tried imagining tiny Pamela Hill glaring up at her sons, who were certain to inherit their father's towering height. Clyde Hill stepped out onto the veranda and eased his sleeping daughter from Aimee's embrace, leaving his wife and her friend on the veranda talking and laughing about the escapades they'd gotten into during their college years. It was after ten when Aimee announced that she was leaving.

Pamela stood up when Aimee rose to her feet. "Why don't you stay over?"

"I can't, Pam."

"But tomorrow's Sunday. You told me that you don't work the weekends."

"Perhaps the next time I come, I'll plan to stay." What she didn't tell her friend was that even though she'd told Leland she would think about going biking with him, she'd decided she wanted to. She wanted to return to St. Simons to spend the night, then get up early enough to catch him before he left to tour the island.

She hugged and kissed Pam and Clyde, then started up her car for the return drive. Fortunately traffic was light along I-95, and when she turned off for the local road leading to the bridge that would take her to St. Simons, her respiration accelerated a little. Meeting Leland at the restaurant and sharing dinner with him made her aware that she liked the reclusive writer. Liked him more than she wanted or needed to.

Leland sat on a rocker near a window in his bedroom, staring out at the night. He'd lost track of time as an occasional ocean breeze lifted the diaphanous creamy curtains away from the open windows. The silvered light of an almost full moon bathed the nearby cottage in an eerie glow. All of the windows were dark, which meant Aimee hadn't returned from Savannah.

Leland didn't know why, but he missed her. And it wasn't that he saw Aimee every day, yet he felt her presence whenever she was in the house. And he'd found himself listening for her departure. It was only after she left that he dared venture into the room where she'd spent the day, savoring the lingering scent of her perfume. The fragrance was so like Aimee—feminine and hauntingly beautiful.

Crossing his bare feet at the ankles, he pressed his head against the cushioned softness of the rocker, and closed his eyes. Scenes from his latest novel flashed through his mind. He'd gotten up earlier that morning to write. What surprised him was that he'd sat for hours typing, his fingers skimming over the keyboard, the words tumbling over themselves in his head before they were transferred to the monitor of his computer. His normal six-hour stint had stretched to more than nine, and when he saved what he'd typed, he was physically and emotionally drained. He'd paused to take a lukewarm shower, change his clothes, and feed Marmalade, then he had hastily thrown together a dinner of a grilled turkey burger on a sourdough roll with sliced tomato, Bermuda onion, and pickle. The butterflies in his stomach would not permit him to eat anything heavier.

It had been a long time since he'd been that inspired to sit and write for hours nonstop. The last time had been when he'd thought himself in love. The excitement of sharing his emotions with a woman was a heady turn-on that had not come often enough in his life.

He opened his eyes at the same time a slight smile curved his strong mouth. There was something about Miss Aimee Frasier, something other than her exquisite beauty, that touched a core of him, which no other woman had been able to stir. She'd been on St. Simons for a week, and he had another three to uncover why he'd fallen under her spell.

Half an hour later, he left the rocker, stripped off his clothes, and lay nude across his large four-poster bed. Within minutes his breathing deepened and the moment he drifted into a deep, dreamless sleep, Aimee maneuvered her car into the sand-littered driveway and parked alongside his SUV.

Marmalade squeezed through the slight opening of the door to the bedroom and sprang up onto the bed. She settled her body near Leland's bare feet, then closed her eyes and joined her master in sleep.

EIGHT

Aimee rang the doorbell to Leland's house at five o'clock the next morning, listening intently for movement behind the door. Less than a minute later she stared up through the lenses of her sunglasses at the expression of surprise on his handsome face.

Her smile was warm, inviting. "Are you ready to go biking?"

He returned her stare, unblinking. "I thought you said—"

"I know what I said," she replied softly, interrupting him. "I changed my mind."

Squaring his broad shoulders under a body-revealing tank top, he flashed a warm smile. "Good." He opened the door wider. "Come in. I have to put my shoes on and get the bikes."

She looked down at his bare feet, and it was not for the first time that she found Leland Monroe a near perfect masculine specimen. She silently admired his broad shoulders, wide chest, muscled arms and legs, flat middle, and well-groomed hands and feet. He hadn't shaved; the stubble on his lean jaw and chin only served to enhance his blatant virility.

"That's all right. I'll wait here on the porch."

Leland nodded, closed the door, and then retreated to an area in the rear of the house to retrieve his running shoes. Marmalade sauntered from her bed, rubbing herself against his bare legs. She meowed softly. Bending over, he tied the laces to his shoes at the same time the orange-colored cat pounced on the dangling pieces of string.

"No, Marmalade. I can't play with you now." He smiled at his pet. "I have a date with another woman this morning." Much to his surprise the feline meowed as if she understood what he was telling her. She flicked her tail around his ankle. "I'll see you later."

He finished tying his sneakers, then made his way to a storage room near the back door. Two bikes were suspended on a rack against one wall. Leland removed one, then the other, checking to see if the tires were inflated with enough air pressure. He perched a pair of sunglasses on the bridge of his nose and pulled on a cap to shield his face from the sun, then cradled one bike on his shoulder, while leading the other one down the back stairs and around to the front of the house.

Aimee rose gracefully from a rocker when Leland appeared with the bikes. She'd expected mountain bikes, not ones usually used for professional races. Adjusting her own baseball cap, she made her way down the porch stairs.

It took less than two minutes for Leland to adjust the seat for her on the bike she'd chosen, and by the time the sun had brightened the sky, they were cycling side by side along the bike path that began at the Fort Frederica National Monument, traveling southward along Frederica Road.

Leland set a leisurely pace, stopping occasionally to point out places of interest. They lingered at the Bloody Marsh National Monument, before making their way along Ocean Boulevard to the Old Coast Guard Station. Once the brilliant rays of the summer sun began to beat mercilessly on their exposed flesh, they decided to return home.

Aimee glanced at her watch. It was nearly seven-thirty. Their bike outing had lasted more than two hours. She removed her cap and rubbed her forearm over her moist forehead.

She smiled at Leland when he held her bike while she dismounted. "I'll treat you to breakfast."

"Where are we eating?"

"At my place." Turning on her heels, she left him staring at her retreating back.

His eyes crinkled in a smile as he studied her swaying hips in a pair of shorts. "I like biscuits for Sunday breakfast," he said.

Glancing at him over her shoulder, Aimee gave him a saucy grin. "So do I."

Throwing back his head, he laughed, the sound floating and lingering on a warm breeze.

Aimee took a quick bath and washed her short hair. She rinsed it with a handheld showerhead she'd attached to the faucet of the antique tub. A quarter of an hour later she'd moisturized her body and face, then pulled on a white sleeveless top with matching slim capri pants that ended inches below her knees.

Walking on bare feet across the cool kitchen floor, she opened the refrigerator and retrieved a package of slab bacon from the freezer. She was so absorbed with selecting the ingredients for her breakfast with Leland that she didn't notice him standing in the doorway to the kitchen until she looked up.

A slight gasp escaped her parted lips. "You frightened me."

He moved into the kitchen and stood beside her. His warmth and scent swept over her, making her weak in the knees. He'd showered and shaved, and the sensual fragrance of his aftershave was a powerful aphrodisiac that pulled her in and refused to let her go. He moved closer, his chest brushing her bare shoulder. He was too close, his body too warm, and much too large. It was as if he dwarfed everything in the small kitchen.

Leland's penetrating gaze lingered on the soft, glossy curls covering Aimee's head before moving down to her enchanting profile. A smile softened his mouth. She was dressed in white—again.

"What's on the menu?"

Aimee shivered when his warm breath swept over her ear. "Bacon, eggs, biscuits, coffee or tea, and a fruit compote."

Curving an arm around her narrow waist, he leaned down and pressed a kiss against her ear. "Do you need any help?"

"Yes," she said quickly. "You can set the table."

He kissed her again, inhaling the seductive fragrance of the perfume clinging to her velvety flesh. "Is there anything else you want me to do?"

Turning her head, Aimee stared up at him, meeting his direct gaze. She was certain he could feel the runaway pumping of her heart. "Yes. You can let me finish cooking."

His eyes shifted to the rapidly beating pulse in her throat. Miss Aimee Frasier was not as unaffected by him as she appeared. Well, it was the same for him. It had taken a week for her to turn his cloistered world upside down. And what he wanted to know was, why her and not some other woman? What was it about Aimee Frasier that made him think about marrying and fathering children? Reluctantly he removed his arm and reached into a built-in antique cupboard for dishes to set the table in the eat-in alcove.

Aimee busied herself rolling out biscuits and placing them on a cookie sheet, while Leland rinsed dishes and dried them before setting them on place mats on the round oak table. She hummed along with the music coming from the wave radio she'd placed on a countertop.

Leland heard her singing and it was as if he noticed the radio for the first time. "That's a powerful little system."

"It's a Bose."

"What's playing?"

"That's the latest Paul Hardcastle CD."

He walked over to the radio and picked up a CD case lying atop a stack of eight. "*The Jazzmasters III*." Turning the case over, he read the selections. "It's nice listening music."

"Do you like jazz?"

"I like it for relaxation. I always listen to classical music whenever I write."

She gave him a sidelong glance. "How's your latest novel coming along?"

He put down the CD case. "I'm ahead of schedule."

Aimee took a pan filled with crispy strips of maple-cured bacon from the oven, replacing it with the pan of biscuits. She quickly and expertly cut up fresh peaches, sectioned oranges, sliced a banana and strawberries, and topped the fruit with shredded coconut.

At exactly nine o'clock Leland pulled out a chair at the table, seating Aimee before he sat down opposite her. The space was filled with the aroma of brewing coffee as they listened to music while eating soft scrambled eggs, bacon, and golden, fluffy, butter-filled biscuits.

Leland's penetrating eyes darkened as he stared at his dining partner. "You can cook for me any day, Miss Frasier."

"Only on the weekends, Mr. Monroe."

He shifted an eyebrow. "You don't cook during the week?"

"Hardly ever."

Both eyebrows shot up. "You don't eat during the week?"

She laughed. "I eat, but most times I eat out, or at my mother's."

What she didn't say was that she usually ate dinner with Jeremy. Either he cooked for her, or they dined at several of their favorite eating establishments in the capital city.

Resting a forearm on the table, Leland stared directly at her. "What if we set up an arrangement?"

Her smooth brow creased in a slight frown. "What type of an arrangement?"

"I'll cook dinner for you Monday through Thursday and Sunday evenings. We'll eat out Friday and Saturday nights, while you can prepare breakfast or brunch on Saturday and Sunday mornings."

She wanted to tell him that she didn't think his arrangement was a good idea, but bit back the words. What she did not want to do was lie to Leland or to herself. She found him attractive, more attractive than she could openly admit. There was something about his masculinity that called out to her femininity. He made her feel things she did not want to feel, only because she had just ended her engagement. But, then there was something about Leland Monroe that made her reckless—made her want to know the reclusive author better.

Reaching across the table, she extended her right hand. "You've got yourself a deal."

Leland grasped her delicate fingers, bringing her hand to his mouth. He tightened his grip, kissing each one of her fingers while she stared at him, her lush lips parted in shock.

He released her hand, smiling broadly. "Thank you. Do you have any food allergies?"

Aimee shook her head, unable to speak. The brush of Leland's lips on her fingers had lingered, sending a shiver up her arm and to her breasts. *It's a crime,* her head screamed. It was a capital crime that Leland was so sexy without even trying.

They shared two cups of coffee before they rose to clean

the kitchen. Leland leaned down from his towering height, kissed her cheek, and told her that he would expect her for dinner at six.

Aimee's second week on St. Simons Island was very different from her first. She'd fallen into the habit of looking forward to sharing dinner with Leland. He'd given her a complete tour of the house, and as she entered and exited each room, the exquisite, priceless furnishings astounded her.

She later discovered with further research of Monroe artifacts that the house had been built on the island as a retreat by Edward Monroe for his mulatto mistress, Sophia. The beautiful young slave woman took up residence in the house, while her personal slave stayed in the guest cottage. Documents also revealed that Edward spent more time with Sophia on St. Simons than he did with his wife and legal heirs in Savannah.

It was the end of her second week that Aimee waited for Leland to emerge from his studio where he'd spent hours writing. He was genuinely surprised to see her when she arose from her sitting position on the carpeted floor.

His hand went to her elbow. "What's wrong, Aimee?" There was no mistaking the rising panic in his voice.

She smiled. "There's nothing wrong. I just want to show you what I found." Threading her fingers through his, she pulled him in the direction of the room where she worked.

"What did you find?"

Aimee gave him a mysterious smile. "You'll see."

He followed her into the room, stopping when he saw the surface of the mahogany table covered with stacks of paper bound in black and red ribbon.

"They're letters."

She pulled her hand from his warm, protective grasp. "I know they're letters, Leland. Have you read them?"

He shook his head. "No. Why?"

"They're love letters. Written by Hayden Monroe and Amanda Lawrence. I checked the postmarks. The first one was written in 1898."

His gaze swept over what were probably hundreds of letters. "Hayden and Amanda were my great-grandparents. Have you read any?"

Aimee shook her head. "No. I wanted your permission first."

Leland gave her a puzzled look. "You don't need my permission, Aimee."

"But they're personal documents," she argued softly.

Curving an arm around her waist, he pulled her close to his side. "If you feel uncomfortable, then we'll read them together. We'll begin tonight—after dinner."

Leland's gaze moved slowly over a letter written by Hayden Monroe to Amanda Lawrence. He and Aimee had sorted hundreds of letters chronologically, separating Hayden's from Amanda's. Moving closer to Aimee on the love seat, he inhaled the haunting scent of her body. The soft light from a floor lamp cast a flattering glow across her delicate features. The crackle of paper shattered the comfortable silence.

"You can begin, Leland," Aimee urged in a quiet tone.

Savannah, Georgia
March 6, 1898
Dear Miss Lawrence,
I would like to thank you for inviting me to share Sunday dinner with you and your family. I appreciate your kindness and generosity.

Best regards,
Mr. Hayden Monroe

Aimee removed a letter from a stack on her lap. A slight smile curved her lips when she stared at the delicate slanting script belonging to Leland's great-grandmother.

Savannah, Georgia
March 8, 1898
Mr. Monroe,
It appears that you are deluding yourself, because it is nei-

*ther kindness nor generosity that compels me to invite to
you my parents' home, but my father's insistence.*

                                    Miss Amanda Lawrence

Aimee stared at Leland, a mysterious smile curving her lips.
"It appears as if Miss Lawrence did not particularly care for
Mr. Monroe."

Leland returned her smile. "It also appears, judging by the
fact that Miss Lawrence married Mr. Monroe, that he managed
to get her to change her opinion of him."

"You forget that many women were forced into arranged
marriages at that time," Aimee reminded him.

Picking up another letter, Leland scanned it quickly.

Savannah, Georgia
March 12, 1898
Dear Miss Lawrence,
*I thank you for your warmth and hospitality. Your charming
presence made Sunday dinner quite a momentous occasion
for me. It was indeed refreshing to find a young woman
who is not afraid to say what is on her mind. I admire not
only your wit and intelligence, but also your exceptional
beauty. Your father has invited me to join your family for
their annual outing this coming Sunday after church services; however, unfortunately, I will be unable to attend. I
have received orders to report to Washington because of
the rebel situation in Cuba.*

                                    Best regards,
                                    Captain Hayden Monroe

Aimee picked up the next one written by Amanda.

Savannah, Georgia
March 13, 1898
Dear Captain Monroe,
*I hope your journey to our nation's capital will be an easy
one. I'm sorry that you will not join my family this coming*

*Sunday, but perhaps you will find time in your very busy
schedule to offer a proper farewell. I await your response.*
                                        Sincerely,
                                        Miss Lawrence

Leland slapped his thigh with an open hand. "He's getting
to her! The famous Monroe charm is working."

Aimee sucked her teeth, and then affected an attractive
moue. "Read the next one, Leland."

Washington, D.C.
March 16, 1898
Dear Miss Lawrence,
*Your letter was delivered to me only minutes before I
boarded a train for Washington. If my hand seems less than
legible, it is because the train is traveling at a very high
rate of speed. I find it ironic that even though I am in
uniform—a uniform that clearly depicts that I am a de-
fender of this nation—I am still relegated to sit in the
inferior Colored coach as I journey northward to receive
orders whether I will have to defend Cuban rebels against
the cruel treatment of their Spanish colonials. As soon as
I am settled in Washington, I will correspond with you
again as often as I can.*
                                Cordially, Hayden Monroe,
                                Captain, U.S. Army

Drawn into the unfolding drama played out in the letters
between Hayden Monroe and Amanda Lawrence, Aimee and
Leland spent the next two hours reading about the growing
attraction between two people whose lives were determined by
forces beyond their control.

The United States declared war against Spain on April 25,
1898, and Hayden was sent to Cuba as an officer for an all-
Colored unit. He was decorated for bravery during the Battle
of San Juan Hill, and returned to the States to enter Howard
University Medical School in Washington, D.C. He and
Amanda continued their correspondence, their letters fraught

with longing and desire that belied their Victorian upbringing. Amanda traveled to Washington, with her two older brothers as chaperones, and was finally reunited with the man who'd captured her heart with only a stroke of a pen after a year's absence.

Aimee smothered a yawn, staring at the stack of envelopes on the cushion beside her. Amanda was prolific, writing an average of two letters a week to her suitor. "I can't read any more tonight."

Leland slipped a single sheet of paper with his great-grandfather's large, bold script into an envelope. "How many letters do you think are here?"

Aimee shook her head. "Thousands. They must have continued to write to each other even after they were married." She gave Leland a direct look. "Were you aware that your great-grandparents were that prolific when you selected your pseudonym?"

He nodded slowly. "My grandfather used to tell me stories about how his father was never without a pen or paper because he felt it was easier to put his thoughts down on paper than verbalize them."

Pushing to her feet, she stood up, Leland following suit. "I'll see you tomorrow."

Leland captured her hand, pulling it into the curve of his elbow. "I'll walk you back to your place."

She tried extracting her hand. "In case you've forgotten, I only sleep about three hundred feet from here."

He tightened his grip on her slender fingers. "I'll rest easier knowing that you're inside behind a locked door."

Aimee gave him a sidelong glance as she followed him out the back door. "What do I have to fear?"

Curving an arm around her waist, Leland pulled her closer to his side. Lowering his head, he pressed a light kiss to her temple. "It's not a what but a who."

Placing one foot firmly in front of the other, she leaned against his solid frame. "Who?"

The sound of their measured breathing punctuated the incessant chirping of crickets, the lapping sound of the tide washing up on the beach, and nocturnal wildlife. The moonless sky provided a black canopy for a warm summer night redolent with the scent of salt water and lush, blooming flowers.

Leland led Aimee up the steps to the lighted porch to the small cottage, then eased her to his chest with a minimum of effort. Her hands came up, providing a modicum of space between their bodies.

He lowered his head and his voice, saying, "I'm the who."

She wasn't given the opportunity to respond when his mouth covered hers in an explosive kiss that shattered her dormant sensuality. What she'd suspected had been manifested. Her hands, pressed against the unyielding wall of Leland's chest, moved up to his shoulders seconds before her arms curved around his neck.

What began as a touch of his lips on hers quickly sent shockwaves of desire coursing through her breasts as her nipples exploded against the delicate fabric of her bra; at that moment she wanted to rip off her clothes to lie naked under Leland. She felt her passion rising like the hottest fire, scorching her body and her brain.

She registered a moan, unaware that the sound had escaped her own parted lips. "Lee . . . Leland."

Leland tightened his hold on Aimee's slim waist, wanting to absorb her into himself. He hadn't realized until he'd taken her into his arms and joined their mouths that it was what he'd wanted to do the instant she stepped foot onto his property. He had fantasized holding her, kissing her, while making love to her all through the night.

Being a recluse for the past six months had prepared him to recognize what he truly wanted. He didn't know how, but he knew instinctively that he wanted Aimee Frasier—not to just share a kiss, but all of her.

He buried his face against the silken column of her long neck, breathing heavily. His arms fell to his sides. "You can slap my face if you want to."

Backing away, Aimee shook her head. "No, Leland. I won't slap your face, because deep down inside I wanted you to kiss me." There was enough illumination from the porch lights to see an expression of shock freeze his features. She offered him a gentle smile. "Good night. I'll see you tomorrow."

She opened the door and stepped into the cottage. "Leland, I also want to let you know that I'm not afraid of you." Turning, she faced him, smiled, and closed the door softly. She shifted slightly, her back pressed to the door, and waited for her respiration to return to a normal rate. It was only then that she pushed off the door and made her way to her bedroom.

NINE

Aimee woke up early the following morning, heard the steady tapping of rain against her bedroom window, and promptly went back to sleep. One thing she did not do was jog in the rain.

When she awoke the second time, it was to the sound of someone pounding, followed by Leland calling her name. A quick glance at the lighted dial on her travel clock revealed it was eight-forty. Pushing back a lightweight blanket, she swung her legs over the side of the bed, walked out of the bedroom, through the parlor, and to the front door.

"I'm coming," she mumbled, quickening her pace.

Unlocking the door, she saw Leland. He stood on the porch, staring down at her, slack-jawed and gaping. A bright yellow slicker flowing down around his long legs provided some protection from the steady downpour.

Running a hand over her short hair, Aimee flashed a wry grin. "I overslept. The rain always does that to me," she continued, apologizing.

Leland moved his lips, but the words were locked in his constricted throat. He'd gotten up early to write, but when the hands on the clock on his desk inched past eight and there was no sign of Aimee, he'd become alarmed. At first he thought she had fallen sick, then the image of her lying injured in the cottage flashed through his mind.

And he hadn't realized until he reached for his rain slicker that he cared about Aimee Frasier—cared enough to make certain she was safe, and in the time it took for him to walk out of his house to make his way to her cottage, his protective instincts were in full throttle.

He knew he was staring numbly at Aimee, but he was unable to speak. His hungry gaze took in the expanse of the flawless, velvety sable flesh covering her throat and shoulders under a floor-length, rose-pink silk nightgown.

An unexpected involuntary tightening in his groin intensified his paralysis. Aimee's full breasts were ardently displayed by the revealing décolletage. He marveled how perfectly the filmy nightgown cradled her voluptuous flesh, the garment appearing to have been expressly fashioned for her lush, feminine body. Closing his eyes, he smothered a groan. When he opened his eyes, he found Aimee smiling sweetly.

"I'll be over in half an hour."

Nodding numbly like an imbecile, he turned on his heel and walked off the porch. He prayed she hadn't watched his retreat, because she would've noticed the stiffness in his gait. The swollen flesh pressing against the front of his shorts was akin to the most intense erotic torture he'd ever experienced.

He wanted her! It had been a long time—a very, very long time since he'd wanted a woman in his life and in his bed. It wasn't as if he didn't have a healthy sex drive, it was just that he'd matured to where he refused to engage in gratuitous sex.

But at that moment he wanted Aimee in his bed and his hardness buried deep inside her until they ceased to exist as separate entities. He knew he wanted her, but what he still hadn't figured out was why. What was there about Aimee Frasier that made her so vastly different from the other women in his past? There was no question that she was beautiful and highly intelligent. But so were a few other women who'd shared his bed. Shrugging a broad shoulder under the yellow slicker, he opened the back door. Marmalade greeted him as he stepped into her space.

"I have two more weeks to find out why I like Aimee Frasier so much," he said to his pet as she brushed against his damp legs.

He slipped out of the raincoat, droplets landing on Marmalade's upturned face. The feline took off like a shot, disappearing under a table. Her gold-green eyes watched Leland warily before she raised a paw to wipe away the moisture.

* * *

Aimee struggled under the weight of the large satchel that held her laptop, scanner, printer, and digital camera. Because she was getting a late start, she'd decided to make copies of what she'd researched. She also planned to begin entering her notes into the laptop.

The case bumped against her legs as she mounted the steps to the porch. The front door opened suddenly, startling her when a large dark brown hand eased the case from her grip. Leland curved his free arm around her waist over a serviceable rain slicker, pulling her into the entryway.

Pressing a kiss to her forehead, he inhaled the now familiar scent of her body. "I thought you could use something warm to drink, so I brewed a pot of tea."

Aimee offered him a warm smile. "Thanks."

Leland left her case in the room where she worked, and then led her to the large, brick-walled, eat-in kitchen. An overhead chandelier and wall sconces blazed brightly, dispelling the gloominess of the cloudy, rainy weather.

Aimee sat at the table in the expansive kitchen, sipping from a cup of excellently brewed Earl Grey tea, while Leland sectioned a grapefruit for her.

Glancing over his shoulder, he frowned. "Are you sure all you want is tea and half a grapefruit?"

"Yes."

She was more than an hour late, and was anxious to begin cataloguing what she'd researched. Her admiring gaze lingered on Leland as he stood at the sink.

"How's the book coming?" she asked once he joined her at the table.

He placed a dish containing the grapefruit in front of her, giving her a direct stare. "Very well."

Her eyebrows lifted. "Can you give me a glimpse of what Xenos will be involved in this time?"

As the author, Hayden Lawrence had created an African-American character, Xenos Sharif, who was a composite of Tom Clancy's Jack Ryan and Walter Mosley's Ezekiel Rawlins. Xenos worked for the United States government, but which branch was questionable.

A slight smile played at the corners of Leland's strong mouth. "This time he infiltrates a small band of international criminals who traffic in drugs, illegal arms, and function as a death squad to the highest bidder."

Aimee wrinkled her nose. "They sound like a very nasty bunch."

"Without a doubt," he replied, deadpan.

"When are you going to give Mr. Sharif a love interest?"

"He doesn't have time for a woman."

"Clancy's Jack Ryan is married, and Mosley's Easy Rawlins has had romantic encounters, while Ian Fleming's Double-oh Seven always finds time to romance a woman, which certainly adds to his celebrated sophistication."

Tilting his head at an angle, Leland regarded Aimee. "Do you really think he needs a woman?"

"Of course. It would soften him a bit."

"He's an independent operative, Aimee, not an international playboy."

She smothered a smile. "I'm not saying you should make him a pimp or a punk; however, you could show a softer, more passionate side of his personality."

Leland picked up his own cup of tea and took a swallow. "I'll think about it."

Aimee concentrated on eating her grapefruit, then got up, Leland rising with her, and rinsed her cup and dish before placing them in the dishwasher.

"I'll see you for dinner," she said.

He nodded, staring at Aimee as she walked out of the kitchen. When he'd walked into his studio earlier that morning, he'd stood in front of the calendar over his computer, staring at the dates. He'd marked the dates for Aimee's arrival and departure. Then he counted the number of days before she returned to Atlanta, and the realization struck him that within two weeks—only fourteen days—she would be gone.

Staring down at the tea in his cup, he smiled, recalling the taste and texture of her soft mouth. He wanted to kiss her—again—her mouth, throat, nape, and the high, full, thrusting breasts whose image was branded indelibly on his brain.

Leland wanted Aimee to share his bed, but he also wanted

her to share much more; and the more was that he wanted her in his life.

St. Simons Island, Georgia
November 30, 1905
My Darling Husband,
I just discovered why I have been feeling poorly these past few weeks. I am with child. It was confirmed this morning. I wanted you with me when Dr. Austin told me, but your absence could not lessen my joy. I miss you terribly, dear husband, and eagerly await your return.

Love,
Amanda.

Leland waited for the soothing sound of Aimee's voice to fade before he removed a letter from the stack resting on his lap.

Baltimore, Maryland
December 6, 1905
My Beloved Wife,
Your letter was waiting for me when I returned to Miss Millie Ryder's boardinghouse at the end of what had become a fourteen-hour day. Although I was bone-tired and in need of a bath, I had to read what you had written. Your letters have become as necessary to me as breathing. I read it three times, my joy overflowing that we are going to have a child. I love you, and I love our unborn child. Your news has given me the impetus I need to complete my studies in advance surgical procedures and return to you as soon as possible. I want you to go to Savannah and remain with my aunt until I return. I would feel more comfortable knowing you are not alone in your most delicate condition. I count the days, hours, minutes, and seconds until we are reunited.

Your loving husband,
Hayden.

Aimee and Leland had shared dinner, cleaned up the kitchen, and then retreated to the living room to continue to read the many letters Amanda and Hayden Monroe wrote to each other over a span of fifty years. She and Leland relived the lives of two people who'd fallen hopelessly in love, and had continued their courtship while Hayden attended medical school. The young couple finally exchanged vows within a month of Hayden's graduation from Howard University's Medical College. Edward Monroe's gift to the only child he'd shared with his Black mistress was their St. Simons Island retreat. Amanda and Hayden had honeymooned on Hilton Head Island a week before they returned to St. Simons to take up permanent residence.

Aimee picked up another letter, the distinctive rustle of paper competing with the soft sound of breathing. Her voice was soft and husky with emotion as she read aloud the words that mirrored Amanda's love and desire for her young husband. It was as if she and Leland had become voyeurs, peering into the lives and bedroom of a couple who loved each other selflessly.

She felt Amanda's loneliness whenever Hayden left St. Simons to attend a medical seminar, or when he was called away at night to care for a sick patient. Amanda confessed to never feeling like a complete woman until she lay next to her husband at the end of a day.

And the emotion in Leland's voice was apparent when he read of his great-grandfather's failure to save his own son's life when he succumbed to complications of diphtheria three months before the child celebrated his second birthday.

Amanda's letters to her husband stopped altogether after the death of their son, even though Hayden continued to write to her. He wrote of trying to coax her from a month-long depressive state that had left her uncommunicative. She spent her days sitting in a chair staring into space. He'd expressed fear that he would have to commit her to an institution for the insane, until he suspected that she was pregnant again. His decision to institutionalize his wife was annulled once her pregnancy was confirmed.

Amanda resumed her letter-writing, thanking God and her husband for another chance at motherhood. Hayden took a week away from his family practice to take Amanda to Hilton

Head for a second honeymoon. They spent the time making love and walking on the beach to talk about what they wanted for their child's future. Amanda gave birth to their daughter in the early spring of 1908; a second daughter followed in 1911, and she delivered her last child—a son—in the summer of 1915. Enduring more than thirty-six hours of labor trying to birth a child weighing close to nine pounds, and losing copious amounts of blood during a difficult delivery, ended any future hope that Amanda Lawrence Monroe would ever bear another child.

But Amanda was content: She was married to a man whom she loved and who adored her; she was kept busy taking care of her home and looking after her three children; and her status as the wife of a prominent doctor with a thriving practice buoyed her social standing not only on St. Simons Island, but also in Savannah.

Amanda's letters were filled with inane chatter as she developed a habit for recapping each day's events for Hayden once he returned home after long hours of treating patients. She related their children's antics, her interaction with the women in her sewing circle, and tidbits of gossip and an occasional scandal she'd heard from a loose tongue.

Hayden's replies were short, filled with effusive compliments of her doing a fine job of raising their children with manners befitting a Monroe. He thanked her for being a warm and charming hostess whenever they opened their home for entertaining. And at the end of every letter he thanked Amanda for their children and her love.

A clock over the mantelpiece chimed midnight, but Aimee did not move. Closing her eyes, she savored the warmth and strength of Leland's large body pressed intimately against hers. The sound of falling rain tapping against the windows cloaked her in a comforting cocoon from which she did not want to escape.

Aimee felt as if she'd stepped back in time whenever she relived an incredible love between two people whose blood continued to flow in the veins of the man she'd found herself drawn to despite her resistance to becoming involved with him.

She'd come to look forward to sharing all her spare time with him. But what she did not want to admit was that she was falling in love with Leland. And what was there not to love about him? He was gorgeous, generous, brilliant, and breathtakingly virile. He was perfect in every way.

Aimee opened her eyes to find Leland staring down at her. His eyes were dark, unfathomable; his expression closed, unreadable. An oddly primitive warning echoed in her head, and within a span of seconds she knew her association with Leland Monroe had changed. A sixth sense told her that Leland wanted to kiss her, make love to her, and that she wanted the same.

It had not mattered that she'd recently ended her engagement to another man. All that mattered was that she was drawn to Leland and she was tired of fighting her emotions.

His head came down at the same time her arms curved around his strong neck, holding him fast. This kiss was not like the other they'd shared. It wasn't tentative, but confident. Leland called and she answered him, her lips parting under his searching tongue.

Tightening his grip on her waist, Leland molded her soft curves to the contours of his body while his tongue plundered the moistness of her mouth. He'd lain awake imagining kissing her until his world stood still, but nothing in his imagination could've prepared him for the sweet taste of Aimee's kiss. He breathed in her feminine scent, wanting to get even closer.

His right hand moved under her shirt, gathering fabric as his fingertips grazed the velvety flesh over her ribs. A soft moan escaped Aimee once his hand closed over a full breast. Pulling back, he stared down at the passion in her eyes.

"Aimee?" Lowering his head, he breathed a kiss under her ear.

He was asking and she knew the answer. *Yes,* her heart sang.

"Yes," her lips whispered, giving him his answer.

She did not remember Leland swinging her up in his arms, or carrying her up the staircase to the second story. But what she did remember was his walking into his bedroom and placing her on his bed.

TEN

It wasn't until much later that Aimee recalled all that had happened before she lay cradled in Leland's embrace, her face pressed to his moist chest.

She'd lain on the bed, staring up at Leland as he reached down and pulled his T-shirt over his head. The diffused light coming from a small bedside lamp cast shadows over his upper body that highlighted the lean, hard contours of his muscled arms and pectorals.

She'd held her breath, her heart fluttering like a frightened bird, as he unsnapped the waist to his shorts and pushed them below his hips. Turning her head, she only caught a glimpse of the solid bulge straining against his cotton briefs. Seconds later he shed his briefs.

Leland forced himself to go slowly. It had been a long time since he'd slept with a woman, and an even longer time since he'd wanted to sleep with one. Leaning over Aimee's soft body, he supported his greater weight on his elbows.

"Please, look at me," he whispered close to her ear. "See how much I want you."

Aimee obeyed, staring up at the passion darkening his face and eyes. Their gazes caught and held before hers eased lower to the swollen flesh jutting between his strong thighs. In the instant when their gazes met and fused, each recognized a silent longing in the other; each aware that they'd met for the first time only two weeks ago; and each was cognizant that whatever they offered the other was fleeting—temporary.

Placing a palm on the center of Leland's smooth chest, Aimee registered the strong, steady, beating of his heart under her hand. She smiled and he returned it. He eased closer, his chest grazing hers as he pressed her lips to his.

Drinking in the sweetness of his kiss, Aimee drew Leland's face to hers in a renewed embrace. She welcomed his weight; drank in the natural scent of his skin mingling with his after-shave; savored the feel of the flesh over his strong jaw and chin. Her mouth moved from his lips to his throat. Her kisses were unhurried, lingering and savoring every inch of flesh on his face, throat, and shoulders.

Leland felt his control slipping, and he forced himself to go slower. His hands charted the curves of Aimee's silken body, discovering her pleasure points as her breathing quickened. He undressed her, arousing her passion as his own grew stronger.

He explored the inside of her thighs, the gentle massage firing her blood. Just when Aimee thought she would scream for him to take her and end her erotic torture, Leland paused to slip on protection; he eased into her body; she emitted a lingering sigh of pleasure as her wet, throbbing flesh closed around his swollen sex.

Aimee felt the heat settle between her thighs, burning, scorching, smoldering. Arching, she rubbed her swollen breasts and distended nipples against the solid wall of Leland's chest, wanting to get closer, wanting to be absorbed into him.

Never, never had she experienced the raw passion he elicited in her. She didn't know Leland—he was a stranger, yet she'd permitted him to *know* her in the most intimate way possible.

She forgot about her research project, forgot that she'd once pledged her future to Jeremy Robinson, and forgot that in exactly two weeks she would leave Leland Monroe and St. Simons Island—forever.

Opening her mouth and her legs wider to permit her lover deeper access, Aimee Frasier opened her mind and heart to offer a love that came from her heart.

Leland closed his eyes and clenched his teeth when he felt the dizzying rush of ecstasy sweeping through him. He'd tried not concentrating on the sexy woman writhing beneath him—a woman who made the blood sing in his veins. The pleasure she wrung from him was pure, soul-searching, and he knew the moment their bodies joined that Aimee was the woman he'd been waiting for.

He'd become Hayden and she Amanda. He wanted to share with Aimee what Hayden had shared with his Amanda—a life filled with love and children. Leland craved Aimee, and for the first time in his life he could openly admit that he wanted children. He didn't want the Monroe name to end with him.

Aimee gasped in sweet agony, her fingers tightening on the firm flesh covering Leland's hips, when the familiar waves of ecstasy raced through her body. The pleasure soared, higher and higher, and she couldn't control her outcry of delight as she succumbed to the rapture that transported her beyond herself. Her breath came in a long, surrendering moan of exquisite completeness at the same time Leland released his own passions, his hips surging powerfully against hers.

His deep moan of fulfillment echoed throughout the bedroom and he collapsed heavily on her body, his heart bursting with love. He loved Aimee, loved her enough to beg her to stay with him—forever. Rolling off her pliant body, he pulled Aimee to his chest and kissed her moist forehead. A deep feeling of peace eddied through his mind. He had time, but not much time, to prove to her that he loved her enough to ask her to share his life and his future.

Aimee awoke the next morning to bright sunshine. Her eyes widened when she realized she'd spent the night in Leland's arms and in his bed.

He smiled down at her, pinpoints of gold firing his large eyes. "Good morning, darling."

Smiling shyly, she pressed her nose to his shoulder. "Good morning."

Leland's right hand toyed with the short curling hair over her ear. "How do you feel?"

She wanted to tell him fulfilled, but said, "Wonderful." She pulled out of his loose embrace. "I have to get up."

Reaching out, his fingers curled around her forearm. "Where are you going?"

Aimee smiled at Leland over her shoulder. "Jogging."

He tightened his grip on her arm, pulling her gently and

settling her effortlessly over his chest. "Don't you know how to relax?"

"Jogging is relaxing for me."

"Stay in bed with me for a little while."

Her eyebrows lifted. "How long is a little while?"

Leland's large expressive eyes crinkled when he smiled up at her. "Long enough for a repeat performance of what we shared last night." A low chuckle rumbled in his chest when Aimee buried her face between his neck and shoulder. "Am I embarrassing you, darling?"

"No." The single word was muffled against his hard shoulder.

Lowering his chin, Leland pressed his lips to Aimee's fragrant short hair while one hand was busy caressing the curve of her hips. The skin covering her body was as soft and delicate as her face. His caresses grew stronger, bolder, as the flaccid flesh between his own thighs stirred, hardening quickly in desire.

Aimee Frasier had unlocked his heart and his soul, permitting him to open himself up to share his existence with her. The rapid pumping of her heart under her breasts kept rhythm with his own; the soft moans of passion coming from her parted lips echoed his own; and the moisture flowing from the source of her femininity matched the emission of fluid from his own hardened sex.

It took a minimum of effort to retrieve the latex protection from the drawer in the bedside table. Sixty seconds later he buried his rigid flesh in her hot, throbbing body. He lost track of time; forgot the names and faces of every woman he'd ever known; and the moment he released his passion in an explosion that hurtled him to another dimension before falling headlong to drown in a floodtide of exquisite ecstasy, he knew he had fallen completely and hopelessly in love with Aimee.

They lay together side by side, holding hands, waiting until their respiration returned to a normal rate. Eyes closed, her mouth curving into a satisfied smile, Aimee let out a soft groan.

"Did I hurt you?" Leland asked softly. Their lovemaking

was strong, passionate, almost desperate, as they'd sought to absorb the other into themselves.

"No." Her breath was low, even as she drifted off to sleep—thoroughly satiated. She didn't know when Leland joined her in sleep, or when Marmalade came into the bedroom to greet her master. The orange feline stood motionless, regarding the stranger on the bed, then turned and padded silently out of the space, leaving the lovers undisturbed.

Aimee felt as if she'd known Leland for years instead of several weeks once she shared his roof *and* his bed. Their relationship was calm, mature, and without an overt angst that their time together was drawing to a close.

She realized that she'd fallen in love with him, but her secret would remain her own. Whenever they made love, each encounter was more intense than the one preceding it. Their bodies communicated what they refused to openly verbalize.

They continued to read Amanda's and Hayden's letters as they were offered a glimpse of the changes in their lives and the world at large. The written missives spoke of the Great War, Prohibition, the Jazz Age, the Great Depression, and World War II. Amanda's letters were filled with the joy of becoming a grandmother for the first time. She and Hayden heralded the birth of their grandson Lee Monroe in 1935, because it meant that the Monroe name would continue for another generation.

Dr. Hayden Monroe divided his time between caring for his patients and researching the advent of modern twentieth century medicine with the discovery of powerful antibiotics and vaccines to eradicate communicable diseases.

The letters stopped completely in 1948 when Hayden, at seventy-one years of age, died while sitting in his favorite chair listening to the radio. An entry in the family Bible indicated that Amanda lived another ten years before she was laid to rest in a century-old cemetery on St. Simons. Amanda was placed between Hayden and her firstborn son, Hayden Jr. The Monroe family plot also held the remains of Sophia, Edward Monroe's mistress. Years later the cemetery would claim another generation of Monroes with Leland's grandparents, great-aunts, and several cousins.

Two days after their relationship changed to that of lovers, Leland surprised Aimee when he walked into the room where she sat entering her notes on her laptop notebook. Even though they'd continued to share meals and now a bed, they maintained the established working protocol not to disturb each other's projects.

A slight frown creased her smooth forehead. Her gaze took in the pristine white T-shirt stretched over his broad chest and a pair of matching walking shorts.

"Is something wrong?"

His impassive expression faded the moment he smiled. "No, but I would like to show you something."

She saved what she'd typed on a disk, and then stood up. Leland extended his hand. She grasped his long, strong fingers and permitted him to lead her down a narrow hallway into a space that had been set up as a music room. It was furnished with tables, chairs, and lamps that predated World War I. An exquisite concert piano that Edward Monroe had ordered from Europe for Sophia was the room's focal point. And despite its age, the instrument's sound was near perfect. Leland had admitted that even though he did not play, he'd had the piano tuned.

He didn't play, but Aimee did. She'd treated him to more than an hour of musical renditions of show tunes, and popular jazz and classical compositions.

He directed her to a tapestry-covered love seat, sat down beside her, and picked up several typed pages from a nearby table. "I'd like for you to read something."

Her gaze moved quickly over the top page. It was from Leland's latest work-in-progress. He was permitting her a glimpse of his next book before it was published. She felt the fiery heat from his gold-flecked eyes as she read the printed words.

A slight shiver raced through her as she read what he'd written, the words flowing fluidly into sentences, phrases that stripped bare the emotions of his protagonist. Within several paragraphs the fictional, larger-than-life, one-man army glad-iator Xenos Sharif became human. And his humanness had come from his yearning for a woman who'd touched a core of him that no other had been able to affect or penetrate.

Aimee finished reading the half-dozen pages, her head coming up slowly. She was hard-pressed to keep her emotions in check. He'd taken her suggestion to give his fictional character a love interest. She had read all of the Hayden Lawrence novels featuring Xenos Sharif, but this was the first time that he made his fictional character real—as real as his creator.

"You gave him a woman." Her voice was filled with awe.

"I've made him vulnerable." There was a touch of irony in the statement.

"You've made him real—human, Leland."

He lifted one eyebrow. "I suppose you're pleased with what I've written."

Leaning closer, Aimee brushed her mouth over his. "Very. And I'm willing to bet that your readers will be pleased."

"That's what my editor said."

"Your editor?"

Leland nodded. "I faxed him the pages yesterday."

Looping her arm through his, she laid her head against Leland's shoulder.

Dropping a kiss on the top of her head, Leland curved an arm around her shoulders, pulling her closer. "Thank you, Aimee."

"For what?"

"For being here. For being you."

Closing her eyes, Aimee refused to think of how little time they would have together. When she arose that morning after sharing a passionate session of lovemaking with Leland, she'd fought back tears. Five days. All they had was another five days, and their idyllic island magic liaison would end.

Biting down on her lower lip, she forced a wry smile. She would share only four weeks—a month—with the reclusive Leland Monroe, but the memories of what they'd offered each other were certain to be ones she would never forget as long as she lived.

ELEVEN

Leland rinsed a dinner plate, and then handed it to Aimee, who stacked it in the dishwasher. His movements were slow, deliberate. He didn't want to acknowledge that this would be the last Sunday dinner they would share, because in another three days she would leave him and St. Simons Island forever.

She informed him that she'd completed her research, and had begun the task of entering her copious notes into her laptop computer. Several disks were filled with images of antique quilts, photographs, legal documents recording bills of sale of property and human beings, birth and death records, and more than half a dozen executed wills.

Whenever he lay beside Aimee after they'd made love, his silent plea to beg her not to leave him and St. Simons remained lodged in his throat. He had no right to and no claim on Aimee Frasier. Just because she'd shared his bed, it was not tantamount to her committing her life and her future with him. He'd become a recluse, a loner. He had no right to ask the woman he'd fallen in love with to give up her career and cut herself off from her friends and all she'd worked for.

A wry smile softened his mouth as he stared at her delicate profile, committing everything about her to memory. And yes, he would have his memories—ones he would treasure for the rest of his life.

The chiming of the doorbell shattered the comfortable silence. Leland reached for a towel, dried his hands, and then made his way to the front door. He wasn't expecting any visitors, but thought perhaps it could be his closest neighbor— the elderly widow who spent the early-morning hours working in her flower and vegetable garden, and evenings on her front porch rocking gently. He approached the door, his brow creasing in a frown. A shadowy image through the screen door revealed a tall, casually dressed, dark-skinned man.

A sixth sense told him that the man standing on the porch of his house was somehow connected to Aimee. And because she was an only child, he knew the stranger wasn't her brother.

Forcing a friendly smile, he said through the mesh, "Good evening."

"Good evening," came a soft, deep-timbred reply. "Is Aimee Frasier in?"

A cold shiver wracked Leland's body. "Who's asking for her?"

"Jeremy Robinson."

He hesitated, then said, "I'll get her." The three words were forced from between his teeth. Turning on his heel, he retraced his steps to the kitchen, leaving Jeremy Robinson staring at his departing figure through the mesh.

Leland knew he was being rude for not inviting Jeremy Robinson in, but at that moment he didn't care. Someone—a strange man—had invaded his island retreat to see Aimee. Walking into the kitchen, he stared at her as she closed the door to the dishwasher, then pressed several buttons to begin the pre-wash cycle. She turned, saw him, and her features softened in the most beguiling smile he'd ever seen her exhibit. His gaze lingered on the soft curve of her lips, the sensual glow in her large, dark, slanting eyes.

Aimee's smile slipped away, a shadow of alarm replacing the expression of love radiating from her gaze as she sensed Leland's disquiet. She'd slept with the man, fallen in love with him, and she had come to know his silent gestures as well as she knew herself. She'd seen the brooding expression whenever she spoke of leaving St. Simons Island to return to Atlanta.

The seconds became a full minute before Leland said, "Jeremy Robinson is asking for you."

Aimee's heart slammed painfully against her ribs as if someone had hit her with a closed fist. Jeremy! What was he doing on St. Simons? Why had he followed her? Her fingers curled to still their shaking.

Leland saw the myriad of expressions cross the features of the woman he'd fallen in love with. First there was shock, then uncertainty.

"Are you all right?" The words of concern were out before he could censor himself.

Squaring her shoulders, Aimee pulled herself up until her spine was straight, unyielding. "I'm fine," she replied in a stilted tone.

He didn't believe her. "Who is he to you?"

"Nothing."

He arched a questioning eyebrow. "Nothing?"

Aimee nodded. "Nothing," she spat out angrily, walking out of the kitchen while struggling to keep her temper under control.

Suddenly she was faced with two dilemmas instead of one. She wanted to tell Leland that she loved him, loved him more than she'd loved any man; and how to convince Jeremy that it was indeed over between them, that there would be no second chances. Her steps slowed as she walked to the door, opened it, and then stepped out onto the porch. Jeremy stood motionless, leaning against a column, staring at her.

His thin lips curled under a precisely barbered mustache. "Hello, Aimee."

She nodded in response, not wanting to waste words. However, she had to admit that Jeremy Robinson was as handsome and imposing out of uniform as he was whenever he wore the standard issue of the Atlanta Police Department. A black-and-white-striped golf shirt and lightweight black slacks failed to conceal the hardness of his well-conditioned body. His close-cut mixed-gray hair, even features, and smooth dark-brown complexion enhanced his attractiveness. For a thirty-eight-year-old man, Jeremy was as physically fit as any man twenty years his junior.

"What are you doing here?"

Jeremy's smile faded. "Isn't it obvious, Aimee?"

"Not to me," she retorted angrily. "I thought I said all there was to say before I left Atlanta. You could've saved your time, gas, and the treads on your tires driving down here."

His eyes narrowed at the same time he crossed his arms

over his chest. "I've spent the past three days in Savannah at a law enforcement symposium—"

"You should've stayed there," she said, cutting him off.

Jeremy dropped his arms. "I made a mistake, Aimee. I'm asking for another chance."

She refused to relent. "What part of 'no' don't you understand? The *N* or the *O*?"

The slight rein Jeremy had maintained on his temper since Aimee had given him back his ring slipped. He took a step closer. "Damn you!"

Her own temper exploded. "Get out of here!"

He took another step. "I'm not leaving until you come to your senses."

"I beg to differ with you," came a soft masculine voice behind them. The door opened and Leland stepped out onto the porch. "Mr. Robinson, you're trespassing on private property. I suggest you listen to the lady and leave."

Aimee moved backward until her back was pressed against Leland's chest. Unconsciously his right arm curved around her waist. The protective gesture was not lost on Jeremy, whose startled expression revealed that he recognized Leland as Hayden Lawrence.

Any and all love Jeremy felt for Aimee dissipated like a drop of cold water on the surface of a heated grill. "I didn't realize you were that easy, Aimee," he drawled in a mocking tone. "I had to wait four months before you took your clothes off for me, but it seems as if your friend didn't have to wait four weeks. Is he the reason you broke our engagement a day before you came down here?" He emitted a snort. "I suppose an honest cop's salary will never match the seven-figure advances of a best-selling author, will it? Good-bye and good luck." Turning, he made his way off the porch and toward his racy sports car parked in the driveway. Less than a minute later, he sped away.

Aimee felt Leland's arm tighten slightly under her breasts before he released her. She stared straight ahead, unwilling to turn around to see his expression.

"Is it true, Aimee?"

"Is what true?" she asked, answering his question with one of her own.

"Were you engaged to him?"

Biting down on her lower lip, she nodded. "Yes," she said when she recovered her voice.

Closing his eyes, Leland remembered the band of lighter color around the third finger of her left hand when she first came to the island. Had she lied? Had she pretended that she didn't know that Hayden Lawrence was a pseudonym for Leland Monroe?

He opened his eyes. "Why did you break your engagement to Jeremy Robinson?"

"The reason had nothing to do with you."

"That's not what I'm asking, darling."

His endearment shattered her resolve to remain in control of her fragile emotions. "We argued about my career."

Career. The word resounded in Leland's head. Had Robinson wanted her to give up her career? Had he issued an ultimatum and she opted for her career instead of marriage?

What Aimee didn't know was that he wanted to tell her that he loved her; wanted her to become Mrs. Leland Monroe; and wanted her to leave her position with the Georgia National Trust for Historic Preservation and relocate to St. Simons Island.

Jeremy Robinson's unexpected visit had become a blessing in disguise, because it had stopped him from making a complete fool of himself.

He was certain Aimee would leave St. Simons within the last three days allotted her, and what he had to do was prepare himself for the inevitable.

"I'll see you later," Aimee said softly. She moved off the porch and made her way toward the cottage.

Leland stared numbly. He knew instinctively that he wouldn't see Aimee later. Both needed time alone—to think and prepare for the end of what had become the most blissful two weeks of their lives.

TWELVE

Aimee's stomach churned with anxiety as she prepared to leave. She moved about the bedroom as if in a trance. She felt like a thief, sneaking away from Leland and St. Simons Island without saying good-bye. Closing her eyes, she inhaled deeply before letting out her breath slowly. She'd completed her research and left a copy of her findings for Leland earlier that morning.

She'd only caught brief glimpses of Leland since Jeremy's unexpected visit to the island. They'd stopped sharing meals and a bed; they'd become polite strangers, barely acknowledging the other's existence.

Picking up the case with her electronic equipment, she walked out of the cottage, stopping suddenly and putting it down when she saw Leland staring into her car's open trunk.

He walked slowly toward her, fingers splayed on his hips. A slight smile curved his beautifully formed masculine mouth. "Leaving so soon?" His hot gaze lingered on the swell of firm flesh under a cotton blouse before moving down to her hips and long legs outlined in a pair of form-fitting jeans.

"It's best that I leave now, Leland."

He moved closer until they were only inches apart. "Why, Aimee?"

She forced a smile she didn't feel. She wanted to cry, not smile. "I don't like good-byes."

Reaching out, Leland cradled her chin in his right hand, the thumb moving over the slight indentation. "It doesn't have to be good-bye."

Her gaze fused with his. "If it's not good-bye, then what is it?"

Lowering his head, his warm breath caressing her parted lips, Leland said, "Until the next time."

Her eyes filled with tears. "Will there be a next time, Leland?"

"Yes, Aimee Frasier. Yes, there will be a next time," he said cryptically.

Turning her head, she avoided his kiss, his lips grazing her cheek. Leland pulled back, his expression revealing disappointment. A swollen silence followed as he picked up her case and placed it in the trunk next to her luggage, closing the lid with a solid slam.

Aimee stared at Leland, committing everything about him to memory. She loved him and would love him—forever. "Thank you for everything. Especially for sharing your family's wonderful history."

He inclined his head. "You're quite welcome."

"Good luck with your book."

"Would you like a personal autographed copy?"

Her expression brightened noticeably. "Yes."

"Give me your address and I'll make certain you receive one."

She gave him the address to her Atlanta condo, then opened the door to her Audi and slipped behind the wheel. She turned on the ignition and headed north, away from St. Simons Island and Leland Monroe.

Aimee maneuvered along the path in the private subdivision community in an Atlanta suburb, pulling into the driveway leading to her home. She'd been back in Atlanta for three weeks, and it had taken two for her to readjust to the crowds and traffic delays in the capital city.

Balancing her shoulder bag and a paper sack filled with a variety of melons, she retrieved her mail from the mailbox. She'd begged off sharing dinner with her mother, deciding instead to prepare a light dinner consisting of fruit and a salad.

She opened the door, the cool air from the central air-conditioning unit greeting her. Kicking off her shoes, she made her way to the kitchen. She went through her ritual of washing her hands and splashing water over her face in the small bath-

room off the modern eat-in kitchen. Then she poured herself
a glass of iced tea, sat down on a tall stool, and opened her
mail.

She sorted various bills before picking up an envelope with
no return address. Her name and address had been typed, so
there was no recognizable handwriting. Her gaze narrowed
when she examined the postmark. It was from St. Simons Island. Her heart lurched. It had to be from Leland. Her hands
shook as she slipped a finger under the flap and withdrew a
single page of large, slanting script. She read the letter once,
then twice before the words sank in.

> *St. Simons Island*
> *22 September*
> *My Precious Aimee,*
> *I hope you are well and that you've settled comfortably*
> *back into your normal routine. I must confess that I've been*
> *unable to do much since you left. I have trouble sleeping*
> *because I don't have you beside me at night. I much prefer*
> *to wake up with you than Marmalade. I skip meals, because*
> *I now realize that I don't like eating alone. I'm behind in*
> *my writing schedule, which has annoyed my editor, who is*
> *expecting the completed manuscript in another month. The*
> *only one who is happy is Xenos. He's having quite a time*
> *with his woman, unlike his creator, who vacillates between*
> *rage and melancholy.*
>
> *I love you, Aimee—much more than I thought I could*
> *ever love a woman.*
>
> *Humbly,*
> *Leland*

Tears filled her eyes and overflowed, staining her cheeks.
She tried wiping away the moisture with her fingers, but she
was unsuccessful. Her hands were shaking uncontrollably as
she retreated to the half-bath to blow her nose and wash her
face. It was another fifteen minutes before she was back in
control.

Picking up the wall phone, she dialed the area code for St.

Simons Island, then Leland's number. He answered on the second ring.

"Hello."

"Leland?"

There was a pause before his voice came through the earpiece. "You got my letter?"

"Yes, I did. Why didn't you tell me how you felt before I left St. Simons?"

"Do you love me, Aimee?"

"You didn't answer my question, Leland."

"And you didn't answer mine."

"Yes, I love you, Leland."

"I'll answer your question when I see you. Will you be home tomorrow around this time?"

"Yes. Why?"

"I've made plans to come up to Atlanta. I've got to go. Good night, darling."

"Wait, Leland! Don't hang up!"

It was too late. He'd hung up; a warm glow flowed through Aimee's body as satisfaction pursed her mouth; the emotion filled her with a weightless joy that made her feel like singing at the top of her lungs.

She had one more day—only twenty-four hours. Then she would come face to face with the man she'd fallen in love with. The twenty-four hours would also give her time to assess her career and her future.

Leland paid the cab driver, then retrieved a small carry-on bag resting on the seat beside him. Stepping out of the taxi, he glanced up at the modern two-story structure that was Aimee's home. Its design suited her—modern, sophisticated. There was no sign of her car, and he assumed she'd parked it in an attached two-car garage.

Waiting until the driver backed out of the driveway, he made his way up the walk to the front door. An oppressive humidity lingered even though the date on the calendar indicated fall. He hadn't realized how rapidly his pulses were racing until after he rang the doorbell. A minute later the door opened.

Aimee stared up at Leland, her heart bursting with love. Her love for him was reflected in her smile and in her gaze. Leland Monroe was more attractive than she remembered. The jacket to his navy-blue lightweight suit hung elegantly from his broad shoulders. A silk tie in a matching blue was tied in a precise Windsor knot under the starched collar of a white shirt. He was elegant in the tailored suit, but somehow she preferred seeing him in his casual shorts and T-shirts.

She opened the door wider. "Please come in."

Leland stepped into a spacious foyer. He placed his carry-on next to a straight-back eighteenth century chair. His gaze swept around the space, surprised to find the modern structure filled with furnishings from a bygone era.

Aimee noticed the direction of his gaze. "Everything in the house came from my mother's antique shop."

He stared at a small octagonal table designed with a rosewood and mahogany inlay. "It's exquisite."

Aimee extended her hand. "Come into the kitchen. I didn't know whether you'd eaten, but I prepared a light repast."

Leland wanted to tell her that he couldn't eat, because he doubted whether he could force a morsel down his constricted throat. He had come to Atlanta to bare his soul, not dine.

He grasped Aimee's delicate fingers, pulling her up close to his chest. Pinpoints of liquid gold shimmered in his eyes as he examined the exquisitely beautiful face that had haunted his days and his nights since she drove away from St. Simons Island.

"You asked me why I didn't tell you how I felt about you before you left St. Simons." She nodded, her lips parting slightly. "I couldn't tell you because I wasn't prepared to ask you to choose."

A slight frown creased her smooth forehead. "Choose?"

He nodded. "I didn't want you to leave. I wanted you to stay on St. Simons with me."

"And do what, Leland?"

"That's what I finally had to ask myself. I have my writing, but what would you have? But then everything changed when your ex-fiancé showed up. When you told me that you argued about your career, I knew then that I'd never ask you to choose between your career and me."

"What are you asking, Leland?"

"I'm asking you to marry me and have my children."

Aimee closed her eyes. He wanted what she wanted—but at what cost? Was she willing to give up her career for Leland when she hadn't been for Jeremy? Did she love him that much to sacrifice all that she'd worked so hard for over the past decade?

She opened her eyes and smiled, realizing that she *did* love him that much. She wanted to go to bed with Leland Monroe and wake up in his arms when the sun rose to herald a new day. She wanted to have his babies—children who were the descendants of a people who had survived against the greatest odds in America's history. The moment she'd walked into the house Edward Monroe had built for his Sophia, Aimee knew her soul had connected with Leland's family.

Moving closer, she tilted her chin and pressed her mouth to his. "Yes," she breathed into his mouth, the single word coming from her heart.

Leland deepened the kiss, fusing his body with Aimee's. Passion—strong and pulsing—threatened to explode. "It's going to take me about a month to close up the house on St. Simons. Will that give you enough time to plan a wedding?"

Pulling back, she shook her head. "You're going to close the house?"

"Yes. After I relocate to Atlanta, we can either live here or look for a bigger house."

"You want to relocate?"

"Your work is here, Aimee."

She emitted a soft laugh. "My work is any and everywhere. I still can work for the Trust as a consultant or researcher on an on-call or as-needed basis."

Leland raised his eyebrows. "You'd prefer living on St. Simons?"

"I'd love to live and raise our children on St. Simons."

"What about your mother? I thought you wouldn't want to leave her alone."

Throwing back her head, Aimee laughed. "My mother's

involved with a man. She confessed that the month I was away forced her to assess whether she wanted to spend the rest of her life alone. He's also an antiques dealer, and a widower with several adult children. Now I know why she's been taking so many trips to Charleston."

Leland sobered. "Are you sure you don't mind relocating to St. Simons?"

"What I do mind is you standing here talking so much, Leland Monroe." Moving closer, she boldly pressed her breasts to his chest. "If you're not too hungry, then dinner can wait. What I'd like to do is take you on a tour of my bedroom. I'm rather anxious to show you how much I've missed you." She knew she sounded brazen, but she was past caring.

Bending slightly, Leland swung Aimee up in his arms. He dropped a kiss on her lips. "What do you think if we got a head start on trying for another generation of Monroes?"

Tightening her grip on his strong neck, Aimee kissed him passionately. "I think that's a wonderful idea."

Walking across the foyer, Leland headed for the curving staircase leading to the upper level. His gaze never left Aimee's face as he walked into the room she directed him to. He lowered her onto a massive brass bed, his body following.

Cradling her face between his hands, he kissed her gently. "I love you, Aimee Frasier," he whispered.

"And I love you," she countered.

The outside world ceased to exist and time stood still as the lovers demonstrated silently the depth of love and emotion that came directly from the heart.

An Officer and a Hero

by Marcia King-Gamble

ONE

"No virgin for me. I want the real deal," Candace Jones said while inspecting bright-red acrylic nails.

"You drink what you want. I'll stick to my Virgin Colada, thank you," Kitt responded, stashing her unpacked suitcase in the cabin's minuscule closet, then carefully placing her underwear and nightclothes into the dresser drawers.

"Be that way," Candy muttered. "Just try to have fun. You're wasting valuable time, girlfriend. We need to be scoping out the upper deck. Checking out the possibilities. Making sure we're seen."

Kitt groaned and rolled her eyes skyward. Heaven help her. It promised to be one long cruise. "I thought you had a boyfriend," she said.

Candy shrugged. "What can I tell you? Boyfriends come and boyfriends go. Brad's in New York, I'm here. When the cat's away——"

"Okay. Got you."

Kitt didn't approve, but she figured Candy was an adult and knew what she was doing. Even as a teenager her friend's vivacious personality and flamboyant good looks drew men like bees to honey. Top that off with a body that could stop traffic and Kitt didn't have a prayer of being noticed.

Not that it mattered anyway; she hated male attention, always had. So what if she felt like a plain Jane next to Candy? She'd come on this cruise to sprawl out on a quiet deck chair and read half a dozen books. Studying for finals had drained her last bit of energy. But it had been worth it. She'd graduated with an amazingly high cumulative average and was now mulling over several attractive job offers.

Kitt felt the vibration of the engines under her feet. The ship hadn't sailed yet, but her stomach felt queasy. What if the wrist bands she'd bought at the drug store didn't work? She'd raced out to purchase them the moment Candy had said they were going on a cruise. The clerk had told her they were effective for motion sickness. Unlike Dramamine, they didn't make you drowsy.

Candy had surprised her with this much-needed graduation gift to the Southern Caribbean. Exotic islands like St. Thomas, St. Lucia, and Aruba were part of the itinerary. Kitt couldn't wait. Candy had won the cruise for being top producer at her travel agency. At least that's what she'd told Kitt. She'd also said it wouldn't cost them a dime, except for tips to the wait staff and cabin stewards, and any incidentals they might purchase. To Kitt, who'd attended school full time and held two part-time jobs, it had sounded like a dream come true.

Candy slipped her feet into high-heel slides. She tugged on too-short shorts and eyed Kitt up and down. "You going like that?"

"Yes. I'm comfortable."

Candy shook her head, clearly disapproving of Kitt's loose ankle-length sundress with the simple scoop neck. "You need a makeover, girlfriend."

Candy's nipples could clearly be seen through the material of her skimpy tube top. It didn't seem to bother her a bit. Tight white shorts hugged a butt that Kitt had once heard referred to as round as an onion, and able to make men cry.

Kitt followed her friend's swishing behind up three flights of stairs, noting that men practically tripped over their feet as she bounced by. Kitt had never been looked at like that. Most men didn't seem to know she existed, and that was fine with her.

On the upper deck, they were greeted by a band playing loud reggae music. Skimpily-clad passengers on their way to intoxication gyrated to the pulsating beat. A group of studs had taken over the spa, ignoring the huge sign that said "No drinking in the Jacuzzi," and noisily guzzled beers. Parading in front of them were several leggy beauties in high-cut swimsuits, one more attractive than the next.

The drinking men in the spa loudly assessed the women,

rating them from one to ten. No one so far had rated lower than a seven. Kitt decided it was definitely time to slink down into her comfortable, loose-fitting dress, and pray to the Lord none of them saw her.

Kitt's attention returned to Candy. Her friend was already seated on a bar stool. She patted the spot next to her. Kitt reluctantly sat.

"What's going on?" Candy asked the bartender, angling her head at the bevy of beauties who'd commandeered lounge chairs.

"Beauty contestants," he responded in a thick Caribbean accent. "Half of the ship's been chartered by the Miss Black Universe pageant. Those fine things represent the world. See the one with the braids? That's Miss Barbados. That's where I'm from."

"Lovely," Candy muttered under her breath. "I'd have to choose a cruise where the women are better-looking than me."

"Hard to top you," the bartender said boldly, wiping a glass and eyeing Candy greedily. "I'd take you over the lot of them, even my girl, Miss Barbados. Now, what would you like to drink?"

Candy brightened visibly. "How about something frothy and cool. Something with a kick to it. What's that?" She pointed to a passing waiter with a tray filled with glasses sporting colorful umbrellas.

"Those are Sun Ship Specials. What does your friend want?"

Kitt spoke up quickly. "A virgin Piña Colada. I don't drink alcohol."

The bartender made a wry face, then set to work. He poured a creamy substance from a blender, added a paper umbrella, then fixed Candy's pink concoction. He placed both glasses in front of them. "Drinks on me. Welcome aboard *The Eternity*, ladies." His attention turned to one of the beauty contestants who'd sidled up to the bar followed by a bunch of gaping men.

"He's cute," Candy said, looking to Kitt for confirmation. "If all the men on board are as friendly as him, even you might land someone."

"I don't want to land anyone," Kitt responded through

clenched teeth. "I especially don't want to land players. I just want to relax."

Candy slid off her stool and crooked a finger at Kitt. "Come. Time to go back to the cabin and get pretty. After dinner we'll check out the singles party and preview the men on board."

Candy's cell phone jingled. Kitt heard her friend say, "Hey, Brad, I miss you already, hon."

She rolled her eyes. It was shaping up to be some cruise.

After a sumptuous dinner, Kitt trailed Candy to the singles party. The nightclub was jam-packed, but they managed to find seats on two art-deco chairs. In the front of the room an overly enthusiastic social host conducted a game of musical chairs. It was the ultimate ice breaker—whenever the music stopped, men and women plopped down on any available lap. Kitt couldn't imagine being out there.

"Ladies, drinks?" A waiter clad in a colorful vest and equally loud bow tie bent over them.

"A Sun Ship Special for me," Candy said. "And my friend will have—"

"A Coke," Kitt said quickly.

"Lighten up. Live a little," Candy said, wrinkling her nose. "Order a virgin or something. Even a glass of wine."

Their waiter, smothering a smile, turned away and went off to do their bidding. Kitt wanted to slap that supercilious smile off Candy's face. Couldn't she just let her be?

Candy's attention had already wandered. She was busy checking out the men in the room. "What about the guy in black? He looks promising."

Kitt gave the man in the form-fitting black shirt, skin-tight jeans, and too much silver jewelry a quick glance. "Looks like trouble to me," she said. "The consummate player."

Something about him reminded her of the man she used to call Uncle, her mother's friend. All style and little substance. An innocent child had once trusted him. Kitt squeezed her eyes closed, willing the memories to go away, burying the hurt.

"Every man is trouble to some degree," Candy said. "That's what makes them challenging. Our job is to stay ahead of the game. Have fun, but keep them dangling." She smiled, but her eyes continued to dart around the room.

"I don't have what it takes to keep anyone dangling," Kitt joked, running a hand with square-cut nails over her short, boyish hair. Candy had convinced her to get her hair cropped prior to coming on the cruise. She'd said it would hold up in salt water.

"What about that one?" This time Candy pointed a ruby-red nail in the direction of a light-skinned man who was dressed in tailored slacks and a crisp oxford shirt. "He looks professional, like he might have money."

Kitt shrugged. What was the point of commenting? Candy would not let up until she'd singled out a man for the evening, and she'd be left hugging the wall.

Her friend sucked her teeth. "Now just look at that."

"What?"

"Check out the entrance."

Every head was turned toward the door. Even the deejay had lowered the music, as if to ensure the troop of leggy beauties prancing in had everyone's attention. A dozen or so young women now draped themselves against the wall. They reminded Kitt of underfed fillies. She apparently was the only one who thought so, because around her, seats were being quickly vacated and offered up. None of the men had done that when she and Candy entered.

"Competition never hurt anyone," Candy said, squaring her shoulders and preparing to do battle. "I'm as pretty as they are, and more intelligent. Time to work it, girlfriend."

Kitt hid a smile. Outgoing, popular Candy had been her salvation from nursery through high school. Kitt, a prime candidate for bullies, had been accepted by the *in* crowd solely on Candy's recommendation. She was now busily eyeing a group of officers in white uniforms in the far corner of the room.

"Gotta get me some of that," she murmured, smoothing the bodice of her red halter dress and tossing back her hair. "Do I look hot?"

"Sizzling."

"Good. I'm relying on you to help me with my mission. We're on our way over."

"No, we're not." Kitt already knew her protest fell on deaf ears. Candy would never take no for an answer. Rather than risk a scene, why not simply follow? It had always been this way.

She followed in Candy's wake, preparing herself for the inevitable. In a matter of seconds Candy would be chatting easily with the officers, while Kitt would do her best to untwist her tongue and grunt something intelligible. In her thirty-five years, she hadn't yet mastered the art of flirting.

"Check out the shoulders on the tall one," Candy said, inhaling audibly as they got closer. "Look at that chest. Bet you anything there's a basketball body hidden under that uniform jacket."

Candy must have set her sights on the dark-skinned man standing head and shoulders above the crowd. Kitt had noticed him, too. The white of his uniform contrasted sharply against his ebony skin. His close-cropped hair had a slight curl to it, and his nostrils, from what she could see, had the hint of a flare. As they approached, he seemed to sense them staring and broke off his conversation.

Up close, he was even better looking. Sleek and long. Different from the muscle-bound jocks Candy usually went for. He smiled at them. A nice smile. Sexy, but not totally intimidating. His eyes were light and sparkled intriguingly, as if he and she shared a joke that no one else got.

For one fleeting moment Kitt wished she'd listened to Candy and borrowed the slinky gold dress her friend had offered. Instead, she'd insisted on wearing her long black skirt and white silk blouse. She'd even worn pearls. She must look like a granny. No wonder the uniformed god had eyes only for Candy.

Candy's walk had grown more bouncy than ever. "Show them your assets," she'd coached before leaving the cabin, and boy, was she ever.

The officer saluted and flashed another perfect smile. His eyes crinkled at the corners. Even though Kitt hung back, she felt the effects of that smile. It warmed her like a sunny day in June. She'd let Candy handle this. She was much too tongue-tied to offer anything but the obligatory hello if she was introduced.

The ebony Adonis was in front of them. She felt an unfamiliar fluttering in her gut. His skin was Hershey's-brown. His cheekbones were sculptured. Those lips were definitely kissable. *Whoops, where did that come from?* She'd never felt such a strong physical attraction for a man, not since she'd stupidly fallen head over heels for a guy in her Adolescent Psychology class. He'd taken what she had to offer and moved on to someone more suitable. Someone perky and pretty, someone with no brains, but lots of style. A trophy he could be proud of. That was years ago, and she hadn't let another man close since.

"Having a good time, ladies?" the object of her interest asked. Kitt swore his eyes were fixed on her, but she had to be mistaken. Next to Candy, she was always invisible.

Candy smiled her come-hither smile. "Yes, we are. So far this has the makings of a wonderful cruise. Now it's getting better and better." Candy was up in his face, assets pointing suggestively.

To his credit, he seemed oblivious to her blatant come-on. His gaze still seemed to be focused on Kitt. "I'm Jared Horne," he said, offering a hand. "You're . . . ?"

"Kitt DuMaurier." She placed her hand in his as if it was the most natural thing in the world. His grasp was firm and reassuring, his palm warm. She sensed he was someone a woman could lean on. Possibly trust.

"As in Eartha?" One eyebrow raised inquisitively.

God, she even liked the timbre of his voice. Not too deep, but deep enough to let you know he was all male.

Kitt shot him an answering smile. Was this what you called flirting? "My mother was a big Eartha Kitt fan," she said. "She loved her. Thought she was the sexiest entertainer in the world."

"I do, too. Your mother has great taste."

"I'm Candy Jones," Candy said, reminding them of her existence. "What is it you do on this boat?"

"Ship," Jared Horne automatically corrected. "I'm the hotel manager."

Candy touched his sleeve and batted her eyelashes. "Is that an important job?"

Jared Horne seemed to be eating up Candy's flirting. "Let's find a seat someplace quieter and I'll tell you all about it. I'll buy you ladies a drink." The eyebrow rose again slightly.

Kitt sensed Candy's struggle. She was never one to place her eggs in one basket. Remaining at the singles party meant keeping her options open, but having an officer drool all over her the entire cruise would win out. It would give her something to brag about when she got home.

"Thanks for the invite, but I'll take a rain check," Candy said, surprising Kitt.

"What about you?" Jared asked. "Would you like to find some place less noisy?" His eyes were on her, the twinkle very evident.

Kitt was momentarily taken aback. She'd assumed Candy had answered for both of them. Much as she was curious about Jared Horne, she couldn't be left alone with him. He was already having an effect on her respiratory system. It would be a challenge holding up her end of the conversation.

Around them there was a sudden flurry of activity. Three of the beauty pageant contestants had joined Jared's friends. Kitt envied their cool and collected personas. They were impeccably dressed, and laughed easily at what the officers had to say. Jared glanced over at the group. Kitt knew that in a matter of seconds he would change his mind and withdraw the invitation. Clearly he wanted to be with them.

"I'd love to," she said, surprising herself and Candy.

Candy gaped openly, but did a quick recovery. She threw back hair that she'd once told Kitt cost half a week's pay. "Nice meeting you, Jared. See you around." With that, she took off.

Gentleman that he was, Jared smiled and called after her, "I look forward to it. I'll need to collect on that rain check."

He and Kitt then faced each other. Kitt's stomach had begun to make embarrassing noises. She hoped he could not hear the rumbling over the loud music. What was there to say to him? Men made her nervous. Good-looking ones even more so.

Jared placed his hand on her elbow and steered her through the crowd. His companions shouted an invitation to come

over, but he ignored them. The roaring in Kitt's ears threatened to drown out the sounds around her. She could barely
hear Jared's voice. She felt a tightening in her chest, and a
sudden shortness of breath added to her light-headedness. Her
stomach felt as if someone were popping corn in it.

They entered another lounge with only a handful of people
in it. A jazz band played a sultry tune while a sleepy-eyed
singer crooned lyrics from another time. Jared found a seat on
a red velvet banquette and he and Kitt sat listening to the
music. A waiter came scurrying over and in a deferential manner asked, "Can I get you something to drink, sir?"

Jared's light-eyed gaze shifted to her. Kitt's mouth went
dry and the popcorn pinged in her stomach. "Kitt?"

"I'll have a Coke, please."

"Same for me."

"Right away, sir."

"You don't drink?" Kitt surprised herself by asking.

Jared's lips twitched. "I wouldn't exactly say that. I don't
drink alcohol when I'm on duty."

"You're on duty now? But you were in the nightclub."

"That's part of what a hotel manager does. Circulate, make
sure everyone's having a good time, and ensure activities are
running like clockwork."

Kitt nodded as drinks and munchies were set down before
them. She sipped her Coke and looked around the room. The
place had filled up, and several striking women now occupied
the once-vacant tables. She and Jared had run out of things to
say, or so it seemed. His attention was no longer on her; he
was scanning the room, assessing the possibilities, as Candy
would say.

"I've taken up quite a bit of your time," Kitt said, preparing
to leave.

"On the contrary. It's not often I get to relax. I'm enjoying
sitting here, being with you."

He was being polite. Men never found her fascinating.
She'd been told she was much too intense. Far too serious for
their liking.

A high-pitched beep got their attention. Jared fingered the
pager at his waist. "So much for rest and relaxation. I'm going

to have to find out what this is about. I'll try to get back as
soon as I can."

What could she say? She hated sitting alone.

Jared unclipped a cell phone from his waist and headed off.
Kitt sipped her Coke and watched the action on the small
dance floor. Several of the beauty contestants had found themselves partners. She was tempted to leave and go find Candy,
or better yet, return to her cabin and finish her book.

"What's a nice girl like you doing in a place like this?" A
man's deep rumble asked, close to her ear.

Kitt smelled bourbon. She looked up to see a heavyset man
dressed head to toe in Tommy Hilfiger and an abundance of
gold. Even his gold teeth glittered. She grimaced. "Uh . . ."

"A woman as beautiful as you shouldn't be sitting alone,"
he said, flopping down in the seat Jared had vacated.

The smell of bourbon was overpowering. Bourbon and the
nasty cologne he'd doused himself in. Time to exit discreetly.

Kitt stood. Her gaze scanned the entrance. She spotted a
tall man in a white uniform. Jared was on his way back.

"My friend's here to take me to the show," she said, exiting
the banquette. "See you around."

Halfway across the floor, she realized Jared wasn't alone.
A slender pecan-skinned woman in a slip of a dress commandeered his arm. She flung her head back, laughing at something he said. Pearly whites sparkled.

Kitt made a U-turn. There was a back entrance somewhere.
The book in her cabin started looking better and better.

TWO

It was part of his job. Be gracious. Entertain passengers. Make sure they had fun. Even so, Jared Horne wished the woman would loosen her grip on his arm. She'd introduced herself as Miss Belize, Hayden something or other. Her last name evaded him.

"Hotel manager sounds like a fun job," Hayden said, brushing the side of her breast up against him. "How long have you been a ship's officer?"

"Ten years," Jared said, stiffening, his guard firmly in place. Even if he had any interest, there was no point in encouraging her. Company rules strictly forbade personal relationships between staff and passengers. Of course, what you did on your own time, off the ship, was your own business.

"You must get to go to some fun places. You'll have to tell me all about it." Hayden slanted elaborately made-up gray eyes at him.

She was beautiful, all right. Especially if you liked the overly glamorous type who worked at staying beautiful. Personally he preferred someone with a quieter style. Someone like the woman he'd been forced to abandon rather abruptly. Kitt DuMaurier in her elegant black skirt and demure white pearls was more his type. A class act, and a far cry from the posturing babes who had taken over his ship. Where was she now?

Jared's eyes scanned the room. He'd left Kitt seated on the banquette alone, now she was nowhere in sight. It figured his pager would go off at such an inopportune moment. He'd been summoned by the staff captain, Giuseppe, to answer some dumb question that anyone at the Guest Relations Desk would have known. Rank and status being what it was, the Italian officer would never lower himself to deal with a front desk employee.

"Jared?" Hayden tugged at his sleeve. "Are we going to sit?"

He managed a smile. "I'm sorry. Of course."

Miss Belize's feet were probably killing her. Walking the decks in those three-inch heels must have taken its toll. He spotted a table about to become vacant. The couple seated were in the process of settling their bill. He took Hayden's elbow and steered her in that direction, swooping down on the table the moment it became free.

A waiter materialized from somewhere, an awed smile on his face. After the bowing and scraping were over with, Jared placed their drink orders. Coke for him. White wine for her. He signed the check, ignoring the envious glances thrown his way. Even the cruise director, Tim, seated at an adjacent table, had his tongue mopping the floor. When Jared caught his eye, Tim gave him the thumbs-up sign. He had apparently scored a big coup. Little did they know that he was bored stiff and was valiantly attempting to hold up his end of a conversation. He couldn't wait to go on vacation. Aruba couldn't come soon enough.

"So tell me about some of the exotic places you've been to," Hayden said, covering her hand with his.

Familiar ground. He could talk his head off and keep the conversation light. "Let's see, my first couple of years with Sun Ship Cruises, I was assigned to the Mexican Riviera."

"The Mexican Riviera? Where is that?"

"Cabo San Lucas, Mazatlan, Puerto Vallarta, that part of the world. Then summers I did Alaska runs: Skagway, Juneau, Ketchigan."

Miss Belize looked awed. "Alaska?"

"Yes, one of my favorite places in the whole wide world. Then I was assigned the Panama Canal and Hawaii. When we started building bigger ships, like this one, I got switched to the Southern Caribbean."

"How many passengers does this ship hold?"

"Twenty-six hundred."

"Oh, my, so many people. You're so well-traveled and so young. You intimidate me."

He doubted he intimidated her.

Miss Belize touched his sleeve and eyed his ringless left hand. "In all this time you never married? There's got to be a girlfriend."

Jared had made a vow never to discuss his personal life with passengers, or guests, as the cruise line preferred calling their patrons. No need to tell Hayden about Sherrie, his four-year relationship, the dancer he'd recently broken up with. He'd fallen out of love with her, realizing that great sex did not a great relationship make. Sherrie had proven he couldn't trust her.

"I'm thirty-seven and single," he said rather abruptly.

"Come on, Jared, a fine-looking man like you must have a girlfriend," Hayden teased. Her gray eyes scanned his briefly. She squeezed his hand. "Tell me the truth."

He tried to discreetly disengage from her grasp. She was coming on strong. Too strong for his liking. He gazed around the room looking for someone to palm her off on. A polite reason to say good-bye and end things on a gracious note. Miss Belize was obviously on the prowl. She needed to find other prey.

Jared spotted Candy Jones, Kitt's friend. She was holding an animated conversation with Arif, the food and beverage manager, from India. Predatory as Candy was, at least she was entertaining. Maybe she knew where Kitt was.

"I'm going to have to leave. Duty calls," Jared said, sliding his hand out from under Hayden's. He tossed her what he hoped was an apologetic look. "I need to go over the week's menu with my food and beverage manager. Drinks are paid for. See you at rehearsal tomorrow." Before Hayden could get out another word, he was up and off.

Halfway across the room, Arif spotted him. The officer acknowledged him with a nod of his head. For one unguarded moment he looked annoyed. What was that about? They got along well and were in fact friends.

Realizing Arif Khoslo had already branded Candy as his own, Jared smothered a smile. Arif was afraid that Candy's attention would be diverted by an officer outranking him. As far as he was concerned, Arif was welcome to Candy. Lovely as the woman was, she was stuck on herself and a tad too pushy for his liking. A far cry from her companion, sweet, unassuming Kitt. He wondered how the two had ever hooked up.

Jared knew that as much as Arif enjoyed Candy's attention, he would never cross the line. It would be nothing more than a mild flirtation. The food and beverage manager had worked too hard to get where he was. Innocent flirtations on the other hand, kept him alive and feeling like a man.

But even innocent flirting was risky. In today's world, complimenting a woman could be construed as sexual harassment, and befriending one sometimes came with a price. Jared had been burned before. That's why he kept his relationships strictly shoreside.

He grimaced, remembering the passenger he'd befriended who'd misconstrued his intentions. When he'd tried to set things straight, telling her they were only friends, she'd contacted the home office and complained that he'd sexually harassed her. The end result had been a six-month suspension and one promotion lost. Top that off with four-plus years of Sherrie using him, boy did he know how much business and pleasure didn't mix.

"Hey," Arif said, greeting him with a thump on the shoulder. "You did well for yourself, huh?" The manager's jutted jaw indicated the abandoned Miss Belize chatting up a new admirer.

Candy Jones squinted at him. "Where's Kitt?"

"I was about to ask you that."

"I left her with you," she said, sounding put out. "I didn't expect you to abandon her."

"I didn't abandon her," Jared said. "She left."

Candy clicked her teeth and drained the remnants of her glass. "She wouldn't just up and leave. You must have done something to her."

What was it with the woman? Why was she so damn prickly?

"Sit," Arif said, pointing to a chair and signaling for a

waiter. He seemed amused at the way the tables had turned. Hotel managers normally didn't get the riot act read to them.

Jared somehow managed to smile through clenched teeth. Candy Jones was one snippy piece. "I was paged," he ground out. "Kitt was supposed to wait, but didn't. I assume something came up."

Candy's arched eyebrows climbed skeptically. "So then you consoled yourself with another?"

"I was doing my job. I speak to everyone." Why was he even getting into a pissing contest with her? Kitt needed to lose her friend, and soon. Jared's innate graciousness eventually kicked in. "I'll buy the first round."

"I'll let you," Arif said good-naturedly, squeezing Candy's shoulder. "Lighten up. We're on a cruise."

Candy simply pouted. Her eyes scanned the room. Jared suspected she was checking out the men. A beat or so later, she said, "I hope Kitt's okay."

"Assuming she's over twenty-one and has a good head on her shoulders, she's fine."

"If you say so."

The woman was impossible. She didn't give an inch. He regretted taking her up on her rain check so soon. But he'd viewed it as an opportunity to get the lowdown on Kitt. He'd even hoped she might return and join them.

"Another Sun Ship Special?" Jared asked Candy when the waiter hovered. She'd been sipping the overpriced drink earlier, and still clutched the neon glass in her hand. "Arif, what about you?"

"Tanqueray and tonic."

Jared ordered his usual Coke.

"How long have you known Kitt?" he asked Candy when drinks were served.

"Almost all of my life. She and I were in nursery school together."

"Who's Kitt?" Arif's singsongy voice interjected. "All I've heard is Kitt this, Kitt that. I can't wait to meet this mysterious Kitt."

Candy flicked an eyeful of hair off her face. "Kitt's a good friend. She came on the cruise with me, but your friend Jared managed to lose her." She sighed heavily. "Look what's on her way over."

Automatically, Jared stiffened. Sherrie, his ex, was doing the late show and didn't get off until after midnight. He'd made it clear he wanted nothing to do with her. She was unpredictable and tended to make scenes. A quick glance reassured him he was in no danger. Miss Belize bore down, another contestant in tow.

"Did you get your business taken care of?" she asked, standing over him and cutting her eyes at Candy. An attractive woman lagged two feet behind. "Your menu's all squared away, then?" Hayden tilted her head, moistened her lips, and waited.

Arif brighten visibly. Candy simply glared at her.

Jared pasted on his professional smile. "Pretty much. Wouldn't you join us?"

"What menu?" Candy demanded, giving the two beauty contestants the once-over.

Arif sputtered gin and tonic and pretended to cough. Jared, glad for the timely distraction, made a huge production of slapping his back. When the coughing ceased, he dispatched him for extra chairs.

Both women now happily sat.

Hayden introduced her friend. "This is Nakia Layne, Miss Martinique. My only competition."

Nakia's brown eyes danced. She appeared to be the more pleasant of the two. "Cocky, isn't she?" She stuck out her hand. Jared found her grasp surprisingly firm. She wore her hair in a sleek knot on the top of her head, and her cheekbones were very pronounced. Exotic as she was, he didn't find her interesting. Another face had superimposed itself on his mind. Kitt's. She didn't try looking like a supermodel. She didn't even wear much makeup.

Jared focused on the women seated around his table. Candy's glares had increased. He could tell she would just as soon rip Nakia's and Hayden's eyes out as look at them. Judging by the expressions on the contestants' faces, they apparently felt the same. Jared found it all mildly amusing.

Faced with all this beauty, Arif was like a kid in a candy

store. Jared had never heard his voice so elated. He was talking a mile a minute, giving the women blow-by-blow details of his job. Jared's eyes scanned the room once more. Everyone seemed to be having fun. Still no Kitt.

"There's Kitt," Candy screamed, jumping up and waving, "Kitt! Kitt! Over here."

Jared's heart actually thudded. Unable to stop himself, he was up and off, heading in Kitt's direction. She hesitantly made her way across the floor. In her tasteful black skirt, she outclassed all the beauty queens dressed in their short, short skirts and wild animal prints.

Kitt hadn't heard Candy and seemed on the verge of bolting. Jared couldn't let that happen. He picked up his pace, shoving past passengers, something he had never done before.

"Kitt," he called when he was almost on top of her.

"Jared?" Their eyes locked and held. Hers were the prettiest shade of hazel.

"We're sitting over there," he said, pointing vaguely to an area behind him.

"We?" Kitt scoped out the area, frowning. "You're with the pageant contestants?"

"And Candy," he hastily reassured. "See, she's sitting directly to the food and beverage manager's right. Wouldn't you join us?"

He could tell she debated. "Look," he said, talking quickly, "before I was paged, I was really enjoying your company. It wouldn't be a late night, I promise. Tomorrow we're in St. Thomas and I'll need to supervise the pageant rehearsal and observe debarkation. One drink," Jared pleaded.

"Okay."

Her acquiescence put him over the moon. He didn't want to think what that meant. Before she could change her mind, he took her hand and guided her through the crowd.

Arif had already found her a seat. Jared's hand lingered longer than necessary on the back of her chair when he seated her. What had come over him? The ship carried twenty-six hundred passengers. He met thousands of women every week. What made this one special?

Introductions were made and more drinks ordered. Jared

tuned out what the others were saying, his attention only on
Kitt. He sensed she was not at ease in this nightclub setting.
She let the beauty queens monopolize the conversation, con-
tributing little. Either she was intimidated or overwhelmed.

He was tempted to whisk her off to a place where they
could talk privately. Get to know each other a little better. But
the only private place was his cabin, and he could hardly take
her there. It was strictly off-limits to passengers, and issuing
that type of invitation would be improper.

"Have you been to St. Thomas?" he asked.

"This is my first time outside the U.S."

"Are you taking a shore excursion?" The question popped
out before he could stop it.

Kitt looked to Candy for confirmation. "Are we?"

"Are we what?" her friend asked, tearing herself away from
her discussion with Arif.

"Taking a shore tour?"

Candy shrugged. "I hadn't planned on it."

"Good," Jared said. "Then if you're not committed, allow
me to be your guide. Yours and Candy's, that is. I'll meet you
at the Purser's Information Desk around eleven."

Kitt stared at him but didn't say a word. His invitation
hadn't gone over well, he sensed. Most female passengers
would be delighted by an officer's attention. Not Kitt. She
remained unfazed or simply dazed. What was it about him she
didn't like?

"Did I hear something about touring St. Thomas?" Miss
Belize asked, breaking the awkward silence. She leaned across
the table and looked directly at him.

Jared refused to bite. "These ladies are. Did you want to
join them?"

Kitt actually smiled. He could tell she was amused by the
way he'd sidestepped the question. Miss Belize looked furious.

"Eleven o'clock in front of the Purser's Information Desk,"
Candy mouthed, rising, and beckoning Kitt to follow.

"Eleven it is," Jared whispered back.

His eyes followed Kitt's retreating back. The slight sway
of her hips produced a tug in his groin. He didn't even notice

another woman approaching until she was on top of him. Even then, all he could say was, "Hi, Sherrie."

Jared's gaze remained on Kitt DuMaurier. Come hell or high water, tomorrow he planned on being at the Information Desk.

THREE

Kitt heard the pulsating steel band music outside. One sandal-clad foot tapped out a rhythm. She tugged on the hem of the black shorts she'd borrowed from Candy, wishing they were longer. They were the most modest item her friend had packed, and Kitt wore them with a white T-shirt, adding a scarf at the neck. Candy had rolled her eyes skyward, declaring the outfit schoolmarmish. Kitt didn't care.

Jared was now fifteen minutes late, and so was Candy. It looked like she'd been stood up. Surreptitiously, Kitt eyed the parading beauty contestants, who, having completed their stint on stage, milled around the Information Desk. Some were dressed in costumes so elaborate, they sometimes required wheels. Others kept it simple, opting for manageable head-dresses and handheld props. Each was lovelier than the next.

A coffee-skinned competitor, with full midriff exposed, slid by, making Kitt feel frumpier than ever. Kitt all of a sudden remembered Jared's role in the pageant—that must be why he was late. She could hear the cruise director announcing the next contestant. She hadn't been stood up, at least not yet.

Outside, the tempo of the music picked up. Kitt's excitement built. She wanted off the ship. Wanted to roam the town. Talk to the natives. Catch some of that uninhibited Caribbean spirit she'd heard so much about.

"Oh, Kitt, I'm sorry." Candy skidded to a stop in front of her. She looked flushed and bright-eyed, nothing like her usual polished self. "Brad called, you know how he goes on and on. Then I ran into Earl."

"Who's Earl?" Kitt asked.

"Someone I met last evening. He's a lawyer. He, his buddy,

and another girl are renting a Jeep. They asked me to join them."

"What about Jared's invitation?" Kitt feared she already knew the answer.

"What about it?" Candy sighed and rolled her eyes to the ceiling. "It's not like we're glued together, girl. You go on your date and I'll have my own fun."

"Jared invited both of us," Kitt reminded her. "It's rude to cancel at the last minute."

"He'll get over it. Besides, it's you he wants, not me. Even a blind woman could see that."

Kitt's face grew warm. Her stomach felt as if Mexican jumping beans were dirty dancing against the lining. "Come on, Candy, please don't do this to me. You know I'm not comfortable with strange men."

"Do what to you?" Jared's voice came from behind them. She hoped he hadn't heard the tail end of the conversation.

Candy spoke quickly. "Jared, I'm sorry, but I'm going to have to cancel. Take good care of Kitt. You two have fun." She wriggled her fingers before racing off.

The expression on Jared's face was priceless. He looked truly bewildered. "Is she always like this?" he asked.

"Always."

"How is it you remain friends?" Jared's smile made the Mexican beans dance.

Breathe, Kitt. Appear nonchalant. Act as if that smile isn't wreaking havoc with your heart. Don't let him know the effect his presence has on you.

Kitt took a deep breath and concentrated on the question. She'd often wondered why she and Candy had remained friends. They were a most unlikely pair, both physically and mentally. Candy was super-attractive and knew it, but still craved attention, while Kitt would just as easily disappear into the woodwork.

"Candy is a little scattered," Kitt agreed, "but overall she has a good heart. She's not the most sensitive person in the world, but she's consistent and loyal." That she was. She'd supported Kitt through some of the most difficult times of her life.

Jared cocked his head, listening intently. He looked completely different out of uniform, less godlike and more human somehow. More handsome than last evening, if that was possible. He'd tucked a form-fitting kelly-green T-shirt into khaki shorts. Kitt risked a peek at his legs. They were long, well-muscled, and had curly hairs. He wore loafers. No socks.

"Ready?" Jared said, slipping sunglasses on.

"Ready." He placed a hand on the small of her back, steering her toward an elevator that would bring them down to the lower deck. His touch set off a chain reaction. She couldn't stop herself from trembling.

"Cold? Maybe you should stop by your cabin and get a jacket," he suggested.

"I'll be fine."

What was she thinking of, going sightseeing alone with him? Her therapist had said not every man was like her uncle. It was sometimes difficult to remember that.

Jared punched the elevator button and almost immediately the doors flew open. They boarded with another couple, whom he greeted with a hearty, "Hello."

"Nice day," the man answered, his Midwestern twang evident. "You folks on honeymoon?"

"Are you?"

"Yup."

"Congratulations. Hope you're having a good time." Jared eased Kitt out of the elevator before the couple recognized him in street clothes.

As they were exiting the gangway, a photographer aimed his lens at them. Jared placed his arm around her shoulder and drew her close, whispering, "Smile for the camera."

Kitt ignored the fluttering in her gut and tried not to be so tense. Jared's closeness made it difficult to concentrate. The fresh, clean smell of his cologne lay heavy in her nostrils. His strong male presence wreaked havoc with her hormones and scared her at the same time. She concentrated on the steel band music that had grown louder and livelier. Three musicians in colorful shirts and wide-brimmed hats were playing enthusiastically for the tourists.

They walked down the docks a bit. Kitt peered at the shops

sporting signs reading "Duty Free." Jared, sensing her interest, came to a full stop.

"We can go in if you'd like," he said. "St. Thomas is known for great buys on alcohol and perfumes."

"I'm not big user of either, but I'd like to pick up some souvenirs to take home."

"Then we'll go into town." He took her hand and guided her through the milling crowd. "You're different from most women I know. Most make a beeline for the stores. Especially those selling fragrances."

Was she really so different? Luxuries were things she hadn't been able to afford, and so had no interest in. With a little bit of disposable income, perhaps she would feel different. She felt Jared's eyes on her. "I've been scrimping and saving to go to school," she said, knowing she must sound dull compared to the women he knew.

"School?" he repeated, clearly puzzled.

What he didn't ask was, why was a thirty-something-year-old woman still in school?

"It's taken me years to get my degree," Kitt admitted. "I took as many courses as I could afford each semester. Some semesters the money just wasn't there. But I did it. I finally graduated with my masters in psychology."

"That's wonderful," Jared said squeezing the hand he was still holding. "Definitely a reason to celebrate. We'll grab a cab into town. Do some shopping and I'll buy you lunch."

His golden gaze swept over her, leaving her hot and flushed, unsteady on her feet. He was acting as if spending time with her wasn't an obligation but something he wanted to do.

"Jared! Jared!" A high-pitched female voice squeaked. "Wait up."

Shoot, how could that woman have changed so fast?

Kitt looked at him questioningly. He quickly pasted on a smile and turned to greet the women calling him.

Hayden and Nakia were walking toward them as fast as their legs could carry them. Hayden was dressed in ridiculously short shorts that made her look even more willowy. She'd coupled the cut-off denim shorts with a halter top. A sharp-looking straw hat was angled over one eye. Nakia, not to be outdone, had opted for an almost backless sundress with a plunging neckline and outrageously high slides. Didn't beauty contestants have chaperones?

"I thought you two were going on a shore excursion," Hayden said, her attention solely on Jared.

"We're not."

Jared smiled at Miss Belize, the corners of his eyes crinkling. His nostrils flared slightly. *He could model for* GQ, Kitt thought. In fact, he and Hayden would make quite the pair. The sepia version of Barbie and Ken. She wondered how she could discreetly disappear.

"We thought we might get a drink and see something of the town," Hayden continued, flirting outrageously. "Come on, join us."

The invitation clearly didn't include Kitt, but Jared seemed tempted. He surprised her by saying, "We would love to. But I'm on official ship's business and my time's committed. How about we have that drink later, back on the ship?"

"Promise?" Hayden said, moistening already-wet lips.

"Promise."

"Don't let me stop . . ."

Jared took Kitt's arm and hustled her off.

"Really, I don't mind," she argued, "if you want to go with them, it's perfectly fine with me."

"I don't want to go with them. I want to be with you, get to know you better," he said with such finality, she was forced to shut up.

The cab ride into town took less than ten minutes. Every tiny square inch of space seemed to house a store of some kind. Designer boutiques jostled for space with souvenir shops. Duty-free liquor stores offered every imaginable libation there was. As they navigated the mobbed streets, Jared held on to her hand.

"A bit overwhelming, huh?" he said, as they narrowly missed bumping into another tourist with a bulging shopping bag.

"A bit."

"You've got three other ports to do shopping. Let's go to my favorite hideout and have a drink."

"I'd like that."

In less than a minute he'd whisked her into a cab. They drove along a picturesque waterfront he referred to as Charlotte Amalie Harbor.

"Where are we heading?" Kitt asked when the streets became less congested and the buildings less commercial.

"The Crab Hole. It's a local hangout. The owner and I are friends. There wouldn't be another cruise passenger in sight."

"Good." Running into all the beauty queens was beginning to get to her. She felt like one of Cinderella's stepsisters, and probably looked like it, too.

The cab stopped in front of a decrepit building. The taxi driver announced, "Crab Hole. Dis where you want to go, mon."

Jared thanked him and paid the fare.

No pretenses here. The building was nothing more than a brightly painted hole in the wall. Three sleepy-eyed youths rolled dice out front, and inside, a menu board listed a variety of local foods and drinks. The patrons, mostly natives, spoke in loud accented voices, and from the number of plates on each table, devoured their food by the ton. At the back of the room a handful of people danced to a popular reggae tune.

While they were searching for a vacant table, a full-figured woman in a too-tight dress approached Jared. "Long time no see, hon." She clasped him in a bear hug.

Jared's long arms whipped around her. He kissed her cheek. After a while he held her away from him. "Give me a break, huh, Bella? You know how hard it is to get off that ship. In approximately four days, I'm on vacation. I've rented a condo in Aruba. Can't wait to relax. You did save me some of that tasty jerk chicken of yours?"

Bella placed plump hands on ample hips and cut her eyes at him. "You not spending your vacation with me on St. Thomas? That chicken gonna cost you big time, boy. Who's this?" Her dimpled smile welcomed Kitt.

"Kitt's a friend," Jared said, prodding her forward.

"Looks like more than a friend to me."

"Now, now, Bella."

After a few minutes of small talk, their friendly hostess led them to the back of the restaurant and seated them at a scratched Formica table. A waitress soon brought them coconut water on the house and left to get the jerk chicken.

"This is really refreshing," Kitt said, sipping from the straw emerging from the coconut husk.

"Nothing quite like it. Tastes even better with a shot of rum. A long time ago I came looking for a sanctuary, a place to hide. I found the Crab Hole and Bella. She introduced me to coconut water."

"You're so outgoing," Kitt said, finally relaxing in his presence. "Why would you want to hide?"

"Trust me, when you're on a ship six months of the year with everyone knowing your business, or thinking they do, privacy is something you cherish."

"I don't think I could live on a ship."

She couldn't imagine always having people around her. Being forced to talk and be upbeat when you didn't feel like it. Her rent-controlled apartment, humble as it was, provided a quiet haven, affording her the opportunity to come and go as she pleased. She sensed Jared's life wasn't as glamorous as she'd thought. She wanted to hear more.

"How did you get into the cruise business?" she asked.

Jared took a long pull on his straw and closed his eyes, savoring the refreshing taste of coconut water.

"I grew up in Chicago, majored in hospitality, and went to work for Sheraton. One evening there was a bad snowstorm. The hotel was overbooked and the lobby was filled with stranded people. I managed to find a room for an elderly man who'd been waiting for hours. That old man turned out to be Harrison Adams, owner of Sun Ship Cruises. He offered me a job, and the rest, as they say, is history.

"What about you? You just graduated, what are you going to do?"

It was a question she'd asked herself time and time again. She'd hoped to find the answer by the end of this cruise. Still, her mundane life and minuscule problems would hardly be fascinating to Jared, who was used to hobnobbing with beautiful people and making sophisticated small talk. Why would he care about a plain Jane's highfalutin aspirations to be a psychologist for adolescents?

"I'm mulling over a couple of job offers," Kitt reluctantly admitted. "Both would mean I have to relocate."

"And how do you feel about that?"

Before she could respond, their waitress returned with a platter filled with jerk chicken, rice, peas, and plantains. Jared waited until they'd served themselves. "Would you have a problem moving?" he asked.

"I've never lived anyplace other than New York," Kitt answered. "It's all I know. Boston or Chicago have never held much appeal. This is delicious." Kitt bit into the jerk chicken.

"Boston and Chicago are big cities with lots to offer. I'm sure you'll make the right choice." Jared chewed on his chicken leg and smiled at her. His lips were shiny and ever so tempting. It had been ages since she'd felt this alive. He glanced at his watch. "We'll have to hurry if you want to see any of the sights."

Just as she feared, she'd bored him. They finished up quickly, said their good-byes to Bella, and departed with the leftover chicken wrapped in foil.

Out on the street, Jared hailed a cab. While doing a quick tour of the island, he explained that Columbus had discovered it in 1493 and named it Las Virgines. The red-roofed capital was called Charlotte Amalie and got its name from the Danish queen. They made a quick detour into the country and drove by an ancient plantation called Sorgenfri before heading back to the dock.

Kitt offered to pay the taxi driver but Jared would have none of it.

"It's been my pleasure," he said, unfolding his long body from the cab and helping her alight. He kissed her cheek, and that sent the Mexican jumping beans into a mad stampede. Warmth infused her face. She turned away. Why was he deliberately flirting with her?

"Thanks for showing me around," Kitt mumbled, trying to retrieve her hand. She'd taken up enough of his time.

"I've enjoyed it." He still held her hand captive in his.

"Will I see you at the captain's cocktail party?"

"If Candy plans on being there."

Jared was just being polite. But the fact that he'd asked meant a lot to her.

"I'd really like it if you came," he insisted. "You'll sit with me. I'll introduce you to the captain and buy you a Coke." At last he released her hand. "Does seven work for you?"

"Only if it works for Candy."

"Leave your chaperone at home," Jared said, winking as he walked away. "I'll look forward to seeing you later."

In a daze, Kitt watched his retreating back. How could a chaste kiss leave her whirling? What would possess her to trust a man she'd met only a few days ago? How could she be certain that his interest in her was real?

FOUR

Candy's hands fastened around Earl's bucking brown butt. "Yeah, baby, yeah," she said, urging him on. They'd decided to pass on the Jeep ride and had sent his roommate and the woman he'd met at a singles function off on their own.

Earl and Candy had been making love now for what seemed hours. Earl was a veritable sex machine. She'd made a good choice selecting him. An attorney who knew how to screw, literally and figuratively.

Earl's large hands fastened around Candy's more than ample breasts. He stroked her nipples, then took one into his mouth. Lord, the man knew how to love. Candy fastened her thighs around him, riding him fiercely, pretending she was a cowgirl from the wild, wild West. "Hee-haw, you do know how to move that thang, boy."

Brian McKnight's melodious voice crooned from Earl's portable CD player. Time to finish him off. Kitt would be back any moment and looking for her.

Jared stood stiffly on the reception line as he always did. Dressed in his whites, he commanded authority. Respect. Giuseppe, the staff captain, dog that he was, stood next to him, eyeing the pretty women. After shaking each guest's hands, they made mundane conversation, then started the process over again.

Captain Mazetti headed up the line. "How are you enjoying your cruise?" Jared heard him ask a portly matron, pumping her equally plump hand.

"It's been lovely. Just lovely," the woman gushed. "I'm Myrtle Fishbind. This here's my husband, Harry." She pushed

Harry forward. Myrtle was dressed head to toe in pink chiffon. Pink face. Pink hair. A walking, talking wad of cotton candy. Myrtle was beside herself. Thrilled that the captain had singled her out. More words were exchanged before she tugged on Harry's hand, moving him along to meet the next officer.

Jared was used to standing on the reception line, shaking hands and making mundane conversation. He'd learned to plaster a smile on his face, turn up the charm a notch, and greet each guest as if she was the most important person on board. He shook the next hand offered and scanned the line. Seven-fifteen. Still no sign of Kitt.

Giuseppe's sharp intake of breath got his attention. "There is a God," he whispered, loud enough for Jared to hear. "Mamma mia, look at the bella negras."

Jared was used to Giuseppe's theatrics. The officer now straightened up noticeably. His barrel chest practically burst from his short formal jacket. Jared smothered a smile.

"Down, boy," he said following the officer's gaze. Jared had worked with Giuseppe long enough to pick up a smattering of Italian. *Bella negras* was not a derogatory term. It simply meant beautiful Black women. The women working their way through the reception line were certainly that—Black and beautiful. One more comely than the next.

A rainbow of colorful gowns caught his eye. Shimmering banners draped across ample chests announced the women to be Miss Ghana, Miss Costa Rica, and Miss Bermuda. Bringing up the rear was Hayden and her sidekick Nakia. Jared fastened his smile more firmly in place. Inside the Paradise Lounge, Sherrie, in the role of dance captain, had been persuaded to meet and mingle with guests. Avoiding her would be one more thing to worry about.

Giuseppe's second audible breath brought Jared back to earth. Hayden was working her way down the line, chatting up every officer on the way. Her large breasts thrust out, practically brushing the staff captain's face. The Italian officer grew flushed, but to his credit, did his best not to gape. Faced with Hayden's considerable assets, how could he not? Through some remarkable effort—adhesive tape, Jared suspected—her large breasts remained in the dress—barely. Her companion

Nakia's white strapless gown was virtually see-through. In the light, it left little to the imagination.

"Hi," Hayden said when she stood in front of him. She grasped his hand as if it provided an anchor. "I'm here to collect on that drink you promised."

Nakia spoke up. "I'm her witness. You promised." She waggled a finger at him. "You and your friend will buy us that drink, eh? We're thirsty."

Jared was used to blatant come-ons. Single women traveling alone sometimes made it their mission to try to seduce him. These two were barracudas of the highest order. They would not take no for an answer, nor would they simply disappear. He wished Kitt would show up.

The reception line had practically broken up and most of the officers had wandered off to find themselves tables. The captain greeted the last few stragglers and ushered them into the lounge, signaling to a bellhop to close the doors behind them. Jared felt a sinking sensation in the pit of his stomach. Up until now he hadn't realized how much he'd been looking forward to seeing Kitt.

Put the brakes on, boy. Kitt DuMaurier is a guest. He remembered how much trouble the last guest he'd befriended had caused him. Nevertheless, he'd always found vulnerable women irresistible. A flaw in him, perhaps. There was something about a defenseless woman that got his testosterone pumping. Maybe it was this driving need to feel needed. To be Sir Galahad. Time and space would take care of any feelings for Kitt he might have. In less than three days, he would be ensconced in that condo on Aruba. He couldn't wait.

Hayden tucked a hand into the crook of one of his arms. Nakia did the same to the other. What could he do except smile and pretend all was well in his world? His colleagues were all drooling, thinking he'd hit the jackpot. He proceeded into the room, his two trophies accompanying him. With any luck, one or another of the ship's crew would take them off his hands.

Spotting Captain Mazetti and other high-ranking officers, he headed over and quickly made introductions. While Nakia and Giuseppe found a table, he flagged a waiter down and ordered drinks. All the while Hayden's grip on his arm never loosened. She'd branded him as hers.

Across the room, Sherrie's searing glare practically singed him. When would she get it through her head they were over with? She was busy chatting up a man whose expensive suit indicated he might occupy the penthouse suite—you would think that would be enough.

"What's the story with the dog who keeps following you around?" Hayden asked, sipping the drink the waiter brought her.

His attention still on Sherrie, Jared repeated, "Dog?" Whom or what was she referring to?

"The woman you were with last evening. You took her into town today." Hayden's snide smile dismissed Kitt as possible competition.

"Kitt?" *Some nerve this over-rouged babe has. Dog* was hardly the word he would use to describe Kitt. She wasn't glamorous if glamor was measured by an elaborately painted face and well-coiffured hair. But there was a quiet elegance to her that none of these women had. It was called class.

"Kitty, is that her name?" Hayden hissed softly. "Who's called Kitty these days?"

"Kitt," Jared automatically corrected, wondering how he could gracefully escape. In roughly half an hour, dinner would be served, thank God.

A movement at the entrance got his attention. A woman dressed in orange hovered at the door looking uncertainly around. Kitt. Jared raised a hand, waving to her. She didn't notice and seemed on the verge of bolting. Time to gracefully disentangle himself and head over.

Hayden followed the direction of his gaze. When she spotted Kitt, she laughed softly. "Mmmm. Looks like the cat dragged itself in."

That was the final straw. Without apology, Jared pried her hand from his arm. Kitt had done what he'd asked and come alone. He couldn't just leave her standing there.

*   *   *

Judging by her haphazardly-buttoned blouse, Candy had raced in from an assignation with Earl. She'd promptly jumped into the shower, using up most of the warm water. Kitt had waited and waited, hoping that it would replenish itself. Eventually she'd ended up showering and washing her hair in almost frigid water. After she was done, she realized she didn't have a thing to wear.

Kitt had considered wearing the same black skirt and white blouse as the other night, but Candy had come to the rescue. She'd loaned her the dress she now had on. In the process of getting ready, Kitt had poked holes into three pairs of panty hose. It was amazing she'd even made it here.

Candy had finally taken off with Earl, leaving Kitt to make her way to the cocktail party alone. Kitt's still-wet hair clung like a cap to her head. She hovered at the entrance of the Starlite Lounge listening to mood music and worrying about whether the borrowed dress was too tight. She must look a sight.

It had hurt that Candy had been insensitive enough not to wait, but then she reasoned this was typical of Candy. She'd put up with her friend's callous behavior for so many years, why let this one little transgression get to her?

Kitt surveyed the lounge, looking for Jared. It had taken everything she had to walk into the room alone. Even now, she still couldn't believe she'd come on her own. In a far corner, a sea of white uniforms got her attention. She squinted in that direction but couldn't find Jared. Around her, beautiful women were engrossed in conversation with equally beautiful men. Kitt's insecurity kicked in. Why had she bothered to come?

"There you are," Jared's voice boomed into her ear. "I was beginning to think you wouldn't show up."

The jumping beans in her stomach began a sensual meringue. Kitt looked up into sparkling light-colored eyes and knew she was lost. Jared's nostrils flared ever so slightly. His dress whites were a sharp contrast against his smooth, dark skin. Ivory on ebony. No wonder she was completely tongue-tied.

"Come," Jared said, taking her arm. "Let me introduce you to the captain."

Kitt blindly followed him. In a daze, she met Captain Mazetti and the staff captain, Guiseppe. The beauty queen Nakia was practically hanging all over the officer. She didn't bother to acknowledge Kitt's presence.

A handful of people were now heading toward the exit. Tim, the cruise director, mounted the stage and called on the officers to join him. As he introduced each by name and station, loud bursts of applause greeted the crew.

"I'm going to have to leave you, it's my turn," Jared said when his name was announced. "If you haven't made dinner plans, join me at the captain's table."

Awed by his invitation, Kitt could only nod. The captain's table. Even Candy would be impressed.

Kitt's attention focused on the stage, where eight officers stood in line. The sole woman among the crowd was the chief purser. Kitt felt a tap on her shoulder and swung around. Miss Belize glared at her.

"Hello, Hayden," Kitt said, sensing the exchange would not be pleasant.

"What game are you playing?" Hayden began without preamble.

"I beg your pardon?"

"You're out of your league, sister."

Kitt hated confrontation, and didn't think she'd done anything to bring this on. She eyed the statuesque woman in the silver dress. By some incredible miracle, her breasts remained contained in the bodice of her gown.

"Kitty cat's got your tongue?" Hayden taunted. "Short of stripping naked, you've done everything to get that man's attention. Now you're playing coy."

While Kitt disliked scenes, she wasn't about to let this woman push her around.

"You're way off base," she responded. "Jared and I have no relationship. He's a Sun Ship employee. I am a guest."

"A guest he happens to be hot for." Candy's voice came from behind her. "That's what's making this witch crazy. She's worried she can't compete."

Two men in sharp-looking business suits stood behind Candy. Kitt assumed one of them was Earl.

Hayden's manicured index finger stabbed the air. "Stay out of this. I'm not speaking to you."

"Smile sweetly, Miss Belize, and crawl back into the hole you came from," Candy snapped. "Your veneer is slipping. That bitchiness could cost you your crown."

Candy's two men moved forward, flanking her.

Hayden eyed them up and down, assessing whether her charm and assets might work on them. Giving up, she snorted in a most un-beauty-queen-like fashion. "You haven't heard the last of this. Just make sure your friend stays away from my man."

"And if she doesn't?" Candy challenged.

Hayden's eyes flashed dangerously. "I'm not a gracious loser."

"You're not a gracious anything."

Snorting again, Hayden stalked off.

"Dinner, ladies?" one of the men asked, trying his best not to laugh.

"Dinner sounds great." Candy took his arm.

Kitt didn't have the heart to tell them Jared had invited her to join him at the captain's table. It was too late anyway. She just hoped he'd assumed she'd made other plans.

For the life of him, Jared couldn't remember the name of the lady with the pink hair seated next to him. Turtle . . . No, Myrtle Fish-something or other. Fishbind. That was it. Harry, her long-suffering husband, sat across from her, awed by Captain Mazetti. The captain held court at the head of the table, his wife, Theresa, an ex–beauty shop manager, was at the foot. She was cruising for the next three weeks and had brought along their daughter.

Guiseppe and Nakia sat on the same side as Harry, as did Stella, the chief purser, and the ship's doctor. Jared had kept the seat to his right open, saving it for Kitt. Since appetizers had already been served and entrées ordered, he figured it was safe to say she would not show.

He felt a strange hollowness in the pit of his stomach that

he knew had nothing to do with hunger. He'd looked forward to getting to know Kitt better, and now felt strangely let down. Another night of boring conversation lay ahead of him. Maybe it was time to think of another line of work.

"I've heard wonderful things about St. Lu-chee-a," Myrtle said, spearing her shrimp and gobbling it up in one fell swoop.

"St. Lu-sha is a Caribbean dream," Jared confirmed, pronouncing the name phonetically and discreetly correcting her. "It's one of the few remaining unspoiled islands. You should take a shore excursion. See the rainforest and Pitons."

Harry Fishbind spoke up. "We'd love to see the Pitons. From what I've read, they're big mothers. Those twin peaks soar two thousand feet up from the ground. What Myrtle and I really want to see is that volcano."

"La Soufriere should be seen," Jared agreed, his attention momentarily distracted by a handful of guests arriving. A harried maître d' led four people toward the back of the room, Kitt and Candy among them. He felt a pang deep in his gut. Which man was Kitt with?

He couldn't be jealous, not when he hadn't made his intentions clear. What were his intentions, anyway? All he knew was that Kitt interested him like no other woman had before. Three days didn't give him a heck of a lot of time to pursue her. Could he put his career on the line for a woman who'd captured his fancy? What did he really know about her?

FIVE

"Come on, Kitt, humor me. You're smart enough." Candy waved a copy of *The Eternity* under her nose. The newsletter listed all on-board activities. For the last half hour, Candy had been trying to get her to sign up for a game similar to *Jeopardy!*

"What does the winner get?" Kitt asked.

"A makeover at the beauty salon, clothes included, and a two-for-the-price-of-one cruise."

Kitt thought for a moment. She'd just returned from touring St. Lucia. Most of the morning had been spent swimming in a briny Caribbean ocean and hiking through the rainforest. She'd later taken a van into the capital, Castries. She would need at least half an hour to put herself together.

"I hate being center stage," Kitt groaned.

"Come on, just this once. For me. You could use a makeover, and we both could use a second cruise."

Kitt threw her hands in the air. "All right, all right. You win."

Candy smiled triumphantly. "Be at the Starlite Lounge at three o'clock sharp. And be ready to win."

Jared and Karl, the hotel manager replacing him, entered the Starlite Lounge and positioned themselves at the back of the room, their attention on the stage. Tim, the cruise director, hyper being that he was, had quickly introduced the four contestants and now poured on the charm. His assistant retrieved questions from a basket on the podium.

Two men and two women were on stage. Kitt was one of the contestants. That surprised Jared. She didn't seem the type to call needless attention to herself. He moved in closer to the stage, bringing Karl with him.

"What's the name of the *M.S. Eternity*'s interior designer?" Tim asked, reading off one of the questions.

Kitt rang her bell. "Derrick Quick." With that, she put herself ahead by a point.

The questions came more rapidly now.

"How many crew members does the ship carry?"

"Six hundred," one of the male contestants blurted. He was greeted by a loud honk.

"You're wrong," Tim confirmed.

Kitt appeared to contemplate the question while Tim counted down. Her complexion was a warm golden brown. Her hair shimmered under the lighting and seemed more copper than black. Jared attributed the subtle changes to a day in the sun. She'd probably been enjoying her time in St. Lucia, while he and Karl had been supervising electricians and joiners, making sure tonight's pageant went off without a hitch.

"Nine hundred," Kitt yelled, seconds before the buzzer sounded.

How did she know that?

The correct answer had jumped her ahead of everyone. Tim's second round of questions would be tougher. He was already speaking faster, conscious of the bingo players who would infiltrate the lounge shortly. The jackpot was up to a thousand dollars.

There would be a tiebreaker. Jared crossed his fingers, hoping Kitt would survive that.

"Give me the ingredients in a Sun Ship Special," Tim challenged.

Jared silently groaned. Kitt wasn't a drinker—she didn't have a prayer.

"Rum, orange juice, Cointreau, and . . ." the same male contestant blurted.

"You've got ten seconds to complete your answer. Ten, nine, eight . . ." Tim chanted.

"And . . . coconut," the man yelled.

The horn honked. The crowd moaned.

"Rum, O.J., Cointreau, and nutmeg," Kitt contributed.

"We've got a winner," Tim announced, handing Kitt an envelope. "Ladies and gentlemen, behold the winner of the makeover and the two-for-the-price-of-one cruise."

A loud burst of applause followed. A woman screamed, "You did it, girlfriend. Next year we'll be cruising."

It sounded like Candy. Nothing inhibited about that one.

Jared had observed this game more often than he wanted to admit. Still, Kitt's winning filled him with pride. He hadn't expected her to know so much about his ship. He wanted to jump on stage and offer his own congratulations. He wanted to hold her, find any excuse to touch her.

The crowd slowly trickled from the lounge. Several remained to play bingo, encouraged by the thousand-dollar jackpot. A couple, still not acclimated to the ship, stopped to ask directions. Jared told them how to get to Club Eternity, the fitness center. When he was able to break away, Kitt and Candy were nowhere in sight.

Turning, he almost collided with Sherrie.

"I miss you," the dancer said, placing a detaining hand on his arm.

He was immune to her golden gaze. That petulant mouth no longer had the effect it once had. Things must not be working out with her Italian officer.

"You made a choice, Sherrie," Jared said. "You need to live with it."

"Who's the woman you've been hanging out with? Not another one of our guests, I hope."

"Who I hang out with is no longer your business," Jared said, attempting to sidle by.

"We'll see about that. You may think we're over with, but we're not."

Jared decided she wasn't worthy of a response.

"Oh, baby, I think I'm almost there." Candy's legs were in the air. Earl was between them.

He groaned. "If you keep this up, I'll be a dead man."

"If you keep it up, I just might marry you."

"Works for me."

With one last thrust, Earl sent Candy over the top. The

world around her exploded. She lay still for a moment, relishing these new feelings. Unable to think. Unable to talk. A first.

Half an hour later, Candy pounded on the bathroom door of her cabin. "We're going to be late."

"I'm almost ready," came Kitt's muffled reply.

"How much more ready could you be? You had your face and hair done in the beauty salon."

More words were exchanged, and finally Kitt emerged. She stood stiffly in the strapless red dress.

"Girlfriend's got it going on," Candy said, snapping her fingers.

She must have passed inspection. Candy wasn't one to give compliments lightly. Kitt ventured a peek in the full-length mirror and grimaced. The beautician had insisted she get a mild relaxer to take the kink out of her hair and then subtly highlighted it. Her sun-kissed skin had been enhanced by coppers and bronze. A subtle stroke of kohl now made her eyes larger and more sultry. She looked like a vamp.

"Let's go," Candy said, hustling her out.

They entered the main lounge, where the beauty pageant was already under way. It was practically standing room only. After a while, they found two seats at the back of the lounge. Candy summoned a waiter.

"What happened to Earl?" Kitt whispered after drink orders were placed.

"I didn't want him sitting next to me and ogling women. He'll be at the deck party later."

On stage, ten finalists paraded back and forth in high swimsuits, one body more perfect than the next. Kitt spotted Hayden and Nakia and wanted to spit.

"They're such bitches, but you can't deny they're good-looking," Candy snorted, picking up on Kitt's consternation.

Kitt's attention returned to the stage, where an array of stunning evening gowns were being modeled. She watched Nakia and Hayden strut their stuff. They appeared poised and confident. They would finish in the top five, she was sure.

The costume portion came and went, the evening gowns modeled. The cruise director, Tim, accepted a parchment-like paper from the judges, unrolled it, and began asking questions.

Nine of the finalists were led backstage by a social host. The remaining beauty, Miss Venezuela, listened carefully as Tim read off the question.

"If you had it in your power to change the world, what would you do?"

"I'd make it mandatory that everyone would have to learn at least two languages." She tossed a dazzling smile at the audience. "That would surely bring the people of the world closer together."

One by one, each finalist was brought back onstage and asked the same thing. Most wanted world peace and a smog-free environment. Nothing at all unique about their answers.

Kitt could think of a million things she'd do. She'd protect innocent children from being hurt by pedophiles. She would ensure that there was no such thing as adult illiteracy. She'd make sure no one starved. More than anything, she'd fill the world with love. Idealistic, yes. But that was her.

Nakia stood before the mike in a surprisingly tasteful lime-green dress that brought out the cinnamon in her skin. Her top-knot had been moved to the side and two metallic chopsticks served as adornment. She smiled confidently, took a breath, and answered.

"I'd create a world where people weren't judged by the color of their skin or their outward appearance. If the whole world were beige, that would truly give us an equal opportunity."

The applause was deafening. The judges asked for fifteen minutes to confer and the orchestra struck up a lively tune.

"That Nakia's got my vote," Candy said. "I don't care for her, but she's a much better choice than Hayden. All that talk about wanting to be a research scientist and finding a cure for AIDS seemed a bit rehearsed to me."

"Nakia's got mine, too," Kitt answered, refusing to comment about Hayden. She scanned the crowd, looking for a familiar pair of broad shoulders in a white uniform. She spotted Jared at the front of the lounge standing with another officer.

Flushed, her stomach again in turmoil, Kitt forced her attention back on the stage. What was it about Jared Horne that got her hormones pumping? For years she'd worked at keeping men at bay. She'd tried to hide, keeping her clothing simple, her hairstyles nondescript. Now all of a sudden she yearned for a man she'd met just a few days ago?

Tim was calling out the five finalists' names. Kitt held her breath.

"Yes, sirree, we've narrowed it down," he yelled. "Any one of these lovely ladies could be the next Miss Black Universe. Our finalists are . . . Miss Liberia."

His announcement was greeted by a smattering of applause.

"Miss Venezuela . . . Miss Martinique . . . Miss South Africa . . . and last but not least, the beautiful Miss Belize."

The crowd rose to their feet, clapping, stomping, hooting, and hollering. Hayden was a definite favorite. She was self-assured and glamorous, everything Kitt wasn't.

Each woman paraded onstage again. The excitement in the audience built to a frenzy. Kitt was conscious of the whispered commentary around her as people speculated as to who would win.

"We have a decision, ladies and gentlemen," the cruise director boomed, waving a card at the audience.

The crowd grew hushed. The only movement now was coming from the handful of waiters delivering drinks.

With great fanfare, Tim announced, "It is my pleasure to give you our fourth runner-up . . . Miss Liberia."

A couple of boos followed. Kitt had expected the African contestant to place higher, and so, apparently, had the crowd.

"I give you our third runner-up, ladies and gentlemen . . . Miss Venezuela."

Another smattering of applause.

"Our second runner-up—and an audience favorite—Miss Belize."

A loud groan and even louder boos. Hayden's lips stretched into a grim smile. She stepped forward, accepting the trophy from Tim. The thought crossed Kitt's mind that she might whack him with it. Nakia and Miss South Africa were the remaining two. Tears streaming down their cheeks, they clutched hands.

"Only one of these lovely young ladies can be the new Miss Black Universe," Tim announced, stretching out the moment. "Should she fail to complete her term, our first runner-up will take her place. Our first runner-up is . . . Miss Martinique. Miss South Africa is our new Miss Black Universe."

Relatives and friends stormed the stage to congratulate the newly appointed Miss Black Universe. A flurry of people headed for the exit. Security tried valiantly to control the excited people who were determined to get closer to Miss South Africa. Security, realizing they were clearly outnumbered, soon gave up.

Jared crowned the new Miss Black Universe, handing over a lush bouquet of red roses. When he kissed the beauty queen's cheek, Kitt felt a knot settle in her chest. She turned away, blinking back tears, and quickly followed Candy upstairs to the Poop deck, where a loud party was under way. Several people were clearly inebriated. Kitt wished she drank. Maybe it would dull some of the pain.

They stood looking over the railing and down at the gyrating crowd. The calypso band, in the throes of a hot and suggestive song, had gotten the crowd going. Overhead, a new moon beamed golden rays, adding to the festive and suddenly romantic atmosphere.

"I'm not coming back to our cabin tonight," Candy announced.

"Where will you be?" Kitt already knew the answer. Brad, Candy's boyfriend, was old news. Tossed aside for a successful attorney.

"Don't look at me like that," Candy chided, bouncing to the beat, shoulders bobbing back and forth. "You've got your own man. Grab Jared before he slips away."

Candy had misread all the signals, obviously. Jared had just befriended a woman abandoned by her best friend. He'd shown her the sights, and invited her to dinner. No ulterior motive on his part.

"Ladies, what did you think of the pageant?" a voice from behind them said.

Kitt's heart rate tripled. Her legs could barely support her. How had Jared made it to the Poop deck so fast? She worried about the slinky material of her dress, wishing it wasn't so short. Wishing she hadn't let Candy talk her into selecting something strapless.

"Fixed," Candy said with certainty. "I'm no fan of Miss Martinique, but *puh-leeze,* she deserved to win."

Jared cocked his head to the side, his light-colored eyes appraising her. "No comment." He seemed amused, but still hadn't acknowledged Kitt's existence. "It's my last night on board, ladies. Can I buy you and your friend a drink?" His eyes assessed Kitt briefly, brows rising in amazement. "Kitt, is that you?"

Candy's pointy elbow dug into her sides. "Say something, girl, anything," she hissed. "The man's getting off the ship tomorrow. It's your last opportunity to get you some."

"How are you, Jared?" Kitt managed.

He came around to stand beside her. Candy immediately spotted Earl and had to leave. Jared's slender fingers grasped the railing beside Kitt's, hands almost touching. The moon's rays illuminated the planes of his face and played across his dashing white uniform. The subtle scent of citrus emanated from him, making her senses whirl.

"You look different," Jared said. "Glamorous. Stunning."

Kitt's voice came in breathy rasps. "Is different good or bad?"

"I'm not sure."

"You, unsure?" She threw back her head, laughing nervously. "You're the most confident man I know."

"It's just that you look like one of the beauty contestants. Stunning, sexy, a little bit intimidating."

"Intimidating—me?" She laughed again. "I thought you liked the supermodel type."

"Not particularly. A pretty face and shapely body have a certain appeal, but what a woman has to say, her values and ethics, are what attracts me to her."

A rare man, if he was telling the truth. Most were turned on by sex.

"Let's dance," Jared said, putting an end to conversation. He took her hand and tugged her toward the floor. "We'll have that drink afterward."

"I thought you had to pack." She wanted to run away from him, but at the same time longed for that bittersweet feeling of having his arms around her. Stupid to want a man who wouldn't be here tomorrow.

Jared led her down a steep flight of stairs and found them a spot amidst the partying crowd. As luck would have it, the music slowed. The calypso band struck up "Red Red Wine." An oldie. A favorite. Jared's sinewy arms wrapped around her. *For God's sake, don't panic, Kitt. Your reaction has nothing to do with him.* She drank in deep breaths of salty air and willed her heart to slow down. After a while, she laid her head against Jared's shoulder and allowed him to twirl her about. The citrus of his cologne acted like aromatherapy, calming her, lulling her into a state where only the two of them existed. It had taken her over twenty-five years of therapy to feel safe.

She was jolted back to earth when they bumped into another couple.

"Pardon," Jared said, moving her away.

"You promised me a dance," Hayden's accented voice accused. Her hate-filled eyes took in Kitt.

"Later," Jared said.

Hayden's dance partner was clearly annoyed that he no longer had her attention. He quickly twirled her away. At the same time, the calypso band picked up the tempo. Glad for the excuse to put some distance between them, Kitt eased out of his arms. She was relieved when the tune ended and a waiter took their order for Cokes.

"What time are you leaving the ship tomorrow?" she asked.

"Does that mean you're going to miss me?" Jared's fingers trailed down her naked arms.

Kitt shivered but remained silent. No point in confirming that she would.

He continued, "On a more serious note, I'll be getting off in Aruba mid-morning, after the ship's cleared, and my replacement is thoroughly briefed. Stop by and say good-bye. I'll give you tickets for the horseback-riding shore excursion."

As she was about to thank him, a light-skinned woman with a curly mane of hair and an itsy-bitsy skirt sashayed by. Spotting Jared, she made an abrupt U-turn. "I've been looking all over for you," she carped, completely ignoring Kitt's existence.

The accent was proper. British.

"I want to dance," she insisted.

"I'm exhausted," Jared answered. "Maybe some other time."

"Not too exhausted to dance with her." The stranger jerked a thumb in Kitt's direction. "Thought you'd learned your lesson the last time around."

"This isn't the time or place to have this discussion, Sherrie." Jared's voice was modulated, but his eyes flashed. "Who I dance with is no longer your business."

Sherrie cocked her head to one side. "Dancing with me is a better alternative than me telling this woman all about you. About how you prey on unsuspecting passengers."

"That's enough. Even you wouldn't stoop that low," Jared hissed, attempting to walk by.

"Try me."

Kitt saw it as her cue to leave. She didn't know what was going on. She'd sensed all along that guys like Jared were in high demand. But she'd never guessed he was a player.

SIX

Jared had tipped the bellboy handsomely. His luggage awaited him on the pier, and the same conscientious employee guarded it. All he had to do was pick up the leased car and drive to his rented condominium.

Visions of the luxury unit with its balcony facing the white sandy beach brought a smile to his face. Two months of vacation lay ahead of him. Time to relax, unwind, and contemplate what he wanted from life. He couldn't wait.

Karl, his replacement, was already settled in. He sat hunched over a computer, reading e-mails. Jared shuffled the two shore excursion tickets back and forth. Kitt should be arriving any moment. Maybe she would give him her phone number and they'd stay in touch. She'd disappeared after Sherrie showed up last evening, and despite calling her cabin repeatedly, he hadn't gotten ahold of her.

There was a soft tap at the door. Karl tore himself away from his e-mail. "Want to get that? Gotta be for you."

"Sure."

Jared threw the door wide, barely hiding his pleasure at seeing Kitt. She was dressed in baggy denims and an oversized white T-shirt. A billed cap covered her head. She looked nothing like the seductive temptress of last evening. He much preferred her this way.

"Come on in. Where's Candy?"

Kitt shrugged. "I don't know. I haven't seen her since last evening."

"Why am I not surprised? Here's your horseback-riding tickets."

Their fingertips touched lightly as he turned the tickets over.

"I hate to go alone."

Was that a plea on her part? If so, it was easily remedied.

"I'll come with you."

"I'd like that."

He was in pig heaven. "I'll need a couple of minutes to let my car rental company know I'll be delayed."

Another fat tip to the bellboy would make sure his luggage was safe. The condo leasing company couldn't care less if he was late—they already had his money. And he was officially on vacation. Free to do as he liked.

Karl shot Jared an amused smile: he'd obviously listened to their exchange. Jared quickly took care of the car business. He glanced at his watch. "We'll need to go now if we're to make the horseback-riding excursion," he said, taking Kitt's elbow.

They raced down three flights of stairs and joined an excited group of tourists on the pier. Jared found the bellboy, tipped him again, and issued new instructions. He rejoined the group, hoping that in street clothes few would recognize him. It would be nice to spend what little time he had left with Kitt. As luck would have it, Hayden and Sherrie were among the group. One woman was bad enough. Duplicated, they spelled trouble.

Sherrie spotted him first. She was with a male dancer. She nodded in his direction. Possibly last night's conversation had gotten through, finally. He'd made it clear he wanted nothing to do with her. Hayden was accompanied by a man Jared didn't recognize. She ignored him.

People were being herded into minivans. Jared grasped Kitt's hand and took her off to the side. He wanted to be sure they weren't on the same van as Sherrie and Hayden. After everyone had boarded, they piled into the last van and found seats at the back.

"What a gorgeous island," Kitt commented, looking around. "What unusual trees."

"They're called divi-divis. Note their sculpted appearance. Wait until you see where we're heading. The beaches are said to curve like an Aruban smile, something like yours, warm and welcoming."

Kitt sighed heavily. "Now you're making me wish I could stay." Her eyes were round as saucers as she took in the passing desert landscape where cacti grew taller than the average man, and weathered boulders were on guard like possessive gods.

"Then stay. I'd like that."

"If only I could." She sighed again, this time more loudly.

Jared was tempted to invite her to stay with him. Give them a chance to know each other better. Instead, he said, "To quote an Aruban friend of mine, this is not the Caribbean as usual. This is Aruba."

He continued to fill her in on Aruba's history, tuning out the chatter of the others in the van, mentioned the strong Dutch influence and the natives who were, for the most part, trilingual.

"What did you say they speak? Dutch, Spanish, and Papia . . ." Kitt's voice trailed off.

"Papiamento," Jared completed.

The van stopped in front of an impressive-looking building; a Marriott that had recently been remodeled. A dark-skinned tour guide waved a yellow flag and flashed a smile that could only be described as warm and welcoming. She had long black hair that was smooth, silky, and luminous. Her cheekbones were high, her eyes slightly slanted. She was a definite descendant of the Caquetios Indians, the original inhabitants of Aruba.

"Many of the locals are of mixed heritage," Jared said, by way of explanation. He placed an arm around Kitt's waist, drawing her close. He could tell by the stiff manner in which she held herself that his presence made her uneasy.

Enormous hazel eyes locked with his briefly. He'd never met anyone so skittish in his life. What had happened to make her so uncomfortable around men? Didn't she know she was beautiful? Certainly more attractive than their guide, and a heck of a lot more appealing than either Hayden or Sherrie.

* * *

The note burned a hole in Kitt's pocket. She'd wanted to take it out and show it to Jared, but was reluctant to ruin the mood. The note was the reason she was late. The official-looking envelope with her name on it had been slid under her door and had immediately gotten her attention. She'd thought it held the tour tickets and was Jared's diplomatic way of saying good-bye.

She'd picked the envelope up with such trepidation, ripping the flap open, then not so eagerly devouring the contents. The message inside had been to the point.

If you know what's good for you, you'll stay out of Jared Horne's life.

Only a couple of people would perceive her as a threat—Hayden and the woman who'd accosted Jared last night. It should have been funny, especially since she didn't see herself as competition. She'd never in her life been the object of envy, and she wasn't quite sure how to handle this. Best to ignore it, perhaps. Focus on the here and now. Enjoy what little time they had together.

"I've never been riding before," Kitt said. "It's hard to find stables in Park Slope."

"Is that where you live?"

"Yes, Park Slope, Brooklyn."

They'd come to a white sandy beach. Jared quickly removed his socks and sneakers, then offered her his shoulder. She leaned against him, slipping out of her sandals and wriggling her toes. Underfoot, the sand felt like silt, and a cool breeze ruffled the pastel umbrellas dotting the beach. Waiting in the surf were the horses controlled by a number of attendants.

Kitt was led to a gray horse called Daisy. Jared, after close inspection of several horses, chose a handsome palomino called Ed. Before mounting, he was cautioned that the horse might have a mind of its own, but given a firm hand would obey.

At last they were off, heading up the beach in a long line. Neither Hayden nor Sherrie were anywhere to be seen. Kitt assumed they were riding with another group farther ahead. She sat cautiously astride Daisy, enjoying the exhilarating feeling of being up high. An ocean breeze whipped across her face as she viewed the scenery from her exalted position. Jared dug his heels gently into Ed's sides, prompting his horse to come alongside Kitt's. From the look on his face, he seemed to be having a good time. Kitt's heart thudded. From behind her, she heard the pounding of hoofs. What could be more perfect? She was on a Caribbean paradise, the man of her dreams beside her. She beamed at Jared.

"How are you doing?" His voice came at her over the roar of the ocean.

A swishing sound cut through the air. Daisy's front legs reared and a series of high-pitched neighs followed. The docile gray raised its head and bolted. Kitt's frantic screams were interspersed with the horse's neighs. The last thing she remembered was coming to a six-foot fence before darkness enveloped her.

Digging his heels into Ed, Jared urged his horse forward. One of the attendants, a more experienced horseman than he, quickly overtook him. As Daisy's front legs rose into the air, Kitt's body catapulted backward. Jared's heart stopped as she landed in a heap on the sand. Adrenaline kicked in and Jared pushed his horse to the limit. Nothing bad could have happened to Kitt, he wouldn't let it.

An attendant had tethered his horse and was crouched down next to her by the time he arrived. The man held two fingers against Kitt's neck, trying to pick up a pulse.

"Is she—" Jared began.

"She's alive. I'm not sure she's conscious. Call an ambulance," the man ordered no one in particular.

Jared barely registered the horrified faces. Some of the women who were on tour with them started to cry. Where was a cell phone when you needed one? He'd left his on the ship. Spotting Sherrie, Hayden, and their respective companions, he yelled to them.

"For God's sake, do something. Run back to the hotel. Page a doctor. Get an ambulance. Help."

His shouting mobilized Sherrie into action. She was off and running. Jared bent over Kitt, hoping with every fiber of his being that she was all right. That she would wake up, so he could tell her he loved her.

SEVEN

Kitt awoke to a hushed silence and the faint smell of antiseptic. She sensed someone else's presence but couldn't be sure. Even the slightest movement made her head ache. It was an effort to open her eyes. To concentrate.

"How's she doing?" a male voice asked.

"As good as can be expected. Your fiancée is one lucky young woman. She's only got lacerations and a mild concussion."

Fiancée? Kitt tried to place the voices. No luck.

"Did the doctor say when she would be released?" the male asked.

"Even if she regains consciousness, he'll probably want to keep her another night just for observation."

Yikes, they were talking about doctors. Talking about her. She was lying in a bed on cool sheets. The pungent smell that wouldn't go away must be some type of antiseptic. Kitt willed her eyes to open and tried to struggle into a sitting position. It was too much. None of her muscles would cooperate. Her head felt like someone was drumming a nail into it. She let out a frustrated moan.

"Did you hear that?" The man sounded elated.

"She's coming around. Yes, yes, she's conscious. Look at her eyelashes blinking. Talk to her—you're her fiancé, maybe she'll recognize your voice."

"Kitt," the man called. "It's Jared, Kitt. Can you hear me?"

All she could think of was how much her head hurt and that her mouth felt dry like cotton. She was groggy and ready to fall asleep again.

"Kitt? Talk to me."

Why wouldn't the man let up?

The female's voice penetrated. "Honey, look at me. Open those beautiful eyes of yours, tell me how many fingers you see."

Kitt couldn't summon the energy to open her eyes, not when her lids were heavy and felt as if they had pennies on them.

Cool palms were placed on her forehead. A familiar citrus scent stirred a vague memory. An image of a man in white uniform filled her vision.

"Kitt?" the man's voice said. "You had a bad fall. You're in the hospital now. You missed the ship."

She'd fallen—how had that happened?

"I went back to the ship, found Candy, and told her I would take care of you."

Candy. There was a familiar name. Candy had been her best friend since nursery school. The pieces slowly began to fit themselves together. Not perfectly at first. Some clicked, others didn't. She'd left the ship with a man to go horseback riding.

Kitt's eyes fluttered open. She moaned.

"Oh, God, baby, I was so scared," Jared managed.

Who was the handsome man standing over her? There was something about him that was familiar, safe. Visions of a white uniform and a luxury ship filtered in and out. Kitt's mind blanked again. Something wet and cold was laid against her forehead. The room wobbled, then righted itself. Flashes of memory came back more vividly now. She'd gone on a cruise with Candy, met an officer called Jared, and fallen in love with him. The shock of that realization brought Kitt into a fully seated position. Nausea hit. She fell back.

"Grab a washbasin," the nurse ordered. "She's going to be sick."

Jared's strong arms held her upright. The nurse placed a container under her wobbling head.

After a series of dry heaves, she successfully ejected what little there was left in her stomach. How humiliating to get sick in front of Jared.

"Feeling better?" the nurse asked.

Kitt managed a nod. Gentle hands pressed her onto the pillows again.

"How's my patient doing?" another male voice inquired.

Kitt spotted the man at the door. Judging from his attire, he had to be a doctor. A whispered conference took place at the foot of her bed. The doctor moved closer to press a cold stethoscope to her chest. "How do you feel?" he asked. "Bet your head hurts like crazy. But your vital signs are fine. You've got no fever. No broken bones. Just a mild concussion."

"How soon can I take her home?" Jared asked.

"That hasn't been determined. I'll come by in a couple of hours and we can discuss it. Ms. DuMaurier, you need to keep your fiancé, he's totally devoted to you."

Fiancé? This was the second or third time Jared had been called that. What exactly had Jared led them to believe? The thought suddenly occurred to her that she had no idea how long she'd been in the hospital. It might be hours, days. The ship had probably sailed, and here she was stuck on a strange island where she knew no one. Better to let everyone believe Jared was her fiancé. That way she might stand a chance of getting out of here.

"I think I just might, Doctor. There's not the slightest chance of me giving him up.

"You said something about me falling. How did that happen?" Kitt asked, after the doctor departed.

"For some inexplicable reason, your horse bolted. You were thrown."

Kitt remembered the threatening note. It had made her nervous and jittery, maybe the horse had picked up on that. She decided to tell Jared about the note.

His brows knitted together. "I wonder . . ." he said.

"Yes?"

"Never mind. You need to concentrate on getting better."

Kitt did not protest when he hugged her close. But she had the sneaking suspicion he knew who had written that note and was unwilling to tell her.

* * *

Two days later an Aruban aide wheeled Kitt to the entrance of the hospital. There she accepted the arm Jared offered and leaned her head against his shoulder, allowing him to half carry her to the rented Jeep. As she breathed in the familiar scent of his cologne, she wondered what she would have done had he not been around.

"Take care of yourself," the brown-skinned nurse's aide said, waving them off. "We love you, but don't want you back. Jared we might take." She eyed Jared longingly. Hungrily.

"I won't be back," Kitt hastened to assure. "Neither will he, if he can help it."

Jared had spent most of his time at the hospital with her. He'd been the perfect fiancé, bringing her toiletries and a change of clothes. He was probably sorry he'd become involved. She'd ruined his vacation.

When Jared's hands wrapped around her hips to boost her into the passenger seat, she didn't protest. The cherry-red Jeep's canvas top was rolled back and a cool breeze ruffled the leaves of the divi-divi trees as they took off.

"How's your headache?" he asked.

"What headache?"

Jared's warm smile washed over her and a familiar tingle began at her toes and slowly worked its way up. Already she was in big trouble.

"You are feeling better."

Jared's long athletic legs flexed as he settled more comfortably into the vehicle. He wore black linen shorts and a turquoise designer polo shirt. A billed cap had been placed backward on his head. How could she have thought him safe?

Kitt sighed heavily. "I still can't believe Candy abandoned me. And all because of some guys she met a few days ago."

"She didn't abandon you. I talked her out of getting off the ship. We packed your clothing together. She trusted me with your passport, airline ticket, and money. She trusted me with you."

Kitt felt warmth infuse her face. She was trying her best not to read more into his words than there was.

Jared ran the tip of his tongue across full lips. Kitt won-

dered what it would feel like to have that tongue in her mouth.
To have it circle and explore.

"I'm looking forward to you and me spending time together. Getting to know each other," Jared said, reaching
across to her, long fingers caressing her thigh.

The tingling began again. Her entire body was on fire. The
warmth had nothing to do with a lingering fever. How could
she stay in the same house with him and not touch him? Sleep
with him? Why couldn't the doctor have given her a clean bill
of health, and let her fly home? A hotel was always an option,
she supposed.

"Did we ever find out why my horse bolted?" Kitt asked,
changing the subject abruptly.

"Something spooked the horse. It's not been proven what."

Again Kitt had the feeling he wasn't telling the whole truth.
She remembered a swishing noise: milliseconds after that,
Daisy had bolted. Either Hayden or Jared's attractive friend
was responsible. Both had gone on the horseback-riding adventure.

Kitt remembered the note telling her to stay away from
Jared.

"How much longer?" she asked. They'd already been driving over ten minutes.

"Patience, my love. On an island roughly over nineteen
miles long and six miles wide, nothing's that far away."

Miles and miles of pristine white beach were on either side
of them. Jared rounded one corner a tad too fast and Kitt was
thrown against him.

"I'm sorry," he said, grabbing her thigh to steady her. "I
didn't bring on another headache I hope?"

Even if he had, she would have lied. It was much too nice
a day to be ushered into an apartment and put to bed. Besides,
the ache wasn't in her head, it was farther south. Her whole
body throbbed. Jared's shoulder had felt solid as a rock when
she'd bumped into him. The heady scent of his cologne
wreaked havoc with her senses.

"We're here," Jared announced at last, swinging the Jeep
into a bougainvillea-filled courtyard whose apartments had
been built around the yard. Each unit had its own balcony

from which trailing ferns cascaded down. Gushing water came from a secret place adding to the feeling of tranquility. There was a delightful smell of salt in the air.

Kitt sighed loudly. "This is wonderful. I'm dying for a swim."

"And you'll have one. You're on the beach, babe."

He helped her down, his hands brushing her buttocks briefly. Intentional or accidental, she didn't care. Jared removed her overnight bag from the backseat and took her hand. "Wait until you see the view from the bedroom."

Kitt's fear and distrust of men, which had been placed on hold temporarily, returned. It had taken ten-plus years in therapy to feel confident enough to have her first sexual experience. She'd been twenty-five then, and had chosen a man she thought she loved. What a disaster. What a player. But Jared, a virtual stranger, made her feel like she might want to try again. Could she trust him? The thought of sharing his bed, scary as it was, wasn't exactly unpleasant.

They entered an airy second-floor apartment. White walls. White tile floors. White rattan furniture. Not particularly expensive decor, but very Caribbean. The living room looked down on the courtyard, and the back rooms had expansive views of the ocean. Kitt wanted to open the sliding glass doors and race out to the balcony and drink in that salty air.

"I'll put your things in the bedroom," Jared said, nimble fingers massaging the nape of her neck. "You go change and we'll meet on the balcony. We'll discuss what we want to do about dinner."

With trepidation, Kitt followed him into a spacious bedroom suite. Jared set her overnight bag down on the bed and pointed to the closet. "The rest of your stuff is in there. I'll meet you outside in a few minutes."

The bathroom held an oversized roman tub. Kitt bent over the washbasin and splashed cold water on her face. She'd come to a sudden decision. Time to grow up. Jared was about to get the surprise of his life.

She pulled on a pair of black capri pants Candy had talked her into buying, buttoned up a red mandarin-collared blouse, and stepped into red platform mules. A quick spritz of CK1 gave an added jolt of confidence.

Jared was sprawled on a lounge chair when she came out. "Hey," he said. "Love the outfit. Very tropical."

She thanked him. He continued to stare at her. She was almost glad when her stomach rumbled.

"Oh, my. That hospital food must be worse than I thought." Jared's eyes twinkled.

"It was."

"Better get you something to eat quickly, then. Your choice. Want to eat in or out?"

"In," Kitt said quickly.

"Your wish is my command." Jared rose from the lounger and came to stand beside her. She wanted to melt into him, have those arms hold her close, lose herself in his chest. "What's your pleasure? French? Japanese? Italian?"

"Local. When in Aruba . . ."

". . . Do as the Arubans do." Jared kissed her cheek. His fingers toyed with the toggles of the fire-engine-red blouse. "Eating in might be dangerous."

"Really?"

His warm breath fanned her face. "You're intoxicating, tempting, dangerous."

Coming from any other man, it would have been bull. He kissed her again. Gently at first, then with an urgency that surprised her. She responded with a passion she didn't know she possessed, opening up for him, making space for his tongue, allowing their tongues to touch in an intimate and titillating dance that could only lead to trouble.

"I've wanted to do that from the moment I met you," Jared moaned, surfacing for air.

"But?"

"But I couldn't. Sun Ships has a no-fraternization policy. The last time I befriended a guest, I . . ."

"You what?"

"Well, she misunderstood my intentions and became angry and vindictive. When I clarified our relationship and told her we were friends, she wrote a letter to the cruise line claiming I sexually harassed her. I was suspended pending investigation. The truth eventually came out, and although I was vindicated, it was a horrible six months, and a painful lesson learned."

"What an awful person."

"She was."

"Then how can you be sure I'm trustworthy?" Kitt asked. "We hardly know each other."

"Sometimes you take a chance. From the moment I met you, I knew you were someone I wanted to get to know better. You were different from the flashy types that come aboard. More reserved. Classier. I hoped you'd find me attractive." Jared ran the back of his hand across her cheek. Kitt trembled.

"I don't know what to say. I didn't think you'd want me."

"You of little confidence. Kiss me again and I'll show you just how much I want you."

And she did.

Jared knew he was in trouble the moment their lips touched and their tongues entwined. He hadn't expected to feel like this. He'd known he was attracted to Kitt, but hadn't known he was in love with her. He couldn't take advantage of a woman convalescing. He hurriedly broke the lip-lock and put her away from him.

"Why are you stopping?" Kitt surprised him by asking.

His hands found their way to the front of her blouse. Cupping a breast through the material, he worried a nipple. Kitt groaned. The nub hardened under his fingers. She began to pull away.

"Don't be afraid, honey. We'll take it nice and slow. We won't do anything you don't want me to do," he reassured, easing her down onto the lounge chair with him. Kitt seemed to be going through a mental struggle. He wrapped his arms around her waist hoping to silently communicate that he would do nothing to hurt her. "Want to talk?"

"Yes. I should explain what I've been through. Maybe it would help you understand why I'm the way I am."

Jared kissed her cheek and waited.

"I was forced to have sex with my mother's boyfriend when

I was ten years old," Kitt announced. "I used to call Malcolm Uncle."

"Oh, Kitt." No wonder she was skittish and wary of men. He'd sensed there was something in her past that affected her deeply. He'd never imagined this.

"Uncle Malcolm lived with us. Those nightly visits went on for years. Eight, actually, until one day my mother walked in and found us together." Kitt's voice broke. "He told her I seduced him."

"Did she believe him?"

"I don't know. All I know is that hours later, he was gone. Packed and out. My mother's only question was whether I had protected myself."

"I'm sure finding you with him was painful for her as well."

"Maybe so. But I wanted her understanding. Her love. I wanted her to listen to my side of the story. I had been too scared to tell anyone what was going on. Malcolm said no one would believe me. I felt guilty, too, because as much as I hated being forced to have sex with him, I shouldn't have closed my eyes and allowed him to do it. For a long time I pretended he was the real deal, a man I loved. When it got really bad, I would imagine that a handsome Black knight would ride off with me on his midnight stallion. He'd take me to a safe place where I was loved."

"God, Kitt. How awful." Jared kissed her cheek again. "To think you endured that abuse for years. That man should have been strung up, his manhood cut off." Jared slammed a curled fist into his palm. "I'd like to hunt the dog down and emasculate him." Catching himself, he ran his hand up and down Kitt's arm. "No wonder you equate sex with pain, not pleasure."

Kitt sat up, looking at him saucer-eyed. "You understand."

"Absolutely."

She wrapped her arms around his neck and buried her head in his chest, admitting, "I've never had a satisfying sexual experience."

"We'll change that. You'll see what it's like to be loved,

not taken advantage of. I want you, Kitt. All of you, body and soul." He kissed her on the lips.

"I want you, too, Jared," she said, clinging to him.

"Let's feed you, then make this a night to remember." He held her close. Kitt snuggled into him.

EIGHT

"To new beginnings. To you in my life." Candlelight flickered as Jared raised his crystal flute and clinked it against Kitt's.

The intensity in his voice got her attention. Although they were only toasting with spring water, she felt flushed. Neither were drinkers, and since she was still convalescing, they'd decided to pass on wine.

"Kitt?"

Jared's voice broke through the haze. He was seated across from her, waiting for her to say something. How could he be so certain this was a new beginning when she viewed it as an impossible dream? Sure she cared for Jared, but his life was on a cruise ship. She'd be lucky to see him twice a year, if that. She had choices to make. A job awaited her in Boston or Chicago. Long-distance relationships seldom worked, or so she'd been told.

Kitt stared at the full moon, hoping that it would beam down some answers. Help solve all her problems. Most of her life she'd waited for someone like Jared to come along. Now here he was offering a possible future, yet all she could think of was how impractical their relationship was.

Muted pinks and corals danced across the sky, promising a beautiful sunset and an even more beautiful tomorrow. Why couldn't she simply live for the moment and enjoy what little time they had together? The truth was, she wanted more. Wanted all he had to offer. Wanted him in her life.

On the table before her was mouthwatering lobster. Tantalizing smells escaped from under the covers. She'd called a restaurant, ordered an appetizing rice pilaf, tasty asparagus, and curried jumbo shrimp wrapped in slivers of mango. Now she'd lost her appetite.

"Is something wrong?" Jared's voice penetrated again.

"Look, I don't even know if you're available or have a girlfriend on that ship," she said. "That British woman, the same one who went horseback riding, accosted you last night. Acted like she owned you. Is she someone special?" Better to know up front what she was getting into.

Jared reached across the table and around the butter dish to hold her hand. "I'm not a player, if that's what you're asking. Sherrie's a dancer on the ship, she was my girlfriend at one point, but our relationship was long over before you arrived."

"Could she have written me that note?"

"I wouldn't put it past her."

"But why?"

"Because she doesn't want to let go. For years I put up with her bad behavior. Forgave her every time she stomped on my heart. I guess she figured we'd work this out once more and get back together. She'd seen us together on the ship. She certainly saw us dancing on the Poop deck. Only an employee would have access to your cabin number."

"Sending me a note was a pretty evil thing to do. How did you hook up with Sherrie to begin with?"

Jared's smile was a mere stretch of the lips. "She targeted me. I was vulnerable and recovering from another disastrous relationship. Sherrie had no problem stepping in, offering her consolation and considerable charms. Stupid me bit, and for several years, if she said jump, I said how high. Ironic that everyone knew she was sleeping around except me."

"I'm sorry," Kitt said, meaning it. "You must have been terribly hurt."

"Devastated."

She could tell by the gruff tone of his voice that even now Sherrie's betrayal still rankled. What if he wasn't over the dancer? What if he'd simply sublimated his feelings and was using her as an outlet for all that male aggression? She squeezed his hand.

"And you think she might have gone as far as whipping my horse?"

"Possibly. Thank God you weren't seriously hurt. Eat," Jar-ed ordered. "Your food's getting cold."

As they ate, he filled her in on his life story. He'd been an Army brat and lived all over the world. His three sisters had married military men and they all resided abroad. He even told her about his ne'er-do-well brother, who'd been incarcerated and now made a living selling automobile parts on the Internet.

Kitt had never met a man so honest or open about his feel-ings and his thoughts. Most of the men she knew spoke about things and events, not feelings, hopes, and dreams. With every word Jared uttered, she fell more deeply in love with him. What a mess. How could there be a future with him?

After a delicious dessert of mango ice cream, Jared left to turn on the stereo. He returned to the balcony and they sat on a teak glider, his arm draped around her shoulders, his fingers playing with her earlobe. "Don't you have hopes and dreams?" he asked.

None of her previous boyfriends had given a hoot what she thought.

"I've always wanted to be an adolescent psychologist," she answered. "Of course, that would mean going back to school and getting a doctorate."

"Then do it."

"Not until I earn real money and pay off all those student loans."

He leaned over and kissed her. "You will in time. I believe in you." Stars exploded in her head. The sun and moon were suddenly in reach.

Jared's hand toyed with the toggles of the mandarin-style blouse. His breath came in little bursts.

"Let me help you," she offered.

Forgetting that they were sitting outside in the dark, she unbuttoned her shirt. Thank God she'd heeded Candy's advice and bought a few sexy bras and underpants before leaving on this trip. Thank God.

Jared's hands were inside her blouse, palms cupping the lace bra, fingers playing with her nipples. When his lips locked around hers, she kissed him back urgently, capturing his tongue between her teeth, and biting down gently.

"You do that well," he said huskily.

He was fast losing control, and she felt herself panic. Counting to ten slowed down her breathing, and at the same time gave her time to think. Did she want to move forward? No one was forcing her to. She was well over the age of consent and could end this anytime. Knowing that gave her an exhilarated sense of control.

"Kitt, honey, are you all right with this?" Jared asked.

"Yes."

His face was flushed. She knew it would take every bit of willpower to stop. Still, the fact that he'd asked made it all better. Malcolm hadn't asked, he'd just taken.

Jared unfastened the clip on her bra, bent his head, and captured a nipple in his mouth. His free hand worked the other breast. Kitt thought she would go out of her mind. She wanted to take off all her clothes. Not just her shirt. Get naked next to him. But they were seated on the balcony, albeit a dark one, and anyone could be watching.

"Time to go in," Jared said, picking up on what she was thinking. "It's more comfortable in the bedroom, much too hot out here."

Kitt managed an, "Ummmm-hmmm." Without another word they headed inside.

A huge sleigh bed covered with a multicolored comforter dominated the bedroom. A couple of Eileen Seitz paintings kept the ambience Caribbean. On the top of the dresser were several unlit candles, and rattan baskets filled up the empty spaces. Economical but pretty.

Jared lit one of the scented candles. The smell of vanilla wafted its way over. He joined her on the bed, took her chin between his palms, and kissed her. The decision was made. Time to let go and trust. Time to get over this crazy fear, stop acting like a victim and take responsibility for her life. Kitt kissed him back, putting everything she had into it. She grasped a handful of comforter, hoping it would steady her. Jared's hands were now on her breasts, stroking, smoothing, soothing. She fell back on the bed. He fell on top of her.

Kitt could feel Jared's wicked erection against her thigh. Right about now she used to squeeze her eyes closed and fantasize, wishing that Malcolm was someone else, that when she opened her eyes, she wouldn't feel ashamed. But Jared's loving was a far cry from Malcolm's. His touch was easy, not demanding: it soothed her fears. She didn't need fantasy when reality was here. This was the real deal.

Kitt's hands cupped the bulge that held the promise of a new tomorrow. She'd never been this bold with any man and had always allowed them to take the lead. Jared stirred and shifted his weight, giving her full access to his considerable assets. Their lovemaking continued fast and furious—touching, tasting, sniffing, nibbling, bringing each other to incredible heights.

With each new discovery and shared kiss, they established a better comfort level. Finally, Jared fitted himself into Kitt. Each thrust brought with it bittersweet agony. She'd never been made to feel this way, like she could never get enough.

"I love you, Kitt," Jared said, holding her so tightly, she could hardly breathe.

"I love you, too," Kitt admitted. "But this is an impossible dream."

"Then make it a reality," he challenged.

He was giving her choices. Letting it be her call. Why was she stalling?

"What about your career? You can't just walk away from it."

"What about my career? Sun Ships has satellite offices in Boston or Chicago. Pick a city and I'm there. If that doesn't work out, both places have a million hotels that would snap me up in a minute."

"I can't expect you to change your life because of me." *Ah, but how I want you to.*

"Honey, you're not asking me to do anything, I'm telling you I want to. It's time for me to settle down, start thinking about having a wife, planning a family. Meeting you only helped me decide."

"Is this a proposal?"

"It could be."

Jared kissed her again. With that kiss, all doubt receded. He was the man she wanted in her life. He'd accepted her for the person she was, giving her that much-needed boost of self-confidence. She didn't feel like a plain Jane anymore. She loved him with all her heart.

Kitt's kiss held the promise of a shared tomorrow. Trailing her fingers across Jared's wide shoulders, she ground herself into him.

He stirred beneath her. "Feels good having you love me," he said.

"Feels good letting you love me," she responded.

He kissed her again.

Heroes came in all shapes and sizes. Hers wore a white uniform.

Our Secret Affair

by Carmen Green

ONE

"May I offer de lady Paradise Resort and Spa's world famous strawberry daiquiri?"

Toni Kingsley looked up from the informative brochure she'd been reading about the island of St. Croix to the bartender who'd been trying to convince her to try something exotic for the past half hour. "What makes your daiquiri so world famous?" She loved the island accent and listened intently.

"It's a resort secret. But I'll tell you dis much: It's so good, you'll nevah be de same. How 'bout it, Queen?"

A challenge? Never one to back down, Toni shoved the brochure in her bag and met his sparkling smile with one of her own. "I'd love to." She swiveled on the stool and considered the near-empty bar. Several couples lounged in plush seats over drinks, relaxing to the distant strains of a band that played music from the pool area.

"I'll take it over there," she said, and weaved her way to a comfortable table for four in the corner.

Toni settled in her seat and lifted her face to the ocean breeze, unable to believe she had won this fabulous trip to Ziotech's president's club.

Earned was more like it. She'd been the top sales manager for Ziotech Information Systems four straight quarters, and had beat every other sales manager by at least a hundred thousand dollars.

In the computer world, that wasn't a lot of money to lose by, and most of her male colleagues had been royally pissed that she'd won.

But that was life in the big city. All the top executives at

Ziotech were on this trip, but because she'd had top sales overall, she'd get extra-special treatment.

For one, she'd been given the master suite. With the exception of the presidential suite, which she assumed was booked to her boss and his wife, she had the best room at the all-inclusive resort. Second, she had a limitless expense account, plus a twenty-five-thousand-dollar bonus.

To top off the fabulous vacation, she knew for a fact that Ethan Westminister, the current VP of sales, was leaving to head up the London office. Toni wasn't surprised he'd taken the offer. His wife was from England and they visited at least once a year.

According to Ethan, Toni was on the short list of candidates for his job, and he'd wanted to feel her out before speaking to Willis Fletcher, the company owner.

Toni accepted her strawberry daiquiri and sipped. At the time, she hadn't wanted to seem too eager, but with Ethan's blessings, she had cast her hat into the ring. They'd spoken about the job's responsibilities, but he'd also wanted to let her know she was in for a fight. Especially when he mentioned the only other name being considered.

A tingle started at the base of her spine and Toni clenched her thighs, denying its power of reminder. She pushed a loose curl from her ear and took a healthy swallow of her drink to only clench again as the roof of her mouth froze, then thawed.

I can say his name without acting like a silly female, she thought, carefully taking more of the rum-based drink down. "J—" the tingle started and she shook her leg.

"John—" A ripple of pleasure danced up her spine and Toni sucked greedily from the straw.

"You wan' sumtin', Queen?" The bartender in a red floral shirt smiled brightly, his eyes suggesting infinite possibilities.

She tapped the rim of her glass. "Another, please."

"Dat's de spirit! Comin' right up."

Toni looked around at the other patrons who were scantily dressed, and challenged herself to finish what she started.

She sucked the last of her drink and let it slide down her throat. Fortified, Toni closed her eyes, pictured her biggest adversary, and took a deep breath.

"John L. Roberts. Over him," she sang aloud, victorious.

"At your service."

Toni's eyes flew open, and if she could have fallen into a sand pit, she would have. Her archrival stood before her, enjoying her discomfort.

"Here you go, Queen. Whatchu wan', Bruda?"

The bartender slapped a napkin down and looked at John expectantly.

Toni regretted ordering the fresh drink when he sat.

"A rum runner and some chips, mon."

"Excellent." The bartender sauntered away, greeting new customers who'd just arrived.

"I guess I'm like a genie in a bottle. You call my name and I appear."

Embarrassed, Toni closed her eyes. *Vamoose! Yah! Abracadabra, make this person disappear!* She opened one eye, and was greeted by John's hundred-watt smile. *Whatever.*

"When did you get here?"

"Why were you calling my name?" They both spoke at once.

Toni stayed quiet. John leaned back, his long butterscotch-colored legs extending past her chair. He wore expensive black Kenneth Cole sandals and matching Tommy Hilfiger shorts and top. As her eyes scanned his long limbs, she tried not to think about his legs and the one reckless time a month ago when they'd been stretched on top of hers, intimately.

She had to put these thoughts out of her mind. Especially since she might one day be his boss.

"You got here when?" she asked again, squinting into the sun, trying to clear the sudden haze from her mind.

"An hour ago. Still dreaming about me, Toni?"

Toni stabbed her top lip with the straw but smiled through her grimace. "No reason to."

John accepted his drink and chips and maintained an amused expression. "That's a relief. You decided it never happened, so why," he asked, as if considering it for the first time, "would I be in your dreams? Or a whisper on your lips? *No reason,* the woman says."

Toni hated his casual demeanor almost as much as she hated her increased heart rate.

John looked at her as if during the night they'd been together, she'd shared all her deepest secrets.

His voice stroked her and he sat up in his chair and raised his glass in salute. "If the woman says my name means nothing when it drips from her lips tinged with the juice of the sweetest berry, then I should believe her."

He drank and gave an appreciative "Ahh." But his eyes said he didn't believe her.

Why did he have to go there? Why couldn't that night be chalked up to too much liquor and way too much lust?

Why did they have to be at a romantic resort instead of in the office, where they both maintained a professional distance, and would never consider broaching the subject of their one-night stand?

She recalled that one sweet time together vividly.

Toni and John had worked late, having spent many evenings trying to finalize a deal with IBR Industries. At first, they'd been ultra-professional, denying the attraction that sparked between them.

But once they closed the fifteen-million-dollar deal, they'd made it to IBR's parking garage before falling into each other's arms.

Toni ended up at John's place, loved intimately, cherished thoroughly, and satisfied completely. They'd had one night. And that was all.

Why instead of quenching her curiosity had that night piqued it? She and John were co-workers and that combination didn't mix, Toni thought as she dragged her gaze away from his long legs. The only way to get over the intimate glow John had cast over her was to bring up a subject that would be sure to give her system a shock.

Just then the band began to play a Billy Ocean tune, "Get Outta My Dreams, Get into My Car," and Toni choked.

John pounded her three times between the shoulder blades. "You all right?"

"Def—" she coughed, clearing her lungs, and attempted to

change the subject. "Definitely. So who's the lucky woman who got to accompany you on this trip?"

John grinned full, the same way he had the quarter he'd beaten her sales by ten thousand dollars and won a handsome Rolex watch. "You're going to love her."

A rush of jealousy collided with the drink and Toni reclined in her chair. Her head swam, so she ate two chips and offered what she hoped was a pleasant face. "What's to love? Who is she?"

"The most beautiful woman in the world."

Envy strangled the words she was about to speak, so Toni sipped her drink from the bottom of her glass and ended up with a mouthful of 150 proof rum.

"Really? Well." She swallowed the shot and ate a couple more chips. "Does this diva have a name?"

He nodded, his gaze on the ocean.

Irritated at the cat-and-mouse game, Toni tried to stay calm and not think about the night he'd told her *she* was the most beautiful woman in the world. Men were such liars.

Jealousy zinged through her veins. The woman was probably some big-tittied yahoo from Georgia, who'd blind her with a full bar of gold teeth and stones that spelled out her name on her fingernails.

That would be most excellent, Toni decided, signaling for a glass of water. Then Willis would question John's judgment and wouldn't give him the job. "I can't wait to meet her," she said.

John finished his drink and stood, leaving a generous tip. "Good, she was settling in when I left. Let's get together later and have drinks."

"Sounds lovely," Toni said, hating the burning in her stomach as much as she hated John's nonchalance.

Not trusting herself on her heeled sandals, Toni slipped them off and grabbed her straw purse.

If she could just get back to her room and sleep for a couple of hours, she'd be ready for anything John L. Roberts and his tootsie had for her. Standing slowly, she wobbled a bit.

"When was the last time you ate?" he asked, reaching for her.

Toni pushed away his arm of support. "I'm fine. Have to get used to walking on sand."

The hotel concierge, Ron, approached them, a look of apology on his face.

"Mr. Roberts, your room has been reassigned because the lady deemed it unfit, and I must say I agree." He clasped his hands together. "If you'll follow me to the presidential suite, I'll make sure you're comfortable as well."

Tony blinked in surprise. The presidential suite? That was supposed to be the boss and his wife's room, and if not theirs, *hers*! She was the top sales manager! She won the twenty-five-thousand-dollar bonus! She was being considered for the VP job! Just who did this woman think she was?.

"Your companion has a lot of nerve making waves," Toni murmured to John.

He stroked the small of her back, sending tendrils of longing throughout her nervous system. "What can I say? I'm a sucker for a woman who knows what she wants and won't accept anything less."

Toni moved away from his touch and accidentally dropped her sandals. Kneeling, she groped behind a potted plant, and heard the concierge greet someone. "Here she is now. Madam, does everything meet your specifications?"

"Why, yes, it does. Hello, darling."

Prepared to hate her, Toni turned, still on her knees, and came face to face with a wheelchair.

"Toni Kingsley," John said, "meet Beverly Roberts, my mother."

TWO

Toni stared into eyes identical to John's. "You're his mother."

The statement stemmed from embarrassment rather than disbelief. Toni tried to get firm footing, all the while wishing she wasn't eye level with the woman's knees. "Glad to meet you, Mrs. Roberts."

The disabled woman offered her a hand. "Likewise."

John and the concierge hurried around the chair and helped Toni up. "Find what you were looking for?"

"Yes, my sandal. . . . Thank you." She damned the rum for slowing her cerebral functions, and ordered herself to shape up. Inebriated was not the way her colleagues would want to see their future vice president.

The concierge excused himself to help another couple, but promised to escort John to the new suite momentarily. The three glanced at one another, so Toni decided to break the awkward silence. "I'm sorry for my current state. I haven't eaten your son—I mean I was at the bar drinking." *Oh God, please kill me.* "N-not that I drink and not eat." Toni pulled in a deep breath. "I was at the bar, had a drink, and haven't eaten since I arrived in St. Croix this morning." Toni scrubbed her eyes with her palms. "I'm not a drunk, I promise."

Where was a typhoon when she needed one? Toni was sure she looked like a drunk and sounded like one, too.

The older woman, who reminded her of Weezie, George Jefferson's wife, dismissed her excuse with a wave of her hand. "I believe you, darling. In the summer evenings, my friends and I get together and sit on my porch and have a little nip, too. John's come by a time or two and joined us. Haven't you, honey?"

"Mom, I'm sure Toni doesn't care." He sounded more adolescent than man.

Toni wanted to kiss Mrs. Roberts, but thought of how her breath must smell and decided against it. "John, I admire the fact that you hang out with old—older ladies, drinking." Heat raced up Toni's skin at the insult. "No offense, ma'am."

This time Mrs. Roberts laughed aloud. "None taken. We know how to have fun."

"Are you enjoying your stay, ma'am?"

"Call me Beverly, and what's not to love? My son won this fabulous trip and instead of bringing someone whom I'm sure he could have more fun with, he brought me."

Suck up. "That was very sweet of him," Toni said, hoping she'd masked her sarcasm.

John took the handles of his mother's chair and gently turned her around. "Don't let my mom fool you, she begged to come." Warmth and love emanated at the gentle teasing.

"That I did."

"Mom, I suggested Toni join us later for drinks."

Mrs. Roberts grasped her son's hand. "Honey, I already made plans to go to the beach with some of the ladies I met. They're going to have a bonfire and a band by the ocean at dusk."

John regarded his mother for a long moment and Toni wondered why. He'd always struck her as an independent man who strove to succeed, but now she couldn't help but wonder why John would bring his mother along on a company trip. This was the Presidents' Club! The elite trip all salespeople wanted to attend but had to earn. And when they earned it, they usually shared it with a spouse or significant other.

Questions rattled in her befuddled mind, but Toni didn't want to ponder too much. She, too, had considered bringing a guest, but none of the men she casually dated warranted a promotion to "vacation lover."

She was glad to have the week alone, because when she got back to Atlanta, work would take priority over everything else.

Still, awareness of John kept her slightly off kilter. Nothing a nap wouldn't take care of, she decided.

"I don't know if it's safe for you to go down to the beach without me," John said to his mother as he pushed the wheelchair through the lobby.

The older woman shushed her son. Toni watched the interplay between mother and son and felt a longing inside her awaken.

Widowed and in her sixties, her mother clearly made it known how much she wanted Toni to settle down to a more traditional life of husband and children, like she had done.

But that was completely wrong for Toni. She couldn't sacrifice her happiness and freedom in the name of love like her mother had. Her father's emotional and verbal abuse was not something she ever wanted to put up with again. She'd made her decision, but she also sought her mother's approval.

"You don't have to coddle me." Mrs. Roberts greeted another elderly woman with a wave. "There's a wheelchair ramp that leads down to the beach, and from there I'll have assistance to the bonfire."

"Are you sure you'll be okay?"

"Yes, John," she insisted. "I did come to have fun, not sit in the room under you the whole time. I'll be fine."

"As long as you're back by a reasonable time."

Beverly had the grace to laugh as she patted her son's hand. "Now, I would think those words would be coming from my mouth. I thought your company was having a dinner tonight."

"We are."

"Well, then, you have plans, too." She reached out and took Toni's hand. "Toni, would you make sure my son has a good time tonight?"

Startled, Toni looked down at their joined hands and didn't know what to say. "Uh . . . well," was all she could manage.

"Mom, what are you cooking up now?"

"I'm just saying, you're worried about me having a good time and I'm worried about you. At least this young lady knows how to party. Get loose, John. Stop being so serious. Toni, make sure he dances and laughs tonight, okay?"

The woman didn't know what she was asking. "Sure. Piece of cake," Toni said, keeping her gaze averted from John's.

"Great!" Mrs. Roberts exclaimed, and released Toni's hand.

"All settled. What do you do for Ziotech, Toni?"

"I'm a sales manager."

"Mom, Toni is Sales Manager of the Year."

"So, this is the young woman who beat you." Mrs. Roberts gave her an admiring smile. John looked as if someone had run over his feet. "Excellent! In order to have won, you had to work hard to beat an old mule like my John. He'll work 'til he drops, so I'm glad he came to the island to play. What about you, Toni? Did you bring a guest?"

"Quit being nosy, mother."

"Oh, come on now. I just want to know about the woman I asked to entertain my son." Beverly quickly sized her up. "So, are you married?"

Toni laughed. "No."

"Boyfriend?"

"Mom," John warned when they stopped outside the bank of elevators. "Toni, don't answer her. She's worse than the FBI when it comes to getting information on people. She's nosy and proud of it. And"—he cut off his mother, who'd raised a finger to interrupt—"you can't hurt her feelings by saying nicely 'Butt out.' "

"I always wanted to be an FBI agent," Mrs. Roberts said, still in good humor despite her son's warning. "But they don't recruit older women in wheelchairs with multiple sclerosis. I guess I'll have to limit my surveillance to the Neighborhood Watch."

Toni bit her lip to keep from laughing. Clearly embarrassed, John looked relieved when the elevator arrived.

The concierge hurried up to them. "Sorry for de delay. I'm ready to escort you to your room. Mr. Roberts, I just took a message from Mr. Willis Fletcher. Your tee-off time is confirmed for two o'clock."

"Thank you."

Toni's thoughts raced as swiftly as the ascending elevator. Why was John getting a private audience with Willis and she wasn't? The group from Ziotech wasn't supposed to officially meet until seven that evening. But John had finagled a golf date. Why? To talk about the job?

Toni knew she had to do something, but what, exactly,

escaped her. The doors opened and everyone stared at the cheerfully-decorated hallway.

"Ms. Kingsley?" the concierge said.

"Yes, I'd love to go golfing." Toni realized her mistake too late.

Ron cleared his throat, looking confused. "Dis is your floor."

Heat flooded her face and she stabbed her toe trying to get past the wheelchair. "Excuse me. Sorry. My golf date is tomorrow," she said, then chastised herself for lying.

"No, ma'am. Dat can't be so," the concierge said regretfully. "De course is closed tomorrow for repairs and de rest of de week is booked solid. I can try to add you to a two- or threesome, if you wish."

Toni stood inside the doorway of the elevator and knew they knew she was lying.

She wracked her brain for alternatives. "I was sure our tee-off time was for three o'clock tomorrow," she fibbed. "They probably booked the reservation in my boss's name. Well, Beverly, it was a pleasure to meet you, and—" The elevator started buzzing from being held open too long.

An amused expression marked John's face. "Toni, would you like to join us?"

Angry with herself for becoming a spectacle, Toni squared her shoulders. The last thing she needed was a mercy invitation from John Roberts. Getting the VP job was the biggest deal she'd close this year, but butting in on John's golf game wasn't how she was going to get it. *Let him have his time,* she thought, as the elevator door clattered against her hand and the lights started flashing.

Toni shot him a derisive look. "Ron and I will work out the details later. See you at the dinner."

THREE

The sunset off the Pacific Ocean stole Toni's breath away and made her realize what she missed by living in Atlanta. During the past four years, Ziotech had transferred her to Dallas, Paris, California, and back to Atlanta, and she wouldn't trade those experiences for the world. Only sometimes, she got lonely.

Happens to everyone, she thought as she walked along the resort's beachfront, luxuriating in the feeling of not having to rush.

The nap had revitalized and prepared Toni to defend her unprofessional behavior from this afternoon. Only rum could make a perfectly normal woman crawl on the floor in front of a wheelchair and tell hideous lies.

John would surely comment on her behavior, but she'd already mulled her response while she'd pulled on her short sundress and slipped into low backless sandals.

She'd shock him by laughing at herself and pretend it was all part of the plan. When he'd look at her with eyes that had seen the intimate spasms of her orgasm, she would hold her head up and treat him with such professional courtesy, the National League of Women would use her as a model for all to aspire to.

Music from the band filled the air as Toni headed up the sandy shore. The smell wafting from the area tantalized her taste buds and she hurried to the group of tables and greeted her co-workers. "How's everyone this evening?"

The men stood. Willis Fletcher approached, handing her a fruity drink with a red umbrella hanging off the side. "Our star has finally decided to grace us with her presence."

"I'm fashionably"—she glanced at her gold watch—"five minutes early."

A round of applause went up and her boss made a grand gesture. "She's never been late a day to work," he boasted. "Maybe that's the key to her success. Take notes," he said to the assembled co-workers. "This lady has got something special."

More whistles and whoops as well as good-natured ribbing went up. Toni waved them down. "Sit down, get comfortable. Is anyone sitting here?" she asked, referring to the empty seat on her boss's right.

"You are."

Score one for me, she thought, as she joined Marjorie, Willis's wife, the CFO Dean and his wife Holly. Other managers and spouses were seated at various tables or mingling around the open bar.

Toni settled in and listened to snatches of conversations. She smiled at the appropriate times, and offered an occasional comment, but her mind wandered. Where was John? Even as she slept, she'd dreamed of him. She shook off the inappropriate thoughts.

In order to maintain the careful distance she'd created since the Christmas party, she had to stop dreaming and thinking about him. Because even *she* didn't know what she'd do if he touched her.

How she'd managed to avoid touching him was, so far, a mystery. Hell. He'd made her body sing. And that had never happened before.

"Toni, you're daydreaming. The island must be relaxing you," Willis observed.

"St. Croix is beautiful," she offered, intent on focusing on the present.

"We were going to wait for John, but I'm starving. Let's eat," he announced to everyone.

A long buffet table had been spread with fruit, assorted pastas, salads, and island favorites as chefs worked on the opposite side grilling the meat to perfection. Toni fixed her plate and joined the others at the table.

A four-member group with congos provided musical entertainment as one brightly-dressed bartender brought Toni a fresh drink. The first had been delicious, but she had to keep her wits about her. When she tried to push it away, he insisted.

"I remember from earlier, Queen. Dis drink is your favorite. Enjoy!"

Everyone at the table gave her sly looks. "Having fun without us?" Dean, the CFO, asked.

Toni was glad the sun had set, or else they'd see her blush. "I thought this was supposed to be a time to party, right? Isn't Ziotech number one?"

Everyone raised their glasses and hooted.

"Now, that's what I like. My executives know when to work and when to play. Drink up," her boss ordered. "This is costing me a fortune. Only kidding," he said when Marjorie shot him a look. "Ah, here's John."

Toni couldn't blame the rush of sensitive feelings that coated her skin on having seen John, because Willis blocked him from view. John hadn't spoken yet, so it wasn't due to hearing his voice. She couldn't smell him or touch or taste him.

Her hand trembled and she realized that just being in John's presence upended her senses to the point he didn't have to *do* anything. Being near him was enough.

John slid into view, and her body began to tingle as if an electrical current had touched her. She set her fork down and watched as he fixed a plate. The closer he got to her, the more active her senses became. She hadn't felt like this since the night they'd made love.

John sat beside her and their shoulders touched. "Hi."

"Hi."

With John seated, Willis finished his speech.

"We're here today because each and every one of you gave one hundred ten percent to your jobs. You deserve this vacation. This is your playtime. If Marjorie or I or the staff here at Paradise Resort can do anything to make your stay better, let us know."

Willis sat and everyone began to eat. He waited for Toni to finish her silent prayer, then leaned toward her.

"Speaking of playing, I heard we missed a golf date."

Toni choked on her corkscrew pasta. "That's okay, sir."

Willis thumped her twice. "I'm sorry that got screwed up. The hotel offered me an early fishing trip in its place because the course is closed tomorrow. It's at four A.M. Interested?"

How could she tell him that she hated fishing? That one of her father's favorite pastimes had been to take his kids on a monthly fishing trip? She couldn't tell Willis just as she hadn't been able to tell her father. The trips were never fun. Her father, a perfectionist, overdid things to the point that once they arrived at the lake, she and her siblings just wanted to escape his lectures.

"Sure. Love to."

"Excellent! Anyone else?"

Marjorie threw up her hands. "Not me. Just bring him back in one piece. That's all I ask."

Willis waved her off. "You don't know what you're missing, but that's okay. Maybe John wants to go." Willis put on a self-deprecating smile and lowered his voice. "I really creamed him on the golf course today. He's probably still licking his wounds."

"Honey," Marjorie said, "do you think just because the man is chewing, he can't hear? The Senior PGA already turned you down. Give it up."

Everyone delighted in the older couple's playfulness. Willis tapped his unlit cigar. "If I had a little more practice, they'd be begging me to join. One of these days, I'm going to give John a good one out there."

Laughter erupted as John caught up on the conversation.

"Is Willis lying about winning again?"

"I was just telling everyone how I cut you a break today," Willis said, changing his story. "There's always the day after tomorrow."

As John talked, Toni took the opportunity to study him. When he moved, it was with the power of a lion, and when he looked at her, it was with an intensity that threatened to melt her resistance.

Why did John's actions speak promises to her inner woman? Toni couldn't understand her mental and physical reaction.

Growing up, she'd experienced the public face men often put on, but she identified most with the confinement women like her mother endured for their men.

Mrs. Kingsley often spoke of how her husband had swept her off her feet, but to Toni, her mother lived in an era as aged as dinosaur bones. It wasn't until a year after Toni's father died that her mother had gotten a driver's license. Her father had wanted it that way. When he flew into one of his rages, he made it known he was the man, and without him, she was helpless.

Once upon a time, Toni had fantasized about what marriage would be like with John. But her mind kept returning to her mother standing in the window as each of her children drove out of her life, and the air of dominance her father possessed because he'd been a good provider, but not a nice person.

John made her feel too good. Their one night of pleasure awakened emotions she'd vowed never to have. The power John had over her mirrored the power her father had over her mother, and it scared her. All he needed was the attitude, and she'd be staring at her father's shadow—and Toni wasn't going to have it.

Toni couldn't risk that type of pain, but that didn't stop her heart from echoing a frantic drumbeat in his presence.

Willis rose and reached for Marjorie's hand. "Let's go mingle and let this food settle before we tackle dessert. Dean and Kelly, care to join us?" The younger couple rose and headed for the other tables.

The drum music made Toni want to dance, but she settled for a gentle sway. She wiped her mouth and placed her napkin beside her plate, pulling back her unsteady hand.

John washed down his dinner with bottled water. His Adam's apple bobbed, and she wished his skin were beneath her tongue. Toni stifled a sigh. She simply couldn't go *there* again with John. The key was not to touch him, and she'd be fine. She inched away and he turned his intense gaze upon her. "You look beautiful."

John always spoke in definitive language that appealed to her as a pragmatic woman. The last time her undoing was John uttering three simple words: "I want you."

To make matters worse, his leg brushed hers and the hairs tickled her smooth skin. "Thank you." Toni noted the singsong melody of her own voice and cleared her throat. "You don't look so bad yourself. Rested?"

"With my mother?" he laughed. "Not likely. She had to get her hair braided. Do you know how long it takes women to get their hair done?"

Toni gave him a knowing look. "Why don't you enlighten me?"

His gaze swept the finely retouched roots of her dark-brown hair, drifted to her face, worked its way down to her feet and back up. He took in a deep breath and Toni was flattered. She'd never made a man sigh before.

"How come you didn't get your hair braided?" His tone implied intimacy while his eyes conveyed desire. "Your hair always makes me want to run my fingers through it." A smile played around his mouth. "It just does something to me."

Every instinct in Toni's body warred between two factions—to stay or to flee. Toni chose the latter. She tried to stand and John caught her hand. "Stop running away. Sit and talk to me." He released her hand before she could react, and she sat back down.

John slid his elbow on the table and propped his chin on his hand. "Why didn't you get your hair braided?"

Toni didn't know how to handle the sudden change in subject. For several seconds she was silent, then decided to go with the flow. She'd always loved to talk to John, his wit and intelligence qualities she most admired in a person.

She swept her hand through her shoulder-length hair and scooted a couple more inches away. "I thought about it, but I didn't feel like sitting for six hours in a salon."

"I thought all women liked going to the hairdresser. My mother would go every three days if my father let her."

She'd wanted to ask him why he'd brought his mother along on a company-sponsored trip, but hadn't had the nerve. But he'd opened the door and she stepped in. "Where is your dad?"

John's face closed down and he looked down the beach to

a distant spot of red-tipped flames. Beverly was probably living it up. "Home. Alone."

Toni did her own private inventory. His soft blue cotton shirt open at the throat gave her a peek of the strong muscles beneath. His arms were bare, and he had on pressed navy shorts and sandals. She wanted to touch the line by his mouth and watch his lips turn up in a smile, but she didn't, too afraid of the consequences. "Why didn't they come separately and join you for a few days?" she asked.

"Because my mother needed a break."

The dynamics of her own family rushed into her mind. Her mother still operated as if under her husband's control and wouldn't even take a vacation without a man as a protector. She'd only go on short trips with Toni's older sister, Veronica, and her husband, Winston. "You're kidding," Toni finally said.

John met her gaze evenly. "My father is spoiled rotten. She finally got fed up and decided to take a vacation. Since I was coming here, I felt it better to bring her with me instead of sending her on a cruise with her girlfriends, the way she wanted."

His tone and his words rubbed against her fierce independence. Suddenly the conversation between John and his mom made sense. Beverly had emancipated herself from one ruler, but had gotten another in return.

"Your mom might have enjoyed the cruise," she suggested in Beverly's defense.

"She's happy."

His reassurance aggravated Toni. Just like a man to think he knows everything. Fully prepared to fight for a woman's right of free choice, Toni jumped in with both feet.

"How do you know? If she was trying to get away from your father, maybe she needed a break from *all* the Roberts men."

John considered her words, then shrugged. "Too bad. She's stuck with me."

Although she knew this wasn't about her, Toni took his careless attitude personally. "Typical."

Willis and Marjorie walked up, followed by several other

couples. "We're going to watch fireworks for a while, but we'll be back for dessert."

There were enough fireworks between them, and Toni thought it best to leave before she told John how she really felt. "I'll come with you." She half rose, but her boss pushed her back down.

"You two look as if you were involved in a serious conversation. No hurry. Join us when you're done."

Trapped, Toni clenched her teeth. There was no graceful way to tell her boss that one of his managers had a 1950s value system. So she sat. Silent.

When everyone was out of earshot, John asked, "What do you mean by *typical*?"

A crab popped up from the sand and scampered toward the ocean. She watched the crustacean until he disappeared into the inky water.

"Maybe you don't know everything. Maybe your mother would have loved a cruise alone with her girlfriends so she could hang out in her pajamas, eat at any hour, and go to the beach without her old-fashioned son telling her to be home by ten."

John's laughter seemed to mock his mother's push for independence, therefore invalidating her desires. On the one hand, Toni realized she knew nothing about Mrs. Roberts or her wants, yet John shouldn't assume *he* knew what was best for his mother, either.

Toni thought of her sisters and how most conversations centered around how the men didn't listen, and how things *had* to be their way. None were abused, but sometimes they looked defeated. Toni was suddenly proud of Mrs. Roberts and the way she'd handled John this afternoon.

John surprised Toni by sliding his thumb down her cheek. His touch sent a rocket of awareness across her chest. "You're angry."

"Yes. I am." He waited patiently, and when she didn't elaborate, he pulled her to her feet and guided her along a winding path, sheltered by tall leafy plants and colorful flowers. Behind them, fireworks lit the sky, but Toni didn't care. She was still angry, but the power of his touch could overrule her good sense.

"Want to talk about it?" he asked.

"You're way off base when it comes to women, and," she added, pointing at him, "you're bossy."

He caught her fingers. Toni flexed her hand, and much to her dismay, John laced his fingers with hers.

"Considering what I do for a living, I'll take the latter as a compliment."

"Not from where I'm standing," she argued. "I hate when men make assumptions instead of really listening to what women are saying."

"Who doesn't listen to you, Toni?"

His astute observation stunned her into silence and she stopped walking. John was not only looking into her eyes, he was also looking into her heart. He'd tapped into feelings she'd had since she started dating at seventeen. She had always wanted the man in her life to not only listen to her, but to hear her.

And from what she'd seen, men, including John, were incapable of doing that. She tried to turn the tables. "This isn't about me."

"Yes, it is."

"No, it's not."

"Then I'm making it about you," he said. "You know what a woman's problem is?"

Toni laughed. "You're crazy if you think you can bait me."

"I always thought you were fair, Toni. Hear me out."

Toni nodded, her curiosity piqued. "Give it your best shot."

"Women don't ever say what they mean." Now John seemed frustrated. "Women talk in code to confuse men so they can use whatever happened against them at a later time."

"That might be the women you hang out with, but that's not me." Toni tried to reclaim her hand to no avail.

"Wanna bet?"

"Ye—" Before Toni could finish the word, John's mouth closed over hers in a sensuous kiss that practically lifted her feet off the ground. His tongue laved hers to the beat of the drums, and all her resistance surrendered under the tutelage of his mouth.

When he broke the kiss, John didn't immediately let her go, and for that Toni was glad. She wasn't sure she had complete control of her motor functions.

"To further demonstrate my point," he said as he pushed their twined hands behind her back. "Are you attracted to me?"

Toni reluctantly shook her head.

"Another example of saying one thing and meaning another." He covered her mouth again, and then trailed delicate kisses down her neck. Despite herself, Toni's head fell back, aching for him to go further. Thin straps held her dress together in back and John's fingers trailed over her bare flesh. She arched toward him.

John's hands stirred memories of the twelve hours they'd shared not long ago. She remembered how it felt to be in his arms and the pleasure he'd given her again and again. "Tell me what you want, Toni," he demanded, in a way that promised fulfillment.

Before she could continue down this path of ecstasy, she had to make him understand her feelings. Toni broke the kiss and put her finger to his lips.

"Respect."

He threaded his fingers through her hair and looked into her eyes. "I do respect you. Doesn't mean I'll always agree with you."

"What about your mother?"

Toni knew she had stumbled into forbidden territory. She really had no right to ask John about his own mother, but she felt oddly protective of the feisty older lady, and she needed to know where John stood.

"She's happy to be here, Toni. If you don't believe me, watch her for the next few days and draw your own conclusions."

Toni closed her eyes to hide her surprise. She hadn't expected John to offer her a choice. In her mother's household, her husband's word had been final. John wasn't making the final decision, but leaving it up to her. The newness of this shared power washed her with warm feelings.

His lips caressed her neck with slow, seductive kisses and she leaned weightlessly into him.

"What do you want, Toni? For me to stop?"

He embraced her tightly. John had her and she was safe. She allowed herself to let go of a little control. "No."

He claimed her mouth again, leaving in the wake of the kiss unnamed promises. "I want more," he said.

Like a train screeching to a halt, reality stopped her head from spinning. She looked through her lust-induced fog and saw the earnest expression on John's face. "I can't make a commitment."

His eyes said he believed her, and he palmed her face. "I want you. Not just in my bed, Toni. I want this week. No titles, no competition. Just you and me."

The idea both thrilled and scared her. "What would I gain?"

With his mouth he charted a path of passion and desire. His hands offered greater incentive when he cupped her butt and pulled her tight against his erection.

John stared into her eyes. "Give me this week, Toni."

She swallowed, tempted to follow the command her body and mind sang in unison, but she wasn't the top sales manager for nothing. She negotiated. "With conditions."

He widened his stance and used a very enticing grind as a negotiation tool. "And they would be?"

"One week," she said, barely able to speak.

"Agreed."

"This is our secret affair." The sky burst into sparkling red and white lights. "No one can know."

John undulated her hips, pushing her to the brink. "Agreed."

"When we get home, it's o—"

John's mouth sank onto hers and absorbed the shocking burst of her orgasm just as the fireworks finale blasted the sky. Toni's head fell back and all she could feel was her body at the height of pleasure.

John's hand slipped up her back to her neck, and he held her close. "If a week's all we have, let's get started now."

Toni's feet barely touched the ground as she followed John into the hotel.

FOUR

The ride up the crowded elevator to Toni's room gave her a chance to let the fog clear a bit. She moved to the opposite corner, determined not to embarrass herself or John. Because if they were alone, they wouldn't have made it out of the glass elevator the same way they had entered.

Toni had wanted him since the night they'd spent in wild abandon a month ago. For twenty working days, she'd seen him dressed in tailored Armani, tight Hugo Boss, or bad-ass Kenneth Cole, and still, she'd kept her hands to herself.

But that didn't stop her ears from seeking his voice and the resulting shiver that snuck up on her whenever he entered the conference room for their weekly meetings.

Her eyes would feast on how the clothes made the man, as a part of her rejoiced that she'd had the man beneath the clothes.

With extreme self-control, she'd inhale his cologne, the scent seductive, liquid sex. Women in the office swooned behind his back, but only Toni knew the smell of him, how his skin felt against her taste buds, the texture of his sex, the pleasure of his kisses.

One week.

John stood across the elevator, his hands balled in his pockets, a poor attempt to disguise his swollen desire.

Could she love him and leave him in seven days?

She'd have to. She cherished her freedom, loved her independent lifestyle, and was afraid of the lives her married friends, sisters, and mother had lived. Although most seemed happy, Toni saw characteristics of her father in the men and didn't want that type relationship.

Yes, she could let her guard down for a week and be the same Toni she was when she arrived. Happy, single, independent, and satisfied.

John gave her the nod, the look on his face so sexually roguish, she wanted to strip and open for his pleasure.

The elevator opened and they walked to Toni's room. John slid the card home, pushed down the door handle, and let her enter first.

In the center of the room, Toni turned to offer him a drink, but one look at his eyes, and the inconsequential gesture slipped away.

Toni unzipped her dress and shrugged, the filmy material falling to her feet.

John watched, but didn't move.

The half bra and matching panties covered her, and she unsnapped the hook and let her breasts spill forward.

His eyes widened.

She let the material fall.

He exhaled.

The fire in his eyes smoldered as she thumbed off the silky panties.

He groaned.

Deliberately John laid the card key on the armoire and walked toward her. His look said it all. It declared her beautiful, sexy, desirable.

As he stripped, Toni watched, a shudder rippling through her belly. He was muscular, his warm skin smooth beneath a peppering of dark hair.

Naked, John was even more than she remembered. There were no illusions of his desire, and before Toni could stop herself, she launched herself into his arms.

Their mouths met, seeking satisfaction as their tongues laved and explored. His hands moved confidently over her, bringing her against him, igniting her body everywhere.

John used his hands and tongue in conjunction to drive her to the edge and back, and she held to him, her arms finding his back as he buried his head against her breast.

Like a pirate seeking a treasure, he stroked her gem until she begged for release. John pushed her against the wall and she straddled his leg, as his teeth played crazy games with her pebbled nipples.

Toni heard herself call his name, and for a second their gazes locked. Then John wrapped her waist with his hands and slowly pulled her across his strong leg. Sparks shot up from her feet to her thighs, up her chest, and made her head fall back. She cried out, wanting release to come, yet wanting it to last forever.

John leaned into her, rocking until Toni thought she'd explode. When she thought she couldn't endure any more, he positioned his legs between hers and impaled her.

The first climax zigzagged up her back so fast, Toni couldn't stop from arching into him, her fingers digging deep into his shoulders, her face tossed in the wind.

She heard her guttural cries, but Toni couldn't stop herself. The spirals of release tore up her body and she fell back, her mouth open, his to command.

She wasn't aware they'd moved, until her butt touched the cool bedsheets.

Toni opened her eyes and looked at him. John stood over her, his erection angled north, his fingers stimulating her knot of ecstasy.

She reached up, clasped him first with her hand, then her mouth, and drove him into the stratosphere.

Toni slid from bed at 3:30 A.M., her muscles sore from the night's activities. She searched among their clothes for her robe, the items telling a story of pleasure and romance.

Unable to find the garment, she gave up and tiptoed to the bathroom. At the door, she couldn't resist a look back at John's sleeping form.

God hadn't been playing when He'd made the man. John was the finest work of craftsmanship she'd ever seen.

Behind the closed bathroom door, Toni drew on a shower cap and let her mind traipse through the events of last night.

When she'd rejoined the group an hour and a half later, no one mentioned their disappearance, probably because the rum and good times had been flowing steadily.

She'd tried to stay away from him for the rest of the evening, yet found herself gravitating to whatever group he was in. He captivated a crowd, but what touched her was how well he listened.

Later, when the group played charades around the bonfire, Toni was tickled when John tried to act out *Titanic,* and caused his team to lose. He, along with his team, took their dunk in the ocean in good spirit, coming back wet and laughing.

Instead of retiring for the night like many of the other wet executives, John joined the remaining night owls, listening to their stories and sharing some of his own.

Toni stayed, too, until her eyes grew heavy, then stood to excuse herself. Casually, John offered to walk her back to the hotel.

Toni panicked, but the others rose, ready to turn in after a long day, and she realized he was being a perfect gentleman.

They strolled through the lobby of Paradise Resort, letting the group get ahead of them, not wanting the end to be so near.

She'd just had the night of her life, the best sex she'd ever known, and according to John's gaze, was in store for more.

Whitewashed tile covered the expansive floor, decorated by floral cushioned couches. Tall trees fanned the air with green leaves, and reggae music filtered in from the disco.

Toni was aware of John's powerful physique, but it still shocked her when he kissed her neck. "Ready to go up?"

"Is everybody else gone?"

He turned her and kissed her slowly. "Yes, everyone else is gone."

As the elevator ascended, the tension grew, and when they were finally alone, John kissed her as if they'd been apart for a lifetime.

That passion had fueled their heated coupling and had driven her to new heights.

Now she stared at her face in the mirror and wondered how she was going to survive the week without blowing their secret. John had a way of making her want him without regard to the rules she'd insisted upon.

She showered, wrapped herself in a towel, and slipped into

the darkened bedroom. She didn't want to wake John unnecessarily, and dressed quickly in the dark.

Her heartbeat thundered. Who was she kidding? If John woke up and crooked his finger, she'd be in his bed in a flash, the fishing trip forgotten.

She stabbed her feet into sneakers and grabbed a baseball cap. On her way out the door, Toni looked back again. The rumpled sheets and his long, muscular body beckoned her in a cacophony of caresses against her skin.

Was every night going to be like this? Would she awaken another morning not wanting to separate her body from his? Probably, she told herself as she slipped out the door and caught the waiting elevator.

But they were adults, and they agreed to a one-week affair, nothing more.

And if there was one thing Toni hated, it was a person who broke a contract.

The sun had risen high in the sky, bringing the temperature to a balmy eighty-five degrees. John sat alongside his co-workers on *The Singapore* as they cruised to a private island where the group from Ziotech planned to spend the day hiking and relaxing.

His mother hadn't wanted to come, and for that he was glad. He needed some quiet time to think. What had he started with Toni?

He sipped orange juice and let his gaze slide to where she lounged. A one-piece white swimsuit accentuated honey-brown skin in such a way that left little to his imagination.

She'd shielded herself with a wide-brimmed straw hat, pink sunglasses, and flat sandals. Around her waist, she wore a net skirt. The garment offered no protection from the sun, and added sensuality to an already sexy body.

Toni pulled sunblock from her bag and asked Dean's wife, Kelly, to smooth some on her back.

John jumped to his feet. "I'll do it."

Toni's sunglasses slid down her nose, a stricken look on her face. "Thanks, but Kelly can handle it."

He felt as if everyone were looking at him, but he couldn't

resist an opportunity to touch her. He squeezed between the two women and sat. "I don't mind. I need to borrow some anyway. I forgot mine back at the hotel," he said, ignoring the fact that he had a small bottle in his bag.

Kelly popped up, her porcelain skin already a toasty brown.

"Honey, go ahead and take my seat," she said. "The last thing I need to do is confuse my tan by getting sunblock on my hands. You guys want something to drink? I'm going below deck."

"Water," they said in unison.

Kelly looked at them strangely. "Did anyone ever tell you that you make a cute couple?"

The sunblock slipped from Toni's hand and hit the deck. The bottle skidded across the floor and John snatched it up before it flew down the stairs.

"Nobody but you," Toni said, her eyes alarmed. "We're just friends. Not right for each other," she continued, talking faster. "We work together, for goodness' sake."

Kelly waved off her objection. "How do you think I met Dean? Honey, that's the place to meet guys nowadays, besides the Internet. Be back in a minute."

John took his time pouring lotion into his hand, trying to get over the flash of disappointment at Toni's statement. What was he to assume, that last night meant nothing? That what they had couldn't carry over and bloom into a successful relationship? He'd tried for the better part of a month to get her attention, but she'd sidestepped his every advance. Until now.

Was it just sex?

Was he that good?

John smiled. Perhaps, but realistically there was something deeper going on inside Toni that had made her commit to a week of fun on the island, but not at home in Atlanta.

John perched the bottle of sunblock between his feet and smeared the lotion between his hands, when the realization hit him.

The way she held him throughout the night should have been a dead giveaway.

Toni wanted to feel safe. The anonymity of being on the island and insisting on secrecy was a way to insure that.

Toni was a great manager and she was number one for a reason, but he was number two, and he knew how to give this woman a run for her money. He could and would win her over, and he'd use every weapon in his considerable arsenal. John poured more lotion into his hands.

"I'm burning right here." She pointed to her left shoulder.

John smoothed on the cream in even strokes, her skin delicate beneath his fingers. He massaged, applying pressure to her shoulder muscles, relieving strain. She held herself erect for a while, but John didn't stop. He kept smoothing it in, one hand over the other until she leaned her head back and purred.

Her spine curved under his hands and he stroked her until a contented sigh seeped from her lips. Her suit dipped low in the back and John took advantage and let his hands roam freely. "All done," he said, when he couldn't take any more.

He wiped lotion on his legs and gave her the bottle. "Thanks."

Her eyes popped open and she glanced around looking guilty. "You didn't have to do this."

"I know."

"What will the others think?"

He fixed her shoulder strap, but made himself pull his hand away. "Nothing. It's our secret, right?"

She nodded, looking confused. "Right."

"Well, let's not talk about it. I'll see you later." He got up.

Toni's hand caressed her strap, and when he looked into her eyes, he saw desire. His heart soared, but he kept his face impassive.

"Let's just behave in public, please, John," she pleaded.

"You could have awakened me this morning."

"Do we have to talk about this now?"

He looked around the boat. "Who's listening to us? You know, people will think it's odd if the only two Black people on the whole trip aren't being nice to each other."

"So now you're worried about race relations at Ziotech?" She sucked her teeth. "That's hard to believe."

"No. Just my relations with you."

Toni looked out over the ocean and finally at him. "I thought we agreed to one week of fun. No attachments."

"I'm sticking to our agreement. I'm acting normal."

Her look said otherwise. "Caressing my back while everyone is down below is normal?"

John slid on his sunglasses. "You set the rules and I agreed to them, so let's move on. How was the fishing trip?"

Her mouth quirked. "Oh, no, Mr. Roberts. Don't change the subject."

"Are we renegotiating our deal? Do you want to up the ante? Because there's a heavy penalty for changing the terms of our agreement."

A smile bloomed. "I am not renegotiating." She hesitated, then asked, "What are you doing to me?"

John couldn't tell her because he didn't know, but he was glad to know that she was affected, too. "Having fun, baby? Did you catch any fish?"

"A few. We had a great time, when I wasn't being eaten alive by mosquitoes. I should have listened to Marjorie. Willis is a good boss, but I won't be doing that again soon."

"So, was it worth leaving me in bed, alone?"

Her gaze slid past him, and he knew she was taking a mental count of all the passengers. Nobody was within earshot, but she obviously wanted to be sure. Somehow he'd have to get her past that fear.

Toni finally looked at him again. "I wished I'd stayed in bed with you."

John's stomach fluttered. "Be careful what you wish for. It just might come true."

Kelly appeared from below deck, followed by several other wives. She handed John and Toni bottled water, then took a long sip of her drink. "Toni, we're going up to sunbathe. Want to come?"

"I'd love to." Toni hesitated before she took the hand John offered and stood. "Thanks," she said tightly.

"You're welcome."

Toni pushed up her sunglasses, shielding her eyes from his. "Bye."

"Bye," he whispered, thinking, *Until later.*

FIVE

Toni slipped into a sleeveless peach dinner dress, the soft material perfect for the tropical island. Her thoughts drifted back over the past three days.

Her main goal had been to talk to Willis about the promotion to VP, but so far that hadn't happened. During their fishing trip, Willis had wanted to talk about John and get her impression of his aggressive management style.

Toni praised his training initiatives and for providing his team with resources from tech support to customer service. John was goal-oriented and did whatever was necessary so that his people exceeded them.

While Toni could understand why Willis would be interested in hearing her opinion, she'd wanted to steer the conversation to her skills and discuss her ideology about management. But that opportunity never came. As soon as she'd successfully turned the conversation, Willis stated that Ziotech had to downsize to be competitive, and that the new VP would be responsible for both manager positions. One manager would be promoted and the other let go. He told Toni he could do little else, then announced he needed to concentrate so that he could catch the biggest fish ever off the island of St. Croix.

Toni groaned as she dug at a mosquito bite on her leg. Why hadn't she pushed harder, or been more direct? Why hadn't she questioned the profit and losses of the company and suggested where things could be strengthened?

The answer came as she gathered her purse and slipped into her shoes.

John was too powerful a distraction. She'd been thinking too much about him, and not about the job.

After their talk yesterday on *The Singapore*, he'd backed off. She'd wanted to talk about Willis's announcement, but there never was a good time.

And when they'd gotten to the island, her thoughts had strayed far away from work, and focused on watching John, wanting him to acknowledge her in some way.

At one point, she'd flirted with him by caressing his shoulders as she passed by. But he hadn't responded to the overture with more than a look in her direction.

But last night in her bed, he'd been so attentive, so focused on her pleasure, he'd driven her to new heights.

Toni straightened her hair and glanced through the mirror at the well-made bed. What delights would tonight bring? Anticipation curled through her.

A tap on the door broke the spell. "Just a sec."

Toni smoothed her hand over her dress and opened the door. "Oh, hello, Beverly. I'm surprised to see you. How are you this evening?"

"Just fine. Can I come in?"

Bewildered, Toni stepped back. "Of course. Can you manage?"

The woman wheeled in. "Yes, thank you. Toni, I won't take up much of your time, but I wondered if I could speak to you a minute."

"Of course. Come into the living room." Toni sat in one of the easy chairs. "May I get you something to drink?"

"No, we're about to have a fine dinner. I'll wait to fill up there. Toni," she began, "I wanted to find out if you would mind if I used you as a sounding board before I talk to John."

"Sure, but is there something wrong?"

"No." Beverly fidgeted and didn't catch Toni's eye. "I'd like to go home."

Surprised, Toni struggled for words. "Beverly, I thought you were having a good time."

Mrs. Roberts chuckled. "I am, but I miss my husband, and he misses me."

"I see," Toni said, not really understanding. "But why do

you need me? You and John seem to have the type of relationship where you can talk about anything."

"We can, but not when it comes to his father. You see, John's father was so strict on the kids when they were young, and I guess he's still got a little Army in him, so he and John disagree a lot when it comes to me."

"I see. I can listen, but I'm not sure how else I can help you."

Beverly adjusted her beaded purse on her lap. "I wanted to bring it up real casual-like after dinner and say, 'John, I had a good time on this trip, but I miss your father and I want to go home.'"

Toni gave her an encouraging smile. "That sounded great."

Beverly shook her head, unsure. "I don't know. Maybe I should say I'm not feeling well. I don't want him to think I'm not grateful."

Toni patted her hand. "You'd worry him needlessly if you didn't tell him the truth."

The older woman nodded slowly and a smile formed. "You're right."

"Can I get you something to drink?" Toni asked again.

"A Coke would be nice," Beverly said. She moved her chair forward. "Toni, would you mind if I asked you to stay nearby so I can look to a friendly face for encouragement?"

Toni poured the dark liquid over ice and pulled out a white wine for herself. She didn't know what to say. "J-John and I are colleagues. We don't discuss, well, get into personal . . . uh, issues." Toni wished she'd worded that differently, because even Beverly looked confused. Beverly's head hung for a moment, then she gave Toni a small smile.

"I understand. I just thought I'd ask." She set her glass on the table and slowly rolled her chair back. "Don't worry, I can handle this on my own."

Toni felt terrible. How could she *not* help Beverly? For all she knew, John might agree with his mother, but even if he didn't, Toni couldn't turn her back on the request.

She stood. "You know what? No problem. If you need me, I'm there. Now, how about some dinner?"

The older woman looked relieved. "Yes. Let's make my

last night on the island memorable. Lots of dancing and dai-
quiris."

Toni couldn't help but think she'd need at least a couple
of drinks before the night was over.

The restaurant where dinner was held had been transformed
from a daytime brunch hangout to a fine dining establishment.

Linen cloths covered the tables, and candles flickered in the
moonlight.

The men had dressed in coats and ties, while the women
all wore short dresses to show off their tanned legs. John was
especially handsome in a camel-colored jacket that showcased
his broad shoulders.

Toni couldn't tear her gaze away. He was talking to the VP
of marketing, and she watched as he seemed totally absorbed
by what the man was saying. Were they talking about jobs in
the marketplace?

Beverly rolled her chair to her son's side and he made room
for her to join the conversation. As Toni watched the scene,
anxiety kicked up. While she wanted to approach in case Beverly needed her, her feet remained rooted.

Toni tried to be a woman of her word, but as she walked
toward the three, she detoured to the buffet table and snacked
on fresh vegetables.

Every once in a while Beverly would give her an encouraging look, but Toni couldn't face her. She couldn't find the
right words to say.

She snagged a glass of rum punch from a passing waiter
and drank. This night was about fun, but also about her securing, at least, a breakfast date with Willis where they could
talk privately about the VP job.

But first she had to follow up on her commitment to Beverly. Then she could talk the night away. Squaring her shoulders, Toni headed over to the small group.

Austin, the VP of marketing, smiled when he spotted her.

"Toni, glad to see you. John, I'll catch up with you later."

Toni started to back away. "Please, don't let me interrupt."

"No, no," Austin said. "I've got to find my wife anyway.
Will you all excuse me?"

They all nodded and Beverly touched John's hand.

"Son, I need to freshen up before dinner. I'll be right back."

John bent and kissed his mother's cheek. "Okay."

They watched the woman roll away. Toni bit her lower lip. "I hope your discussion with Austin wasn't too important."

"It was interesting, as a matter of fact. We were talking about you."

Now, that was news. Great news! She didn't want to pry, but she couldn't help herself. "What about me?"

"Ethan is leaving to head the office in London. His wife is from there."

"I'd heard." Toni didn't want to appear as if she knew too much. "What did Austin say?"

"He said your name has been tossed around regarding Ethan's position."

"Really?"

"You had to know," he said, and she finally nodded.

"I thought it was confidential." Toni bit her tongue and decided to go for it. "I understand you're up for the same job."

He turned to her, his body blocking all but a halo of light. "I'd heard that, too. I also heard there'll be an elimination. One of us will lose our job."

"How do you feel about that?" she asked.

"There are other jobs. But the VP job is something I've worked hard for. I know that I'm qualified for the position, and I know the competition is tough."

"I hadn't heard of any other candidates," Toni said, batting the compliment back to see if it was really intended for her.

"I was talking about you." John's lips twitched, hiding a grin.

"How can you smile at a time like this?"

"Because I know that whatever goes on next week, I can't control. Only now. My outlook is like a weather forecast. My days are breezy and sunny. My nights are humid and warm." His words caused her to blush. "I'm a happy guy."

"What did you tell Austin?"

"I told him you were highly qualified for the job."

She gazed up at him, not believing her ears. "You said that, even though we're competing against each other?" Toni couldn't help but laugh. He seemed so calm and reassured.

"It's the truth. They're aware of your qualifications and they know how successful you've been. Restating the obvious doesn't threaten me."

Toni couldn't hide her surprise. "I can't believe you'd do that for me. Thank you."

"It's the truth. Anyway, I didn't knock myself out of the race. I just made sure they know my skills are comparable."

She laughed. "Oh, did you?"

The dinner bell rang and John guided her toward the tables. "Definitely."

John held her chair, and when she moved to sit, he lowered his voice. "I'm expecting to be showered with gratitude later."

Shivers of longing slid up from her feet to the roots of her hair. She raised her hand to caress his face, but stopped herself. What was she thinking?

Toni held her hand on her lap, unable to look at John. He'd seen the movement and, she was sure, wanted to know why she hadn't followed through.

She kept her gaze on her menu as John talked to his mother, who was seated across from them. Beverly seemed in good spirits, not at all the woman who'd asked for moral support to give her son news he might not take well.

Butterflies took flight in Toni's stomach when Beverly started talking about home.

The waiter appeared and took their drink orders, followed by another who explained the specials and took their dinner orders.

Toni busied herself talking to Kelly, but felt John's leg occasionally brush hers.

She sighed when his hand squeezed her knee.

"You okay?" Kelly asked.

"Fine. Long day on the boat yesterday. The sun wiped me out."

"You look gorgeous. Doesn't she, John?"

"Gorgeous," he agreed, his hand squeezing hers beneath the table.

Kelly leaned over to see John more clearly. "Then do something about it, man! Ask her out."

Toni swatted at Kelly. "Be quiet."

But she wouldn't be deterred. "Come on, she's gorgeous, got a great body, and she's intelligent." She ticked on her fingers. "She's single. No warts." Toni and John started laughing. "She's a hottie. Ask her out."

Beverly chimed in, "Well, son?"

John looked at Toni and she wanted to hide her face. If they only knew what was going on during the wee hours of the morning, they wouldn't be pushing a date, but a fire hose to cool them off. Would John be gracious and decline, or would he reveal their secret affair? Toni tipped her head.

"You don't have to do this," she said, trying to keep her smile from trembling. "Kelly is drunk."

John quirked his mouth. "I'd like to have drinks with you later."

She couldn't believe they were playacting in front of everyone! A thrill tickled her spine at the knowledge that he'd go to this much trouble so as not to embarrass her.

She graciously accepted.

"Dean," Kelly gushed, ending his conversation with Austin. "Honey, I've made another successful match."

Her husband kissed her cheek affectionately. "Honey, you are perfect at what you do."

"Aren't they cute?" Kelly smiled, gazing at John and Toni.

"Yes, dear," he teased. "I especially think John is cute."

Everyone at the table laughed, but Toni could only sit, a smile frozen to her face.

"About eleven?" John said, ending her reverie.

"Fine."

Dinner arrived and the delectable food comforted her. The effects of the wine and good company made her wish she never had to worry about returning to work. But the reality was that in order to be on this special trip, a hard year of work was necessary.

For the first time Toni wondered if she really wanted to beat out John for the job. Not only would she still be responsible for her own sales quota, but also the sales of a team of managers and the account executives below her.

She separated personal from professional. She did want the

job. She'd worked hard for it, and although it would involve more responsibility, she was ready.

On a personal front, she didn't want to hurt John. Nor did she want to be hurt. But this was where they were, and she could do nothing more to sway the vote in her favor. She might as well enjoy the remainder of the trip.

Many people were turning in early in preparation for their long day tomorrow. Toni thought of going to bed, too, but she still hadn't helped Beverly with her problem.

Her thoughts weighed heavily as she walked inside the hotel lobby. A voice brought her out of her fog.

"Toni," Beverly said, as she wheeled from the concierge stand. "I thought I'd tell him now. Do you have a minute?"

Toni felt more anxious than she let on, but she followed Beverly and wondered how John was going to take his mother's news.

SIX

John couldn't believe what he was hearing.

His mother wanted to go home. To his father. He didn't know which he felt more, relief or remorse. Granted, he'd wanted to spend time alone with Toni, but he didn't want his mother to return home to her old routine of waiting hand and foot on his father.

His mom sat before him, and occasionally, her eyes would wander. "Mom, do you need Toni for something?"

"Now that you mention it, I'd feel more comfortable if she were sitting here with us, John."

Confused, he asked her to join them. Toni sat, but her leg shook nervously and she kept rubbing her hands together.

"Mom, what's this about?"

"Nothing, son. I'm just ready to go home."

"Why now? We're not scheduled to leave for another four days."

Beverly chuckled. "I know, but *I'm* ready."

"But why? Has something happened I don't know about?"

"No, honey. I love it here. It's just that"—his mom shrugged and looked pensive—"I miss your father."

How could that be, when all she'd done before the trip was complain about what her husband wasn't doing? And how hard she worked even in her wheelchair and he didn't appreciate it. How if she left for a week, he would survive. When had all that changed?

"That's not good enough. You were ready to get away and now you want to leave. Do you know what's going on?" he asked Toni.

"Your mother and father have decided to work on their

problems together, but your mother feels that they have a better chance of coming to an understanding if they are face to face. Your mom's going to be okay."

John watched Toni from the moment she started speaking. She'd met his eyes with sincerity and truth punctuating each word. She squirmed until she was barely able to perch on the couch cushion, but there she sat, and had unconsciously reached out and grasped his hand without regard to who might see them.

He looked down and tenderness engulfed him, followed by understanding. For whatever reason, Toni didn't want to be here confronting him, but on his mother's behalf, here she was.

He couldn't explain the shift in his feelings for her, but the tightness in his chest lessened and was followed by welcoming heat.

John reached for his mother's hand. "If you want to go home, I'll send you home."

"Thank you, son."

"With conditions," he said evenly.

Beverly beamed. "I didn't expect anything less." She began to slowly turn her chair. "Well, I'm beat. I've got to pack for my early flight in the morning, so I'm going to turn in. Thank you, Toni."

John didn't want to let go of Toni's hand, but he did as she bent and kissed his mother's cheek.

He reclaimed her hand. "Give me half an hour, then you and I should talk."

"I'll be right here."

Contentment flooded him. He couldn't let this good thing go. "Thirty minutes."

John followed his mother to their suite, where he dialed his father. "Dad," he said, glad to hear his father's voice, "Mom wants to come home tomorrow, but I think you should do some things to make her more comfortable."

"I will. I miss Beverly," his father said, emotion in his voice John had never heard before. "How is she?"

"Missing you."

"I miss her, too. I thought I'd get some things done around here, but everywhere I went, no Bev. Will she talk to me?"

"Of course. But I was thinking she might like a maid service to come in so that you both don't have to worry about caring for that big house yourselves. And maybe get a computer so she can shop online."

John smiled at his mother's bright smile.

"Join a senior center," Beverly whispered and John laughed.

"Anything, honey!" his father yelled in John's ear.

"I think you're both going to do fine. Dad, I'll talk to you soon."

"Good-bye, son."

"I love you, Dad," he said before he could stop himself. He didn't expect a response, but he heard the muttered, "I love you, too." And the day brightened.

Satisfied that his mother would be fine, John left her packing.

He returned to the lounge where Toni waited. As he strolled toward her, he noticed the tension in her body. She didn't see him, but he could read her expression. She was afraid. John thought his heart would explode.

He'd had deep feelings for Toni even before she'd agreed to the affair, but now as he witnessed the mix of bravery and vulnerability, he could only conclude the beginning of a love affair had transformed him.

He sat beside her and took a sip of her drink. Peach Schnapps neat. Sweet with a bite. Just like her.

"I'm sorry," she said.

John couldn't find his voice. Why was she apologizing when he should have been the one making amends? "For what?"

"I had no right to interfere in your family business."

"I thought my mother asked for your interference."

"She did."

"Then you came into my business honestly. So why are you apologizing?"

"I should have let you two handle it."

She looked troubled, as if the penalty for taking up for his mother was to face a firing squad.

John tried the only thing he thought would shake her. "I don't accept."

A spark of challenge lit her eyes. "John, accept my apology so we can move on."

Anger surged through him. "Who are you?" Toni's eyebrows shot up and he blasted her. "I don't recognize this passive female who won't tell me I'm selfish for wanting my mother to stay. The Toni I know is tough and confident. She never saw a boardroom fight she couldn't handle."

"Work is different," she declared softly. "I'm in my element there."

He was starting to understand, but he needed to know more. Had to get through to the real woman beneath. "Why not here? What's holding you back?"

Her eyes shone like clear glass. "My family is old school. I was raised to believe that the man is the head of the household and the women are docile and obedient. My mother is only changing her lifestyle out of necessity. My father passed away a couple years ago."

"I remember," he said. "I'd just joined Ziotech." John was taken aback. His father had the same beliefs, but that hadn't kept his mother from voicing her opinion. He could see how Toni misinterpreted his desire to keep his mother with him, and how her interference might be seen as disrespectful of him.

"I'm glad you told me, but you weren't disrespecting me by siding with my mother. You helped me understand her feelings."

She turned, and all he could see was her troubled profile. "I should have refused, but I wanted to offer her moral support."

John rubbed his hands together. "Like you've never done before." He knew he'd hit the mark. "To whom? Your father?"

"You're on a roll. Maybe you should try your luck in the casino." She moved to stand, but John stopped her.

"I'm not your father. You can say anything to me."

All pretense slid away. Toni had opened up and he wasn't about to let her walk away and close herself off again.

The leaves rustled as the breeze headed inland, taking the

tension from Toni's shoulders. "I know," she said. "But a lifetime of habits are hard to break."

"Is that why you never let me get close to you? We had something special last month and you just cut it off."

She nodded. "That's part of it."

"Have you ever been in love?"

"Sure," she said, but he didn't know if he believed her. "You?"

"I have." John didn't care what the admission cost him, because he wanted to know the real Toni. Not the one he'd slept with for the past three nights. He wanted to know the secret woman who lived inside her skin. "I can't help the way you were raised," he said. "I can only imagine how oppressive it must have been not being able to express your opinion. But as an adult, you have the power to make choices. You chose to stand up for my mother and you chose to wait for me tonight."

Toni's lips quirked into a smile. "What does that mean?"

John couldn't help himself. "You want me."

She laughed and raised her delicate hand. A waiter appeared from the shadows. "What can I get de queen and her man?"

"Water, please."

"Nothing for me," John said.

"Right away," the waiter answered with a lingering look.

John hid a small smile as he watched the man go. Toni was beautiful and she didn't even know it. He wanted to make love to her more than anything.

Her water was delivered and when she finished, they stood.

"What are you doing, Mr. Roberts?"

He slid his arm around her back. "I always tell my account executives, planning and execution are key to a successful sale."

John guided her toward the elevator, her pulse kicking up in anticipation. "What does that have to do with me?" she said.

They stepped inside and rode the elevator to her floor. "I'm planning to execute a night of seduction and then move on to plan B."

He loved the catch in her breath when she said, "Plan B?"

Behind her suite door, John unzipped Toni's dress and touched his lips to the curve of her shoulder.

"You're going to love it. I guarantee it."

SEVEN

Toni lay spent in her bed, the cool cotton sheets feeling delicious against her warm skin. John hadn't let her get a bit of rest all night. Just the thought of his mouth and hands working wonders on her body made her want him again. But she was glad for the respite, no matter how brief.

John had left an hour ago to escort his mother to the airport, and had promised to return to finish what he'd started. He'd made love to her like a man possessed, a man intent on leaving his mark. And he had. Indelibly, unmistakably, he'd branded her, and she wanted him like an addict craved a fix.

Toni rolled onto her back and stared at the ceiling. What was happening to her? She'd wanted John from the moment she'd seen him approaching her their first day on the island. But the difference now was that she wanted him not only in her bed, but permanently, in her heart.

Sex wasn't supposed to be that good. She sighed, knowing it wasn't just the physical love that had suddenly been fulfilled. John was the answer to questions that had lived inside her heart for her entire adult life.

Toni bunched the pillow beneath her head. She'd lied to John when she'd said she'd been in love before. She hadn't ever felt love like this.

The breath she expelled hurt. She had fallen in love with a man whom she'd resisted for a long time. A man she found wildly attractive. A man she had more in common with than not. A man she could imagine living in her world, in her life.

A man who might one day soon be the cause of her first unemployment check.

The weight of the dilemma rushed in on Toni as she filled

the tub and soaked in lavender-scented water. How was she going to get herself out of this fix? She was in love with John and one of them was going to be out of a job.

No matter how often John had reassured her that he was a modern man and didn't have a problem with her taking up for his mother, she wasn't so sure about how he'd feel if he were to get fired. It bothered her that John wasn't more concerned. That he was relaxed in front of the executives by day, and attentive to her every need at night.

She'd watched him last night with his mother. He loved and respected her in the way Toni wished her father could have for her.

On the one hand, Toni felt liberated. The nagging fear of crossing the line with John had dissipated like a cool front passing over the tropical island.

John had helped her. Part of the night, they'd talked about the differences and similarities of their upbringing, and where they now stood with male/female relationships. The other part of the night, he'd made crazy love to her.

The soft click of the suite door closing signaled John's return. He sauntered in, his gaze lighting up when he saw her.

"Good morning."

"Good morning," she replied. Toni couldn't look at John, fearing that her warring emotions would be all over her face. Therefore, she reached for the one skill she'd perfected: politeness. "Your mother get off okay?"

"Let's not do this."

Toni's stomach flopped. What was happening? "Do what?" she asked calmly, afraid John saw what she wanted to hide.

"Let's not act like polite strangers when you've seen me naked and I've seen you naked." His voice hitched and his words drove at her heart. He walked toward her, his intentions reflected in his smoldering gaze. "If we can't be expressive in public, damn it, I want it in private. I love holding you in my arms. Watching your face when I give you pleasure. I love teasing you crazy and I love tasting you. I love the feel of your nipples against my palm and how they taste against my tongue. You're a hottie." John reached out and touched her lip with his thumb. "I love watching you come."

Every worry that had plagued her in his absence disappeared as she slid up on tiptoe. She loved the freedom he offered by being a generous lover, and she looped her arms around his neck. John met her mouth in a lingering kiss.

"I—" she started, then drew in a deep breath. "I love the feel of your tongue when it slides inside my mouth. I love to feel it against my neck, arms, and legs." Her voice grew husky as his lips drew a diagram from her words. "And everywhere in between. I love the feel of you inside me, the smell," she said as she pushed off her panties and he lifted her and laid her on the bed.

When he moved over her, she looked into his eyes.

"The swell. The feel. The—oh—" He entered her in one swift motion. "The depth. Yes. You. I love how you make me feel."

Toni uttered words in time to the thrust and retreat of John's body with hers. She heard herself, could see the pleasure her words brought in his eyes. She couldn't stop until they reached the plateau and he crushed his mouth to hers, their final burst sending them into paradise together.

Toni lay beneath him, her face wet, his breath hot against her damp skin. This man was *the* man for her. Her heart knew, but her mind was taking its time catching up.

John pulled from her and slipped from the remainder of his clothes. He seemed so serious. As he stripped her skirt and top from her body, Toni reached for him.

Her thoughts had returned to the job and the "what ifs" of tomorrow. John also seemed preoccupied, but Toni left him alone with his thoughts.

She wanted to ask him what was wrong, but couldn't find her voice, so she settled for the tranquility of the moment. The whisk of the fan above their heads. The buzz of a lonely mosquito. The feel of her man's arm around her waist. Toni couldn't deny the solace in her heart. She wanted this. The pleasure and the responsibility of loving someone and having her love returned. She wanted this with John and she would tell him once they got home.

Toni fell asleep content with John wrapped around her.

* * *

John boarded the plane heading back to Atlanta and started through first class to his seat in business class. Toni sat alone, one of the perks of being the sales manager of the year, her gaze on the distant sky.

She'd withdrawn the past few days, even though he'd tried to make it damned hard for her.

They'd made love every day and spent every moment together, which didn't go unnoticed by the other company executives, but John didn't care. He'd reached the Toni he'd known was there. The hidden woman. The woman who'd occupied his thoughts and filled his heart.

He couldn't resist reaching out to her once more. He turned and headed back up to first class. Sitting beside her, he held up a hand to stave off the flight attendant. "Sir, that seat is reserved for another passenger."

"I'll only be a moment." She nodded and assisted another passenger.

Toni looked amused as she gazed at him. "John, what are you doing?"

"Where are you, Toni?"

She knew what he meant. It was just like John to cut to the heart of the matter. Mentally she was back in Atlanta, in her office, closing deals, possibly the one of her lifetime. She'd talked to Willis, but he'd been noncommittal. She had expected at least a clue, something to let her know of his decision.

"I'm right here," she finally answered. "Heading home."

"Is that all?"

Toni didn't want to be pushed, but John didn't heed nonverbal warnings. He wanted what he wanted when he wanted it, and she respected that, because he also knew when to give her space.

"If you must know everything, Mr. Roberts, I'm thinking—"

"Worrying," he added.

Toni nodded. "About you and me. About the fact that one of us will get the job and the other won't."

He stared into her eyes and took her hand. "Let me ask you something. Can you do anything about it today?"

Possibilities ran through her mind and Toni knew she'd exhausted all of them. "No, I can't."

"Then worrying needlessly isn't going to get you anywhere. Tomorrow will be here soon enough." His gaze burned into her. "I'm not worried, Toni."

"You're right. I know I shouldn't worry, but I've wanted this for a long time. We both have a great chance to make a difference. You're smart and have lots of experience."

"Stop."

Toni dropped her head. "But I want to win. Is that so terrible?" she whispered.

John leaned in and spoke gently into her ear. "No, that's what makes you the best at what you do."

A woman boarded and gave John a quizzical look.

He started to rise, then leaned over and kissed Toni on the cheek. "Have a good flight and get some rest."

She grabbed his hand. "My place or yours?"

His eyebrows rose in surprise. "Mine."

She stood and kissed him full on the lips. "Good."

EIGHT

"Toni, congratulations! You're the new vice president of sales."

Toni counted back from five, letting the words sink in. They echoed inside her body and settled at the bottom of her empty stomach, filling her with double doses of delight and disappointment.

"You worked hard, and I recognized that," Willis said, his eyes expectant. "So what do you think?"

Toni hoped her response sounded genuine. "Thank you, Willis. I don't know what to say."

Her boss gave her an understanding look. "I know rumors have been circulating for weeks about the company and this difficult transition. We've hit a rough patch, but with you as the head of sales, we can't go wrong."

Toni shook his hand. "I won't let you down." He walked with her to his closed office door.

Hollow, Toni felt as if her face was going to fall off from the false smile she managed to keep in place. She'd gotten the job.

At one time, that was all that mattered. But now she felt sad, scared and anxious. *Where is John?* The repercussions of her success left only one alternative for him. "Sir, when is everything effective?"

Willis drew his hand over his jaw. "Immediately."

Toni held herself erect when all she wanted to do was sit down with John and talk. "Was there no other way?"

Willis shook his head. "There wasn't, Toni. We're losing some great people, but we can't duplicate talent. Your team outperformed every other division. With you in the lead, the sales force will do well. I'm expecting results."

"You'll get them."

Where is John? Has he left? She didn't want to seem ungrateful, but she was worried about her man. "Thank you, sir," she said, and hurried down the hall. The other managers that had been let go occupied conference rooms one and two, giving pertinent information to their superiors. Toni felt nothing.

The halls were quiet, the atmosphere heavy as she passed two of the administrative staff. They gave her pleasant smiles, but this wasn't a day to celebrate.

As employees of Ziotech, everyone enjoyed the comfortable work environment, but the backlash of the layoffs would mar the easygoing atmosphere for quite a while.

She rounded the corner and stuck her head into John's empty office. Emotion flooded her body and tears stung her eyes. She would not cry, she thought, as she headed back to her office. He was still in the building somewhere.

John wouldn't leave without saying good-bye.

Since they'd returned from the President's Club two weeks ago, they'd spent every night together, and had talked about everything except this inevitable moment.

John had wanted to, but Toni had refused, not wanting to face this moment before now. *Some leader,* she thought as she sank into her visitor's chair and rubbed her temples.

A promotion wasn't supposed to feel this rotten.

Her door clicked just before she heard his voice. "I hear Ziotech has a new, sexy VP of sales."

A sad smile curled her mouth as she lifted her head and looked at him. She nodded. "I got the job."

John came around the chair and dropped down on one knee in front of her. "You've got to work on your celebratory skills."

Toni's gaze came to rest on the man who by his actions had dispelled the myth that men in positions of power used it against women. He'd treated her like a queen and won her heart. "How can you be so calm? What are we going to do?"

"Let's not do this," John said, so serious, for a second Toni thought he was ending their romance.

After he'd stolen her heart, did he want to break up? a

scared little voice inside her wondered. She'd fallen in love with him and she wasn't going to lose him. "Do what?" she asked.

"I'm not going to let you change the subject. I came in here to congratulate you, and I intend to do just that."

His mouth molded to hers in a slow, languid blend of love and desire that ended in a fierce hug.

"Thank you," she whispered. This wasn't at all how she imagined love could be, and Toni considered herself very lucky. She held his face between her hands and kissed him softly. "Thank you, John."

"For what?" he grazed her ear and held her close.

"For caring about my feelings. For being so kind. For being you." A tear slipped down her cheek. "What are we going to do?" she repeated.

John brushed her eyes. "We're going to take a long lunch and celebrate your new job. And then . . ." He smiled mischievously.

Toni liked the way his voice dipped low in secrecy. "Yes, Mr. Roberts? Don't keep me in suspense."

"Much later tonight, we can strategize about the future."

"But what about you?" Toni felt anxious again. This time it was she who wanted to talk things through.

John grabbed her purse from her desk drawer and slipped it under her arm. "All my life my father gave every bit of himself to the world. His best work, his time, his energy.

"He never had anything left for his family. My mother was a hard-working woman, and when multiple sclerosis landed her in that chair, she didn't stop. My father took advantage of her willingness to fight her disease and didn't spend any time with her until she couldn't get around. She regrets not having done more for herself."

John laced his fingers with hers. "I don't want to be my father. I want a family. A wife and children who are going to love me and I'll love them back. But they'll always come first."

Toni's heart leaped in her chest. She loved this man with all that was within her, but she didn't feel complete knowing her dream had come true and his hadn't. She took both his hands in hers and gazed at them.

"What is it, Toni?"

"I'm worried about you. What will you do?"

"I love you."

She nodded. "I know, but what will you do?"

"I've got that covered. Will you marry me?"

"John," she pleaded, hating that his smile was so reassured and calm.

"I asked you a question."

"Yes, now, what do you have covered?"

John loved her tendency to worry about him. Instead of leaping for joy at her own success, Toni's compassion healed him from not having been chosen. That had always been a possibility, and he'd taken the precaution of putting out feelers weeks ago.

He drew her close. "I'm going to love you forever. Respect and adore you and take the offer I received yesterday from Technology Specialist Corporation. Now can we go celebrate your promotion?"

John laughed when Toni playfully smacked his arm. "You are so bad for keeping that from me." Tears blurred her eyes. "I love you. Did you ask me to marry you?"

He wiped her tears, kissed her lips. "Yes, woman. What's your answer?"

Toni felt joyous. "Yes, Mr. Roberts, yes."

Heart's Desire

by Felicia Mason

ONE

"Ooh, I like that one," Allie Reynolds said as a woman in a sarong bathing suit walked by. "Let's pick her."

"Nah. Her legs are too skinny," seven-year-old D.J. said, rejecting his big sister's pick. "Remember, Dad's a leg man."

"Yeah, chicken legs. He likes wings, too," Karenna added. The four-year-old hovered behind her siblings, waiting her chance to spy through the binoculars. "When's it gonna be my turn?" she whined.

"Shh," Allie warned. "If Dad catches us, we're goners."

"Check it out! Check it out! New group at three o'clock." D.J.'s excited whisper sent three curious gazes toward the reception desk, where a large group of tourists gathered to check into the Caribbean resort.

The three children, tucked behind an indoor grove of palm trees and tropical plants, commanded a bird's-eye view of the hotel lobby. They'd promised their dad that they could manage to stay put and out of trouble in the few minutes it took him to grab the snorkeling gear needed for that afternoon's lagoon foray.

"I can't see," Karenna complained.

D.J. handed her the binoculars. "Don't drop 'em, either."

"I'll bet we find somebody in this group," Allie predicted.

"Yeah," D.J. said. "Look at the lady with the big earrings. She's pretty. I can't see her legs, though, suitcases are in the way."

"I still can't see anything."

"You're looking in the wrong side." Shaking his head, D.J. turned the binoculars the right way and held them out to the little girl. "Look at the one with the big bird earrings."

* * *

A pounding headache didn't exactly qualify as the best way to launch a week-long Bahamian vacation. But a couple of aspirin, a hot shower, and an escape from Mile-a-Minute Millie sounded a lot like heaven to Lucia.

Hoisting her garment bag on her shoulder, she glanced around. Sunshine spilled through the lobby atrium. Tropical plants, some in full bloom, boosted the already alive-with-energy atmosphere of the resort. This place was really nice, exactly what she needed. Winning that WJAM contest had been a stroke of luck.

"Lucia Heart Allen."

Lucia winced at the way the woman pronounced her name, like Lucy with an A tucked on the end.

"It's Lou-CHEE-a," she said, stepping forward.

"Sorry about that," the woman said with a smile. "It's going to take me a day or so to get everyone straight."

"Maybe we'll be in adjoining rooms," Millie piped up from just behind Lucia.

Lord, please don't punish me that way.

The radio station's on-site coordinator handed Lucia a small envelope. "Remember," she said, facing the group, "you'll need to wear the purple wristband tonight to get into our mixer. It's at the pavilion adjacent to the hotel. You'll find the wristbands, the key to your room, a map of the resort, and some other information in your packets."

"Christian Ambrose," she called out next. As the man stepped forward to claim his room key, Lucia took the chance to scope out the rest of the Bahamian Getaway contest winners. Fifteen in all, the small group would spend a week in the Bahamas courtesy of WJAM-FM, "Where we jam so you can."

The contest winners were easy to pick out; each one carried a tote bag with the station's call letters and slogan emblazoned in orange and purple. She'd met Millie—who'd apparently gathered a dossier on each person in the group—on the plane and had said hello to the hunk with two earrings as they hailed a cab to the resort. Lucia wondered if he was single, straight, and available.

She smiled. She had plenty of time to find out.

A young couple holding hands were next up. The contest prize was a week-long trip for one person, but some people had opted to pay a reduced fee to bring along their partners or friends.

Cisco Rollins pimped his way to the tour coordinator to snag his room key, multiple gold chains gleaming on his chest between the edges of an open-neck shirt.

"Mack Daddy thinks he has it going on," a woman said under her breath.

Lucia smiled. "Well, the seventies are alive and well in the new millennium. Hi, I'm Lucia," she said, introducing herself.

"Vonda Drake. I live on the Peninsula. Love your earrings. Are those parrots or macaws?"

"Thanks. And parrots," Lucia said. "I wanted something tropical to get in the mood. I'm from Virginia Beach," she added.

"Where are you?" Vonda asked, holding up her room key.

Lucia lifted the envelope to look at her room assignment. "I have 805. What about you?"

"Eight-oh-seven. Looks like we're next door to each other. I'm gonna head on upstairs. See you tonight at the party."

Deciding that getting settled in her room sounded like a good idea, Lucia lifted the handle on her rolling bag and headed toward the bank of elevators.

"Hold up there, Lucy, and what's your name, Vanna. Ah don't think Ah introduced myself to y'all."

Vonda kept right on walking. Lucia wanted to ignore the man, too. Particularly since he'd called her Lucy. But manners won, at least for the moment. Planting a tolerant smile on her face, Lucia waited to hear him out.

"What are you all doing?"

As one, Allie, D.J., and Karenna Reynolds whirled around.

"Uh, hi, Dad," D.J. said. "We're just standing here. Waiting for you."

David Reynolds raised a brow. His offspring looked guilty, very guilty. Allie's smile shone a bit too bright, D.J.'s words came too fast, and Karenna had something tucked behind her back.

"What do you have there, pumpkin?"

"Nothing, Daddy."

D.J. snatched the binoculars from her hands and held them up. "Just these. We, uh, thought we'd take them along in case we wanted to see what's on the other side of the lagoon." The boy steered his father away from the direction where the surveillance had been taking place.

David handed a blue mesh bag filled with flippers and snorkeling equipment to Allie. "I don't know what you guys are up to, but let's get going before you get into whatever trouble you were brewing."

"Dad," Allie said, planting small hands on small hips, her voice carrying an insulted edge. "You left me in charge of the little kids. Everything's fine."

"Who are you calling a little kid?" D.J. accused. "You're nine years old."

"And you're seven," she said. "That still makes *me* the oldest."

David shook his head. "All right. Enough of that. Let's get this show on the road."

The Reynolds brood headed toward the door. David paused to let a hotel guest pass by. He smiled at the woman's giant parrot earrings as she wheeled her luggage behind her. Had he been interested in women again, she'd be the type he'd want to date—someone with a vitality for life who didn't fear or mind making a bold and grand statement.

Quick on that thought emerged a prick of guilt. Shouldn't the very idea of dating another woman bring a sharp pang of disloyalty racing through his heart?

The absence of it gave David pause. Literally.

"Dad, what's wrong?"

"Huh?" he said, snapping out of the reverie. The tourist with the earrings had stopped to chat with a man. Karenna tugged on his arm and the two older kids stared at him.

D.J. leaned toward Allie. "He must be having what Grandma calls a 'senior moment.' "

Allie nodded her agreement with the assessment.

With a final look at the stylishly attractive—not to mention sexy—woman, David fell in step again. He didn't know whether to be relieved that the level of guilt had diminished through the years or appalled that he no longer carried the weight of grief as heavily as he once did.

His kids had a lot to do with that. Being a single father with a demanding job and three smart and lively children kept him plenty busy. Little time remained to dwell on occasional pangs of loneliness and isolation.

Besides, David was looking forward to spending the day with his children. That, after all, was what this spring vacation was all about—spending time with family, something he aimed to do even more of. He'd presented a proposal recommending a four-day workweek to the operating group at the company where he worked. The plan, developed out of his desire to spend more quality time with the kids, turned out to be a terrific idea for other employees as well. By the time he returned from vacation, the senior management group would have made a decision on the proposal.

"Hey, Dad? What if I scare all the fish away?" Karenna asked.

He chuckled as he scooped the four-year-old into his arms and planted a big, juicy kiss on her cheek. "Not a chance of that happening, pumpkin. They'll see your pretty face, tell all their friends, and you'll have *all* the fish around you."

"Ooh. Maybe we'll see a great white shark," D.J. exclaimed.

Turning around, he made a ferocious face, opened his jaws, and with fingers clawed, advanced on Karenna's bare leg. With menacing sound effects that rivaled any from a Hollywood studio, Allie aided the shark attack.

Karenna yelped and wrapped her arms tighter around her father's neck. But the "shark's" mouth found its target and gnawed on the tasty morsel of young brown flesh.

"Daaad!" Squealing and squirming in his arms, Karenna clutched David's neck in a choke hold while trying to kick away from D.J.'s mouth.

"D.J., stop it." But a hint of laughter in David's voice took the sting out of the reprimand.

"It's okay, pumpkin. No shark is going to make lunch of you today. And if one tries, we'll just give him D.J. instead. Deal?"

The four-year-old nodded, then glared at her older brother. Laughing together, the four made it to the beach lagoon without any further sightings of Jaws.

The WJAM group had the rest of the afternoon free to relax and unwind before the first group activity began at the pavilion at six. That left a little less than three hours, and Lucia knew just how she planned to spend the time.

She made fast work of unpacking her bags and quickly discovered she'd brought way too many clothes.

"But who cares, mon?" she said in her best Rasta accent. "A girl's gotta have some fun and be prepared for anything under the sun."

She'd tuned the radio to a station playing reggae and bopped around the room. From her carry-on bag, which was actually the tote from WJAM, she pulled her sketchbook as well as a small case filled with her graphite and colored pencils. Those two items had been tossed in at the last moment. This week was about vacation, not work. But since inspiration could strike at any moment, she wanted to have her tools handy just in case. The tropical atmosphere might yield an idea for a new line or theme of her specialty jewelry.

Seven bathing suits lay spread across the bed. Her biggest worry over the next six days would be which one to wear each day.

Lucia grinned.

The Millie-induced headache forgotten, she contemplated her options. Four of the suits, including two naughty wisps of string ostensibly called bikinis, were brand-new, purchased just for this trip. The radio station's instructions had been pretty generic: resort casual.

Luckily for Lucia, the wasted days spent with her country-club set cousins and ex-husband had finally served a purpose. Resort casual meant relaxed and comfortable, yet stylish.

Choosing a blue tone-on-tone maillot with its matching

cover-up, Lucia headed into the bathroom for a shower before finding the pool.

A little while later, she decided poolside had been an excellent choice. She'd claimed a chaise and a large fluffy white towel. A golden-brown waiter whose name she didn't catch kept her plied with a non-alcoholic fruit concoction that tasted like more—which, of course, he obligingly kept bringing.

The sun didn't beat down too oppressively, and the splash of people in the water added just the right level of background noise.

Now if she could just get the *main* noise to go away.

"So, I told him if he didn't want to pay the four hundred dollars to join me, I had every intention of going by myself. Stella got her groove back in Jamaica or somewhere out here. I can get mine in the Bahamas even if I'm married. Don't you think?"

Lucia turned to face Millie, who'd unfortunately claimed the once-empty chaise closest to her. The woman had dragged it over so they could talk. "I don't know," she answered.

"Are you married, Lucia? That's such a pretty name. Did I tell you that already?" Millie took a sip of her own drink. "Did you see that gorgeous fellow with the earrings? He's in our group, you know. I bet the two of you could, you know." Millie raised a suggestive eyebrow.

Lucia sighed.

This was not how she'd planned to spend the afternoon. The plan, a simple one, had been to soak up some rays and get into a very relaxed Caribbean state of mind.

"No, Millie. I'm not married. But I am a little tired. I'd like to spend the rest of the time before our event taking a little nap."

Was that polite enough? Lucia could only hope that Millie would get the hint.

"Oh, look!" the woman exclaimed. "There's somebody with a WJAM beach towel. I'm going to go introduce myself."

Millie bounded off her chaise to go greet the new arrival.

"Thank goodness," Lucia muttered.

But the goddess of goodness had apparently turned off her pager and wasn't answering emergency prayers that afternoon.

Millie returned a moment later dragging a hapless fellow in her wake. He would have been cute if not for the thick glasses, the sharply receding hairline, the braces, and—yes, there was even an *and*—the green plaid fashion-faux-pas-at-the-golf-course shorts.

"Lucia, meet George. He's in our group. And guess what. He's single, too."

TWO

The rhythms of the steel band called to any and all takers. The contagious melodies created a get-up-and-dance atmosphere that defied even the staunchest wallflowers to keep still.

No shrinking violet, Lucia swayed into the pavilion with a crowd of people, several of them wearing the purple WJAM wristband. She'd changed into a purple and white sarong skirt with a white T-back shirt that left most of her back bare.

"Hmmm, what do you think the wristband is for?" George asked. "There doesn't seem to be an admission charge."

"Probably food or drinks," she said.

Despite the clothes, George turned out not to be so bad. *Which yet again proves you shouldn't judge a book by its cover.* She'd done that once before and had gone so far as to marry the pretty packaging. When the wrapping came off, though, boy, had she been in for a rude surprise.

George was a computer tech back home. And home—or the airport—seemed to be where his luggage got left. The plaid shorts had been a joke gift from his co-workers, one he'd planned to change out of just as soon as he reached the resort. With assurances from the concierge and the radio station representative that his bags were indeed on the island, he'd purchased a pair of tennis shorts and a polo shirt from the gift shop and changed into them. The new look, all in white, was a marked improvement over the getup he'd sported earlier in the day.

"There's a WJAM sign. Our group must be over there." He led the way to the section where resort-clad people with purple wristbands had gathered.

After determining that everyone had been accounted for,

the radio station's deejay, Jeff, asked everyone in the group to gather in a circle.

"No mike here, so y'all got to get close together and share some love so everybody can hear. My name's Deejay Jeff, and before we get started, I want to introduce to y'all the rest of the WJAM crew. Shontae here was in charge of getting all your arrangements and gift bags and badges and stuff."

Pointing toward a woman in a polo shirt with the station's logo, Jeff continued the introductions, ending with "And that there is Gretchen. Since she's paying all the bills, y'all need to be *real* nice to her."

The crowd gathered around and Lucia noticed that the man with the gold chains had his arm draped around a woman's shoulders. Lucia looked around for Vonda and spotted her standing next to the very attractive earring guy.

Vonda smiled and ever so slightly tilted her head toward him. Lucia grinned and mouthed, "Work it, girl."

It obviously didn't take *some* people long to make hookups.

Four of the radio station contest winners brought spouses or friends along on the trip. Not counting Mile-a-Minute Millie, who was mad at her husband, that meant the remaining ten winners were single. Lucia quickly did the rest of the math. George was single. She herself was available—but not looking, thank you very much—which left three people, two of whom were female.

So much for matchmaking, she thought.

"Tonight we're just gonna have some fun," Deejay Jeff said. "Your wristband gets you all the food and alcohol you can stand. This is a party the hotel throws every Wednesday, Friday, and Saturday night. So you're welcome to come on back while we're here. But you'll be picking up the tab for your eats and drinks if you return some other night. Right, Gretchen?"

"That's right," she called out.

"Y'all need to try some of the conch fritters before you leave. That's some good eatin' that you ain't gonna find in Norfolk and Virginia Beach. There's a terrific band playing and I'll be watching to see that everybody gets on the dance floor."

The group started to disperse. "One more thing," Jeff said. "When the band takes their first break, which should be in about forty-five minutes, y'all will need to make your way back over here. Miss Shontae has some games and prizes planned for you."

George turned to Lucia. "Food or dance floor?"

"Sustenance first. Then we'll work it all off," she said with a grin.

Everyone in the WJAM group must have made the same decision, because the line at the buffet tables had plenty of purple wristbands reaching for plates.

"Daddy, let's go to the music."

Karenna emerged from the bathroom and joined her father, brother, and sister on the balcony of the hotel room. Their two rooms overlooked the ocean. The sound of the steel band and the smoky sweet scent of barbecue tempted them to join the festivities in the resort's tent-draped pavilion.

"We were just talking about that," David said, as Karenna settled near his feet on the chaise.

"So we can go, Dad?" D.J. asked.

"Why not? Go get dressed," he said.

"Yippee!"

The Reynolds children were up in a flash and off to change into clean short sets. David crossed his legs and tucked his arms behind his head.

"Now, this is living."

The kids had done well snorkeling. They all swam like fish, so the only problem came when he finally called it quits. Coaxing the three out of the water had taken some effort—as well as a promise from Dad that they'd snorkel again before leaving.

David, however, was the one closest to throwing a tantrum. He'd enjoyed their first two days on the island and found himself a little reluctant to turn his kids over to the activities director. When it came time to pick a hotel, this one beat out the others because of its extensive kids' program. David signed them up to attend two of the five days the family would spend on Freeport.

Now, with almost three of those days already gone and him enjoying the kids' company so much, that didn't seem like such a terrific idea.

"Dad!" Allie called from inside. "Somebody's knocking on the door."

David swung his legs over the chaise and went to answer the summons. Since he hadn't ordered room service, he could only wonder who was knocking. Karenna, D.J., and Allie knew not to open doors to strangers. The three, after calling for him, went about the business of donning shirts and sandals while David saw to their caller.

"Ahoy there, mate. I'm looking for my recruits."

David laughed and opened the door wider for the pirate to enter the room. "Hey, guys. Somebody's here for you."

The three kids came running and all screeched to a stop when they saw the pirate decked out in black knee britches, a red-and-white-striped shirt, tricorn hat, and eye patch. A large sack draped across his chest featured a cartoon skull and crossbones. The pirate consulted a clipboard with the resort's logo stenciled on the back.

"Well, shiver me timbers. Look at this. Not one, not two, but three buccaneers to join our merry band."

D.J.'s mouth dropped open. Allie grinned and Karenna clutched David's leg.

"Which one of you mates is Allison Reynolds?" the pirate boomed.

Eyes wide, Allie stepped forward. "I'm Allison. But everybody calls me Allie."

"I already know that. Says so right here," the pirate said, tapping his clipboard while sizing her up. "Hmmm. You'll do just fine. Stand there," he said, pointing toward a wall.

With a glance toward her father, Allie marched to the designated spot.

"David Reynolds Jr.!" the pirate hollered.

D.J. jumped forward and gave a smart salute. "D.J. at your service, sir!"

"Oh, you give a pirate a free 'sir' and you make me work for it," David said.

D.J. shrugged and grinned at his father.

"Ah, I like enthusiasm on my crew. Excellent. Excellent. You'll be a fine mate."

The pirate then crouched down to get eye level with Karenna. "And you must be Karenna Reynolds," he said, the ferocious thunder gone from his voice.

Karenna nodded but didn't let go of the safe harbor of her father's legs.

The pirate nodded toward the two older kids. "They're gonna join my merry band and have some fun. Would you like to come along, too?"

The little girl bit her lip and looked up at David.

"It's okay, pumpkin."

"Yeah, Karenna. We're headed for adventure," D.J. said.

With one eye on the pirate and the other on her brother and sister, Karenna slowly made her way to the place where her siblings waited. She nestled between them and clutched one of their hands on each side.

The pirate nodded. "Well, looks like I've captured another three recruits for my merry band." The pirate handed the clipboard and an ink pen to David and approached the three children.

"Our adventure begins tomorrow at 0900 hours. You'll need to bring your kits with you," he said, reaching into his sack. He pulled out three small red duffel bags and handed one to each child.

Then he reached in again and produced three tricorn hats, just like the one he wore. Each black hat had a name embroidered in gold thread on the side, one for Allie, one for D.J., and one for Karenna.

David handed the signed release form back to the pirate as the kids settled their hats on their heads.

"Thanks, Mr. Reynolds," the pirate said in a normal voice just loud enough for David to hear. "We'll have them back at five o'clock each day. If you want to join us for lunch or any of the activities, here's a copy of the schedule. The concierge can direct you to the Pirate's Den and Cove."

The pirate whirled around. "As for you, me fine buccaroos," he said with a menacing finger surveying each child, "I'll see you tomorrow at 0900 sharp!"

He swept out of the room and the kids tore straight to the beds to dump their pirate kits. David closed the door and then went to see what kinds of goodies they had.

"Dad, what's 0900 hours?" D.J. asked.

"Nine o'clock in the morning. That means you have to be up, dressed and to have finished your breakfast *before* he comes for you."

"Okay, cool," Allie said. "Ooh, look, a treasure map."

David just shook his head. It took them until eleven to get up and at it this morning.

And it took another thirty minutes before he could round them up to head to dinner and the music.

After the pirate's performance, David knew the kids would probably have a ton of fun with other vacationing children. He hated admitting it, but he felt a bit jealous. Where was a pirate or activities director or someone to come plan *his* next two days?

"Okay. This is a good spot. All we have to do is find somebody we all agree on," Allie said.

"And remember to look for wedding rings. We don't want any of those," D.J. added.

"Daddy's not going to like this," Karenna said.

D.J. threw up his hands. "Look at him. He's pathetic." The boy's outstretched arm guided the girls' view to where their father stood several yards away. A woman clearly eyed him, but David appeared oblivious.

"That woman is all over him and he's acting all janky," D.J. said.

"What's that mean?" Karenna asked.

Rolling his eyes, D.J. just pointed. "Watch, you'll see."

The three watched as a woman in a black skirt and bikini top sidled up to their father at the buffet table. The two exchanged a few words.

"Come on, Dad. That's it. You can do it," D.J. coached from the table where they waited.

A moment later, though, the woman snatched a roll and walked away in an obvious huff.

"And he fouls," D.J. said, his shoulders slumping. "Again."

Allie shook her head. "The man is without a prayer." She turned to her sister. "Karenna, we all agreed. You can't back out now."

"Well, let me pick."

"Fine," D.J. said. "There's a room full of women here. Pick one."

Karenna looked around. "What about her?" she said, pointing to a curly-haired woman wearing a white shirt and a purple and white skirt. "Oh, never mind. She's with her husband," she said, after spying a man sitting next to the woman. Karenna bit her lower lip and gazed around the pavilion. "There's one. And she's by herself."

Allie and D.J. honed in on Karenna's pick.

"Not bad," D.J. said. "Nice smile. No ring. Let's make sure she's not with somebody. If not, we can go to work."

"Here you go," David said, returning to their table. "More barbecue for Karenna. Fruit for Allie and punch for me."

Karenna looked at the proffered food. "I want my own plate. My food is touching hers."

"The food is clean. The plate is clean, Karenna. So stop that whining."

The two older kids shared a look. "I'll go get her a plate, Dad," Allie offered.

"And I think I'll grab some more punch, too," D.J. said.

David took a seat facing a still-pouting Karenna. "All right," he told them. "Sit down, Karenna."

Behind his father's back, D.J. gave Karenna the thumbs-up sign as he and Allie went off on their surveillance mission.

In the cordoned off WJAM section, Lucia sat at a table eating dessert with George, one of the married couples, and Gretchen from the radio station.

"Does everyone like the resort?" Gretchen asked.

"Oh, the hotel is lovely," one of the older ladies enthused. "I had a massage this afternoon." She batted her eyes and wiggled her fingers in delight.

Gretchen and the others chuckled.

"We looked for a place that had a good mix of options for families, singles, and couples," she said. "The last time we did this, the trip was to Jamaica and about five of the winners brought their entire families with them."

"What happens after this?" George asked.

"This dinner and the mixer is all we've planned for tonight. But before everyone leaves, Shontae has an updated itinerary she wants to pass out. There's a group tour tomorrow morning and the afternoon is golf or tennis. We'll also do sign-ups for the deep-sea fishing trip and scuba-diving lessons."

George nodded. "You can count me in on the fishing trip. I plan to land a big ol' something. What's out there? Cobia, tuna, marlin? I'm going to get one of them."

Chuckles were shared around the table, but Lucia didn't laugh. The last thing she wanted was to get bogged down in a lot of running all over the place. The most strenuous activity she planned to partake of on this trip was guiding the straw from a tropical drink to her waiting mouth.

"Of course," Gretchen said, "some people just decide to lay out on the beach and soak up the sun."

"Now you're talking my plan," Lucia said.

"I brought a new bathing suit with me," the older woman told her husband. "Did you see how pretty the water is?"

The table conversation shifted to the look of the water in the Bahamas versus the beaches back home in Virginia. A few minutes later, Lucia excused herself to go in search of the ladies' room.

At the Reynoldses' table, Karenna had had an accident.

"Oh, pumpkin. Look at your shirt," David said, surveying what appeared to be an impossible mix of red fruit punch and barbecue sauce dripping down the girl's lemon-yellow halter top.

"Come on, let's see if we can get you cleaned up." Taking her hand, David headed toward the rest rooms.

At the doors, he paused facing a men's room and a ladies' room. He'd gotten used to either Allie seeing to her younger sister's rest room needs or the third option available in the States: a family room for single parents and others who had need of mixed gender facilities.

"Uh, pumpkin . . ."

"Ah, it's the age-old problem for dads. Which rest room to use."

David turned around and a smile spread across his face, a slightly embarrassed one, but nonetheless a smile. It was the woman he'd seen in the lobby. And she was even prettier up close and personal. The soft curls in her hair matched the soft look of her skin.

"Daddy, I think I have to go now, too."

"Oh, uh . . ."

Lucia stepped forward. "I'll take her. And just so you don't panic or think I'm a child molester, my name's Lucia Heart Allen. I don't have any kids, but I do have all of her parts, which is what matters right this moment."

"Her shirt . . ."

Lucia glanced at the sticky mess, then offered him a bright smile. "Don't worry. We've got it under control."

Taking the little girl's hand, Lucia led her into the ladies' room. "What's your name?"

"Karenna."

"Well, that's a very pretty name. When I was growing up . . ."

David couldn't hear the rest of their conversation. Apparently a second door separated the actual rest room area from where he stood. Grateful that the woman had come along, he was even more surprised to discover that in just that brief moment, he'd memorized everything about her.

A riot of soft curls framed her face, which had the reddish undertones of a summer sunset. He'd missed the color of her eyes, but only because her smile was so sweet, it tempted him like ripe fruit on the vine. The curve of her hips evident from the form-fitting sarong skirt sent his thoughts racing along corridors that hadn't been traveled in a while.

Suddenly, he cleared his throat and shoved his hands in the pockets of his slacks. "Oh, boy."

He ran a hand over his hair and looked around, ever so grateful that mind-reading was just a thing of fiction.

David couldn't remember the last time he'd noticed a woman. That's because he hadn't paid much, if any, attention at all to women in the past few years. He'd been too busy raising his kids and making a living.

There was no real reason he didn't date—well, except for the really big one. And that gave him considerable pause, about the same effect as a bucket of ice water over his head.

Still, Lucia Heart Allen had the most delightful twinkle in her eyes . . .

THREE

A few minutes later, Lucia emerged from the rest room holding Karenna's hand. David stopped short when he took a look at his daughter. His gaze went from Karenna to Lucia then back to Karenna.

"What happened in there?" he asked, wagging a finger between the two.

"Look, Daddy, Miss Lucky made a new shirt for me. Isn't it pretty?"

"I see, pumpkin." David's gaze connected with Lucia's, the questions obvious in his eyes. "Lucky?"

Lucia glanced down at the girl, then smiled at David. "Short for Lucia, I suppose." Then, "I don't think there's too much hope for her halter top. If it hadn't been yellow . . . Maybe you can just dye it another color."

"But . . ."

"Miss Lucky worked magic, Daddy."

David slipped a hand in a pocket and covered a smile with the other. Karenna was wearing a new halter top, one fashioned from the same material as Lucia's purple and white skirt.

"So, how did this magic work?"

"I had a scarf tied around my waist, just an extra flourish for a bit of pizzazz. A quick twist on the scarf, though, created magic for Karenna."

"Thank you," he said, smiling at Lucia. Her easy grace charmed him. This woman had pizzazz with or without a scarf.

"Anytime," Lucia said. "You have a good evening now, Karenna. And nice meeting you, Karenna's dad."

With a smile, Lucia started walking away.

"Dad, don't let her get away," Karenna whispered.

David stared down at the girl holding his hand. Then his gaze focused again on the woman, whose hips swayed to the beat of the steel band's island music.

"Lucia!"

She stopped and turned.

Suddenly at a loss for words now that he had her attention, David merely waved and said, "Thank you."

Lucia waved back, then disappeared into the crowd.

Beside him, Karenna slapped her forehead. "Poor Dad. You blew it again."

His attention focused on the place Lucia last stood, it took a moment for him to again focus in on Karenna.

"What was that, pumpkin?"

The little girl just shook her head.

An hour later, the pavilion party was in full swing. The band opened its second set with a trio of tunes for the young and the young at heart. From the sidelines, David watched his children shimmy, shake, and jump with all the other kids. Adults ringed the room shouting support while clapping to the beat.

Across the way, David spied Lucia Heart Allen. Her infectious smile made his own broaden. Had someone asked, he didn't know if he'd be able to determine whether it was the woman and her smile or the music and the night that had lifted his spirits in such a glorious way.

Then he saw something that took his breath away.

Karenna ran up to the woman, grabbed her hand, and dragged her onto the dance floor. Holding hands, Lucia and Karenna did the Twist and Shout.

A second later, David himself was yanked onto the dance floor.

"Come on, Dad. The deejay said every kid should grab an adult."

"When did he say—"

A woman bumped into him and David's words were cut off. He grabbed for her waist to steady her and found himself face to face with . . . well, to be kind, not the most attractive woman on the planet.

"Hey, I like it like that," she said a moment before wrapping her arms around his neck and grinding her pelvis into his.

David scooted his rear end back, trying to get out of her clutches, or at the very least, to get some much needed air between their bodies.

"Ma'am, it's a G-rated program tonight. My kids—"

But the woman thrust forward, shimmying her bosom in his face. David's eyes widened.

Watching the fiasco, D.J. quickly grabbed another partner. He met Allie, who twirled her own partner toward the woman attacking their dad.

"Ready?" D.J. hollered above the music.

Allie nodded.

As the beat switched to a conga rhythm, Allie twirled her dance partner off to the woman D.J. was dancing with. Allie went into her father's arms and that left D.J. to dance with Jungle Woman.

"Oh, no. Not me," he said before ducking away.

Nonplussed, the woman turned and started dancing by herself.

"Having fun, sweetie?" David asked Allie.

"This is great!"

A shout and cheer rent the air and all eyes turned toward the noise.

"Come on, everybody. Join the pretty ladies," the deejay said. "Everybody now, party!"

Leading the conga line was none other than Karenna, who had Lucia Heart Allen right behind her. David threw his head back in laughter as he watched his daughter shuffle-kick her short legs to the beat.

"Come on, Dad." Allie tugged on his arm and a moment later, they, too, were attached to the snaking line that traveled around the pavilion. At one point, David and Lucia made eye contact, the air between them crackling with laughter and fun. Then the beat changed, the tempo increased, and he lost track of her.

The revelry continued for some time. Karenna conked out right in the middle of it all. Cradled in her father's arms, she slept soundly. David let the older two enjoy themselves a little while longer, then called it quits for the entire Reynolds gang.

"But, Dad . . ." D.J. whined.

"*But, Dad* nothing. You three have an early start tomorrow. Karenna's been knocked out for half an hour. You two need to follow suit. Come on."

D.J. and Allie said good-bye to some friends they'd made, then followed their father out of the pavilion.

Lucia watched them leave and blew a kiss to Karenna, who'd shifted in her father's arms.

The little girl waved, then settled her head on her dad's shoulders.

"Cute kid," Vonda said. "Do you have any?"

"No. None of my own. My ex had two demon seeds he called children. They live with their mother."

A hint of a smile curved Lucia's lips as she thought about the little girl named Karenna who'd asked the same question while they were in the rest room.

The girl shortened Lucia to Lucky, and for the first time, Lucia didn't mind, particularly when, unprompted on Lucia's part, the girl automatically added Miss in front of it.

If children were like Karenna, well-behaved and mannerly, she might like them a little better. Unfortunately, Lucia's personal experience with her former stepchildren had taught her all she ever wanted to know about children. And that, in a nutshell, was that she didn't want any.

Much later that night, after the children were all asleep, David sat in a chair on the balcony, his feet propped on the edge of the chaise. In his hands he held the length of material Lucia had fashioned into a top for Karenna.

The scarf still had the faint scent of a light perfume, and he wondered if the scent would be stronger on the woman or if her skin would be as soft as it looked.

Closing his eyes, David ran the cloth across his face and under his nose. The image of her dancing and swinging Karenna in a joyful circle had been indelibly stamped into his memory. The music tonight had been fast and fun and frenetic. But David wondered what it might be like to dance a soulful melody with Lucia Heart Allen, just the two of them in the sand while the Caribbean surf lapped at their feet.

When he opened his eyes, a full spring moon shone bright onto the beach below. With a realization that was both surprising and personally illuminating, David admitted that right now, in this particular moment, the thing he wanted most was to see Lucia dancing in the moonlight.

In her room, Lucia glanced at the WJAM itinerary for the week, a copy of which had been under her door when she returned from the pavilion. The nonstop, jam-packed schedule left little time to just kick back and relax.

"I don't think so, people," she said, tossing the schedule onto the desk top.

In the morning, she'd decide if she'd spend the day at the pool or on the beach.

Right now, though, as she listened to the waves break on the shore, she thought about the little girl Karenna. Well, actually, she thought about Karenna's tall, dark, and handsome father. Notwithstanding the fluke that had been her husband, who'd been a fair-skinned pretty boy of average height, Lucia liked her men tall and very dark.

A second later, she laughed.

"Yeah, right, Miss Lucky. More like unlucky." Her less-than-stellar track record with the opposite sex was proof positive that some people needed to focus on other talents.

She reached for her sketchbook and a pencil. A few minutes later, the image of Karenna's father stared back at her: finely sculpted lips, a broad nose, wise, dark eyes. But something was missing. She stared at the sketch trying to determine what didn't feel right about it.

Rolling a malleable eraser between her fingers, she thought a minute longer. Then, with a nod, she erased a small section and with quick strokes, added a touch here and there.

It was the mouth that she'd worked on. A hint of a pleased smile now played at his lips. That's what she remembered most about Karenna's father. He looked content and at ease with life and his family.

As she put the sketchbook away, Lucia wondered what it might take in her own life to have that look of contentment.

* * *

The next afternoon David wandered around a bit. He even peeked in at the Pirate's Cove to see what the kids were up to. They waved and kept right on playing with about twenty other children.

"They must make a killing on kids alone," he said of the resort's twelve-and-under program.

Moving on, he thought about, then rejected, the idea of taking in a few holes of golf at one of the resort's two courses. What he really wanted to do was find Lucia Heart Allen.

He'd spent much of the night thinking about her. And since that was such an abberration in and of itself, he wanted to see if maybe the light of day changed his thinking. It had been so long since the opposite sex sparked genuine male interest in him, he felt it necessary to see if the magic, as Karenna had put it, was for real, or simply a product of the sultry Caribbean night and the elemental rhythms of the steel drums.

With a mission, he headed back toward the front desk.

"Excuse me," he said to a woman sitting behind the concierge desk. "Could you tell me what room Ms. Lucia Heart Allen is in?"

"I'm sorry, sir. We don't give out guest room numbers."

David frowned. "Oh. Well, I guess that is wise. And safe," he added. "Well, thanks anyway."

Not sure what to try next, and suddenly wondering why he was acting like a sixteen-year-old, he made his way to the lagoon where he and the kids had snorkeled. Slipping off his sandals, he walked along the beach taking in the sights. A few people splashed around out in the water while others walked along the sand searching for shells and enjoying the day.

Facing the ocean, he stared at the incredibly blue water and sighed.

"Well, that's not the sort of sound people usually make on vacation."

He turned to face the voice, and there she was—just as beautiful and vibrant as he remembered. Today a long white cover-up trailed behind her, lifting when the breeze did. A grin split his face.

"Hello."

"Hi, there, Karenna's dad. So, why are you out here sighing into the wind?"

His smile, self-deprecating, gave witness to his thoughts.

"I cannot believe this. I'm at a resort and I'm bored."

"Maybe that's because you haven't found the right activity yet," she said.

He nodded. "Could be." Then, reaching for her hand to shake, he said, "I'm David. David Reynolds. And thank you again for last night. I'll get your scarf back to you. As a matter of fact, I just asked about you at the front desk but they wouldn't give me your room number."

"I know."

For a second he looked confused. "You know the policy or you know I was asking about you?"

Lucia smiled. "Both, actually. The policy is pretty standard at hotels. And I heard you say my name, so I followed you. I'm not a stalker, though," she quickly added. "Just curious."

"What were you curious about?"

She laced her hands in front of her and looked out over the expanse of the lagoon. "A lot of things," she just said.

"Hmmm."

Small talk had never been his forte. He could talk for hours about Disney's latest animated movie or the best way to get bubble gum or peanut butter out of a girl's hair. And experience taught him that after the first few words explaining his job, most people's eyes glazed over and plastic, polite smiles appeared. So adult conversation had its limits as well.

"Karenna is an angel. She told me she's almost five."

David smiled as they began to walk. "That *almost* is very important. She wasn't quite sure if declaring that she's four and three quarters was the thing to do. So she makes sure she lets everyone know that five is quickly approaching."

"You have other children?"

"A son who's seven and a daughter who is nine."

"Oh."

He glanced at her. "You don't have children?"

She spread her arms wide and let them glide through the warm air. "I'm free as a bird," she said. David smiled at her antics until he heard her next words. "I like it like that."

The joy he'd been feeling faded a bit. It would be a tad much to ask a woman to accept three children. Maybe that was why he'd never really pursued a relationship.

"Children are gifts from God," he said.

Lucia stopped walking and she faced him. "Yes, I suppose they can be. I never thought about it quite that way, probably because . . . Well, that's not important." Then, "Are you married, David Reynolds?"

"No. My wife died four years ago."

She reached for his hand and squeezed it. "I'm sorry to hear that. It must be tough being a single parent."

Now he was really confused. One minute she seemed anti-kid, followed by something that sounded a lot like philosophical longing. And now, the touch of her soft hands on his sent what just may have been a tingle up his arm.

"I'm sorry. What did you just say?"

Lucia smiled. "Come on, David Reynolds, single dad. I'll buy you a drink."

They'd reached a tropical stand at the far end of the lagoon, an area separating the lagoon from the deeper water of the ocean. If not for the resort's insignia stamped on the napkins and hardboard coasters, the bamboo hut would have looked as if it had always been there as a refuge to thirsty beachcombers. A resort waiter stood behind the bar.

"What can I get you folks?"

"Something tropical. With all kinds of fruit in it," Lucia said. "No alcohol, please."

"I'll have one of what she gets," David said.

"Two Tropical Sunrises coming up."

The bartender mixed their drinks. Lucia signed the check, then led them to two low lounging chairs strategically placed on the beach to get a good view of a man-made reef.

"Ah, I see your plan now," David said.

Lucia sipped from her drink. "Mmmm," she said on a half sigh, half moan. "This tastes like heaven. What plan is that?"

"You're going to get me in your debt and then call in an extremely high chit."

She chuckled, the sound, to David's ears, a siren call—just like her moan of pleasure had been a moment ago. Turning in her chair to face him, the ribbed edge of her cover-up fell open. David's breath caught. He'd gotten glimpses of her legs as they'd walked. But this . . . this was spectacular.

A silver bathing suit cut high on her thighs exposed a tantalizing length of honey-brown skin. Her legs looked smooth to the touch, like satin. David suddenly and desperately wanted to find out just how her skin felt.

His gaze met hers.

Electricity danced between them. David recognized in her eyes an intimate curiosity that matched his own.

He swallowed. "I . . . I . . ." He set his glass in the sand, securing it deep enough so it wouldn't topple over.

She didn't say anything.

"You're very beautiful, Ms. Allen. And I think I'm out of my element. Excuse me."

With that, he was up and gone.

Lucia stared after him, at first in wonder and then with growing pleasure.

She'd seen the very male evidence of his attraction to her.

"Tall, dark, handsome, and a shy gentleman to boot," she said, settling into her seat. "Imagine that."

FOUR

"Lucia, there you are. We've been looking all over for you!"

Biting back a groan, Lucia turned to see whom Millie referred to as *we*. Shielding her eyes from the sun, she squinted up. "Oh, where's everybody going?"

Eight of the WJAM contest winners all decked out in radio station T-shirts grinned down at her.

"We're headed over to the straw market. There are supposed to be some great deals. Want to come?"

Lucia got up so she didn't have to strain to see everyone. "Why is everybody dressed alike? Where'd you guys get those T-shirts?"

"Shontae was handing them out in the hospitality room. Don't worry. She said there's one for everybody," George informed her.

"We all decided to wear them so nobody gets lost," Millie said. "The man at the front desk says it can be really crowded sometimes, especially when the cruise ships come in. So we thought we'd all wear our new T-shirts."

While most of the island's visitors were tourists, walking around advertising that fact didn't seem like a good idea, at least in Lucia's estimate. And that went doubly so for going to a market where bargaining for prices was standard operating procedure.

"I think I'll take a pass today. I'll get down there before we leave. Have fun, though."

Some of the others waved and headed back in the direction of the main buildings.

"You feeling all right, honey?" Millie asked. "I have a bag full of over-the-counter medicine in the room. I stocked up before coming over here. You never know in these foreign countries," she added in a whisper with a look around, as if one of the native foreigners might overhear.

Lucia smiled, but gave Millie the reassurances the woman needed to hear.

"All right, now," Millie said. "I don't want anything happening to you. By the way," she said with a wink and a nudge, "I think George is a little sweet on you. He's single, you know."

"I know, Millie. You told me yesterday."

Millie waved a hand. "Oh, that's right. I did. Well, I don't want you to let a good one get away. So many of our men are in prisons or they're a little funny, you know," she said, twisting her wrist. "My cousin Bertha's boy . . ."

Okey-dokey now, Lucia thought, taking a deep breath. *I've definitely heard enough.*

"They're waiting for you," Lucia said, pointing toward the group.

Millie threw her hands in the air. "Land's sake. Let me get on now. You try to have some fun. I'll scope out the best bargains for you." The woman took off in a run-jog toward the waiting shoppers.

"You do that," Lucia said, shaking her head.

She ordered a refill on her Tropical Sunrise drink, then settled in her chair to compare David Reynolds with George, the WJAM contest winner.

"Well, that was pretty easy," she said a moment later.

There was no comparison.

One had the look of a man who thrived in his masculinity, was comfortable with life and his place in it, and seemed to be a loving and caring father to his kids. The other, a man who paraded around in a purple and orange T-shirt with dancing stick figures proclaiming "We jam so you can!" just didn't spark her elemental female interest.

Since she barely knew either one of them, the first impressions and initial conversations carried a lot of weight. Even with three kids in tow, she realized she wanted to know more about David.

George was a nice enough guy. As a matter of fact, he

reminded her of the UPS driver who made sure her jewelry supply shipments arrived on time. David, on the other hand, well, something about him exuded a wary sex appeal. And it wasn't just the erection he'd attempted to conceal from her.

She doubted if he even knew just how sexy he was. He stood a little taller than six feet and had broad shoulders. His legs were built like an athlete's; she wondered if he'd played ball at some point. The thought of his legs made her wonder what it might feel like to have her own wrapped around his waist.

"Whew." Lucia fanned herself.

The thorny—make that horny—path her thoughts decided to take surprised her. Since her divorce, she hadn't been in the market or on the prowl for male companionship. But one look at David Reynolds and she was ready and willing.

And from the looks of things earlier, so was he.

"All right, now. Get a grip," she said. Her mind immediately settled on just what she wanted a grip of.

Lucia got up, slipped out of her cover-up and ran straight into the water thinking it might cool her off.

But the naturally warm Caribbean water enveloped her body in a cocoon of sensual heat. She closed her eyes, floating on her back, her face to the sky. As the water gently lapped around her, she imagined what David's hands might feel like caressing her legs, her thighs, her breasts.

Smiling her pleasure at the image and the exquisite feel of the water, she let the fantasy run its course. They'd make love on the beach, reenacting the famous kiss scene from that old movie. Slowly, he'd peel the bathing suit from her body, pausing to worship with his mouth each inch of newly exposed flesh. Then she'd run her hands along the broad length of his—

"Tag! You're it!"

Lucia went down gulping water. A moment later someone pulled her up, coughing and sputtering.

"Sorry, lady. Here, let me help you."

The teen guided Lucia to shallow water, where she got her footing.

"You okay?" he said. "We didn't see you out there."

Lucia bent over, taking deep cleansing breaths. "I'm . . . fine. Thank you."

But it took her a few moments to recover from the experience. Only then did she see the group of teenagers playing with a big striped beach ball near the spot where she'd been floating.

She plopped onto the sand and put her head between her bent knees. "I'm going to take that as a sign," she told the beach.

If just thinking about the man stood to get her drowned, David Reynolds obviously wasn't the one.

Cold water sluiced over David's head. He turned in the shower, not believing what had happened at the beach. The last time he'd responded to a woman like that had been . . .

"So long, I can't remember," he said as he leaned his head on the tile. Water fell across his back.

Eventually, he straightened up, turned off the water, and reached for a towel to dry his hair and body. As he did, he caught a shadowed glimpse of himself in the large mirror. His wet feet slapping on the floor, David went to the mirror and wiped off a circle of space.

He studied his reflection, wondering what Lucia Heart Allen saw when *she* looked at him.

Then it hit him. Lucia Heart Allen. The woman had three names, two of them last names. Sort of like Hillary Rodham Clinton or Marian Wright Edelman.

"Oh, God," he said, dropping his head into his hands. "I've got it for a married woman."

A knock on the door ceased his torture, at least for the moment.

"Just a sec," he called.

He wrapped another towel around his waist and snatched one of the robes the resort left in each guest room.

"I'm coming," he said as he neared the door and secured the robe's belt around his waist.

"Yes?" he said, finally opening the door.

"David Reynolds?"

He stared at the woman. She seemed about his age, mid to

late thirties. Cute and a little plump, she looked like a kinder-garten teacher or someone who used to be the captain of her high school's pep squad. Her hair, cut in an asymmetrical bob, flattered her face. She wore a short-sleeved polka-dot jumpsuit and held what looked like a picnic basket in her hands.

"Yes?" he said, looking beyond her down the hall to see if someone stood either behind her or with her. "Are the kids okay?"

She smiled. "Oh, they're fine. As a matter of fact, they sent me."

He stared at her. "Sent you?"

"Aren't you going to let me in?"

He looked down the hall again. "Uh, I was just getting out of the shower."

"Okay," she said. "I'll wait."

She walked right by him and into the room.

David shook his head, trying to clear the cobwebs that had suddenly taken up residence. He left the door wide open and followed the woman into his own hotel room.

"Do I know you?" he asked, even though he was one hundred percent sure they'd never met.

"I was at the pavilion last night," she said. She placed the picnic basket, a finely made pale wicker hamper, on the round table near the window and started unpacking it.

"I'll just put this right here," she said, moving D.J.'s Game Boy cartridges to an adjoining chair.

She whipped out a red-and-white-checked tablecloth and smoothed it across the expanse of the table, then started pull-ing sandwiches, fruit, plates, and cups from the basket.

"Hold it right there," David said.

She paused. "Yes?"

"Who are you?"

The woman smiled. "Oh, I'm sorry." She came forward and stuck out a hand to greet him. "My name's Marcia Perkins."

Habit made David take her hand and shake it. "Pleased to meet you, Marcia Perkins. Now, why are you here and *what* are you doing?"

"I'm just setting out our lunch. I hope you like grilled tuna. The chef here makes it into a scrumptious salad."

"*Our* lunch?"

She turned and smiled at him. "Of course, silly."

She didn't look crazy. Maybe he was the one going crazy, David thought.

He'd been womanless for nigh on four years, and all of a sudden two pretty ones popped up out of nowhere showing definite interest.

"I wasn't sure if you'd like wine, so I brought a bottle of white and a bottle of sparkling cider."

David glanced at the door, waiting for, at any moment, the television camera crew to run into the room. When none arrived, he chanced a peek at Ms. Perkins. She arranged a small bouquet of flowers in a vase she produced from the basket.

"It doubled as storage space for the corkscrew and silverware. Inventive, huh?"

David folded his arms across his chest. That's when it dawned on him that he wasn't dressed, while a woman he didn't know made herself comfortable in his hotel room, a room he shared with his seven-year-old son.

"All right, Ms. Perkins. The game's over. I don't know who sent you. As a matter of fact, I'm pretty sure you've got the wrong David Reynolds. It's a common enough name. There are probably two of us at this hotel this week."

In his towel and robe, he marched to the table and started repacking the lunch she'd placed out.

"But—"

"It's okay," he said. "I'm sure you and your David Reynolds will have a good chuckle over this."

After tucking the last plate back in the picnic hamper, David guided Ms. Perkins by the elbow and saw her to the door.

"Have a nice day," he said, shutting the door. He applied the security chain and then leaned back on the closed portal.

"Now, *that* was too weird."

"So, Jamar, are you here with both your folks?" D.J. asked.

The two boys were resetting the obstacles on a game they'd been playing with six other kids. Each wore a bandolier, D.J.'s red and Jamar's gold, the sashes indicating they were team captains. Their pirate hats sat at jaunty angles on their heads.

"Nope. Just my moms. Pops lives in California with his new wife. Well, they will when they come back from their honeymoon in Hawaii."

D.J. glanced back at Allie and gave her a thumbs-up sign. So far, so good.

"Is your mom, like, you know, seeing anybody?"

Jamar looked at D.J. "Why you asking?"

D.J. put his arm around the other boy's shoulder. "Let's go over here and talk man to man. Away from the women."

"D.J.," Allie called.

With one hand behind his back, he waved for her to be quiet while he went to have a conversation with the other boy. When they were out of earshot of the other kids, D.J. turned and faced Jamar.

"Here's the story. We, that's me and my two sisters, we're trying to get our dad hooked up. He knows nothing, and I mean *nothing* about trying to get a lady. So we're helping him out, you know."

The other boy stroked his chin. "Yeah, I see where you're going. But I tell you, my moms ain't been too down with the homies lately. That's why we're out here."

"Whatcha mean?"

"My aunts paid for this trip for us," Jamar explained. "They said she needed to get out of town before she killed every Black man on the street. She's still kind of P.O.'d at my dad."

D.J. groaned and made a face. "Oooh. That doesn't sound too good."

"She might be ready in a couple of months. But right now, man, she'd probably bite your pop's head off."

"All right, I understand. Keep an ear out for us, though. We've been scoping the place since we got here. There has to be somebody on the island we can hook him up with."

"You know, Maria's mom is divorced. They're here for a family reunion, a whole bunch of 'em. And her mama is *fine*. I saw her this morning."

"How fine?" D.J. asked.

"I'm talking apple brown betty with sugar on top."

This sounded promising. "That good, huh?"

"You ever seen Jennifer Lopez?"

D.J.'s eyes widened. He nodded.

Jamar leaned closer, the two looking like pirates conspiring about a raid. "Maria's mama could be Jennifer Lopez's twin sister."

The two boys grinned and high-fived each other.

"Now you're talking." Comrades in arms, the two headed back toward the obstacle course where the other children impatiently waited.

"I think it's time Allie and Maria had a little conversation," D.J. told the other boy.

"Hey, D.J., your sister Allie is kinda cute, too."

"Watch it now," D.J. said, yanking his arm from around the other boy's shoulder and balling his fists. "That's my sister you're talking about."

FIVE

"WJAM, the station where we jam so you can, would like to welcome you to our beach party volleyball bash." Deejay Jeff had a microphone this time and was obviously in his element. "Step right up, anybody who wants to jam out here on the beach. Grab a number, evens to the left, odds to the right. Let's make some noise out here!"

Music blared up from speakers the resort set up for the volleyball games.

"Gonna play?" George asked Lucia.

"I'm game," she said, whipping off the shirt that covered the top of her bathing suit. "What about you, Vonda?"

"I don't know," the other woman said. "I haven't played volleyball since I don't know when. And definitely not in the sand. Besides," she said, frowning and inspecting her hands, "I might break a nail."

Lucia laughed and held up her own hands. "That's why it pays to be an artist. Short nails."

"Natural ones, too," George said on the sly as he passed by Lucia's ear.

She smiled but didn't say anything.

"Oooh wee. Volleyball. Now, how do you play this game?" Millie asked, eyeing the net and the assortment of people who'd gathered. "Where'd all these folks come from?"

"The game's open to anyone, Miss Millie," Deejay Jeff said. "Come on out here and show us what you've got. You got game, don't ya?"

"What is that boy talking about?"

A few people laughed, but Millie paid them no mind as she worked her way across the sand in her sneakers. "You just put me on a team and I'll show you some game, all right."

David chuckled at the comment. He'd happened onto the beach after getting dressed, and heard the announcement about the game. His intention had been to watch for a few minutes. Until, that is, he spied Lucia. Then he wondered about his own volleyball skills.

"Hello there."

She turned, a smile transforming her face.

"Well," she said. "Fancy seeing you here."

The man looked even better than he had the last time she saw him. A mesh T-shirt covered well-formed pecs, and white shorts led her gaze along the length of strong legs, well-shaped and muscular—like a runner's.

She hoped her thorough inspection of his physique came across as casual curiosity, particularly since at the moment, she felt anything but casual.

When her gaze finally locked with his, he didn't give any indication that her perusal had been too forward. Except, that is, for the hint of a smile at his mouth.

"Are you joining in?" he asked.

"I am. And you?"

"If you're in, I'm in."

Lucia cocked her head at him. "Well, Mr. David Reynolds, let's see you do your stuff."

They wound up on opposing teams. Deejay Jeff gave the ground rules for participants, then acted as sideline sports commentator as the teams squared off. Lucia and George stood next to each other in the first rotation. When it came her time to serve the ball, encouragement came from the opposite side of the net.

"You can do it, Lucia. Just send that puppy right over here."

Lucia nodded at David, ignored a backward glance from George, and lobbed the ball over the net and straight onto Millie's head.

"Owww!"

"Time! Time," Deejay Jeff called.

Millie rubbed her head, the volleyball now between her feet in the sand. "Girl, you're trying to kill me. I wasn't ready."

Her team members chuckled, and one of the men reached for the ball. "You all right, Miss Millie?"

"I'll be fine. Just wait 'til I'm ready."

"Point for the left side," Deejay Jeff called. Protests ensued, but he was hearing none of it.

"Lucia, you're up again."

Someone tossed Lucia the ball. She leaned into serving position. "You ready, Millie?"

"Send it on over," Millie called back.

Lucia served and the teams played an intense round before the other team took possession.

Before long, Lucia found herself in the front row, facing David on the opposite side of the net.

"Nice form, Ms. Allen."

"Not bad yourself, Mr. Reynolds."

"All right now, stop consorting with the enemy up at the net," Deejay Jeff called out.

David laughed. "I'm just getting their strategy down."

"Unh-huh," Jeff said with a knowing nod.

The ball was served, and Lucia and David faced off. A high jump on Lucia's part spiked the ball into the sand at David's feet.

"Ah, you'll pay for that," he said.

"Promises, promises."

In the end, Lucia's team took the game.

George ran up to congratulate her. "Nice job. Where'd you learn to play like that?"

"Summers at the beach with my cousins," she said.

"How about grabbing a drink together," George suggested, sidling closer. "I could go for some ice water about now."

Lucia glanced over her shoulder toward David, who was coming around the net. She placed a gentle hand on George's arm. "I don't think so," she told him. "But thanks."

George eyed David with barely veiled hostility. A grunt passed as greeting between the two men before George, with a final look at Lucia, trotted to join the others at a WJAM cooler filled with cold drinks.

"Here you go," Shontae from the radio station called out to David. "Compliments of WJAM." He caught two purple and orange hand towels and passed one along to Lucia, who wiped sweat off her face.

"So," David said with a nod toward George. "Is there something I should know?" He pointedly looked at her ring finger, which was void of any rings.

Biting the inside of her mouth to conceal a smile, Lucia toyed with him. "That depends."

David nodded. "I told you I'm more than a bit out of practice at this sort of thing. So, please, would you help a brother out. Explicit directives are preferred over mixed signals."

"Explicit, huh?"

"Crystal clear," he said.

Lucia edged closer to him. While her gaze met his head-on, one of her fingers met the bare skin of his chest, traveling down more than a few inches of the broad expanse. The hair on his chest, still damp from the exertion of the game, glistened in the afternoon sun.

She stopped when he sucked in his breath.

"I came on this trip alone, David Reynolds. Is that clear enough?"

Lifting her finger from his hot skin, she placed it in her mouth, her unwavering gaze still locked with his.

She took David's shaky exhale as a yes.

"I don't usually come on quite so heavy," she said a while later.

They sat sharing a salty-sweet treat and Tropical Sunrise drinks at a small table on a terrace overlooking the beach. Opting out of the second volleyball match gave David and Lucia the opportunity to get to know each other, so they decided instead to find a quiet place to talk.

"So, why am I the exception?"

"I don't know," she said. "I've been asking myself the same question since I met you." She shrugged. "Maybe it's the tropical setting. But I think it's your smile."

He put forth a valiant effort to avoid it, but a smile spread across his mouth at her comment.

"That's exactly it," she said. "Very sexy."

Shaking his head, he leaned forward in his chair. "You're

something else, Lucia Heart Allen. Tell me about yourself."

She fingered the fruit-laden straw in her tall glass, then plucked off a piece of pineapple. "What do you want to know?"

"Start with your three names," he said. "You said you're not with that guy on the beach. What's his name? George or something? Is there an ex or a former lurking around?"

"You do get straight to the point, don't you?"

He quirked his head.

"Well, there is an ex. His name was . . . well, I guess it still is, Gerard. We got married when I was twenty-seven and was feeling the pressure of my family, a group of the most over-bearing manipulators you'd ever want to meet. But I love 'em anyway," she added with a shrug and a smile.

"You just have to know how to maneuver around some of them," she said. "Particularly my uncles and a great-aunt who considers herself the matriarch of the Heart clan. Anyway, more than that, though, I was getting kind of stressed that thirty would be knocking at my door soon, and I hadn't done the husband, kids, and house thing."

David sat back and folded his arms. "And so?"

"And so I married Gerard Baldwin and became Lucia Heart Allen Baldwin. We bought a huge house in an exclusive gated community, hired a nanny on retainer for when his kids came for their visits, and parked a Mercedes-Benz, a BMW, and a sport utility vehicle in the three-car garage."

"I'm taking it didn't work out?"

Lucia tilted her head. "Oh, it was working out just fine for Gerard. Marrying a Heart, even one slightly removed from the main money line, gave him a certain carte blanche. Instant entrée with the country club set. He'd already cultivated the image, he just needed the Heart connection to gain access."

"Who are these Hearts?"

She grinned, grabbed his hands, and planted a kiss on them. "For that gift, I could kiss you. Thank you."

David's brows furrowed. "What?"

"Well, without getting into the long, complicated stories of their lives—and believe me, a writer could come up with books about them—suffice to say, the Hearts control a significant portion of the African-American wealth in southeastern Virginia."

"Then that's where you're from, Virginia?"

She nodded. "Many of them, particularly my aunts and uncles, not so much the ones in my generation, think the sun rises and sets because they proclaim it."

"So what happened with you and Gerard?"

"Several things. Unfortunately, all at once. It got ugly. His business deals fell apart and he blamed me when my uncle wouldn't bail him out. His children lied about me, a lie that to this day, I believe, he still clings to despite overwhelming evidence to the contrary. And in the midst of it all, a balloon payment came due on the house—a payment we couldn't make. The last couple of years have been a real struggle. I've had to rebuild my life."

She leaned forward, peace evident in her eyes and her smile. "But you know what, I'm a better person for having gone through it all. I grew up, learned a lot about who I really am and what I want out of life."

Taking another sip from her drink, she looked at him. "And that, David Reynolds, is the sorry tale of Lucia Heart Allen. Your turn."

David took a breath. "Well, after all that, my sad little story pales in comparison."

Lucia smiled. "You don't look like a man who's spent much time being sad."

He leaned forward, placing his elbows on the table and clasping his hands together. "That's because you didn't know me when my wife, Denise, got sick and died."

"Oh, David. I'm sorry. Cancer?"

He shook his head. "Lupus. It's been four years now. The kids and I have been on our own, and you know what's so amazing?"

"Tell me," she said.

"This horrible thing that happened to us is the stuff of sitcoms. I was amazed when I found out how many television shows are based around single fathers. Of course, the laugh tracks don't typically address the why of the mother's absence."

At a loss for words, Lucia remained silent.

"What hurts the most, though, is that the kids don't really remember her. Allie does. She was five when Denise died. D.J., who is just seven now, has vague recollections. And Karenna, well," he said, shaking his head. "Karenna has photographs. Denise left a videotape for each one, though. It's for when they turn sixteen or whenever I think they need it."

Lucia, touched by his story, reached for David's hands. They sat together, quiet for a while, occasionally looking at the water, sometimes at each other.

"Well," David said after a few minutes. "Now that we've significantly depressed each other with the low points of our lives, let's pick up the energy a bit, shall we?"

"I'll drink to that. Garçon!" Lucia called, lifting up her empty glass.

Laughing, David took hers and his and went to the bar for refills. When he returned a few minutes later, a frown marred his face.

"What's wrong?" Lucia asked.

"My kids. They'll be back from their day program in about ten minutes. I need to be at the room when they're dropped off."

"Mind some company as you head back?"

He put their drinks on the table and held out a hand for Lucia. Hand in hand they walked toward the resort's main buildings.

"I enjoyed the afternoon with you," he said.

"I did, too."

David paused. Lucia turned, her outstretched arm the distance separating them. David closed the gap.

"Thank you," he said drawing her closer. He wrapped an arm around her waist. When she didn't protest or pull back, he clasped the other one around.

Lucia's open palms rested on his chest. "What am I being thanked for?"

He smiled. "I don't know. It seemed the right thing to say."

Her laughter, an enchanting melody, lifted his spirits and further brightened his day.

"Lucia?"

"Um-hmmm?"

"I want to kiss you."

"Then we have something in common," she said. "Because I was thinking the same thing about you."

His mouth lowered to hers. The first touch was as light and as sweet as the spring afternoon they'd shared.

Lucia's arms slid up his chest and circled his neck. With a hand caressing his head, she pulled him closer. Opening her mouth to the tender assault, Lucia's heart sang with an incredible lightness and rightness. In David's embrace, she felt cherished and beautiful, like a princess on holiday with the man of her dreams.

His kiss, exquisite in its simplicity, filled her with a sense of joy and wonderment.

When finally he released her, Lucia stared up at him, words temporarily failing her.

Then, speech came again. "Wow!"

David threw back his head and laughed. Then he hugged her close for a moment.

"I gotta go," he said.

He waved as he backtrotted toward the sliding doors.

"David. Wait. When will I see you again?"

He stopped for a moment. Then a smile spread across his face. "Tomorrow. At the pool near the aquarium. Ten o'clock."

She nodded, then grinned. "It's a date."

Lucia watched him dash through the doors. Then she hugged herself, delight evident all over her face. "It's a date, David Reynolds."

"Mr. Reynolds," a hotel clerk called out.

David's sprint across the lobby toward the elevators stopped. He made haste toward the guest reception desk."

"This just arrived for you, sir."

The clerk reached under the counter and pulled out a small gaily-wrapped box and handed it to him.

"What is it?"

"I don't know, sir."

David pulled a couple of dollars from his pocket and tipped the clerk. Walking to the bank of elevators, he turned the package this way and that, trying to figure out who would leave something like that for him.

He made it to the adjoining rooms he and his children shared just a moment before they arrived. The next forty-five minutes were spent listening to the tales of adventure the kids had had during the day.

"And tomorrow, Dad, we go out on a treasure ship," D.J. exclaimed.

"Is that a fact?" David said, feigning surprise.

He already knew that a glass-bottomed boat would take the kids in the Pirates program out for a three-hour tour and lunch. They'd see what was purported to be the wreck of a sunken treasure ship and would search for the pirates' buried gold in a "secret" hideaway on the opposite side of the resort's property.

The family ate dinner in one of the hotel's six restaurants. It wasn't until they'd returned to their rooms and the kids settled down in the girls' room with a board game, that David remembered the package.

He pulled it from the drawer where he'd placed it and went on the balcony to tug off the wrapping.

Tucked in the box was a note and a hard plastic key card that looked like all the other room keys at the resort. David raised an eyebrow at the key, then opened the small piece of paper.

A hotel baby-sitter will arrive at 8:55 p.m. I'll be waiting for you at 9 p.m. Wear something comfortable.

The handwritten note bore no signature, just a room number: 1503.

SIX

The subtle scent of a woman's earthy perfume wafted to his nostrils. David lifted the note to his nose and a moment later confirmed the scent definitely as perfume, and obviously from the sender of his suggestive gift.

A smile tilted the corners of his mouth. "Lucia, you devil, you."

She'd never let on that she'd planned this little surprise.

David glanced at his watch, amazed at how eager he was for the kids to finish their game and go to bed. Then a thought crossed his mind. While the hotel did offer a baby-sitting service, he needed to make sure this wasn't some plot. When it came to his kids, David could be, as Allie had pointed out on more than one occasion, more than a smidgen overprotective.

He tiptoed to Allie and Karenna's room. The three, deeply embroiled in Candy Land, didn't see or hear him. Pushing one of the connecting doors closed a bit, he went back across his room and picked up the telephone receiver. He dialed guest services and asked to be connected to the childcare office.

"Good evening, Mr. Reynolds. How may I help you?"

David glanced at the note inviting him up for what seemed to promise some adult entertainment.

"I was calling to confirm tonight's appointment," he said.

"Yes, sir. We have you down for eight-fifty-five P.M. Zoe will be with your children. I believe they met her this afternoon at the Pirate's Cove. If they're not already asleep, she'll have some story books and quiet activities for them."

Pretty sure that Lucia was behind this, but still wondering at the identity of his mystery date, David asked another probing question of the helpful guest relations receptionist. "The woman who booked this, her last name is . . . ?" He let the question hang.

"I don't know anything about that, sir. It says you requested baby-sitting service from nine until you called us. Would you like me to insert an ending time?"

Thwarted, David said no, then thanked the receptionist.

It looked like he'd have to wait another hour or so to see Lucia . . . and pick up where they had left off on the beach.

In the other room, the Reynolds children snickered together. Karenna, playing the role of scout, checked the door to make sure their dad wasn't listening in.

"It's okay," she said, a bit too loudly.

"Shhh," came immediate twin admonitions from the older two.

"Get back over here," Allie said.

When Karenna settled on the bed, Commander D.J. reviewed the operation thus far.

"Well, he didn't say anything about the lady today. Do you think she did it?"

Allie shrugged.

"Why don't we just ask him?" Karenna said.

D.J. rolled his eyes. "We can't do that, silly. Then he'd know we'd been up to something."

"Oh," Karenna said with a wise nod.

"The good news is we have two more lined up."

"I don't know about Maria's mom," Allie said.

D.J. cocked his head at his older sister. "What's not to know? She's a babe. And she thought the idea was great."

"Yeah," Allie said biting a fingernail. "But that was after she stopped laughing."

Karenna shook her head. "And I didn't get the joke. What was so funny?"

Pacing the floor between the bed and the dresser, D.J. considered that wrinkle. The two girls watched him think. Finally, he stopped, faced them, and shrugged.

"Maybe she just thought we were cute kids."

It was Allie's turn to roll her eyes.

"So, what's the plan if these next two don't work?" she asked. "We're running out of time."

"I don't know," D.J. said. "But we'll think of something. There's got to be at least one lady in this hotel who'd wanna date Dad."

"Lucia," Millie called. "Lucia!"

"Huh? I'm sorry. Were you talking to me?"

Lucia, Millie, and some of the WJAM gang sat together in the resort's all-you-can-eat buffet restaurant.

Millie sent a knowing wink across the table. She and Lucia sat on the end. The woman leaned over and beckoned Lucia to do likewise.

"I saw that fine brother you were hanging out with at the beach today. You work it, girlfriend. He looks the way I like my coffee, dark and strong."

Coming here had been a mistake, Lucia realized. She should have ordered room service. The last thing she needed or wanted was to have her jumbled feelings about David dissected by this busybody.

"Of course," Millie said, "that means poor George is left out in the cold. I tell you true, if I didn't have that good-for-nothing husband of mine back home, I might give old George a whirl."

"What are you two whispering about?" asked one of the married ladies sitting next to Lucia.

Millie sat up. "I was just telling her how–"

Lucia's eyes widened. She reached across the table and grabbed Millie's hand. "Millie, please."

The red lipstick highlighting Mile-a-Minute Millie's smile broadened. "Ah, look at that. I done made the child blush." She patted Lucia's hand. "Don't worry. Your new flame will just be our little secret. 'Course now, I wasn't the only person who saw y'all out there locking lips. I remember when it was new with my man. We couldn't wait to get back to the car or a room to, you know. Did y'all do it in the sand? That's something I haven't tried. Seems like it might be kind of gritty, you know."

That's it. I'm outta here, Lucia thought.

She dabbed her mouth with a napkin, excused herself, and made haste.

"What about your dinner? No need to get all in a huff," Millie called after her. "I'll keep your little secret."

"What secret?" three people at the table turned and said.

Millie cut a piece of roast beef, dabbed it in a little plastic cup filled with horseradish, and met the curious stares of the others.

She took on an air of superiority as she held the fork near her mouth. "I can't say."

Lucia took a walk around the resort complex, her thoughts and emotions as mixed up as if she'd dumped them in a blender set on whipping speed. She hadn't come on this Bahamian getaway to meet anyone. And she definitely hadn't come to get the nonstop earful from Millie, even though, in her own well-meaning but misguided way, the woman was just trying to be friendly.

If anything, Lucia had come to get some much-needed rest and relaxation.

Being the fifteenth caller on the WJAM contest hotline and then winning one of the coveted spots for this Bahamian vacation was validation for the last two years she'd spent rebuilding her credit, her confidence and her life post-Gerard.

He'd demanded alimony, telling the hearing officer that Lucia commanded considerable wealth that she'd consistently denied him during the course of their two-year marriage.

"Thank God for competent judges," she said as she walked.

The court, after reviewing her financials, ruled that Gerard had to pay her. Running from creditors, though, he'd hastily filed bankruptcy, leaving a tangle of bills and balances that somehow she got stuck with. Gerard couldn't, "more like wouldn't" she told the surf, pay her one dime in support. So the only income she had was what she made selling her handmade jewelry at art shows and in a few specialty shops.

With a lot of hard work and a small, no-interest loan from one of her cousins, Lucia had gotten her life back on track.

The last thing she needed was to fall right back into a relationship.

Clouds covered the sky. Before arriving in the Bahamas, Lucia identified with the feeling of being covered up. A few days in the sun, though, and a few hours with a certain single dad had chased the clouds away.

She shivered despite the evening's warm air.

David Reynolds had three kids. That alone negated the possibility of there ever being more than an island fling between them.

Granted, her two former stepchildren were definitely the products of their scheming, manipulative parents, but Lucia had had more than enough of the mom role.

No way would she *ever* again get seriously involved with a man with young children.

At nine on the nose, David stepped out of the elevator and walked up to Room 1503, the sexy invitation and room key in his hand. He positioned the beige hard-plastic key at the electronic slot, then thought better of just barging in, invited or not.

He rapped on the door, then picked a stray piece of lint from the light sport jacket he'd donned. A linen shirt, a pair of slacks, and dress sandals completed the ensemble for his date with Lucia.

After a moment, a woman opened the door and smiled at him.

"Hello. You must be David. I was surprised and a little intrigued when I got your note."

"I beg your pardon?"

"Come on in," the woman said.

David stood right where he was in the hall. "You're not Lucia."

"No," said the tall Asian woman wearing a flowing caftan with a red and gold dragon woven into the silk fabric. "My name's Camille. Come on in."

David stared at the key and at the note he'd received. Then his gaze went back to Camille. She was beautiful. Of mixed race, she'd gotten the best of whatever genes flowed from her parents to her. David's best guess was that she claimed a Chinese and either African or Latin heritage.

She held the door open for him, the invitation in her eyes one that no living, breathing male could resist.

Taking a deep breath, David followed her. It was time to find out just what in the world was going on.

Forty minutes later, he appeared back at the rooms he

shared with his three meddling offspring. David tipped the sitter, who closed the book she'd been reading and told him they were all sound asleep. After closing and locking the door behind her, he went to look in on his sleeping daughters.

The girls looked like little angels nestled in the big double beds. Their matching white lacy nightgowns had been purchased just for this trip. He leaned over and pressed a kiss to Karenna's cheek, stroking her hair.

She looked a lot like her mother. Knowing that Denise watched over them from heaven each night eased the loneliness he'd felt in the months following her death. As the years passed, the ache in his heart diminished. He still missed her and he'd always love her, but time had helped him create a new life and place with the children.

Karenna turned over and David smiled. He smoothed the crisp white sheet that covered the girl, then turned his attention to Allie.

Allison was the oldest, named for Denise's grandmother, who'd also been called Allie. His eldest child was growing so fast. She'd be a teenager soon, a young lady all grown up.

"Where'd the time go?" he whispered into the dark room.

He pressed a kiss to Allie's forehead, then crept out of the room and back to the one he shared with D.J. The doors between the two rooms remained open so he could hear if they needed him or vice versa.

David stood over his son for a few quiet moments. D.J., the middle child, bore his name and his looks. Unlike many boys his age, D.J. had skipped the "girls are yucky" stage. He had an eye for the ladies and already claimed a "girlfriend" or two at school.

"Boy, you are something else. You and your sisters keep my life interesting, that's for sure."

Shaking his head, David adjusted the sheet, pulled off the pirate eye patch on D.J.'s head and gave his son a kiss.

Then he tugged off his shirt and padded into the bathroom for a shower before bed.

When the water started running, D.J. rolled over. He peeked open first one eye, then the other, and stared at the sliver of light shining from under the bathroom door.

"Uh-oh. I think he's onto us."

SEVEN

"Hold it right there, mates."

Allie, D.J., and Karenna all stopped in their tracks at their father's command. D.J.'s hand dropped from the room door he'd been about to yank open and rush through.

"Dad, we have to hurry if we're gonna make breakfast before the cap'n comes for us."

Wagging a finger in front of the three, David smiled, the expression as diabolical as any seafaring buccaneer. "You have plenty of time," he said.

"I think we're in trouble," Karenna whispered to Allie.

The older girl tried to size up her father's mood. "Let me handle this," she whispered to the other two.

"Come on back," David said. "Have a seat."

He indicated the edge of the bed. The trio sat, oldest to youngest, and waited.

Standing before them David stroked his chin. He glanced at them, drawing out the silence. Sure enough, the children started to squirm under his intense perusal.

David cleared his throat and folded his arms. "There have been some odd things going on around here the last couple of days. I thought one of you might be able to shed a little light on the situation."

The three kids shared a glance, then the spokeswoman lobbed the first return.

"Odd things like what, Daddy?" Allie asked.

David chuckled at the innocent-sounding question. "Oh, things like picnic lunches and a late-night rendezvous."

"What's Ron day food, Dad?" Karenna asked. "Are we going to eat some today?"

"Rendezvous," D.J. corrected. "And it's like a date."

David raised an eyebrow. "Oh, you know that word, son?"

D.J. folded his hands and looked at the ceiling.

"Oh, I know," Karenna exclaimed. "A date like what we–"

Allie erupted in an outbreak of very loud coughing. She leaned into D.J., who also suddenly got a frog caught in his throat. He pinched Karenna in the process of hacking to clear his throat.

"Oww." She rounded on her brother. "Why'd you do that?"

"Knock it off," David told them. He crouched down so he could face them. "Thanks, guys, for what I think you're trying to do. But I'm all right. Okay? You can cease your little campaign."

Allie and D.J. looked at each other.

"What campaign?" D.J. asked.

David stood up. "No more," he said. "Understand?"

The two nodded, but David could have sworn he saw fingers crossed behind their backs.

"You guys need to get some breakfast. Let's roll."

The children raced for the door, while David got his wallet and the room key.

"I don't see why you had to pinch me," Karenna said as they left. "All I was going to say was–"

Allie yanked her sister's arm. "Let's go ring for the elevator."

Shutting the door, David just shook his head.

"My kids are trying to set me up," he told Lucia less than an hour later.

He'd skipped the meal while the children ate, figuring–correctly–that he and Lucia might share a late breakfast. They sat on a terrace, tropical flowers in bloom between the tables of the outdoor poolside restaurant.

"Set you up with what?" she asked, slicing into a ripe, juicy melon.

"A date."

David paused in the act of pouring juice from a carafe. He looked at Lucia, his gaze narrowing as he considered a possibility that suddenly crossed his mind.

"What?" she said.

"Don't tell me you're a setup."

"What are you talking about?"

He eyed her. "When you took Karenna to the bathroom, what did she tell you in there?"

"She didn't *tell* me anything. I told her my name and told her about my idea for her top."

"Oh!" David said, hitting his head with his palm. "I completely forgot about your scarf. I'll get it back to you today."

Lucia shrugged. "That's not important," she said. "But what are you talking about being set up?"

David quickly told her about Marcia Perkins, the picnic lunch lady, and Camille Ling, the wine and roses woman.

"You sent her roses?"

Lucia didn't want to admit it, but she felt insulted and jealous to boot. Here they were getting to know each other and he was sending another woman roses.

"No. I think the kids did, though."

He explained about the package and how he thought it had come from her. He also told Lucia what Camille had revealed, that she'd received three red roses and a typewritten note asking if she'd like a little company. She'd followed the directives and handed her gift-wrapped key over to the reception clerk with orders to see that it got delivered.

"See, this is what comes of having children who obviously watch too much cable at their grandmother's house. It also doesn't pay to have them computer literate. I wonder how long it took them to weasel their way into the hotel's business center and then—"

"Aren't you overreacting?" Lucia asked.

David faced her.

"I don't see the harm, really," she said. "As a matter of fact, I think it's kind of cute."

He closed the distance between them by leaning forward. "Even though I've already found the woman I'd like to get to know better?"

Lucia smiled. "Hmmm. Since you put it that way." She nodded. "We'd better put a halt to their diabolical machinations."

David chuckled. "Okay. You've made your point. I've blown this way out of proportion." He plopped back into his chair next to her. "I just hate that they think I'm so pathetic, I can't even attract a woman."

Lucia stood up and opened her golden coverall. "I don't think you're pathetic, Mr. Reynolds."

She let the material slide down her body and pool at her feet. In the time it took David to stop breathing, she stood before him in an itty-bitty leopard-print bikini.

Leaning forward, she taunted him. "I don't think you're pathetic at all. As a matter of fact, I think you're downright sexy."

He reached for her, but she moved just out of reach and walked a few steps away. Humor danced in her eyes as she regarded the virile man. She detected more than a gleam of interest in his intense gaze. As a matter of fact, Lucia decided, heat and fire smoldered in his eyes, and she felt a need to get closer to the flames.

"Did I tell you how lovely you look today?"

"Too late," she said. "You've already seen my feminine wiles."

Suddenly glad she'd brought along the near scandalous bikini, Lucia gracefully moved in a slow pirouette, making doubly sure that if he hadn't seen everything before, he definitely would now.

David's eyes tracked the sway of her hips and the curve of her legs. "I didn't know you could see wiles," he said.

She looked over her shoulder at him, a sensual invitation in her eyes. "Well, then, maybe my assets interest you more."

She slid out of the high-heeled gold mules and made a tantalizing production of slowly walking to the edge of the pool.

"Come on," she invited. "They say the water feels great."

Breakfast forgotten, David stood, shedding his shirt and shorts to reveal swimming trunks unable to conceal his growing desire for her.

Lucia gave him a once-over, raising her brow as her gaze meandered over certain parts of him. Her mouth curved in an unconscious smile, and then, without a word, she dived into the water, her body a perfect arc into the crystal clear depths.

She swam a lap and a half before she encountered an obstruction in the water. Rising to investigate, water sluiced from her skin. She wiped her face and ran her hands through her hair to clear her vision, but she already knew what obstacle impeded her progress. They stood in about four and a half feet of warm pool water.

"Are you a fisherman out to get the morning's catch?"

David smiled as he curled an arm around her waist. "Umhmmm. And I think I just snagged a beautiful mermaid."

"Aren't mermaids supposed to be magical, granting wishes or something?"

"I don't know," he said as his mouth lowered to hers. "Don't care, either."

His demanding lips caressed hers. Lucia thrilled at the sensation. They stood together in the water, their bodies pressed so close, she could feel the hard evidence of his arousal. His lips seared a path from her mouth to her neck and then the hollow of her shoulders.

Lucia moaned, then drew his face back to hers to again taste the sweet nectar of his kiss.

"Ahh, look at the honeymooners, dear," came a voice from the edge of the pool. "Isn't that sweet?"

David smiled into the kiss. "I think we're attracting an audience."

Lucia gazed into his eyes as she ran a hand along the side of his face. "Then I think we should explore our options in a more private setting."

For a moment, no words were spoken between them. Lucia knew what she wanted. And she knew that taking this next step with David was possibly committing to more than she'd bargained for. But those problems would have their time and day. Right now, she wanted David.

"Come with me," she said, her gentle words both statement and plea.

David lingered for a heartbeat longer, enough time to raise her from the water and let her body slide down his. The embrace ended in a kiss, a meeting of two hearts beating to the same rhythm.

He held out his hand, and she followed him from the pool. Pausing a moment to scoop up their clothes and her shoes, Lucia led the way.

In her room, he closed the door, secured the locks, and pulled her into his arms. A delightful shiver of wanting raced through Lucia.

"David, you should know this isn't something I do. I mean, I haven't since my husband—"

"Shhh," he said, raining kisses along her neck.

Lucia arched into him, the feel of his tender lips a balm to her attention-starved senses.

"I want you, Lucia," he whispered. "I need you."

The two shared urgent kisses as they backed farther into the room, heading toward the tangle of sheets on Lucia's unmade bed.

David made quick work of escaping his swimsuit. When Lucia reached for the tiny string of her bikini top, he halted her.

"Let me."

Unable to speak, she nodded. David sat on the bed and pulled her between his legs. He ran his hands up and over her stomach before cupping breasts that completely filled the swimsuit's bra top. Lucia's heartbeat throbbed in her ears and she swayed into his embrace. The touch of his hands enflamed her senses.

Wrapping her arms around his neck, she threw her head back while he worshipped her navel with his tongue and teased her breasts with his hands.

"David." His name trembled from her lips.

A moment later, she felt cool air on her skin. But the sensation lasted barely a moment before his mouth covered a bared breast. He suckled her, and Lucia thought she'd die of the tender ache.

"David."

He ministered to her other breast before inching the barely-there bikini panties from her thighs.

They tumbled to the bed and in a moment, Lucia lay under

David's strong body. He whispered unintelligible words in her ear, praise songs to her beauty and his desire.

And then they were one, sharing the rhythm of lovers lost in each other's arms.

Later, they lay together, listening to the soft breathing in the aftermath of their passion.

Lucia propped an arm up and hovered over him, her free hand drawing curlicues in the whirls of hair on his chest.

"I didn't have any—"

He silenced her with a finger at her mouth. "I know. It didn't cross my mind, either."

"That makes us bad adults," she said.

A rueful smile curved his mouth. He edged out of the bed and went to retrieve his shorts dropped somewhere near the door.

Lucia tugged a sheet up to cover her nakedness.

"What happens now?" she asked him.

David swung a chair around and straddled it at the end of the bed. Lucia scooted up, the bed's headboard supporting her back, the sheet tucked firmly under her arms.

"I don't know," he said. "But I want you to know that this was . . ." He paused. "I never expected to find someone like you."

"What does that mean?"

"It means," he said, pulling on his shirt. "It means that right this moment, the one thing I want to do the most is crawl back in that bed and love you all day."

A smile trembled over her lips. "Then why don't you?"

He got up, walked over to her, and kissed her with the controlled passion of a man confident in himself.

Lucia dropped the sheet that concealed her breasts from him and wrapped her arms around his neck. He lingered for a moment, then he pulled her arms away from him and rose.

"That's why," he said. "We just met. I have the kids." He shrugged. "This is . . . I don't know what happens next."

With a final look at the tempting display, he picked up his swim trunks, then let himself out of her room.

Lucia stared after him as the door clicked shut behind him. She wished she could claim ignorance, but she knew exactly what David meant. They didn't know each other well.

The tropical sun, the soothing surf, and an undeniable chemistry between them had led to this. She leaned back on the headboard and pulled her knees up to her chest. In David's arms she'd come alive with every fiber of her being. Even now, she wanted him, just as he'd professed to still wanting to be with her.

Was it truly possible to fall for someone so quickly?

Lucia didn't know, and frankly, with the way she felt right this moment, with the memory of their passion fresh on her mind, she didn't much care.

She'd dated a couple of times since divorcing Gerard. But neither of the men inspired her to spend the late morning making love.

"Of course, I wasn't in the Bahamas with either of them, either," she said.

But Lucia doubted the setting had much, if anything, to do with her attraction to David. She'd have had the same visceral reaction to him had they met in an art gallery or in a grocery store in the States.

She tried to pinpoint a specific attribute that made David Reynolds so different from the others. A warmth shone in his eyes. A hint of a smile at his mouth gave him a touch of introspective whimsy that invited her to explore the possibilities.

Then, of course, there was the thing he did with his hands and his mouth. It was too easy to get lost in the way he looked at her, the way he worshipped her body like a supplicant at the altar of a goddess.

Lucia closed her eyes, trailing a hand along her waist and up to her breasts, remembering the feel of David's hands on her body, aching to know again the pleasure only he could give her, and she him.

After a moment, she stretched like a contented feline, her hands reaching for the ceiling, her toes wiggling. Reaching for a pillow, she hugged its softness to her, then rested her head on its cushioned comfort.

She didn't know what would happen next with David. But for the first time since she'd gotten her life back on track,

Lucia felt blissfully happy and fully alive. And that was a state of being she wanted to keep for a little while.

David slammed the door behind him as he stormed into his hotel room. At what point had he lost all control?

"Not to mention your mind," he said, tossing his damp swim trunks on the bathroom floor.

He paced the floor, trying to get a handle on the conflicting emotions that raced through him. Unlike some men, sex wasn't something he took lightly. The communion of bodies was as important as the communion of spirits between two people who cared about each other, who were committed to their relationship.

Right this minute, though, with his body still humming for her and his head recalling every exquisite inch of her golden-brown body, David had to question himself: Did he want her because she spoke to him on another level or did he want her because she made him hot and hard?

No answer came, but David instinctively knew that Lucia Heart Allen was the best thing that had happened to him in years. Being with her, making love to her made him feel. . . . strong, invincible, not old.

David hung his head and plopped onto the bed.

"That's it," he said. "You're old. Too old to be having a meaningless fling with the first pretty woman who says more than two words to you."

But in fact, he'd been approached by other beautiful women, even stunning ones like Camille Ling. But they didn't move him the way Lucia did.

In addition, David wasn't old, even though keeping up with three growing kids sometimes wore him out. At thirty-three, he had the rest of his life in front of him.

The guilt slammed into him with that thought. He and Denise thought they had the rest of their lives to live and love together while raising their three young children.

He fell back upon the bed, waiting for the mental lashing and the emotional turmoil he expected would wreak havoc on his state of mind for being unfaithful to Denise.

He'd been unfaithful. Right?

He waited, but no demons chased him. No "how-dare-you" voices rang through his head or his heart.

David sat up, suddenly aware that the pressure he was feeling wasn't guilt at all, not even a vague notion of desecrating the memory of his wife. Time had done its healing in that regard. With a sense of wonder, he realized that rather than those soul-bashing feelings, he was experiencing an odd mixture of relief and excitement.

He jumped up and leaped into the air. "I'm alive! I'm alive!"

A moment later, embarrassed as if he'd been caught in his exuberance, he settled down.

A silly grin spread across his face.

Lucia Heart Allen was a woman he could get to know better, a lot better. He wanted to introduce her to the other children. Even if nothing came of the bliss they shared together on this Caribbean isle, no harm would be done if Allie and D.J. met her as well.

A nagging something played at the back of his consciousness, though. Lucia had had a bad experience with her stepchildren, something so negative that she didn't want children. She was good with them, though, if her experience with Karenna was any indication. Maybe she just needed a different experience.

Stripping off his clothes, David took a shower. The phone rang as he tied the laces on his running shoes.

"Hello?" he answered.

"Hi, David," a woman said. "I'm waiting in the lobby. If you don't hurry, we're going to be late."

EIGHT

"Oh, no. Not again," he mumbled. "I told those kids—"

"Hurry up. They're waiting for us."

"Ma'am. I think you have the wrong room."

"Come on now, David Reynolds. I'll be waiting."

Before he had a chance to say anything else, she'd clicked off the line.

Determined once and for all to put an end to whatever the children started, David marched to the lobby. When he reached it, though, he realized he didn't know whom he was looking for.

A woman in a tan and brown shorts set walked up to him and smiled. "Hi, David. You look just like they described."

He stared at her. "Did anyone ever tell you you look just like—"

She smiled and held up a hand. "All the time. But I'm not. My name is Natalia Sanchez. I'm Maria's mother. Pleased to meet you," she said, holding out her hand. "Come on, we don't want to miss the ferry."

"Who's Maria and what ferry?"

"Maria is my daughter and the ferry to the Pirate's Treasure Island." She grabbed his hand and tugged toward the door. "Come on. Having lunch with the kids will be great."

Confused—yet again—but willing to go along if it finally meant confronting his offspring about their matchmaking schemes, David willingly followed.

Lucia stepped out of the elevator and into the lobby in time to see David dashing out the door with a leggy beauty with sun-streaked hair. Lucia faltered, her steps suddenly unsure. The woman looked back at David, laughed, and then linked her arm in his as they hopped onto one of the resort's open-top courtesy shuttles. Lucia's body stiffened in shock . . . and hurt.

Anger. Confusion. Jealousy. The three warred within her. Taking a deep breath, she fought for equilibrium.

He'd lied.

And she had in turn been played by a man.

"Again."

David, Allie, D.J., and Karenna Reynolds sat at a weather-bleached wooden picnic table with Natalia and Maria Sanchez.

"All right," David said. "Who's going to do the explaining?"

D.J. and Allie glanced at each other, silently communicating. After a moment, Allie sighed.

"I guess I will, Dad."

He folded his arms, waiting.

Allie looked at Natalia Sanchez. "Thanks for agreeing to come, even though it looks like we're in a heap of trouble."

"Stop stalling, Allison."

"Dad, we didn't want you to be lonely," Allie said. "You never go out. You always stay at home with us."

"I go out," David said in his own defense.

"Dad," D.J. said. "Leaving us with Grandma so you can go to a game with Uncle Freeman is not going out." He nodded toward Natalia. "*She's* going out."

Natalia smiled. "Let me get this straight. You guys have been setting your father up with dates?"

Allie nodded. D.J. had the grace to look embarrassed.

"I told 'em it wasn't a good idea," Karenna said.

"Start at the beginning, Allie," David said.

"Well, we were at Grandma's and she was watching the Travel Channel because she's going on her big trip to London. And when it was over, she and Karenna went to make cookies."

"Chocolate chip with raisins," Karenna clarified.

"Anyway," Allie continued after a glance at her sister, "after the London show was over, another one came on about the Bahamas."

"And the announcer said lots of 'single women flock to the island paradise,' " D.J. said, deepening his voice to mimic the program's narrator.

"And that's when we got the idea to get you a date from the Bahamas," Allie finished.

Shaking her head, Karenna said, "I told 'em you weren't gonna like it."

David sat dumbfounded. Maria giggled. And Natalia, after a moment soaking it all in, burst into delighted laughter.

Natalia turned to her daughter. "And your role in this was what?"

"Just to get you two to meet," Maria Sanchez said. "Allie told me her dad was really cute. And you like to go out with cute guys. So I figured, why not?"

The adults shared a glance, David trying not to smile, Natalia not even aiming to make the effort.

"Well," she said. "He is cute."

"Thank you," David cut in.

Allie and D.J. brightened up. "So that means you guys are gonna go out on a date? Cool beans, man."

Natalia looked at David, who subtly shook his head.

"I don't think so, darling," she told him. The endearment made the boy grin.

"Guys," David said. "Thank you for your concern and your considerable sacrifice and effort. But I can do all right on my own. As a matter of fact, there's someone I want you to meet later on."

"Really?" Allie said. "Who is she?"

"We'll talk about that later," he said. "Right now, I think you owe Ms. Sanchez an apology. And when you get back to the hotel this evening, the same goes for Ms. Perkins and Ms. Ling."

The children nodded, and then mumbled a halfhearted apology to Maria's mother. For Natalia's benefit, David filled in the blanks about his two previous blind "dates."

Later, as a picnic lunch was set out for them and the other treasure island inhabitants, D.J. leaned over and whispered just loud enough for his father's ear alone. "But, Dad, you have got to admit, she is a babe."

"You and I, son, will be having a little talk when we get back to the room."

The junior lascivious smile fell off the boy's face. D.J., familiar with that tone of voice from his father, slumped in his seat.

The two families shared lunch. Then, along with a handful of other parents, David and Natalia caught the ferry back.

In the lobby, they shared a laugh and then a hug before going their separate ways.

From the lobby restaurant where she'd spent the last couple of hours nursing her jealous spirit and wounded pride, Lucia watched the pair.

"Win some, lose some," she said, holding a drink up in toast to the couple standing just a few feet away. She'd barely touched her salad. This Tropical Sunrise, though, like the two others she'd already downed, differed from the other ones she'd had while at the resort. This one had plenty of alcohol listed in the ingredients. Unfortunately, the liquor wasn't drowning the hurt she felt.

And just why David's treachery made such a difference to her was something she didn't want to investigate too closely anyway.

Several hours later, a ringing phone disturbed the sound sleep Lucia had fallen into, aided by her lethal liquid refreshment. She inched across the bed and picked up the receiver, trying at the same time to glance at the clock to determine the time.

"Hello." The muffled word came out a mumble of sleep and pillow mouth.

"Hi, Lucia. Did I wake you?"

"I don't want to talk to you," she told David.

"I understand if you're upset that I left this morning. But I needed time to think."

"Well, I saw your thinking," Lucia said. "She had long legs and honey-red hair. Good-bye, David."

"Wait!"

But Lucia slammed the receiver down and rolled onto her back. The improbably competitive part of her wondered how she compared to his other conquests and if he'd thought of her while in that other woman's arms.

The expletive that came from her mouth summed up exactly how she felt.

Several minutes later, knocking on her door interrupted the pity party.

"Lucia, I know you're in there. Please open the door."

It took her a while, but she finally came to the door and opened it a crack.

"I told you, I don't want to talk to you."

It may have been a while since David had been in a relationship, but he still knew women. Had it not been the jealousy in her voice when she said "long legs and honey-red hair," he'd have taken the rejection, chalking it up to a bad choice. Since David knew himself to be a pretty good judge of character, he'd come to the conclusion that Lucia had seen him with Natalia Sanchez and had jumped to an early and incorrect assumption.

"She's not my girlfriend," he said through the tiny opening she'd allowed. "My kids, thinking I needed to get out more, set me up. It's how they've been spending their free time on the island."

Lucia eyed him for a moment, then her mouth eased into a smile. "Little Karenna is picking out your dates?"

David nodded. "Her older sister and brother appear to be the masterminds. She was just along for the ride."

Lucia opened the door and let him in.

"That explains it," she said.

"What?"

"Her questions."

Shutting the door behind him, David followed her into the hotel room. His eyes took in the rumpled bed and his thoughts returned to the love they'd shared there together earlier in the day. Forcing his attention away from that direction for a moment, he faced her.

Lucia's curly hair had a finger-combed look to it. He wanted to run his own hands through it, drawing him again closer to her warmth and vitality. She'd donned a sunflower sundress, but her legs and toes, with fire-engine-red polish on the nails, remained bare—tempting him.

David cleared his throat.

Lucia's perusal of him, just as intense, ended when their gazes met. "Will it always be this way between us?"

"I don't know," David said. "I've never felt this way before, so I'm not able to say. What do you think?"

Lucia took a shaky breath; just being near him made her achy, if not for the touch of his lips or of his hands, just being close to him, sharing space and togetherness.

"I . . ." she started. Then, folding her arms, she said, "I'm not surprised your kids had no problem finding you a beautiful woman."

"Actually," he said, "they found three, four if you're added to the number."

"I beg your pardon?"

She sat in the deck chair while he, leaning on the sliding glass of her balcony door, told her about his three mystery women.

"Each one a different ethnic background," he said. "And each one *very* pretty. But that they were so willing to go out with a stranger, a date set up by a bunch of little kids is strange. What kind of woman would do that?"

Lucia smiled. "Well," she said, the word a lingering consideration. "When we were in the rest room that night, Karenna asked me if I was married. She also wanted to know if I had a boyfriend and any children."

"You're kidding."

Shaking her head, Lucia glanced at her nails. "I think I may have been having my initial interview."

That made him laugh. "Probably, knowing my kids."

He paused for a moment, sobering. "I'd like you to meet them, Lucia. All three of them."

It was Lucia's turn to get serious. "I don't think that's a good idea."

"Why not?"

"I'm not good with children. We don't speak the same language," she said.

"Half the time I have to ask for a translation to figure out what my son is talking about."

He closed the distance between them and placed his hands on her shoulders. "Earlier today, I wondered what happens next in our relationship. I don't want what we've started here to turn into just a nice memory of a few pleasant hours while I was on vacation. I know there are people who take sex lightly, as just another way to express themselves. I'm not like that. I never have been and I never will be."

She turned, facing him. "But your children—"

"Are the greatest part of me," he said. "If I'm going to be serious about a woman, they need to know."

Lucia looked up at him. What he said both intrigued and frightened her. "You're talking like this, us, is more than a vacation fling."

"I hope it is."

She took a deep breath. "Things are happening too fast. We need to get to know each other better. I need time to think."

"Okay," he said. "Think about this."

The kiss was hard and urgent, needy and demanding, and oh, so right. She ran her hand along the contour of his face, seeking and searching and imprinting his essence on her psyche.

"Tomorrow," he said against her lips. "Just give me tomorrow. We can all go to the straw market. You haven't been there yet, have you?"

"Unh-uh," she murmured.

"Then we can make it a day. It'll be light," he said with a nibbling kiss.

"It'll be fun," he said, as a slow hand traced the outline of her breasts.

"It'll be—"

She pressed her mouth to his, effectively swallowing his next words of enticement. Her heart fluttering wildly in her chest, Lucia once again found herself captivated by this man.

Was she so sex-starved that just his touch could make her burn?

"No," she said, answering her own question.

Slowly, reluctantly and breathing heavily, he backed away

from her. He swallowed, trying to regain his composure.

"I . . ." She opened her eyes. "What happened?" she asked him, her voice husky with desire. "Why'd you stop?"

David turned to leave. "You said no."

For a moment, Lucia stood confused. Then, she realized that she must have verbally responded in the negative to the question that had been on her mind all day, even when she thought he was seeing another woman. She wasn't merely starved for male companionship. There *was* something about David.

She reached for his hand and drew it to her breast. She guided his palm along the tender places, the hardened nipple, the fullness of her. Gazing into his eyes, she dared him to leave her again.

"What are you saying?"

"Stay with me," she said. "Make love to me."

"I thought you'd never ask."

But as she led him to the bed, Lucia remembered the obstacle that stood between them: the responsibility of being a parent.

"You shouldn't stay," she said. "I know you have to get back to your children."

A mischievous glint lit his eyes.

"What?" she asked.

He reached into his pocket and pulled out the scarf she'd given Karenna and a small plastic bag bearing the resort's gift shop logo. "I stopped at the guest services desk and arranged for a sitter."

Lucia eyed the bag in his hand. "And then?"

"And then I found some adult responsibility in the personal items section of the gift shop."

"Personal items?" she echoed, even though she guessed what he'd purchased.

David reached into the bag and pulled out a small package of condoms.

"Well, now, weren't you leaping to some conclusions?" she asked.

He snaked a hand around her waist and pulled her close to him. "No, sweet Lucia. I was being ever hopeful."

NINE

"Now, I want you guys to be on your best behavior," David said.

D.J. paused in the act of brushing his hair.

"Oooh, Dad's all nervous. She must be really special."

"She is," David said as he wiped traces of shaving cream from his face and neck. The two Reynolds men were getting dressed for their day in the town.

Sometime later in the night, after he'd returned to his room and tipped the baby-sitter, David finally acknowledged his concern about Lucia's flippant attitude and tone on "the husband, kids, and house thing." She'd had an awfully bad experience with her ex-husband and stepchildren, so bad that she'd been willing to throw away what they were developing just because David came as a package deal.

"Try not to do anything . . ." He paused, searching for the right words.

"That might scare her off," D.J. added helpfully.

David dropped his towel on D.J.'s head. "Exactly."

"We had a vote last night," the boy said. "We'll be judging your mystery lady on looks, poise, and gifts."

"Looks? Gifts? Poise? Now wait just one minute—"

"Heh, heh, heh. Just joking, Dad." D.J. leaned out the open bathroom door and yelled across the way to Allie and Karenna. "He's got it bad, girls. He can't even take a little joke."

"D.J. . . ."

But David's fears were put to naught. Lucia waited for them in the lobby, wearing a bright-red tank top and walking shorts. The colorful parrot earrings adorned her ears, and she clutched a small wallet purse with a long strap that draped across her body.

David saw her and a smile transformed his face. Watching her father, Allie's gaze darted toward the object of his attention. A frown marred the girl's face for a moment, then she folded her arms and openly glared. D.J. let out a low whistle that earned him a sharp glance from his father.

Karenna, however, was the one who surprised them all.

"Miss Lucky! Look, Daddy, it's Miss Lucky."

Arms wide open, the girl ran straight to Lucia and launched herself into Lucia's embrace. Unsure for just a heartbeat, Lucia caught the girl and hugged her.

"Well, hello again, Karenna."

A grin split David's face at the sight of his youngest child in his lover's arms. He liked the picture they made.

Allie and D.J. shared a glance.

"How does she know Karenna?" Allie whispered.

D.J. shrugged in answer.

Taking Lucia's hand, Karenna led the woman to her waiting father and siblings.

"It's Miss Lucky, Dad."

"I know, pumpkin." But the intimate hint of a smile was strictly for Lucia. He noticed her take a deep breath when he placed a hand at the small of her back. It was time to meet the other two.

"Allie, D.J., this is Miss Lucia Heart Allen."

Lucia greeted each child, her smile bright even though it felt as though eight hundred sixty-five butterflies danced calypso through her stomach.

Meeting David's other children shouldn't have been a traumatic experience. Yet she'd worked herself into an emotional frenzy with thoughts of what-ifs—for example, what if she and David really got serious and she had to deal with these children on a regular basis?

That thought alone was enough to keep her safely locked in her room. But staying docked in a safe harbor wasn't what the journey of life was all about. She needed to make this next step.

If they were all like sweet little Karenna, everything would be just fine. Then memories of her former stepchildren plotting against her came to mind. Those two had been a united coalition of brat-dom wreaking havoc on her nerves and her already-in-trouble marriage.

"Hi there," D.J. said, breaking into her thoughts. "You're pretty."

Lucia blushed and smiled, this one a true smile. She relaxed and a chuckle bubbled forth. "Well, thank you," she said. "And I do see where your Dad gets *his* good looks."

David shook his head at his son's antics. They'd already had that little talk, but D.J. seemed bound and determined to become a ladies' man.

"And you're Allie," Lucia said. "It's very nice to meet you."

Lucia didn't know if she should shake the girl's hand or not. Allie stood there stiffly, staring her down, almost willing her to turn away.

But something in Lucia refused to be intimidated. Not by a child, ever again. If resistance was what Allie planned for her, Lucia had another idea: honesty.

She leaned forward a bit and beckoned the girl to her. Wary, but curious, Allie acquiesced. Lucia didn't touch her, but she got close enough to whisper.

"I'm nervous, too."

Allie's eyes widened a bit and she stepped back. Lucia smiled. The girl's answering smile, if not quite completely welcoming, at least wasn't hostile, like her stepdaughter's had been.

"Well, is everyone ready to head out?" David said.

"Dad, we're going shopping," D.J. said, a world of distaste lingering at the curl of his mouth. "Cool this is not."

David rubbed his son's head. "Poor D.J. Forced to spend the afternoon outside in the sunshine, watching all the pretty ladies go by."

D.J. brightened. "Oh, well, come on, guys. I know you don't want to miss the good bargains."

Looking like any traditional American family, the five set off to the straw market. When they arrived at the tourist trap, they paused from a vantage point across the street to survey the scene.

"Wow," Allie said. Straw products beckoned at every turn. Stalls overflowed with hats and scarves, bags and totes, gadgets and toys and musical instruments all designed for visitors to take home a memento or two . . . or three or more . . . from the Bahamas.

Music blared from loudspeakers at a corner, and the smell of conch fritters frying filled the air.

"Let's go that way," Allie said, charging off toward a vendor featuring oversized sunbonnets and ribbons.

"Hold it right there, Allison Reynolds," David said. "Come back here."

Allie obeyed and the Reynolds clan huddled. "The ground rules," David started. "No dashing off alone. Make sure you keep sight of one of us," he said, indicating Lucia and himself. "And hold your sister's hand."

"I'm not a baby," Karenna said, pouting.

"I know, pumpkin. But there are a lot of people out here and even more probably coming. I don't want you or anyone else getting lost. Okay?"

The three children nodded.

"All right, then," he said. "Where shall we begin?"

"I think Allie had a great idea with that booth," Lucia said.

The girl glanced up at Lucia and smiled. David looked at the row of displays and shrugged. "Off we go."

The first hour zipped by. Allie, Karenna, and Lucia had no problem deciding which of the tempting wares should go home with them. D.J., however, was holding out for something better. What, exactly, he didn't know.

D.J. and Allie hung back a bit as they walked along one of the corridors of the straw market. In front of them Karenna strolled between David and Lucia, one of her small hands tucked securely in each of the adults'.

"What's wrong?" D.J. asked his sister.

"I don't know. I guess it's different," she said.

"What?"

Allie shrugged, then kicked a stone in the walkway. "Seeing Dad with somebody. I mean, it was fun talking to all those ladies and you know, setting him up with dates and stuff. But now that he's like, you know, actually interested in some-body . . ." The troubled words fell off.

D.J. stopped walking. "I don't get it," he said. "You're the one who came up with this whole idea of finding a lady for Dad."

"I know. But I can't help the way I'm feeling." Allie started walking again and D.J. fell into step beside her.

"Well, give her a chance. I mean, we just really met her. And look at Karenna. She's cool with her."

The little girl's delighted laughter drifted back to them, even though the growing crowd shielded their view of the three for a moment.

"D.J. Allie." David's call to them came over the general hubbub.

"We're coming, Dad," D.J. answered. "Come on, Al. It'll be okay." Taking his sister's hand, D.J. and Allie caught up with the other three.

"Ooh, Daddy. Look!" Karenna tugged away from David and Lucia and pointed toward a group of dancers performing in front of a small steel band. She started to mimic one of the women's movements.

"She likes music and dance," Lucia observed.

"How'd you guess?" David said on a chuckle. "She's en-rolled in ballet, jazz, and tap, but the girl likes nothing better than freestyle jumping around."

"She did a great job leading the conga line the other night."

"I'm already saving up for Juilliard."

Lucia nodded. "Smart man."

David slipped his hand into Lucia's.

Noticing, D.J. nudged Allie. "Let's give 'em a little pri-vacy."

"We're watching Karenna, Dad," Allie said.

"Stay in my sight," David reminded them.

"We will." The children went to the edge of the horseshoe circle to watch the performance.

David and Lucia strolled to a fruit stand that overlooked the area where the dancers danced. D.J. turned and waved, keeping true to the directive to stay in sight.

"You have good kids," Lucia said, staring at the place where the three youngsters stood enjoying the show.

Could it be that all children weren't like the ones she'd been exposed to?

"Thanks," he said. "But I'm detecting a but, or a however."

Shaking her head, Lucia faced him. "There are no buts. I just . . ." She shrugged. "My experience with kids hasn't been great."

"I don't believe you," he said. "You've been terrific with Karenna."

"My stepchildren, former stepchildren," she said clarifying the past relationship. "Well, they tended to be manipulative. They lied, they even stole from me."

"What happened?"

"I'm a jewelry designer," she said. "I made these earrings."

David smiled and touched one of the whimsical parrots. His fingers brushed along her neck and Lucia quivered.

"You know," he said, "these earrings were the first, well, one of the first things I noticed about you. A vibrant woman wearing vibrant accessories."

"I wasn't wearing these that night at the pavilion."

He leaned down, his breath a whisper along her skin. "I know," he said. "I first saw you in the lobby, the day you checked in."

The wanting returned, but now was neither the time nor the place for intimacy.

"I," she started again. But David's hand replaced his finger. He slowly caressed her. Lucia sighed into him.

"You know we can't do anything here," she said.

"That doesn't mean I can't think about it," he replied.

Lucia captured his hand in hers and pressed a kiss into his palm. "Behave," she murmured.

David smiled and dropped his hands. "If you insist. Finish telling me about your ex-husband's kids."

The smile fell off Lucia's face. "I don't generally work with gemstones, but I'd been commissioned to do a piece for a client. She wanted a matching brooch and a necklace. Well, without getting into the long, ugly details, those brats stole the gemstones, then baldly and boldly told me they did so."

"I don't get it," David said.

Shaking her head, Lucia faced him. "That's just it. They knew that when I confronted their father about it, he'd take their side. Gerard said I'd probably 'misplaced' the stones. Like I'm going to lose three thousand dollars' worth of loose diamonds and emeralds."

"What happened?"

"I had to take a loss. A big one. That commission would have . . ." She paused. "There's really no need to get into all of it now. It's water under the bridge. When Gerard and I divorced, I had nothing but a pile of debt, his included in the mix. But I knew one thing for sure. I hated those kids, and I'd never had that strong of an emotion about any living thing. Children—his children—were lost souls. They'd grow up to be people just like their parents."

David took a deep breath. He didn't know quite where to begin.

"Lucia, I'm sorry you had such a bad experience. But you shouldn't judge every young person you meet by the standard of your ex's kids. Most kids, when given a loving and nurturing environment and some training at home, do know right from wrong. I'm in no way condoning what they did to you, but it sounds like they were products of their environment."

Lucia just shook her head. "They're teenagers now. They were twelve and fourteen when I married Gerard. I tried to be a nice stepmom. I tried . . ."

He took her by the arms. "Lucia, you yourself said it's over and done. Let it go. Just remember that all children aren't cut from the same cloth. I know that from raising my own three. They each have different personalities, different strengths and weaknesses. My job is to applaud their strengths, help them build their weaknesses into positives, and show them, through my example, what it means to be honest, dependable, and trustworthy. What it means to be a person of good character."

"Well, you've definitely got my ex beat on that score."

"Being a parent is hard work. But it's also fun. You learn a lot. And," he added, "you finally figure out just what your own parents put up with. You probably gave your folks a few scares."

A grin spread across her face. "I was a perfect child, thank you very much."

"I'll just bet. You know what's funny, though? Every time I think I've got this parenthood thing down, they do something that completely throws me for a loop."

"Like what?"

"Like this whole island setup thing."

She tried to suppress a giggle. "Well, I think that was cute."

"Cute, my foot," David said. "It was downright diabolical."

She cocked a head at him. "Those three, diabolical? Maybe Gerard's kids. But yours? Not what I've seen so far, Mr. Hyperbole. Yours seem grounded in reality."

"Hmph. You be the judge," David said. "Consider the evidence. You have three little kids. Nine, seven, and almost five. What one place in the world do kids that age want to go?"

Lucia thought about it a minute. "I don't know. Disney World?"

"Bingo!"

"And the point?" she prompted.

"We're here in the Bahamas," David said, spreading his arms wide, encompassing the straw market area and the fruit stands all around. "I told them this year we'd go somewhere special for their spring holiday. Usually we just do things in and around Atlanta."

"You're from Atlanta?"

He nodded. "I told them they could pick the place. Since I *knew* Disney would be their one and only choice, I had all the brochures all ready to whip out. I'd even gotten a video from the Disney Store so they could see all of the things Disney offered at the theme parks. I," he said, pointing to his chest, "I, David Reynolds, thirty-three-year-old single dad was hyped about going to Disney World."

"Poor baby," Lucia said, barely able to keep the laughter from her voice. "What happened?"

"They hatched an evil plan," he said, lowering his voice in an imitation of a dastardly villain.

Outright laughing now, Lucia pushed for the rest of the story. "And after they had you in their clutches . . ."

"They picked the Bahamas! What kind of kids choose an island paradise over Mickey Mouse?"

"Well," Lucia said, circling her arms around his waist, "I, for one, am glad they did. We'd have never met if they'd chosen Florida."

David's arms surrounded her. "And for that, I am eternally grateful to my interfering offspring."

His lips then pressed to hers, hungrily feasting on the sweet temptation. As they kissed, Lucia realized there *was* a difference between the trying-to-be-helpful clean fun of David's children and the deliberate malice from her ex-husband's children. She wondered if D.J., Allie, and Karenna could or would ever do anything deliberately mean.

David deepened the embrace and all thoughts of children and plots fled from Lucia's mind.

His demanding lips caressed hers and she answered the call and the plea. She pressed herself closer to him and gave way to the ecstasy of his touch.

Several yards away at the street performance, Allie looked around, her brow furrowed.

"Where'd Karenna go?"

TEN

D.J. glanced about. "I thought she was standing next to you."

"Oh, wait," Allie said, ducking down to peer through an opening in the throng. "I think I see her over there."

The girl pointed toward a cluster of people. A flash of blue and green, the same color as Karenna's seashell print T-shirt and shorts, moved through the crowd.

"Stay here," Allie directed D.J. as she gave chase.

"Karenna! You know you're not supposed to wander off."

The figure in front of her turned, and Allie's mouth dropped open. It wasn't Karenna!

Now what?

Allie's anxious gaze darted around the crowd. Karenna was nowhere in sight. She looked back at the place where D.J. waited, only to find him gone, too. All of a sudden, the crowd erupted in applause and a moment later, wild cheering. People pushed forward and someone bumped into Allie.

"Do you see her?" D.J. asked.

"Unh-uh," Allie said, absently sticking a finger in her mouth while scanning the crowd, looking for her little sister. "You go that way. I'll look over here."

The two went in opposite directions, each hoping to locate Karenna even as the spectators around the horseshoe crowded closer.

Several yards away at the fruit stand, Lucia and David stood hand in hand.

"You know, David Reynolds, I don't usually do this."

"Good," he said. "Neither do I."

Lucia smiled, then took a deep breath, inhaling the scents of a perfect day.

"Look, fire dancers," Lucia said.

David watched the three men enter the circle with lit torches.

"The kids will like this," he said. But when he looked at the place where the three of them had been just a few minutes ago, he didn't see any of his children.

David scanned the area and a frown marred his face. "Now where'd they go?"

"They were just there a minute ago."

"You go that way. I'll check over here."

A few minutes later, David spotted Allie and D.J. Allie's nerves were shot, David knew, because she was biting her nails. Her distress wasn't lost on him.

"Where's Karenna?"

Allie burst into tears. "I don't know."

"She was standing right there," D.J. said. "And then, the next minute she was gone."

David took a deep breath. "All right. Come with me. She probably went to look at something that caught her eye. Lucia's over there, we'll hunt in this area."

Together, the three searched, calling the girl's name in the crowd.

Behind a large yellow and white umbrella propped up to shade the afternoon sun from a vendor, Karenna sat talking to one of the original dancers.

"I'm a dancer, too," she told the woman.

"Are ya now, sugarpie? What kind of dance do ya do?"

As the woman changed shoes, Karenna demonstrated a jazzy move.

"Not bad. Not bad at all. Can you do this?"

The dancer did a fancy step, then repeated it, slower, for the girl. Karenna followed the lead, faltered at a point, and looked to the woman for clarification of the move.

"Try it like this, sugarpie," the woman said, spreading her arms out for balance.

"Karenna! Oh, my God. There you are."

Lucia ran up to a startled Karenna. She reached out, but stopped short of hugging the girl to her.

"Hi, Miss Lucky. I'm learning how to do a new dance." The girl demonstrated by showing the step to Lucia.

The other woman clapped her hands. "There you go, sugarpie. You did it!"

Lucia's anxious gaze took in everything about the woman, her height, weight, hairstyle, clothing, just in case she needed to make a statement to the police. But then she realized Karenna appeared to be in no harm.

"Well, your dad is very worried about you. So is Allie and D.J."

"Oh," the girl said. "Well, I have to go now. I liked your dance."

"Thank you, sugarpie," the Bahamian dancer said.

Lucia held out her hand and Karenna took it.

A few minutes later, Lucia and Karenna united with the others.

After a scolding about wandering off and a promise exacted from the girl that it wouldn't happen again, David called an end to the afternoon excursion. D.J. decided on a straw hat and the group headed to the shuttle that would return them to the resort.

Back at the hotel, David sent the children up to their rooms while he saw Lucia to hers.

"I enjoyed today," he said.

"Me, too," she said. "Except that part about Karenna being lost."

With a finger at her chin, he lifted her head to meet his gaze.

"What are you thinking?"

She shrugged. "I don't know. You handled this afternoon so well. I'd have been half out of my mind with fright."

"I was."

Raising an eyebrow at him, she said, "Well, you didn't look or sound like it," she said.

"That comes with practice. The fear is a vise in your gut that clenches tighter until you think you can't bear it one minute longer."

"Well, that doesn't sound like a wonderful recommendation for parenthood."

"The joys outweigh the tense moments."

"If you say so," Lucia said. She inserted her card key in the slot. When the indicator light turned green, she turned the door handle.

"Want to come in?"

He smiled at her. "I'd love to, but I can't. I need to supervise the packing."

"Packing?"

"We leave tomorrow, after a late breakfast."

Lucia grabbed his shirt. "You're kidding, right? Tell me you're joking."

"No, we had five nights. I wanted the kids home Saturday so they could have a day to unwind and settle down before heading back to school Monday."

"I didn't realize."

Despite his earlier words, David followed her into the room and pushed the door closed.

"So this is it?" she said, the statement coming out in the form of a question, much like a convicted felon getting his sentence clarified.

"Lucia," he said, taking her hand. "It doesn't have to be."

She shook her head. "But you're in Atlanta, I'm in Virginia Beach."

"Did you know they have these really big mechanical birds these days? They whisk people all over the place and the birds take off every day."

She hit his shoulder, then went to gaze out at the window. "I'm being serious."

"So am I, Lucia. When we get home . . ."

Lucia blinked back the moisture that sprouted at her eyes. Maybe saying good-bye and letting it go at that was best. The bliss they'd shared on this Caribbean island was just that, a magical interlude—just what she needed to start her new life.

"When we get home, I think it's best if we just remember the good times here," she said.

A moment later, she felt him come up from behind.

"You don't mean that," he said.

Lucia nodded. But she was grateful she didn't have to look him in the eye. The differences that stood between them while here on vacation didn't seem so insurmountable. But Lucia knew the divide would be tremendous back on the mainland, when they each returned to their real worlds.

She'd spent almost two years rebuilding her life, organizing it in a way that let her enjoy the sweet taste of freedom, unencumbered by the drama and trauma of contorting her life to make it fit around three other people, two of whom were spoiled, rotten brats.

She'd been down this road before, and it led to a dead end.

Grabbing hold of her courage, Lucia turned to face him.

"Yes, I do mean it, David." When her voice cracked, she swallowed, cleared her throat, and met his gaze head-on. "You have your life to live and children to raise. I have my own issues."

David nodded. "All right," he said. "If that's the way you want it."

"I think it's best."

For a moment, he didn't say anything. His eyes, with a depth of experience and spirit in them, probed hers. Lucia wondered what thoughts filled his head. Then, with a blink, his gaze held something else. She read in his dark eyes a soul-deep longing—one she didn't want to admit mirrored her own. But the chance on loving him was too high a mark to reach.

As his mouth lowered to hers, Lucia realized what she'd just acknowledged. She loved this man. As impossible as that could be, she'd managed to fall in love with him.

His lips pressed to hers and she told herself it couldn't be love, just longing coupled with the heady setting of a tropical island.

His tongue traced the softness of her lips and she told herself it was just the sweet attention from a sexy man that she'd fallen for.

His lips seared a path down her neck and shoulders, then back to lavish her mouth. Lucia told herself how good it felt to be in his arms.

Too soon, though, he ended the kiss and pulled away from her, the reluctance evident in his eyes as his gaze took in all of her.

"Well, I guess this is our farewell," he said. "I've enjoyed your company, Lucia Heart Allen. Thank you for giving me memories to cherish forever."

He reached in his pocket, pulled out his billfold, and plucked a small white card from it. He wrote something on the back, then capped the pen he'd picked up from the desk.

"If you change your mind about us," he said, handing her the business card, "don't hesitate to call or e-mail me."

When Lucia didn't move to take it, David placed his card on the desk, then quietly let himself out of the room. For a long time, Lucia stood staring at the card, wondering if she'd just let the best thing to ever come into her life walk out the door.

Later that night, she sat up dissecting her reaction to spending the day with David and his children. She didn't want to admit it, but she'd been scared when they couldn't immediately find Karenna.

Was that the heartache parents went through all the time? If it was, it sure was draining.

Lucia fell back on her bed and stared at the textured ceiling. She'd never have believed it, but fear lanced through her where David was concerned. The courage she'd found to pick up the pieces of her shattered life after her failed marriage seemed to have completely escaped her.

The possibility of a new, serious relationship frightened her; not so much the one-on-one relationship with David, but the package he'd bring to the table.

"Maybe it's too soon," she whispered in the dark. "Maybe it's just not emotionally time for this."

The sleep she sought eluded Lucia. Finally, close to midnight, she gave up the pretense of getting any rest. She turned on the light and reached for her sketchpad. So far, she'd done not a lick of real work on the jewelry designs she'd hoped the tropics would inspire. But there was an image she wanted to capture.

"Come on, guys. We're gonna be late. If we miss this plane, you're going to have to swim back home."

"I'm ready, Daddy," Karenna said. "I don't want to swim home. The sharks might eat me."

"I won't let them, pumpkin," David assured as he closed the latch on his suitcase and secured the luggage lock. "D.J. Allie. Let's get going."

The Reynolds family had eaten breakfast in one of the restaurants. All that remained was a final check of the rooms to make sure they hadn't left anything behind.

"I can't find my Game Boy," D.J. whined.

"It's in the bathroom," David told him. "Let's get a move on, people."

Ten minutes later they made it to the lobby. David had the kids sit on one of the rattan sofas while he checked out and settled their bill.

"These were left for you, sir," the front desk clerk said, handing over three packages gaily wrapped in the resort's signature wrapping paper.

Wary that his children had yet another surprise date lined up for him, David eyed the bundles with suspicion. But closer inspection revealed not his name on the envelopes, but his children's. Taking note of Lucia's address on the cards, he quickly jotted it down at the bottom of his hotel invoice. He signed off on the resort bill, pocketed the receipt, and took the packages.

"I hope you enjoyed your stay. Come see us again," the clerk said.

David thanked the man, then made his way to where the three sat, surprisingly quiet.

"Looks like someone decided to give you parting gifts," David said. He distributed the packages, Allie's was small, D.J.'s thin and flat, and Karenna's soft.

"What is it?" Allie said.

"Open 'em and see. I'm as curious as you are."

The kids wasted no time ripping off the paper. Allie squealed in delight when she discovered Lucia's very colorful parrot earrings. D.J. let out a whoop when he saw the small sketch of himself decked out in pirate gear. Karenna found the scarf Lucia used to fashion a top for her the night they met.

"Dad, look!"

"Can I keep them?"

"Ooh."

David smiled at the exuberance of his children and at Lucia's generosity. That she'd been thoughtful enough to leave mementos for the kids conflicted with her assertion that she didn't know how to handle children. That she'd take the time to choose, and in D.J.'s case create, something that would be precious to each child, spoke volumes about her innate nurturing ability.

An awareness shivered through him. He glanced up, and there, across the lobby, he spied her standing next to a balustrade.

She smiled at him, but when he made a step to approach her, she shook her head and disappeared. He watched her flight, realizing that she'd probably been right about them. The vast differences between their lives and the distance between their homes *was* an obstacle.

But the moments they'd shared here would always bring him a special joy. A ghost of a smile crossed his lips at the memory of the passion between them.

"Daddy? Daddy?" Karenna tugged on his hand.

"Yes, pumpkin?"

"What did you get?"

Staring at the place Lucia had been, David shook his head. "Apparently not my heart's desire."

ELEVEN

THREE WEEKS LATER

Lucia's work on a new line of jewelry progressed well, even though it hardly looked like anything she'd ever produced before. Kid-inspired, the bangles and necklaces she'd sketched had a whimsy that might appeal to the preteen set as well as young-at-heart adults.

"No surprise where that came from," she said as she bent over her worktable. Trays of beads and feathers surrounded her. After a moment, she sat up to survey her handiwork.

She stretched a knot out of her back and studied the funky hairpins she'd created.

That her days were filled thinking about and sketching designs that would appeal to girls like Karenna and Allie wouldn't have been so bad if her nights hadn't been crowded with restless energy and longing for David. Much like a preteen with a serious crush might do, Lucia found herself writing his name in the margins of her sketchbook.

The constant e-mail from the children didn't help her get over the longing. As a matter of fact, it just made it worse. D.J. explained how he used his pirate sketch for show and tell. Karenna pleaded her case for a puppy. And Allie asked a question about boys that Lucia thought long and hard about before crafting her e-mail reply.

Except for a quick note thanking her for the gifts to the children and a postscript adding that he'd love to see her again, David's voice had been silent from her world.

"Well, you made yourself pretty clear about where the relationship was going," she muttered.

Deciding it time for a break, Lucia went to the kitchen for

a snack, then booted up her computer to check e-mail.

She smiled at the little voice that told her mail was, indeed, waiting. A couple of familiar screen names appeared in the listing of about fifteen messages, including a message from Vonda. In the time since she'd returned from the Bahamas, she'd been in contact with a couple of people from the WJAM tour.

Vonda's interest in some of her jewelry had sparked a bond that led to a developing friendship. The two women had even had lunch together. Millie, who in a moment of weakness had wrestled out of Lucia an e-address, tended to forward long strings of recycled jokes at least three times a day. Lucia didn't even bother reading most of them. She deleted the forwarded jokes as well as a couple of spam messages.

Oddly disappointed that no message awaited her from the Reynolds clan, she quickly read and responded to the other messages. When Lucia moved her mouse to escape from the mail program, an instant message popped up on her screen.

RCREW: Miss Lucky, are you there? We need help!!!

Alarmed, Lucia quickly typed in a return message.

HEARTART: I'm here, guys. What's up?
RCREW: Dad's depressed. We think he's gonna do something crazy.
HEARTART: Crazy like what? Your father's a pretty level-headed guy.
RCREW: He's always frowning and he looks really bad. We think he needs some vitamins.

Lucia grinned. These three were a mess. She could just picture Allie, D.J., and Karenna huddled around their computer. While a part of her wanted to believe that David looked bad, as the children said, because he missed her as much as she missed him, the reality was that he'd probably not given her a second thought. If he looked haggard, it was probably from work.

The thought flashed across her mind that he may have

picked up a bug while on the island. But three weeks had passed already. If that had been the case, he'd have had symptoms before now.

HEARTART: Pour him some orange juice and make sure he drinks it. Are you guys staying up late at night and keeping him up?

She waited, but no message popped back on the screen. Maybe their connection had been lost. Then . . .

RCREW: Maybe we should call ammb . . . . dj_sklzz

Alarmed, Lucia sat up. What was going on down there?

When no additional message popped up, she sat for a moment, growing increasingly alarmed. Did the kids just run out of things to say, or were they trying to tell her David was truly sick?

And was that last coherent string supposed to be "call an ambulance"?

A thousand scenarios raced through her mind, each one more horrible than the last. Lucia reached for her cordless phone and flipped through the box of index cards she used as a phone directory. She'd slipped David's card in there.

The line was busy, though. Probably tied up by the kids on the computer. Lucia glanced at the clock, then at her computer, the last message from the children staring back at her like a cry for help. Two minutes passed. Then five, ten. She tried to call again, but still got a busy signal.

Her mind suddenly made up, Lucia printed out the message log on the monitor, turned her computer off, and grabbed her purse.

A little more than four hours later, she stood at the front door of a tidy two-story house on a tree-lined Atlanta street. A white Chevy Blazer with red trim sat parked in the drive.

Suddenly, the enormity of what she'd done hit her. Without any confirmation that an emergency had actually happened, she'd hopped on the first plane to Atlanta.

No luggage.

No thinking.

No nothing.

David or his children needed her. That was the only thing that mattered.

She rang the doorbell and waited.

"Clean that mess up," David said. "Then to your room, every one of you. Go to bed."

"It wasn't my fault. I was just—"

David held up a hand. "I don't want to hear it," he told D.J. "Wipe the paint up, then go upstairs. You all are just in destructive mode today. First, juice all over the computer, now finger paint all over the carpet."

"But, Dad—"

David cut a glance at D.J. as the front doorbell pealed again. "Coming!" he hollered toward the door.

He'd gotten no work done today, on top of yet another bad night of tossing and turning in a too large bed that used to be just right. And now the kids were bouncing off the walls. With summer vacation coming up soon, David was starting to rethink the idea about residential camp for the oldest two.

Tossing across his shoulder the towel he'd grabbed to mop up the rainbow mix of paint, David yanked open the front door, ready to send the solicitor packing.

"Oh, thank God. You're okay."

Lucia fell into his arms.

Sure that the day was closing on a hallucination, David sighed. It couldn't be Lucia standing at his front door. But if it wasn't Lucia, how could he embrace the soft feel of her? How could he inhale the sweet, earthy scent of the perfume he remembered? How could his body respond like a parched man at a desert oasis?

He pulled back and framed her face in his hands.

Then he kissed her.

His kiss sang through her veins, filling all the empty places that had languished without his touch. His mouth did not become softer as they kissed, the stake he claimed was hard, fast, and thoroughly devastating.

Lucia's hands wandered to his face. She wanted to feel him and touch him even as their lips merged. Pleasure radiated through her and she knew that no matter what happened between them, this was right.

As he aroused her passion, his own grew stronger. Lucia felt the evidence of his arousal and thrilled at the sensation of his welcome.

"What are you doing here?" he murmured against her lips.

Lucia took the moment to compose herself, to put a little air between their bodies. With an arm at her waist as if she might change her mind and flee at any moment, David ushered her into the house.

He closed the door behind them and stared at her.

"I've missed you," he said.

"Not half as much as I've missed you."

"Why are you here? How did you get here? Why didn't you tell me you were coming?"

As the questions tumbled from his mouth, the enormity of what she'd done *really* hit Lucia. She glanced around the foyer, then clasped her hands together.

"I . . ." she started. "The kids . . ."

Lucia looked at the floor, at an umbrella stand in the corner, anything to keep from admitting that she'd hopped on that plane because she could no longer bear to be away from David.

"Don't tell me those three have been playing matchmaker again. They're all about to be on punishment for their antics today."

"Punishment? What happened?"

David explained about the orange juice on the keyboard and then the finger paint project on the dining room table and floor.

A light dawned with Lucia. "Were they by chance on the computer, oh, about three-thirty or four, maybe after school?"

"Yes. They get an hour computer playtime before homework and dinner."

A chuckle bubbled up from Lucia. A moment later she was laughing out loud.

"What?"

Lucia told him about the e-mails she'd been receiving from the children, then she told him about the "emergency" message. Pulling the folded page from her purse, she handed the log of their instant message to him.

"I thought you were hurt or ill."

David studied her, his eyes sharp and assessing. "And so you came running. Why?"

This was the part Lucia hadn't quite worked out. On the plane ride south, she'd tried to formulate an articulate speech to rationalize her actions. The only problem was, she couldn't. She'd listened to her gut and her heart. Now it was time to face him, and she didn't know what to say.

"David, I . . ."

She glanced up at him, but his closed face and expression offered no hint of what he might be thinking.

Taking a deep breath, Lucia took the plunge.

"I've spent the time since we all left Freeport thinking about what I told you on the island. I'm still afraid of what it might mean to be a stepmom again."

He raised an eyebrow and she held up a hand.

"Even though our relationship is nowhere near that point," she hastily added. "It's just that, well . . . David, what I'm trying to say is, I handed over a credit card and got on the first plane to Atlanta because I wanted to see you again. I needed to see you. Yes, the e-mail from the kids alarmed me at first. But that was just the smoke screen I needed to propel me into some action. If the offer of pursuing whatever we have here still stands, I'd like to submit a different answer."

A gleam of interest—or was that mischief?—danced in his eyes.

"Are you sure?" he asked, his voice a balm to her anxious nerves.

Lucia held out a hand to him. "More than sure."

He smiled. "I'm glad."

David took her hand and led her into the family room. "One of the things about having kids is that moments of silence and privacy like this can be rare. Right now, they should be getting ready for bed. That's if they're not conspiring to get me another girlfriend."

"And what does the moment of silence mean?"

He tugged her to the sofa, where they tumbled together onto its softness. "It means," he said with a smile, "that if you're serious about us, we have probably ten minutes before one of them breaks something or yells downstairs."

Lucia smiled. "Well, we'd best use the time wisely."

This time it was Lucia who sealed their words with a kiss.

She felt a warm glow flow through her. Regardless of what might happen in the future, they had right now—and it was this moment that would begin all their future ones.

The bond with David's children started on a firm foundation and would only grow deeper. She looked forward to the experiences they might eventually share as a family. But even more importantly, she anticipated the love she'd share with David.

Turn the page for an excerpt from
Blackboard bestselling author Francis Ray's
next emotionally powerful book

I Know Who Holds Tomorrow

Available soon in trade paperback from
St. Martin's Griffin

The Wilshire Ballroom in the Hyatt Hotel was filled with lavishly dressed people, scrumptious food, and breathless anticipation. A hush fell over the room that seated close to five hundred of the top journalists in the country. The biggest award of the night, that of Broadcaster of the Year, was about to be announced by the legendary Walter Cronkite. The nominees' names had already been given. Wes Reed's name was among the four.

Opening the envelope, Cronkite's mouth curved into one of his rare smiles, then he lifted his head and said in that distinctive voice, "For Broadcaster of the Year, the award goes to Wes Reed."

Wes, known just as much for his jubilance as his tenacity, surged to his feet. People from his table and around him quickly came to offer handshakes and robust pats on the back. He acknowledged them with a flash of the killer smile that had made him a favorite of women viewers. But as the award testified, he was respected by men as well for his hard-hitting commentary.

As applause continued, he turned to Madison sitting beside him, then leaned over and kissed her on the cheek.

"Congratulations, Wes," Madison said, still applauding. She more than most knew how much this award meant to him. Finally he had been validated by his peers, recognized as a great reporter, not just a great black reporter. This award capped off a year when he had won several, including the Ma'At Award from the Regional Association of Black Journalists. He had succeeded in his career, if not in his personal life.

With a final wave of acknowledgment, Wes started toward

the stage, then whirled and came back to Madison. His manicured hand extended toward her. Applause erupted again. This time louder. Only Madison, who was watching, saw the almost imperceptible tightening of his mouth, the glint in his hazel eyes. Dutifully, she placed her hand in his. This was his night.

As they made their way toward the stage, Madison heard the comments that always made her wince inside.

"Aren't they a beautiful couple?"

"They're so happy."

"They're perfect."

With difficulty Madison kept the smile on her face. Louis's PR had succeeded beyond any of their wildest dreams.

In her mind's eyes, she could see Wes, tall and elegant in his tailored tuxedo with a patterned vest, black tie, and snow-white pocket square. Her red Valentino slip gown highlighted her honeyed complexion and chocolate-brown eyes. The gown also picked up the red in Wes's vest and the red in the rose in his lapel. If you didn't look past the surface, they did indeed look good together.

Onstage, Wes accepted the award with one hand and shook Cronkite's hand with the other. Then he reclasped Madison's hand, drawing her with him as he stepped in front of the Plexiglas podium. "Few times in my life words have failed me. This is one of those rare times." As expected, the audience laughed. Wes had earned his reputation as the great "talker."

Finally releasing Madison's hand he ran a long finger over the award. Then his head lifted, his soothing voice was deep and serious. "There are only two occasions that I will treasure more than this one, and since the first is the day Madison agreed to marry me and the second is the day we were married almost five years ago, it is right and fitting that she be with me to share this third occasion." Turning, he stared down into her eyes.

"Thank you for putting up with me and my crazy schedule, for letting me follow my dream, and most of all for loving me."

Applause erupted. People stood to their feet. Madison swallowed, unable to say anything. Wes placed a kiss on her forehead that bespoke of tenderness and love. Curving his hand around her slender waist, he led her from the stage.

It wasn't over.

Backstage, more press waited. Microphones were thrust in their faces, cameras flashed, the glaring lights of the television cameras focused on them to catch every nuance. Well aware of how the media game was played, Wes keep his arm around her waist. Madison's bright smile never faltered. She also knew the routine, knew the questions that would follow, knew the choreography of tender looks that were expected.

They were the perfect couple and it was show time. And she wanted to scream.

CHECK OUT THESE SOUL SISTERS!

BUTTERSCOTCH BLUES
by Margaret Johnson-Hodge

At the age of thirty-four, Sandy Hutchinson wonders if love will forever elude her, until the day she meets Adrian Burton, a Trinidadian with caramel skin, naturally wavy hair, and eyes the color of butterscotch. Together they share a whirlwind romance—until the night of a fateful call from the hospital and she learns of his ailing ex-wife. Now, Sandy must decide if her love is strong enough to help get them through what may be their darkest hour.

A FAMILY REUNION
by Brenda Jackson

It's been fifteen years since the Bennetts were all in one place at one time, and now at a total blowout of a reunion, three generations will gather to remember old memories and reestablish deep roots. But for four special cousins, hidden desires and long-kept secrets will challenge their bond, test their courage, and change their hearts forever . . .

FAR FROM THE TREE
by Virginia DeBerry and Donna Grant

Struggling Manhattan actress Ronnie Frazier has come home to Buffalo for her father's funeral. In Ronnie's opinion, Celeste English already has it all as a doctor's wife and a mother. But when the sisters journey to their newly inherited North Carolina family homestead, the startling truth about Celeste's perfect life and Della's murky past begins to emerge.

TRYIN' TO SLEEP IN THE BED YOU MADE
by Virginia DeBerry and Donna Grant

Gayle Saunders and Patricia Reid have been best friends since they were children. Gayle, the beauty pampered by her working-class parents, believes a man will make her world complete. Pat, the brainy one, is the hand-me-down child whose mystery parentage haunts her. And then there is Marcus Carter, linked to both women from the moment a childhood tragedy bonds them in secrecy.

THE TURNING POINT
by Francis Ray

Desperate to escape her abusive marriage, Lilly Crawford files for divorce, then slips away from her small east Texas hometown. When her car breaks down on a back road in Louisiana, Lilly seeks help and finds unexpected employment as a caregiver to Adam Wakefield, a former prominent neurosurgeon who is now blind. As the two spend long days together, an unexpected bond develops that can offer the promise of healing . . .

**AVAILABLE WHEREVER BOOKS ARE SOLD FROM
ST. MARTIN'S PAPERBACKS**

AA 8/01